PENGUIN BOOKS

DEAREST DOROTHY, ARE WE THERE YET?

Charlene Ann Baumbich is a popular speaker, journalist, and author. Her stories, essays, and columns have appeared in numerous magazines and newspapers, including the *Chicago Tribune,* the *Chicago Sun-Times,* and *Today's Christian Woman.* She is also the author of the second novel in the Partonville series, *Dearest Dorothy, Slow Down, You're Wearing Us Out!,* and six books of nonfiction. She lives in Glen Ellyn, Illinois. Learn more about Charlene at www.welcometopartonville.com.

ALSO IN THIS SERIES

Dearest Dorothy, Slow Down, You're Wearing Us Out!

Dearest Dorothy,
Are We There Yet?

Charlene Ann Baumbich

PENGUIN BOOKS

PENGUIN BOOKS
Published by Penguin Group
Penguin Group (USA) Inc., 375 Hudson Street,
New York, New York 10014, U.S.A.
Penguin Books Ltd, 80 Strand, London WC2R 0RL, England
Penguin Books Australia Ltd, 250 Camberwell Road, Camberwell, Victoria 3124, Australia
Penguin Books Canada Ltd, 10 Alcorn Avenue, Toronto, Ontario, Canada M4V 3B2
Penguin Books India (P) Ltd, 11 Community Centre,
Panchsheel Park, New Delhi – 110 017, India
Penguin Books (N.Z.) Ltd, Cnr Rosedale and Airborne Roads,
Albany, Auckland, New Zealand
Penguin Books (South Africa) (Pty) Ltd, 24 Sturdee Avenue,
Rosebank, Johannesburg 2196, South Africa

Penguin Books Ltd, Registered Offices:
80 Strand, London WC2R 0RL, England

First published in the United States of America by Guideposts Books 2002
Published in Penguin Books 2004

PUBLISHER'S NOTE
This is a work of fiction. Names, characters, places, and incidents either are the product
of the author's imagination or are used fictitiously, and any resemblance to actual persons,
living or dead, business establishments, events, or locales is entirely coincidental.

ISBN 0-7394-4324-0

Printed in the United States of America

Set in Berthold Garamond
Designed by Sabrina Bowers

Dedicated to the real *Oldster Characters
in my life who inspired creativity;
taught sensitivity; modeled kindness,
acceptance and wahoo fun;
were unabashedly their own True Selves;
and cheered me on—all the way from heaven.
Especially my Dearest Dorothy.*

Acknowledgments

How do I begin to thank everyone who helped wing these books to life? I mean, the cast of characters (real ones) is huge! Although I have already written my dedication page to the Masters of My Inspiration, there are OH! so many more friends, family and just plain good folks who helped knit these books together. Their range of contributions is nothing short of astounding: inspiration ("I know you can, I know you can"); education (teaching me details about stuff I know nothing about so that my fiction doesn't get too many "I don't think so!" responses from you astute readers); cheerleading ("Great chapter!"); shrink duty ("Yes, sometimes 'reality' is slippery, Charlene"); hysteria stopping ("Snap out of it!"); listening to me whine (yes, I do my fair share). And a WAHOO! thanks for friends who never gave up on me, even when I was impossible; who provided laughs when I needed them, breaks when I needed them, tolerance when I needed it, mercy when I needed it and a kick in the butt when I needed it.

Without Terri Castillo, there would be no *Dearest Dorothy* books. Her verbalized question became the materialized project. She asked; I knew; it was. (Okay, there were years of hard work and creative flying in the midst of this, but the short and True Birthing Miracle version is this: She asked; I knew; it was.) As I type, I pray blessings upon her journey. She has gently launched me with full spiritual sails into the delicious waters of Story.

Regina Hersey, my editor, was a constant bellows to the all of my all (and she'll probably tell me "'the all of my all' doesn't make sense," but I'm writing these acknowledgments and she'll just have to live with it—HA!). Again, without Regina, no *Dearest Dorothy* books. Simple as that. From the very first e-mail forwarded to me after she read my first draft, to the very last conversation I've had with her (which was probably yesterday, since she's become my True Friend), she has been nothing short of a pure-gold gift. I have no doubt that our synergy was God designed, and 'twas the genius of Terri Castillo who matched us up. Even though I sometimes quake at Regina's ability to be a self-ordained Grammar Nazi who always has "just a few little things" for me to address in my manuscripts, she is, without exception, grace upon grace in my life.

Oftentimes we need a mentor who has honorably journeyed down the road before us. Novelist Terri Blackstock graciously gave me ninety minutes of her time during one frantic, out-of-the-blue phone call. It was ninety minutes' worth of genuine, literal, literary and Big Picture guidance. My journey became instantly lighter and wiser.

Between *Are We There Yet?* and *Slow Down, You're Wearing Us Out!* the following are people who fell into that "education" category I mentioned before, going above and beyond the call of duty to help guide a stranger through the back roads of things like commercial real estate development, long-haul moving, heart conditions, auto repair, demolition derby and a host of other details: Steve Gibson, Larry Alexander, Thomas Wood, Harold Benware, Dave Thompson, Bruce Bradley, Mary S., Donna Manley, Robin

Webb, Joanne Boppart and Gregory Baumbich, who, against his Chevy heart but for the love of family, talked to me about a Ford product. My apologies to anyone I left out before this rolled to press. Your exclusion implies no less importance but speaks to my fuzzy, midlife brain cells.

The folks at Guideposts Books and Inspirational Media Division, especially Elizabeth Kramer Gold and her snappy sense of humor, were definitely guideposts. I thank them for their courage and their ministry.

The first time I met Carolyn Carlson, both my professional and personal life brightened. Her enthusiasm for the first two books in the Partonville series, and her sensitivities to what *really* matters in *all* of life—which is the same message in the novels—made for a rousing combination. When it became official that Penguin Books would be bringing the books into book stores, a shout of joy erupted from my soul (once I stopped freaking out), which has yet to stop twirling with delight.

And to my husband, George, I give my utmost thanks for standing watch at the door to Our World. He has countless times stood there alone, staring down the road (or up the stairs to my office, or into my eyes), waiting for me to return from Partonville. I love you, my Honey Bunny.

Introduction

To be seventy years young is sometimes far more cheerful and hopeful than to be forty years old.
—Oliver Wendell Holmes

And now, welcome to Partonville, a circle-the-square town in the northern part of southern Illinois, where oldsters are young, trees have names and cars don't fly.

Dearest Dorothy,

━ ━ ━ ━

Are We There Yet?

1

A powerful CRACK! broke the pre-dawn hush as a bolt of lightning seared into the field, briefly illuminating the clapboard farmhouse. Dorothy Jean Wetstra's eyes flew open and her body lurched. Up until that moment, she'd been deep in sleep, curled up on her side, nesting in a warm sea of ancient quilts.

She rolled to her back and lay there, stiff as a board, staring unblinking at the ceiling. Once her heart finally stopped hammering, fits of tossing and turning kept her awake long after the booming and rumbling had passed. In the aftermath of silence, the rain-drenched and ripened farmland beckoned her into its respite. She'd once read that nature was a glove on the hand of God, and she knew she'd read Truth. She finally gave up on sleep and decided to take her charged energies for a swift walk, hoping not only to extinguish their dominion over her tired body, but also to rest in the quiet hands of the Creator.

Dorothy swung her legs over the side of the tall bed and slowly straightened her stately five-foot-ten-inch frame, waiting for the night's body kinks to work themselves out. Since she always slept with at least one bedroom window open, the cool, damp April air spurred her into action to pull on her clothes. Pink—her trademark color—sweat suit, white socks and Keds in place, she whisked into the bathroom, put in her partial plate, then looked in the mirror at her sleepy brown eyes and wispy white locks. "Hair, you're on your own until I return."

Sheba, her eight-year-old constant companion—dubbed "Queen of the Mutt Dogs" the day Dorothy discovered the brown-and-black pup in the ditch—raised her head from the end of Dorothy's bed and stared at her. "You're either comin' or not, but I'm going to the creek," Dorothy said, hands on her hips. Sheba stood, stretched back on her haunches, gave a widemouthed yawn and leapt to the floor, right on Dorothy's heels. Sheba wasn't one to be left behind. She needed to spring into action if she wanted to keep up with her energetic master—although some in Partonville might question who mastered whom.

The journey down Dorothy's steep staircase, into the living room, through the kitchen, out the back door, past the giant white barn, then along the cornfields down to the creek was invigorating. Although she could have negotiated the familiar path with her eyes closed, she relished each step. The last moody shades of pink sunrise had finished their dance by the time she stood creekside in the silence.

Like the comforting lullaby of a mother, the coo of a mourning dove spoke straight to her heart. For a moment, a single sound of a moment, she forgot about her predicament, and all that existed was the fresh wind of spring bursting into her worried, wintered soul. In that bright instant, the beauty of the meandering creek and the farmland beneath her feet held her safe.

Just as quickly, the dove fell silent and the rapid beating of Dorothy's anxious heart once again rocked her security. What would, what *could* her life be like were she to sell this farm, which had embraced and nurtured all eighty-seven years of her life?

Dorothy stepped down the slight embankment to the edge of the water and studied its brisk current. Although mud squished up the sides of the rubber trim on her tennis shoes, she never worried about mess or cockleburs when she was roaming the land. The earthy aroma rendered by her very steps was as pleasing as any highfalutin perfume she'd whiffed. Black Illinois dirt was something to celebrate and receive with all your senses. "God's creatures don't melt when it rains or shrivel when they're dirty," she'd often said, and she lived every word.

Dorothy recalled days from her youth when decisions had been made by the simplest of means: a "lefty-or-righty, righty-or-wrongy twig." She grinned at the absurdity of the method, but also at the fun of the process. Of course, what decision did any ten-year-old have to make that really mattered to the grand scheme of life? If Dorothy sold her land to a developer, the ramifications would have much more impact than the youthful consequences of whether or not to dive in the swimmin' hole on a chilly day, or whether or not to tell May Belle she had a crush on somebody. Now, were she to sell her farm, not only would her life change, but so would the entire future of Partonville.

And yet, the true country girl who dwelled within couldn't resist; she began hunting for the perfect "lefty-or-righty, righty-or-wrongy twig," humming the song she and her best friend, May Belle, had composed more than seven decades ago.

Lefty or righty, righty or wrongy,
tell me true while we sing this songy.

Wish we may, wish we might,
have you reveal if we're wrong or right.

No sooner had Dorothy finished the tune than her eyes landed on the perfect twig. She scooped it up and turned to show it to Sheba, who had wandered off somewhere, probably hot on the trail of some poor critter. Holding it firmly, she closed her eyes, created her righty-wrongy choices—which changed from incident to incident—and spoke her decision aloud.

"Left of the rock is wrongy and I don't sell, right of the rock is righty and I accept the offer with Craig & Craig Developers." She stepped back into the squishy mud, leaned over and, with great ceremonial dignity, tossed the stick into the middle of the rushing waters.

Off it sailed toward the Big Rock in the middle of the creek just before the bend, where all righty-wrongy determinations were made. Holding her breath, she squinted to keep the twig in sight, knowing how easily it could be lost in the current. Within a few seconds, the righty-wrongy twig raced into the middle of the rock where it . . . LODGED! It was going neither right nor left around the rock. Immediately after the twig hit the rock, a three-foot-long, three-inch-thick branch pinned the twig to the back of the boulder and a barrage of other twigs and branches instantly joined the dam. It looked like an entire beaver town had broken apart upstream and swallowed her twig alive. Dorothy realized she was still holding her breath, and she gushed a whooshing exhalation, staring, staring. . . .

The pile began to shift and rock and finally broke itself apart, splitting down the middle, some going left and some going right, her twig lost in the shuffle.

"Lord," she said aloud, "You and I know it was just a silly girlhood game anyway. But I'm needing an answer! I'm plumb worn out from sleepless nights, praying and thinking about this decision, remembering all the years of my life on this land—as a girl, a wife . . . a mother myself.

"And yet, I'm eighty-seven, and my children are growed up and gone. Gone. That's the reality. And we both know my old ticker isn't what it used to be and nothing stays the same and change is sneaking up on us anyway and I have this hunch it's just time to move on while I still have my senses and can make the choice myself and . . ." Her voice trailed off as she ran out of breath releasing the exploding thoughts. She walked a few steps, kicking aside twigs and clumps of last year's damp leaves, praying the way it came naturally, with her eyes wide open, just chatting away with Jesus.

"Now You tell me in Your Word that You know every hair on my now mostly pink-scalped head. You know my comings and my goings and You knit me in my mother's womb. Is it too much to ask, in the middle of all Your counting and knitting, that You give me one little answer?" She looked up at the bright morning sky, hands on her hips—like Job, challenging the One who loved her.

"Okay. I'm done talking now and ready to listen. I promise. Amen." Dorothy stood still as a post, watching the waters race to wherever they were going next. The mourning dove cooed, and for a moment, another single sound of a joy-filled moment, she knew she had an answer, even though she wasn't sure what it was.

Dorothy made her way back to the house and fixed herself a cup of tea and a slice of toast slathered with butter and sprinkled with sugar, her personal version of "cooking" dessert for breakfast. She washed her face, fixed her hair and fed Sheba, then finally felt mentally strong enough to try once again to plow her way through the Craig & Craig offer. She sat down at the massive mahogany desk that had served for more than a century as a cornerstone in the dining room. It was once her father's father's; she felt connected to heritage whenever she stroked her hand against the well-cared-for wood. Slowly she opened the file, glanced at the offer's expiration date, May 3—she'd had the offer for nearly a month—and then at her calendar, April 22.

"Sheba!" she yelped. Sheba jumped up off the floor near the radiator and began barking. "It's May Belle's birthday today! I've been so selfish, worrying about me, that I've forgotten my best friend's birthday!" She closed the file, tossed it toward the back of the desk and briskly walked to her kitchen phone, fingers flying over the keypad. After listening to Dorothy sing "Happy Birthday" clear through twice, May Belle happily accepted her friend's offer to buy her a birthday lunch at Harry's.

Lester K. Biggs, "Sole Proprietor of Harry's Grill," as it said on his business cards, grumbled a bit about Dorothy's last-minute fussing around, just when the early lunch crowd was at its height. She'd arrived in a flurry, stormed into the grill, tossed her giant handbag on a chair at the table in the front window—right under the MAXIMUM SEATING 25. NO CREDIT CARDS & NO CHECKS! sign—and retrieved an old-fashioned, pointy birthday hat from her pink nylon backpack. Whisking up to the U-shaped counter, she helped herself to the last of the sweet rolls left in the display near the cash register. She also helped herself to a plate from behind the counter, which was what really got Lester to bristling, since this was definitely his territory. Because it was Dorothy, he let it slide, but not without huffing around a bit to let her know she'd violated the rules of the establishment.

Dorothy took the sweet roll to the table, rummaged through her backpack and produced a box of partially burned birthday candles, which without counting she stuck in the sweet roll, this way and that. *Eighty-six candles would probably burn the place down anyway!* she thought. She alerted everyone at the counter that as soon as May Belle entered, they were to watch for Dorothy's cue to sing "Happy Birthday." Even if they didn't feel like singing, like Lester, they'd make an exception for Dorothy, since she was, well, Dorothy and they all loved and respected this spunky woman who had, over the decades, become a kind of town matriarch.

Seating herself facing the door, she waited for May Belle to arrive. May Belle walked in just a few moments later, accompanied by her son, Earl, another of Dorothy's favorite people in the whole wide world. May Belle and Homer had, much to their surprise, conceived their only child late in life. Never a day passed when Earl wasn't viewed and loved by them as nothing short of a "bright miracle." Although Earl was mentally challenged, he was lovingly described, enjoyed and accepted by folks in Partonville as "slow and particular. That's just the way Earl is."

Dorothy leapt to her feet and welcomed her friend with a hug. As soon as she'd secured the rubber strapping to the birthday hat around May Belle's plump chin, she turned to the folks at the counter. They had all swiveled toward her. Eyebrows up, head tilted back, Dorothy lifted her hand high over her head, held it poised for an attention-commanding moment—she had been a bandleader all her working life—hummed a note suitable to her aged tenor voice, then sliced her hand down through the air with the first of the three-beat motions, leading the entire group at Harry's Grill in singing "Happy Birthday."

May Belle broke out in laughter when Dorothy made them hold the last note so long she thought they might all tumble off their stools, gasping for breath. Everyone clapped, then returned to eating as the two women seated themselves at the table. Earl, who had already eaten lunch at home, had disappeared when all the uncomfortable attention had turned their way. Dorothy and May Belle understood, knowing he'd headed home, one block off the square, where things were normal.

After ordering their food—hamburgers and fries, their favorite since grammar school—May Belle said, "Dorothy, you really look tired, and it's not the first time I've noticed that lately. Are you feeling okay, dear?"

Dorothy silently studied her best friend for a moment, so needing to talk to *someone* about her tormenting decision. But she knew May Belle couldn't be impartial. For years May Belle had expressed how it worried her that Dorothy was so far out in the country, all alone. "At our age," she used to begin, "things can happen, Dorothy, and no one would even know it! Maybe it's time for you to *unburden* yourself from that old farm and move into town." But Dorothy always resisted, unable to put the words *farm* and *burden* in the same sentence. No, May Belle was too devoted to her friend to worry about the community as a whole. And besides, Dorothy knew May Belle had enough on her mind, fretting and praying about what might one day happen to Earl when the Lord took *her* home.

"Do you mean to tell me you slept right through that storm this morning?" Dorothy said, skirting the issue.

"Storm?"

"Oh, May Belle! You could sleep through an earthquake, I imagine." Dorothy was about to ask her if she remembered the "lefty-or-righty, righty-or-wrongy twig" when May Belle thankfully changed the subject.

"Say, did you hear about Tess Walker? Poor thing. I haven't actually seen her for years. I feel terrible she died so alone."

"Yes. I heard. Cora Davis phoned me. I guess she saw the ambulance out in front of Tess's house when they wheeled her body away. Honestly, that woman just seems to have a nose for news. Hasn't changed a lick since she was secretly voted third grade's biggest tattletale!" May Belle and Dorothy grinned, aware they were sitting in Cora's usual seat, right in the window from which at least half of the town square could be spied upon.

Dorothy said, "I imagine Tess's niece in Chicago will be the one who has to come and deal with arrangements and her estate, such as it is. I don't believe Tess had another living relative."

"You'd know better than me. You and Tess used to visit on occasion, the way I remember it. Of course, her baby sister always had to tag along. I just never got to know either of them much more than to say a howdy do."

After hesitating a moment, Dorothy said quietly, "Yes, I guess I got to know those sisters about as well as anyone. They were so close . . ." Her voice trailed off and she swirled her coffee mug, watching the last drops coat the bottom. Somberly, she continued: "I tell you, when her sister, Clarice, moved to Chicago, it about broke Tess's heart in two. Set her into an unlifting depression. And Tess wasn't much of a traveler anyway. Always did like to be home, sleeping in her own bed."

"I can relate to that," May Belle said. "Some of us," and she nodded her head at Dorothy, "just tend to have a bit more gypsy in our souls than others." Although Dorothy loved her farm, she would travel just about anywhere via any means at the drop of a hat, chanting "Road Trip, Road Trip" to the tune of a doorbell and asking within minutes of their departure, "Are we there yet?"

When they'd polished off their last French fry, Dorothy held her mug in the air to catch Lester's attention. She needed one final steaming cup to go with dessert. They lingered a spell, May Belle letting Dorothy eat most of the sweet roll, knowing her penchant for sugary anything.

"Well," Dorothy said, wiping her mouth with her paper napkin, "I better get home to Sheba, though she's probably still sleeping. She plumb exhausted herself during our early morning jaunt to the creek. I had to holler three times before she finally appeared, dripping wet and full of mud, grinning from ear to ear. It must have been quite the chase. I pity the animal!

"I'll see you tomorrow at the Hookers meeting. I hope you're spending the day baking!" Dorothy said as she gathered her handbag and backpack and headed for the door.

2

Dust flew up off the gravel road while rocks clatter-banged their own frenzied rhythm on the exhaust. The Tank, as Dorothy loved to call her rusty-and-white 1976 Lincoln Continental, fishtailed coming out of the thirty-degree bend in the road, the last curve before the half-mile straightaway into town. At least that's the way Dorothy viewed it.

"Full throttle," she hollered to Sheba as the battle-worn Tank finally shimmied and skidded her way due west. Dorothy reveled in the freedom to travel just the way she liked: fast. Her short, thinning snow-white hair rippled in the breeze of the open windows like a field of dried dandelions.

Sheba steadied herself against the swaying backseat, then resumed her position in the window once The Tank flattened out. Tongue sailing, ears flapping parallel with her tongue, twelve-pound Sheba made the perfect copilot. If Lincoln Continentals could fly, undoubtedly she and Dorothy would be airborne by now, such was the height of their exhilaration. But alas, cars didn't fly, not even over the back roads of Partonville.

"Hang on, Sheba! I'm gonna see if we can't make sixty!" As if she understood English (and most in Partonville thought she did), Sheba spread her hind legs a bit wider.

The Tank topped out at sixty-two before Dorothy started backin' her down to make the stop sign for the T intersection at the hard road.

Dorothy was on her way to the monthly meeting of the Happy Hookers Club, and she sure didn't want to miss a minute of this one. Maggie Malone, seventy-two-year-old Hooker member and owner-operator of La Feminique Hair Salon & Day Spa, was back from her annual trek to Chicago for a regional hairdressers' convention, and the Happy Hookers couldn't wait to see what she looked like. Every year's convention presented Maggie with an opportunity for an exciting, outrageous adventure. Though a lifetime resident of Partonville, business owner, wife, mother of nine, grandmother of eight and great-grandmother of three (Maggie was a woman who relished and lived extremes), she truly loved being away where she could let the "Real Maggie" out, as she told her clients. Why, one year she'd returned with mahogany-colored hair!

Dorothy zoomed up in front of May Belle's at the stroke of 7:00 P.M. Nearly simultaneously, she turned off the engine, kicked open the door and began unfolding herself upright. As usual, she was dressed in pink from her turtleneck to the curlicue laces in her white gym shoes. Once erect, she slung her giant black vinyl handbag over her shoulder and then slammed the door. Realizing it didn't close just right, with all that was within her she slammed it again and hollered to the universe, "Arthur Landers! Some mechanic you are! Next time FIX that door!" Then with one swift motion, Dorothy, eyes glistening with mischief, turned toward the back window, steadied herself and held out her arms. Sheba catapulted through the open window, right into them.

"Sheba, if you gain just one pound or I live to get much older, we'll both be going down on this maneuver." No doubt this maneuver was one of the things that kept this oldster so strong for her age. Dorothy rearranged the wiry-haired dog until she held Sheba's head over her shoulder, as though she was going to burp her. "There now. Don't act too stunned when you see Maggie, okay?" she whispered in Sheba's cocked ear.

"Howdy, Dearest Dorothy," Earl said smack up against the back of Dorothy's head.

"Earl!" Dorothy yelped as she turned to face him. "How many times do I have to tell you to announce your arrival, please! Why, I nearly launched Sheba!"

Earl was always excited about seeing Dorothy. Ever since early that afternoon when his mother told him the Hookers were coming to their house, Earl had been watching for her. No sooner was May Belle's announcement out of her mouth than he went directly to the front closet, pulled on his spring jacket and flung open the door.

"Earl!" May Belle called after him. "The ladies aren't coming until after dinner, honey."

"That's all right, Mother. Dearest Dorothy might come early. I just don't want her to miss our house. I better wait out front on the porch so she sees me."

"For goodness sakes, Earl. Dorothy knows where we live. She knows where *you* live, Earl. It's too early to start watching. You'll lock up your eyes, staring down the road for six hours."

May Belle's short, portly figure was framed by the archway that led from the dining room into the living room of her house, which had been built around 1900. She held a wooden spoon covered with frosting in her right hand while wiping the left on her ruffly blue apron. Earl stood holding the screen door open with his back. With both hands, he tugged his Cubs baseball cap tightly down on his head, completely shading his eyes. Mother and son stood frozen, staring at one another for a moment.

Earl often appeared to May Belle stunningly like Homer, aside from her blue-gray eyes. Same square jaw as his father. Same nose. Same thickness, height and rounded-shoulder posture. This was one of those moments. As powerfully as she loved her son, she missed her husband, even though she had been a widow for many years.

After a few seconds, she began waving the spoon back and forth as though to wipe away her thought. Then she began waving it at Earl.

"Earl Justice, come on in now and close that door. You won't miss our Dearest Dorothy. You can wait on the porch after dinner. In the meantime, get in the kitchen. I've got a few things I need you to do to help us get ready for tonight, and I've got a sinkful of spoons and bowls just waitin' to be licked." May Belle knew how to persuade her beloved Earl.

But now spoon licking and dinner were over and his Dearest Dorothy had finally arrived. He followed close behind her, right up the front steps and into the house, repeatedly and intermittently apologizing for scaring her and loudly announcing her arrival.

"Apologies accepted, Earl. You know I can't stay mad at you for even a minute. And where's your mother? And is Maggie here yet?" Maggie only lived a few doors down from May Belle.

"Mother's in the kitchen, Dearest Dorothy. She's been cleaning and cooking all day," Earl said. "I haven't seen Miss Maggie." He always called everyone Miss or Mr. whatever his or her first name was, aside from Dorothy. She was special. When Earl was beginning to talk, Dorothy had plopped down on May Belle's porch swing, drawn him up in her lap, nestled the top of his head under her chin and begun to sing "Casey Jones." Earl, who ordinarily didn't take to anyone not immediate family, softened his little body and melted right into her.

"Oh, my," May Belle had said as she watched this heartwarming sight. "He sure loves his Dearest Dorothy." Earl had smiled and repeated "Dearest Dorothy," and the name had stuck with the Justice family—and a good number of other Partonville friends—ever since. It just seemed to fit.

Dorothy passed Sheba off to Earl and set her handbag down on one of the head chairs at the dining room table, reserving the prime spot. Then she helped herself to a chocolate-covered raisin out of the bridge mix piled in a cut glass bowl neatly centered on a bright yellow floral napkin.

Dorothy gave the table a quick once-over while she chewed, then picked through the bridge mix for another chocolate-covered raisin. Everything was set up just so for the evening's game of bunco: score pads; pencils; two sets of three dice, one set at each end of the table; coasters for the glasses; and, of course, four bowls of bridge mix. Although the Happy Hookers had, aside from Nellie Ruth, long ago stopped hooking rugs together and taken up bunco, no one was willing to let go of their dangerous name. The club had ended its rug hooking thirty-three years ago, the day Dorthy, in a dramatic presentation, shouted, "Bore, bore, BORE," then threw her half-hooked rug and all materials off her lap and into her bag, where it remained until she finally donated the entire lot to the thrift shop.

Earl gave Sheba a couple quick head pats, then set her

down. She made a beeline for the kitchen, skidding to a halt on the green-and-white linoleum floor right in front of May Belle. May Belle always had a goodie waiting for Sheba, and Sheba never missed a trick.

"How's my little darlin'?" May Belle asked, then tossed Sheba a piece of liver sausage held out from lunch just for this purpose. Sheba jumped up on her hind legs and snapped it out of the air. "Do you know you enter a room about like The Tank enters Partonville?" May Belle laughed at her own joke. Dorothy heard the wisecrack just before she turned into the kitchen, still chewing.

"Well, that's a fine howdy do after that grand birthday lunch yesterday!" Dorothy quipped. "You'd think you were happier to see Sheba than me! And don't be picking on my driving, or you can drive yourself to our next hair appointment." May Belle, who never mustered the courage to learn to drive, just grinned at her friend, knowing full well she was pulling her leg, especially since May Belle always enjoyed walking the few blocks to the shop, whether it was nine or ninety degrees.

"The table sure looks great. And I feel real lucky tonight," Dorothy said as she sauntered across the room to the kitchen table, where the dessert cake was sitting on May Belle's beautiful, Imperial Candlewick cake plate. Like a teasing child, Dorothy first ran her little finger across the top of the bumpy glass edging before lightly letting it rim into the frosting, right where the cake met the platter. She scooped May Belle's buttery confectioner's sugar frosting right into her mouth.

"Hey! That'll be enough of THAT!" May Belle yelped.

"Why leave a cake sitting where we can see it if you don't want us to eat it?"

"Dorothy Jean Wetstra. You'd think after eighty-some-odd years of friendship I'd have better sense than to leave a cake out in front of *you*! "

"Sense has never been your strong point, dearie. But cake-making sure has." Dorothy licked her finger to make sure she hadn't missed a morsel of sweetness. "What do ya say we skip bunco tonight and just go right to dessert?"

Before May Belle had a chance to answer, Earl announced that Miss Gladys and Miss Jessie had arrived. Gladys McKern was Partonville's ten-month acting mayor. Many still wondered if her installation was legal. "Could they just declare a wife mayor to finish her deceased husband's term like that?" they buzzed when Gladys wasn't around. Thus, she was hardly ever referred to as anything short of Acting Mayor Gladys McKern, lest anyone mistakenly think she'd been elected. Jessie Landers was known around town for a lot of things, including hanging in there all these years as Arthur's wife ("How *does* she put up with that cantankerous husband of hers?" was muttered on more than one occasion), but mostly for making her mark as a Partonville star when she played semi-professional softball in her heyday. She and Gladys nearly knocked Earl and each other over getting into the kitchen to see if Maggie was there.

"No, she's not here yet." Dorothy figured she would just beat them to the question. Sheba ran between Gladys and Jessie, greedily collecting scratches and compliments.

"Miss Nellie Ruth's here!" Earl hollered from the living room.

"Great," May Belle said. "Just show her in, Earl."

At sixty-two, Nellie Ruth McGregor was the youngest of the six remaining Hookers; Edna and Rose had long been deceased, and no one had come along to replace them. Although Gladys had once recommended that Cora Davis be invited in, the rest of the club vetoed her suggestion, fearing that every word they shared would make the rounds. The girls had simply learned how to create their own version of bunco with six instead of eight, each pretty much playing for herself rather than in teams, the way it was usually done.

Finally, everyone had arrived but Maggie. Just when the ladies were getting on quite the collective chit chatty roll about the latest goings-on and their personal Maggie Malone speculations, in she strolled, making her grand entrance with a loud "Ta Da!" She was dressed in an orange, swishy gauze skirt and top with a two-inch-wide leopard print belt. Her jet black shoulder-length locks (dyed that way, of course; no one knew what color her natural hair was, since they hadn't seen it natural since she was about sixteen) were in an updo, with sprigs of stiff hair jutting up and out of the center like a firecracker in mid-explosion. Between the hair and neckline she was adorned with deep brown eye shadow, lots of black mascara, tangerine blush and frosty orange lipstick.

"Weeell?" she uttered in a slow, dramatic drawl. Although she stood center kitchen, hip cocked and arms up and out, not one of them could figure what was new. She looked, to all of them, perfectly normal for Maggie.

"Well?" she repeated louder, sounding a bit impatient.

"Well," Gladys finally responded, "you look beautiful as ever. How was the conference?"

Maggie's hands dropped to her waist and she let out a big sigh. "It was exciting and . . . and . . . painful." She jutted her right leg out in front of her, toe pointed and lightly touching the floor. Then Nellie Ruth made the discovery.

"Oh, my gosh," she whispered. "OH, my GOSH!" she yelped. "Maggie's got a TATTOO!"

Maggie just stood there, beaming from ear to ear, while the ladies all but stormed her trying to see exactly where and what while speaking those same curiosities aloud. If only Harold Crabb, editor of the *Partonville Press*, had known about this photo opportunity! The flurry of activity and squealing voices caused Sheba to burst into fits of barking. The kitchen so quickly turned into chaos that even Earl, who really didn't much like crowds, came roaring in from the front porch, where he had continued to wait, even though all the Happy Hookers had arrived. There stood Maggie, leaning back for balance into Gladys's arms. Nellie Ruth, who was kneeling down and holding up Maggie's right leg to get a closer look at the tattoo, began hoisting the ankle upward to give Jessie a better view. Dorothy was behind Nellie Ruth, leaning on her shoulders for balance while trying to get a look-see. May Belle was doubled over with laughter taking in this sight. They looked like a pile of elderly cheerleaders whose pyramid had tumbled down.

After trying to view the tattoo every which way, Dorothy, always being the most direct, said, "What the heck *is* it anyway?"

"Why, it's the new logo for my shop!" Maggie shrieked. "See? See the open scissors here are upside down." She twisted herself around and pointed out the details. "And they create the letter A in SPA! It's so obvious!"

Dorothy grinned when she saw Nellie Ruth's head bow and eyes slam shut. Dorothy knew Nellie Ruth well enough to know she'd begun yet more of her ongoing silent prayers for Maggie, not only for Maggie's immediate shocking behavior, but also for the very salvation of her yet unsaved soul. No, there was nothing United Methodist about a tattoo, and for all things, Nellie Ruth prayed.

"What did Ben say?" Nellie Ruth asked when the group had quieted down. Ben was Maggie's husband of fifty-two years and the love of her life.

"Truth is, he doesn't even know about it yet." Eyebrows throughout the entire room raised in a salute to this startling piece of information. "I told him when I phoned from Chicago this morning that I'd probably just make it home in time to park the car and run over to May Belle's for the meeting. And that's just what I did. All he's seen of me since I returned is a twirl of my skirt when I ran in, gave him my 'Hi, honey' kiss and headed back out the door."

"Oh, my!" Nellie Ruth smacked her hands to her cheeks and said, "Oh, my!"

3

It was nearly 10:00 P.M., an hour past most of their bed-
times, aside from Maggie, who was the latest of late-night
owls. The excitement of Maggie's shocking adventure and
all the chatter, explanations and exclamations immediately
following had backed up their playing time by nearly ninety
minutes. By the time they finally moved off the topic of tat-
toos, heard all the details about Maggie's hotel room and
the latest styles and products, there was barely time for
bunco before Dorothy started hinting that surely it must be
cake time.

Even though they got in only two rounds, hardly
enough to qualify for prizes, May Belle had Earl hand them
out anyway. He was nodding off in a kitchen chair, but he
always loved being the bearer of gifts, and May Belle knew
that after all these years he'd be very disappointed—and so
would the gals—if he missed this special duty. There were
prizes for most wins, most buncos and a booby prize, given
respectively to Maggie, Jessie and Gladys. It wasn't Dorothy's
lucky evening after all. Each winner received a proportion-
ate assortment of May Belle's homemade cookies, wrapped
in clear plastic wrap, secured by loops of multicolored ribbons. Everyone was too full to unwrap them, which is just
the way May Belle liked it: full bellies on the way out the
door and plenty to enjoy tomorrow. The last of the decaf

coffee was poured and most had settled back in their chairs when the conversation shifted.

"You all heard about Tess Walker, right?" Nellie Ruth asked.

"Yes," Jessie said, "Cora Davis phoned to tell me."

"She phoned me, too," said May Belle.

Everyone else acknowledged hearing about it from one person or the other, but mostly they'd heard from Cora Davis, Partonville's unofficial town crier. Even her husband called her that on occasion.

"Why is the funeral being held so long after her death? My goodness, she dies on Friday and doesn't get buried until a week later?" Nellie Ruth wondered aloud.

Gladys responded, "There's only one relative left in the family, her sister's daughter Katie, and she lives in Chicago. Said she just can't get arrangements made until then. She's been talking to Eugene." Eugene Casey was the owner and undertaker at Casey's Funeral Home, Partonville's one and only facility for FINAL RESTING PLACE PREPARATIONS, as it said on his sign. Although there were two cemeteries, Eugene was the only one who actually buried anyone in them.

"I didn't know Tess very well. I'm sure I'm not the only one," Jessie said.

"I used to spend my fair share of time with her," Dorothy said, "especially when we were in our late teens and early twenties. Used to have quite the time together, in fact. May Belle and I were talking about this yesterday. She and her younger sister, Clarice, used to come out to the farm, and we'd berry-pick along the creek. Lively girls, those two sisters, and nearly inseparable. Of course, there was never a berry in our basket by the time we returned. Just lots of purple fingers and tongues!" Dorothy laughed at the memory.

Rather than laughing, Jessie looked surprised, then asked, "You mean Tess was normal once?"

"Of *course* she was normal, Jessie!" Dorothy responded. "I'm not sure she wasn't normal, whatever that is anyway, right up to the end. And are any of *us* really normal?" Dorothy paused and glanced around the room, her twinkling, challenging eyes landing on each one of them. Not an argument was rendered, although a few shoulders shrugged. "Tess was just lost after her sister moved to Chicago so suddenly. It shattered her. I remember her telling me right after Clarice left that it felt like a piece of *herself* backed out of that driveway on Vine Street when her sister pulled away, all her belongings crammed into that little car."

"It's surprising they were so close, with that big age difference and all," Nellie Ruth said.

"Well," Dorothy responded after gathering her thoughts for a moment, "their mom died when Tess was only about seventeen, and their dad had died years before in a combine accident, so that left Tess pretty much devoting her life to raising her baby sister. They became bonded on many levels—sister to sister, mother to daughter, what with that fifteen-year age gap. . . . After Clarice's death, Tess's lifeline shriveled up. She got so she wouldn't answer the door for anyone besides Wilbur when he delivered groceries from Your Store. I always asked him to pass along my greetings to her, especially after she stopped answering her phone. He said she did write her own checks, from what he could tell. Obviously she was at least engaged with life enough to take care of her finances.

"The one thing I regret most is not going ahead and getting folks together from the church to at least care for her yard. Yes," Dorothy said in a thoughtful voice, "I regret that very much." She lowered her head and stared for a moment at her entwined fingers resting in her lap.

"Me, too," May Belle whispered.

"Well, I heard the entire inside of her house is such a ramshackle that the paramedics could barely get the gurney through!" Gladys's loud, unsympathetic voice broke the silence. She, being the acting mayor, seemed always to be privy to insider information—something that really rattled Cora Davis! "I've wondered if I shouldn't have a look-see myself, just in case I'd need to get the health department to condemn it or something. That place has been so grown up with weeds for so long that it would be a great beautification to Partonville just to have the entire lot, house and all, bulldozed. I mean, where HAS that Chicago niece been all this time, what with Tess being her mother's only sister?"

"For goodness sakes, Gladys! Don't you think you're getting a bit carried away here?" What Dorothy wanted to say but was checked from doing so by her spiritual side was that Gladys had grown a little too power-hungry since her installation.

"I'm just telling you that there are comments in official documents leading me to believe I might have to get involved, like it or not."

Speculations soon died out as everyone started yawning and could feel the evening coming to a close. It had been a big evening indeed. Jessie nominated it to go down in the club's "Best of Happy Hookers Moments" they shared each year during the Christmas gathering that, since the club's inception, took place out at Dorothy's farm. Dorothy's two sons and her grandkids always flew in for the holidays; her daughter was deceased. Many others from Partonville, whether in or out of the club, were naturally invited to the gala. Dorothy could accommodate quite the crowd in her big old farmhouse, and she had always loved entertaining. Sometimes there were upwards of sixty people at the Christmas party, filling nearly every nook and cranny of her inviting and fully greeneried-for-the-occasion homestead. All the kids, grandkids and now great-grandkids played board games together and ran around bumping into one another while the adults chattered and laughed and ate themselves silly.

"Yup," Jessie said, "although the entire town will probably be talking about this evening within two days, we'll have to give it a blow-by-blow rehash at the Christmas party when everyone's together so they can for once hear the same version!" Everyone chuckled. Everyone but Dorothy, that is. A flicker of sadness crossed her face. But whatever thought had captured her, it only lasted a moment before the mass exit began.

One by one the Hookers said their good-byes and thanked May Belle. Earl had slipped off to bed right after passing out the prizes. May Belle and Dorothy stood together on the front porch, waving.

"Jessie," Dorothy called out to her just before she got into her car, "tell Arthur I'll be bringing The Tank around sometime this week so he can fix that door properly!"

"Oh, I'm sure he'll be glad to hear *that*," Jessie quipped as she fired up her big old Buick and headed toward the country.

Since Dorothy couldn't see well enough to drive at night—even though she never admitted it—she'd stuffed her pj's, toothbrush and Bible in her giant handbag, knowing the Hookers' evenings usually ran late.

"Whew," May Belle said as she closed the door and slid the deadbolt until it locked into place.

"Whew exactly," Dorothy said. She plopped herself down on the couch like a rag doll, then patted her knee for Sheba to come sit in her lap. "Think we oughta wait up and watch out the front window to make sure we don't see Maggie tromping down the street with her suitcase?"

"Nope," May Belle said. "I imagine that after all these years Ben isn't shocked by much Maggie does."

Dorothy nodded her head in agreement. Sheba sat perched on the end of her leg, head hanging down over her knee. Dorothy repeatedly ran her right hand between Sheba's ears. "Lot of excitement for us old gals, wasn't it, dearie? I imagine you're as pooped as we are." Sheba didn't move her head, but her ears cocked back to acknowledge she knew she was being spoken to.

May Belle removed her apron and hung it on the bentwood hat rack next to Earl's ball cap. She then seated herself across from Dorothy in her favorite green wing chair with hand-crocheted doilies on the arms. She studied her friend's face for some time as they sat in silence. May Belle contemplated the fact that somewhere during the evening Dorothy had lost her spunk. She couldn't help but wonder what had caused it. One thing, since she'd known Dorothy nearly all her life, she knew Maggie's tattoo wouldn't be the kind of thing to rattle her. Nope, she figured Dorothy'd have her usual comment about that: "To each his own, and we're each owned by the same loving Father." It seemed to May Belle that Dorothy started getting quiet after the conversation about the Christmas party.

"You okay, old friend?"

"Yup. Just tired."

"So what do you really think of Maggie's latest adventure?"

"To each his own, and we're each owned by the same loving Father. One day Maggie will know that, too, just like you and I do. And goodness knows Nellie Ruth's sayin' prayers for her right now! Yup, we each gotta make our own decisions." She stopped stroking Sheba and rested her hand on the crook of her back. Her eyes never lifted and her expression revealed she was far off in thought. They sat in silence for a few minutes, then May Belle, still wondering what was bothering her best friend but trusting that Dorothy and the Lord would work it out, finally got up and turned on the hall light before turning off the floor lamps.

"Time to hit the sack, as Homer used to say." May Belle waited for Dorothy to signal Sheba and head for her bedroom. "Your room reservation is the first door to your left, madam."

"Ah, my usual." Dorothy patted May Belle on the back as these two white-haired old friends—one tall and dressed in pink, the other nearly a foot shorter and wearing a faded-blue gingham housedress—walked silently side by side down the hall, Sheba close behind. Then they parted ways, each into her own room.

Sheba jumped up on the end of the twin bed and curled up in a circle before Dorothy had even flipped on the ceiling light. She unzipped the giant bag and laid out her pink, one hundred percent cotton, long-legged pajamas. Next she set her worn, burgundy leather Bible, name engraved on it in faded gold print, on the nightstand beside the bed and touched the lamp shade that turned on the light. *Just like in the commercials,* she thought. "Could the Clapper be far behind?" she asked Sheba aloud to no response. She pulled out her brush and ran it through her hair a few times. Rummaging for the plastic bag containing her toothbrush, toothpaste and plate container, she walked to the bathroom.

When she reentered the bedroom, she turned off the ceiling light and changed into her pj's, carefully draping her clothes on the corner ladder-back chair. She whopped the pillows a couple good ones, folded down the bedspread just short of Sheba, then slid under the sheet and worn quilt. Turning to the Psalms, her ritual evening "Moment with the Big Guy," as she liked to refer to it, Dorothy silently read the words of Psalm 139, lips moving to each word. She needed to be reminded and dwell in the knowledge that God knew all there was to know about her. All.

"O Lord, Thou hast searched me and known me. Thou dost know when I sit down and when I rise up; Thou dost understand my thought from afar. . . ."

She read it through twice before turning off the light.

The Tank was bedded down for the night, allowing Partonville's citizens and the surrounding farmers to rest easy. Dorothy wasn't sure if she would, however. After all, like Maggie, she had her own decisions to make.

"Dear Lord," she prayed, "give me answers. Now. Amen."

4

It was eleven-thirty. Sunday night, and forty-seven-year-old Katie Durbin was sitting very erect at the kitchen table, papers stacked up in front of her in neat piles. She had shuffled and rearranged them until she thought her head was going to burst. CNN news blared from the television in the background, and the Braun was empty of its last drop of French vanilla coffee. One of her steadfast rules was no caffeine after 4:30 P.M. She was angry with herself for this lapse; her nerves were already stretched to the max.

Surely, she'd thought when she first received the phone call from the hospital in Partonville early last Friday morning, surely there had to be another relative. Another way. Something or someone who could relieve her of this nightmare. But nothing in her mother's documents that she'd just finished prowling through proved otherwise: she was the only living relative of Tess Walker, her deceased mother's sister. Yes, Tess was her aunt, but she'd rather not have to admit that either backward Partonville or any of its residents, especially one strange and peculiar duck, was remotely related to her. Now not only did she have to admit it, albeit thankfully not to anyone in her circle of friends, but she also had to see to it that Aunt Tess got buried on Thursday.

She sat tapping her Mont Blanc pen on the table with

her right hand while running the spread fingers of her left hand through her hair. A couple loose strands stuck in her cocktail ring between the platinum setting and the sapphire. She squinted up her face as she yanked the hairs right out of her scalp. Revealing evidence of pain wasn't her style, but who was looking now anyway?

"Great!" she spat as she pulled the hairs from her ring and inspected them. "On top of everything else I need my roots done, and my appointment is Thursday!" About three-eighths of an inch of speckles of gray appeared at the scalp end of one of the deep red strands. She continued muttering out loud to no one. "Maybe Jeffrey can squeeze me in tomorrow."

"Mom," Josh said, "are you talking to yourself now?" At fifteen, Joshua Matthew Kinney, Katie's only child from her long-ago failed marriage, wandered over to the refrigerator, swung open the door, stood staring into it for a moment, then grabbed the milk, unscrewed the lid and took a few swigs while holding the door open.

"Josh!"

"I know. Don't hold the door open. Don't drink out of the milk container. Shouldn't you be in bed?"

"Well, if you know the drill, why . . ." Her voice trailed off as she shook her head, clunked her elbows down on the table and cradled her temples in her hands.

Josh silently retreated back to his room, turned off the computer and crawled into bed. He lay there on his back for quite some time, eyes open, staring into the darkness, listening to the sounds of news blaring under his bedroom door in their perfectly remodeled Lincoln Park brownstone.

She could make things perfect on the outside, he thought, but she sure couldn't seem to hide her own internal disaster at the moment. He wondered if his mom might just finally be cracking. Perhaps she was human after all.

He recalled her events of the last week. Fender bender with the Lexus on Wednesday. Canned from her vice-president job with the real estate development firm on Thursday. And then, the call from Partonville on Friday. Oddly, that seemed to be the most distressing to her. Not that her aunt had died, but that she had to do something about it. He felt that he didn't really know his mom at all, nor did she seem to care to know him. This was just one more thing he could wonder about, but not anymore tonight. He finally rolled on his side, punched his pillow a couple times to fluff it under his cheek, then closed his eyes. In two days he would finally get to see this "backward and pathetic Partonville" place his mother moaned about.

Katie rinsed out the coffeepot, then reviewed her notes and checklist. She had spoken with the coroner, had the body picked up from the hospital and talked about burial. She decided cremation was the route to go since Aunt Tess didn't have a plot. She would have skipped a wake and funeral altogether if she hadn't been talked out of it by the pastor. The only details left concerning the arrangements were ordering flowers and meeting with him on Wednesday. What in the world kind of flowers should she get for a crazy aunt she really didn't know and hadn't seen for more than a decade? What could she even say on the card? *For goodness sake, no one will read it anyway!*

No sooner did she have that thought than she dismissed it. Of course people would attend the funeral and go around reading all the cards. What else did they have to do in Partonville? At least Pastor Delbert Carol, Jr., at the United Methodist Church had sounded more normal on the phone than that Eugene Casey at Casey's Funeral Home! He nearly drove Katie crazy trying to get her to have the funeral on Tuesday. No way could she pull that off. Pastor, however, told her not to worry, that he would help her put the details together. He said he'd talk to Eugene and co-ordinate things. *One step at a time. I'll worry about Aunt Tess's house later. One thing at a time.*

Katie sifted through one of the stacks and found the photo she'd intentionally buried at the bottom. It was a black and white of her mom and Aunt Tess. They were stand-ing next to a silo, arms around one another's shoulders, laughing. Her mom looked to be in her early twenties. She studied it, curious about the location, guessing it was taken before her mom moved to Chicago. Before her mom met her dad, thus before Katie was born. She looked first at the face of her mother, then at Aunt Tess. It always startled her that she could never see a family resemblance. Her mother didn't look like her sister, and she herself looked like nei-ther of them. Katie's father had died before she was born, and there wasn't a single photo of him to be found. Al-though her mother said she had his eyes, no evidence could physically prove it. Even her dad's folks had been killed in an auto accident when he was only seven.

She began wishing her mother were here. She would know how to deal with funeral arrangements and churches. Katie hadn't stepped inside a church or ventured back to Partonville since her mother died. The only reason she'd occasionally gone to church the decade before that was to please her mother, who said she prayed for Katie every day. When Katie's worst fears were realized and she learned her husband had been cheating on her, she determined right then and there that prayers were for the weak ones and God didn't answer them anyway, if there even was a God. Yes, she wished her mom were here, not only because she'd know how to deal with church, but because she'd know how to deal with Partonville, since those were *her* roots. Katie, gratefully, was one hundred percent a city girl.

Suddenly her eyes began to sting and a knot formed in her stomach. Must be the caffeine, she concluded. She slid the photo back in its hidden place, remembering why she had put it there in the first place—*emotional rides are for the weak ones, too*—then stacked up the piles, setting her checklist on top. She slowly got up out of the chair, which she'd been sitting in for way too long. Before turning out the kitchen light, she added one more item to her checklist and she made it number one: "Phone Gregory's FIRST THING." Gregory's was the poshest salon in Chicago, and Jeffrey, her colorist, would work at nothing less. Odds of actually getting a color appointment moved this late in the game were slim to none. But she wasn't one to play the odds. She was one to get her way. That is, until recently, it seemed.

At 6:00 A.M. Katie was up prowling through her library of exercise videos. She still had three hours to wait before she could call the salon. She hadn't slept well, and her entire body felt stiff and old. What would it be today? Cardiovascular workout? Yoga? Kickboxing? In an attempt to drown out the craziness in her head, she settled on a routine that was one of her least favorites but that had bouncy music from the sixties. She popped the cassette into the VCR and

pushed the button. While she one-and-twoed it along with the instructor, her thoughts raced between funeral arrangements and her career.

Although she had been blindsided by her sudden dismissal, she was very aware it had been precipitated by her number one rival's power play to dethrone her and capture her job. The risks and cutthroat competition in industrial and residential development could be brutal, but then that's the way she liked to play the game herself. That's why from the get-go she'd introduced herself and signed all official papers as Kathryn C. Durbin, a name with distinction, rather than her humiliating given name of Katie Mabel Carol Durbin. What in the world was her mother thinking anyway, giving her a name that sounded so . . . Partonville! The fact that she grew up hating getting her fingernails dirty, drove a pricey SUV rather than a pickup and preferred the opera and gallery openings to corncribs and coyotes made her given name all the more ridiculous. Her mom had told her that Mabel was a strong name and that her dad had come up with Carol. Katie just groaned when she heard the explanation. She hated her name so much that she'd never even told her son the whole of it.

Katie was mildly embarrassed about her dismissal, but she wasn't worried about finances or her ability to bounce back. In fact, she didn't have to worry about money at all; between her severance, her gutsy real estate takeovers in the last eight years and her prudent stock market investments, she wouldn't have to work another day in her life. It's just that she loved the hunt. In fact, she was already planning how to position herself against Keith Benton, the guy who had caused her temporary fall. Strong, Hart and Cleaver had, for quite some time, been trying to lure her away anyway. She would undoubtedly move one more rung up the success ladder if she accepted their offer. Maybe she would become a full partner in the conglomerate before the year was out.

But first, first she'd have to deal with Partonville.

"Mom, do you think you can turn that TV down?" Josh's auburn hair was askew and his sweatpants were wrinkled from a night's tossing and turning. His five-foot-ten-inch self stood staring daggers at his mother, who was tirelessly bouncing up and down, red hair dancing atop her head, five-foot-five-inch slender frame looking like a pogo stick on speed. How, he wondered, could anyone be so determined so early in the morning.

"Just five more minutes, Josh. My workout will end in five more minutes. You have to get up soon anyway," she said somewhat breathlessly between hops.

"Oh, right. Like I'm not up already."

"Josh, don't use that tone of voice with me," she said as the video moved into its slow-down portion before coming to an end.

"You did phone Latin, right?"

Katie felt a stab of guilt as once again, in the midst of her busy life, she'd dropped the ball handling something for her son. The Latin School of Chicago was the oldest independent school in the city and certainly among the most prestigious and expensive. Although Josh was neither a jock, the artsy type nor a pocket protector kind of guy–in fact, he had yet to discover his "type"–he had been forced by his mother into attending Latin when he would have much preferred the public school near their home. She insisted he

get an education at Latin, believing upper status and "rigorous college preparatory education," as it said in the bro-
chure, would set him up to be a top-notch whatever it was
he'd decide to be.

Well, top-notch wasn't his goal if it meant ending up like
her. And he might as well add his dad to that mix, too. Dad
had become much more concerned with his second marriage's "Daily Kids," as Josh secretly referred to them, than
with Josh. All either of his parents ever wanted to know, it
seemed, was "Are you applying yourself?" Other than that,
he was at the bottom of their lists.

"Mom. You did call them, didn't you?" He'd read the
look on his mother's face that let him know she hadn't.

"It's on my list for today. We're not leaving until tomorrow anyway, Josh. Don't worry so much."

Right.

5

At 5:45 A.M. Wednesday, Arthur Landers parked his 1993 Ford pickup outside Harry's Grill on the Partonville square, turned off the engine and sat behind the wheel staring at the CLOSED sign on the front door. Harry's was the only grill in town and one of the few true greasy spoons left in the county. Even so, Lester would not unlock that door until exactly the crack of 6:00 A.M., no exceptions. Not weather, emergency or complaining could make him change his routine. And he closed at 6:00 P.M. Sharp. Even if a friend was trying to get in to join another, "Too dang bad. Shoulda got here on time." Twist goes the lock in the door. End of story.

Arthur, Jessie's husband for fifty-nine less-than-blissful years and the only mechanic who'd ever worked on The Tank, wasn't much for patience, other than when he was wielding a wrench under the hood of a car. Then there was no end to it. It was the challenge and dance between steel and man that he enjoyed. But for now, he sat in his truck staring at the door to Harry's. If looks could vaporize, all but his steaming coffee would have disintegrated by now.

At five-fifty, Acting Mayor Gladys McKern bustled her way to be first in line, as usual. Heaven forbid Partonville's Queen Lady, as Arthur liked to refer to her, should miss an opportunity to be first. She was immediately followed by Eugene Casey, Harold Crabb, Pastor Delbert and the rest of the regulars. Of this six-day-a-week order of events he could be assured.

Arthur considered this eclectic group, although *eclectic* was a word clearly out of the realm of his vocabulary. They were lined up practically right in front of his bumper. Occasionally, just to get everyone's juices running, he'd roll down his window and spit. Why, sometimes he even cranked over his engine, just to see them jump. Then he'd grin like a fool. It's not that he was a mean person; determined and set in his ways, like Lester, would be more like it. And he definitely enjoyed being an instigator.

Finally, Lester turned the key, flipped the CLOSED sign to OPEN and the swarm entered. Steaming cups of coffee were already waiting at each unofficially designated place. Lester knew who had decaf and who didn't. Who used cream and who took extra sugar. Like Santa Claus on the night before Christmas, Lester spoke not a word but kept straight to his work as the customers plunked onto their stools. Mostly they saw Lester's back, since the grill was located at the end of the U, although they all knew he never missed a word.

Lester had biscuits and sausage gravy and eggs over easy to cook and serve. And this being Wednesday, he had bacon and onions to cook up for the liver special, and spuds to peel for his famous "smashed taters," as they were listed on his hand-scrawled and photocopied menus in plastic page protectors. No time to chat for Lester. No sooner would he be done with breakfast than the lunch crowd would begin arriving at 10:30 A.M. Farmers got hungry early. Then right on into the early supper crowd so he could lock that door at six o'clock, try to get people to hurry and finish up, clean up the grill and head home to his bachelor dwelling by seven.

"Harold," Gladys hollered across the counter, "any news I ought to know about this morning?"

"None that I can think of. Some more garbage cans were smashed, but that's about it," he said without raising his head from his magazine.

"Nothing more on Tess Walker's state of affairs?"

"Like what?" Suddenly Harold stopped looking at his fishing magazine and gave full attention to Gladys. Perhaps she knew something that he ought to know.

"Like have you asked for official reporter's permission to inspect that place?"

"For what?"

"For possible condemnation."

"Gladys, it's my understanding that her next of kin hasn't even had a chance to look. Why should I? No crime has been committed. And whatever could lead you to believe it needs to be condemned? Just because someone lets her lawn grow tall enough to be baled rather than mowed doesn't mean her place ought to be condemned." He stuck his head back in his magazine at the end of that sentence, trying to dismiss her.

Now it was Arthur's turn. "There's always a farmer looking for hay," he said, looking at Gladys. "Think Tess's yard is big enough to get baling equipment in?" Arthur chuckled, having obviously pleased himself with that one.

"Oh, Arthur." Gladys was clearly disgusted no one was taking her seriously. As if on cue and making a social commentary, BANG! Lester thunked down her plate of "two-poached-eggs-no-bacon-rye-toast-with-no-butter-doc-says-I-gotta-watch-my-cholesterol" order, which always came out of her mouth in one breath. The disruption to her thoughts startled her and caused her to give him a good stare. He returned Gladys's look of disgust, crunched eyebrow to crunched eyebrow, and she thought she saw him shake his head when he turned back toward the grill. This didn't stop Gladys from finishing the diatribe she'd started at bunco last night.

"I'm just saying that I read in official documents that they could barely get the gurney through, her place was so piled up with stuff."

"Everyone's got a right to be messy, Gladys." Harold turned the page of his magazine while Gladys looked around, seeking anyone's support but finding no takers.

She spun on her stool thirty degrees to her right, reached across in front of Arthur and grabbed two pats of butter out of the bowl in front of him. She proceeded to unwrap the little foils and spread every last drop of butter onto her toast, scraping the foil with her knife for any remaining signs of cholesterol. Eugene watched her, then shot Lester a glance as Lester slammed Eugene's biscuits and gravy down in front of him. Lester again shook his head back and forth, Gladys's inconsistency having been fully visible to him as well. Same every morning.

"Got any *real* news on that developer I heard has been snooping around our parts?" Arthur asked Harold. Gladys sounded a loud "hmph."

"Nothing official, but I'm hoping to have more infor-mation by Sunday's edition. I sent Sharon over to Hethrow this morning to try and get an interview with anyone from Craig & Craig. From what I've heard, several people have seen one of their red pickup trucks driving in your neck of the woods, Arthur. Seen anything of them?"

"Nope. Can't say that I have." If Arthur had seen them, he probably wouldn't tell Harold anyway. He much preferred talking to that sassy little Sharon Teller. She was as cute as a bug.

"What make trucks are they drivin'?" Arthur asked.

"Toyotas."

"Traitors. I hope they go broke in a hurry." Arthur had definite opinions about foreign cars and the people who bought them. Just wasn't American.

"I can't think of anyone who would sell his home and land at any price on that east side, no matter how much they offered," Harold said. "And that's the kind of information I hope Sharon can come up with, names—although I doubt she'll be able to. Developers always hold their cards close to their vests. So far we've got nothing but talk. But the amount of talk is increasing. Something must be in the wind."

Cora Davis arrived and settled into her usual table at the window. Then they all turned their heads simultaneously at the slam of the screen door. Earl always let it slam. He was the only one Lester allowed to get away with it without quoting the cost of a new door. He'd finally decided to give up stopping Earl from slamming the door when Earl turned twenty and it became obvious the banging just wasn't *going* to stop.

"Mornin', Earl," Lester said.

"Good morning, Mr. Lester." Earl walked around behind the counter and stood about a yard away from Lester, watching him flip eggs and smash bacon with his bacon press.

"Got any deliveries for me today, Mr. Lester?" He sounded hopeful, as he loved to be useful.

"Not 'til lunchtime, I reckon, Earl. Same as always. Come back at eleven, okay? And tell your mother howdy for me." For more than twenty years, Lester had "hired" Earl to deliver food. His pay was per delivery, not time, as occasionally Earl had a way of getting sidetracked, oftentimes to the back pew at United Methodist, where he rearranged the Bibles and hymnals to his satisfaction. Lester now paid Earl fifty cents per delivery, and the people on the receiving end usually slipped him a quarter or so, too. Nearly all deliveries were to store owners on the square.

As Earl was on his way out the door, Arthur called to him. "Tell your momma I sure enjoyed the cookies Ms. Jessie brought home from bunco last night. I believe those snickerdoodles are my favorite."

"Yes, sir, Mr. Arthur. Yes, sir, I sure will. Mr. Lester?" Earl had opened the door but then stopped before exiting.

"Yes, Earl."

"Mr. Lester, what's a tattoo?"

"Well," he said, as he flipped a pancake in simultaneous motion with the swiveling of everyone's head toward Earl. "Well." His voice trailed off, and he wiped his hands on his apron to give himself time to think. "Why do you ask, Earl?"

"I heard Mother talking to Dearest Dorothy this morning, and she said Miss Maggie got a tattoo. That doesn't mean she's sick, does it, Mr. Lester?"

All heads swiveled back to Lester, whose hands continued to swipe mindlessly at his apron. All heads but Cora's, that is, whose eyes seemed to be permanently locked on Earl. It appeared as though her eyelids had flung up into her eye sockets like a retracting pull-down map in an old schoolhouse. Her mouth was agape, and her arm held her coffee cup frozen in midair. Gladys quickly looked from Lester to Cora, then grinned like a Cheshire cat, realizing that this would be one time when Cora hadn't scooped her, and she didn't want to miss delighting in it.

"Well, Earl," Lester said. "Well, a tattoo is just a decoration. I'm pretty sure you didn't hear your momma correctly anyway, Earl. I doubt Miss Maggie got a tattoo. Sometimes we get things confused."

"Not this time," Gladys said a little too happily, considering she didn't approve. But it was just too much fun to spill the beans to Cora Davis.

"Yes, Earl. Miss Maggie *did* get a tattoo, but I assure you she is just fine, honey," Gladys said.

Bang went the screen door.

Crash went Cora Davis's cup.

Dorothy and May Belle sat across from one another at May Belle's kitchen table. The last of the buttermilk pancakes had been scraped into Sheba's bowl, now licked spanking clean, and Sheba was checking under the table just to make sure there wasn't something else for her.

"Sorry, Sheba. Us two pigs ate every last scrap of the bacon," Dorothy said as she patted the top of Sheba's head.

"And wasn't it good bacon," May Belle said rather than asked.

"Yes. Where'd you get that anyway? Best I've had for some time."

"At Your Store. Seems like his meat market slices are thicker than they used to be. And kind of smoky flavored. I'll have to tell the powers that be we noticed the change and like it."

Dorothy had gotten up later than her typical 6:00 A.M., even though Sheba had arrived in the kitchen right on time. May Belle noticed Dorothy still didn't seem her usual cheery self. She had dark circles under her eyes and was kind of quiet, like last night.

"You got a doctor's appointment today, friend?"

"No. What makes you ask?"

"I've noticed you looking at your watch several times this morning as though you have an appointment. And you seem kind of preoccupied or something. Worried, maybe." May Belle was willing to let last night pass, but now Dorothy's somberness had gone on too long.

"No doctor appointment today, although I do have one on Friday that I better make sure I don't forget."

"Is something worrying you about your health?"

"Nope. Can't say that it is. Just got my regular appointment for prescription refills. I'm nearly out of my heart pills, and Doc Streator's nurse said he won't phone another refill over to Richardson's until I come and see him. And don't think I didn't try getting T.J. to slip me in one more refill. You'd think after four years of putting up with his shenanigans in the wind section he'd figure he owed me one."

"Dearest Dorothy, if everyone you taught or conducted in bands throughout the years owed you one, you'd be the most powerful lady in Partonville!" Both of them chuckled at that thought. And indeed, it wasn't far from the truth. Dorothy had been the band director at nearly every level school for more than forty-five years before she retired at age seventy. She was one of the few farm girls in their area who'd actually gone off to college. Partonville residents had been thrilled to have one of their own come home with such an honorable gift to give the community and one that she'd never stopped giving, in one way or another.

To this day, nearly everyone in town knew who Dorothy Jean Wetstra was. Although they most certainly remembered *her* name, she found that she couldn't keep all *their* names straight. Even though that was a great embarrassment to her, she never missed remembering what instrument they'd played, for she remembered each of them as part of the music of her years, the fruit of her teaching and the gifts in her life. She could look at them and name the instrument. Why, T.J. Winslow played nearly four entire high school years of the worst clarinet she'd ever heard. In fact, in Dorothy's opinion, he continued to be the sour note in the community band today, of which Dorothy was also a member. She played first clarinet, even though it wasn't the favorite of her multiple instruments, because, according to her, "they're weak in that section" and she remembered what that was like from the other side of the baton. Next to the Lord, music would always be her passion.

Dorothy pushed back from May Belle's table and periodically continued to look at her watch. At exactly 9:00 A.M., she announced to May Belle, Sheba and Earl, who had returned from Harry's, that it was time for The Tank to venture home so she could check her e-mail. Dorothy was always one to move with the times, aside from The Tank, that is. She was on her third computer upgrade and fourth modem, often laughing and referring to herself as the fastest old lady in Partonville. May Belle took Dorothy's impending departure as her signal to pack her up with a tray of cookies, bigger than any of the bunco prizes. She knew Dorothy had an unending sweet tooth and also that she was the world's worst baker.

Earl walked right behind Dorothy, all the way to her car. She opened the back door and set Sheba in her place, then got behind the wheel and arranged herself. When she closed the door, once again it didn't close right. She opened it up and slammed it again.

"Earl," she said, looking up at him while she fastened her seat belt, "I'm going to get this car over to Arthur Landers and have him fix it right before it plumb kills me trying to shut the door. Either that or I go flying out rounding a corner."

Earl didn't move. He took in what she said and thought about it while she turned over the engine. Then, as if he'd finally figured out the answer to a riddle, he looked first surprised, then worried, then said, "Dearest Dorothy, don't get killed, okay?"

"Oh, Earl, honey, I won't." With that she tromped on the gas and away she went. Earl stood motionless, staring down the road at the backside of The Tank long after it had disappeared around the corner.

6

Dorothy had once flipped The Tank, or rather she had been helpless to keep from doing so. The accident was caused by a "yahoo teenager," as she put it, who hadn't quite mastered the fine art of speeding on gravel and maintaining control the way she had. He'd come toward her, skidding out of control at the bend, leaving her nothing to do but hit the ditch, ultimately rolling down the slight embankment, The Tank settling on its roof, leaving Dorothy hanging like a rag doll by her seat belt. Boy, that was the talk of the week at Harry's and Maggie's, as well as news in the *Partonville Press*. "Dorothy Jean Wetstra Found Hanging," the headline read. That sure got everybody's attention, as well as won second runner-up for the most misleading headline in the tricounty area at the annual district press awards. That was one plaque that didn't hang on the Wall of Honor in Harold Crabb's office.

When Dorothy first told the story to Nellie Ruth, who came to visit her in the hospital where she was held overnight for observation, Nellie Ruth was at last certain that Dorothy indeed had a hot line to Jesus and a legion of angels that followed her everywhere. Thank goodness Dorothy had a reputation for being one of Partonville's most potent prayer warriors, especially when she unleashed what Nellie Ruth referred to as the Do Something Bazooka

Prayer. No dart prayers for Dorothy. Fast. Out loud and LOUDLY. "Just get right to the big guns and let God work," she always said. No one ever prayed more fervently, succinctly or with more faith than Dorothy. It was a good thing, most in town agreed, considering the way that woman drove. In fact, most in town prayed she'd quit driving, since she was beginning to scare them with her lead foot, not to mention her bad judgment. The Tank wore the proud battle scars to justify their concerns. There was a crevice in her rear left bumper the exact shape of the southwest light pole in the parking lot at Wal-Mart, along with scrapes and paint bruises that looked like a giant cat had been clawing on it and enough dents to make it look like she'd been in a demolition derby.

When Nellie Ruth asked Dorothy how in the world she had kept from panicking when she ended up upside down and suspended, Dorothy said she simply uttered her favorite prayer. Even though Nellie Ruth and practically everyone else in town knew what it was, Dorothy repeated it for her anyway: "Dear Jesus, Just DO something. Amen." And the fact of the matter was that He always did, and usually in quick order. That particular time the fire truck just "happened by" almost immediately. It had been heading back to the station from pumping out its hoses in a nearby field. Dorothy knew this was no accident and blew God a kiss when they arrived.

Jessie was putting clothes on the line when she noticed The Tank heading toward its home. Even though she'd never lost her twenty-twenty vision, a person could be half-blind and still know when The Tank was in motion, because it was the fastest thing around. Why in the world Dorothy needed to be getting home faster than a speeding bullet, Jessie couldn't imagine, but then at their age, neither of their bladders was what it used to be. She chalked the speeding vehicle up to a when-nature-calls episode and continued pinching clothespins onto the sheets.

Dorothy zinged on past Jessie's another half mile, then stopped short of the mailbox at the end of her lane. Her original intentions were to pull up to the mailbox, roll down the window, tug open the mailbox door, get the mail, then shoot on up to the house in time to make her appointment. Instead she felt a sudden need just to take in the beauty of the spring land. She sat staring the eighth mile up her lane, thinking about how familiar it was. As familiar as her own face in the mirror.

Dorothy Jean Brown Wetstra had been born on this farm. As the story went, it was during a blizzard on a November evening, the day before Thanksgiving, when her mother, Ethel, went into labor with what turned out to be her one and only child. One minute Ethel was peeling potatoes for tomorrow's gathering, the next she was doubled over the sink clutching the peeler in her hand while taking stock of the fact that life on the Crooked Creek Farm was about to change.

Since the lane and most country roads were drifted over, there was no way for them to get to a doctor or for one to make it to their house. Charles Brown calmly decided he'd helped bring enough farm animals into the world to figure things out as they came. Of this he assured his wife. She had every reason to trust him, since Charles was a man of his word.

At two minutes past two on Thanksgiving morning, Dorothy Jean arrived. She was greeted by the large and gentle hands of the man who would love her until he died at age eighty-two and the smile and joy of a mother who made it to sixty-two before finally succumbing to a yearlong battle with breast cancer.

Even when Dorothy married at age twenty-seven, she didn't leave the farm. Her faithful husband, Henry, had been more than willing to move in and share life with the Browns. He had been waiting for Dorothy to say yes to his many proposals, beginning before she left for college. In fact, he knew perhaps the only way to make sure he would get to see her every evening was to be sitting around the table, in the kitchen, in the house, on the property she loved. He remembered her telling him once that the fields themselves were part of the rhythm of her life and the notes she played. "My music just wouldn't be the same if I couldn't stand in a freshly plowed row of black Illinois earth or watch the sun go down over a field of golden corn," she told him as they sat in the parked car in the very spot Dorothy sat in now. Of course, in those days they parked at the end of the lane so Charles and Ethel wouldn't see them sparking.

Dorothy sat, hands gripping the steering wheel, recalling so many of those moments. All of her family had gone from Crooked Creek but her. Sheba finally hopped in the front seat, put her paws up against Dorothy's shoulder and began

licking her face. "It's a lot to remember, isn't it, girl?" Sheba
cocked her head, lost in her own doggie thoughts.

Just then a red Toyota truck pulled up behind them,
slightly ahead of schedule.

La Feminique Hair Salon & Day Spa sat one block off the
square. Maggie Malone had, at twenty years of age, purchased it from its original owner, whose husband had run
off with the mail clerk at window number two. While tears
and mascara ran down her face, the woman had scrawled a
handmade sign that said, HUSBAND LEFT ME. SHOP FOR
SALE, posted it in the window and within five minutes, Cora
Davis, then Cora Wethersby, saw it and immediately ran
over to Maggie's house to give her the news, knowing she'd
been talking about getting a place of her own. It turned out
that even busybodies have their golden moments, as this
piece of timely information was a turning point in Maggie's
life. Maggie barely beat another buyer to the shop, where
she sealed the deal with a handshake. Ben, three years older
than Maggie and owner of his own hauling company, said
he would help finance her endeavor as long as she would
marry him within two weeks. Two weeks to the day later,
the long time couple became man and wife in a ceremony
that took place in the Partonville square on the hottest day
recorded in the town's history. Ben was so excited to have
finally landed his beautiful Maggie that her profuse sweat-
ing appeared nothing more than "dewy drops of beauty," as
he told her before he wiped her brow for their first of thou-
sands of steamy man-and-wife kisses.

Over the decades, each time Maggie gave birth to one of

her nine children—she and Ben had *always* hoped for a baseball team's worth—or experienced an identity crisis, she closed down the shop, renamed it, remodeled it and had yet another grand reopening, advertising with dollar-off coupons in the *Partonville Press*. Even though it was always the same location with the same owner—and there were usually playpens, building blocks, crunched Cheerios and kids to walk over, most related to her kids' kids—the ladies of Partonville found these reopenings to be just as exciting as Maggie herself did. She always served some exotic snack or gourmet coffee she'd purchased from one of the many catalogs she received. Partonville just didn't sell the type of things that piqued Maggie's buying buds, so she ordered them. Never let it be said that Maggie Malone had slipped off the cutting edge of trends and fashions, even though her waistline had long ago caught up with her hips and she was often surrounded by a gaggle of great grandbabies!

Maggie pulled Cora's hair up between her fingers as she snipped across the gray locks with her scissors. Conversations at La Feminique Hair Salon & Day Spa had been shocking and lively since Maggie's first day back with that horrid tattoo, as everyone was already referring to it—everyone except Maggie. Although Maggie equally adored the energy and sounds of her family and her shop, the shop bustle seemed to hold special excitement for her this morning, the first day her new logo rode shotgun on her leg.

"So *what* did *Ben* have to say about this, Maggie?" Cora asked, after thoroughly inspecting the tattoo she'd so shockingly had to learn about secondhand. Of course, she'd made an appointment the minute she left the grill, just to check things out for herself. "Why, Alfred would probably divorce me if I'd gone and done something like that. Which, of course, I never would. But *gracious*, I still can't believe you are a tattooed lady!"

"I'll answer the Ben question first," Maggie said as she slipped her little finger under another section of Cora's hair and lifted it for the procedure. "Then we'll talk about a few of the things *you* have done, Cora Davis!"

Cora just raised an eyebrow in the mirror as she yielded her head into the hands of Maggie . . . who was holding those very sharp scissors very close to her aging-but-still-pretty-smooth skin.

"All the Hookers last night were so worried about what Ben would say and, truth is, he *loved* it! Although he'd never mentioned it before, he said he'd thought about getting one himself when he first hit midlife. He teased me a bit and said he 'outgrew' the notion but he guessed I wouldn't have a chance to do that, since it was a done deal. He said, 'Besides, at seventy-plus years of age, Mags, you're just too old to ground, honey!' We both had a good laugh trying to even picture him holding me back!"

"Does this new image mean the shop will be closing again for a face-lift? Last time you redid the shop was right after you got new caps on your teeth, remember? I'd just gotten used to it being called Sleek and Sheik when you went and changed it again. The truth is, though, I rather like this purple color. It seems to feel more relaxing in here than that last red-and-black-striped wallpaper. Besides, all your customers are getting too old for those loud colors!"

"I guess I get bored with things more easily than other people," Maggie said as she took another snip and kicked the building wad of hair out from under her. "This is about my favorite, though. I can't see me changing again for quite some time. And day spas are so *in* now!"

Maggie tilted Cora's head down and to the left, forcing Cora to talk into her own chest. "I've been meaning to ask you, Maggie, what *is* a day spa anyway? And the truth is, I'm not the only one who wants to know."

Maggie sighed, swung the chair around so Cora was facing her and said, "It's a full-service salon, Cora! Some day spas even have electrolysis, wax dips and massage therapists in them."

Cora caught her breath and said, "Do tell! And what do you have that makes it a day spa?"

Maggie twirled Cora's chair back around toward the mirror, pushed her head down again, pumped up the chair two notches and sighed loudly. "Me, Cora. I've got me."

7

It was 5:50 P.M. Wednesday when Katie and Josh neared Partonville. *Wake tomorrow, funeral day after . . . not much time to make sure everything is in place but more than enough time to endure,* Katie thought as she sped down the highway past field after field after field, not one tall building in sight.

They had traveled most of the way in silence since pulling out of their driveway nearly two hours behind schedule. Katie had fielded four business-networking calls, each time looking at the caller ID before deciding to put her purse down once again and engage in verbal battle. Although she wasn't worried about money during what she was sure was her temporary unemployment, she did want to plant as many corporate seeds as she could before heading out of town. Real estate was currently experiencing a wild seller's market, and things were hopping.

Neither she nor Josh had eaten lunch, and Josh's stomach was growling louder than the blabbing voices on the public network radio station Katie always had tuned in. He suspected, however, that she wasn't really listening, as the static was getting louder. Josh noticed his mom had been wearing kind of a glazed-over look for the last hour of their five-hour, southbound journey. He reached over and pushed the search button. Three times he pushed it, only to have it cough up three different country-western singers in midsong and a preacher ranting—at least that's the way he saw it—about "REPENTANCE," immediately followed by "SEND US YOUR MONEY!" *This guy probably has* very big hair! he thought to himself. *Man, no wonder Mom never goes to church!* Options being limited, he stuck with pitiful love songs.

"Great," he said aloud in disgust.

"Great what?"

"Great radio selections," he said with as much sarcasm as he could muster.

"So what's wrong with keeping abreast of world situations and unbiased news?" Katie asked. Obviously he was right about her being in her own world. He turned up the volume until the strains of the very sad singer nearly rattled the windows.

"Earth to Mom. You call 'and she left me for a hound dog and a new pair of boots' news? I didn't think you were paying attention, Mom. Should you even be driving?"

After about three more seconds of the bellowing singer's heartache, he punched the button with the side of his fist, turned the radio off and asked, in his best five-year-old imitation, "Are we there yet?" Simultaneously the worn WEL-COME TO PARTONVILLE sign appeared on the side of the road to their right. He looked at his mother's face to see if he could read her.

"Welcome to Pardon Me Ville," she said aloud, as she recalled that the sign was no more than about three quarters of a mile from the town square.

"What? Did you say Pardon Me Ville?"

"It's what I used to call this place."

"I've never heard you say that before."

"Amazing what forgotten memories we have locked

within us until something comes along to trigger them." Her voice sounded far off.

"It looks exactly the same. Honestly, I don't think one fence post has changed." After checking the rearview mirror, Katie slowed down. She glanced from side to side and rolled down the window when she noticed the highway ditches had just been mowed. Deeply she inhaled that fresh, green fragrance, recalling the sound of her mother's breath doing the exact same thing when they used to roll into Partonville decades ago.

Josh put his window down and inhaled. "Well, Pardon Me Ville smells pretty good."

"Yes, that is one of the few perks one can find in the country. Make a note of this, Josh, as this might be the last one we have for the next few days."

"Right." They both inhaled one more time before approaching the square. "So *this* is the square, huh? Pretty obvious when you get here."

"Take a good look, Josh. This is where all the action happens, if you can call it action. I'll give you a once-around before we head down West Main Street to the motel."

Josh was fascinated by the merging ritual. All traffic, two lanes deep, went counterclockwise around what appeared to be a government building in the middle, and people already on the square seemed to have the right of way. Maybe. He noticed that the hands on the large clock protruding off one of the corners of the stone building were stopped at one-fourteen.

"No digital, huh?" Josh quipped. "Do they even have computers here?"

"I couldn't tell you, but I imagine we'll find out when we

check into the motel and I see if their phones have computer jacks for my laptop."

"I brought mine, too. Thought I'd keep Alex posted on my nightlife now that we've entered Corn Country." He laughed at himself. "And speaking of corn, I'm starving! Nice segue, huh, Mom? Can we get something to eat before we check in? I see a sign that has a coffee cup on it. See it, there on the right just past the drugstore?"

"That would be Harry's," she said flatly, feeling her stomach lurch at the greasy memories. "Unless it's changed hands, which I doubt." She drove right on by, not even slowing for the parking place in front. "I really do want to check in first, Josh. Just to make sure we've got rooms."

Josh craned his neck as they sailed past. Indeed, it was called Harry's, and it looked pretty full. He wondered if they'd have to wait long when they returned. His stomach gave another loud growl.

Katie missed her turnoff, unable to get to the outside lane of the circle. When they were about to drive past Harry's for the second time, Josh suddenly said, "Mom, *please* can we eat first? I'm starving! And look, there's still a parking place right in front."

Katie quickly checked her rearview mirror and pulled into the parking spot, deciding to give her son a break.

"Thanks, Mom. I'm about to turn inside out from hunger."

They unbuckled their seat belts and walked toward the cafe door. Just as Josh was about to open it for his mother, a hand appeared on the other side of the door's glass pane. They heard the clicking sound of a deadbolt, and then the bold-lettered, black OPEN sign that hung in the door was quickly flipped to CLOSED, right in front of their eyes. The sign flipper quickly turned his back and walked away. Josh was so stunned he jerked his head, raised his eyebrows and looked toward his mom in disbelief. She nearly knocked him aside, then tapped on the wooden part of the door with her keys. Although several people on stools swiveled toward the door and looked at them, no one moved. They just sat there, chewing and staring like a field of grazing dairy cattle. Next Katie aggressively knocked on the glass with her knuckles. A staring standoff ensued. The smell of fried onions and bacon wafted through the air, further igniting Josh's appetite. Had he known the bacon and onions were smothering liver, his saliva might have stifled itself.

"Would someone let us IN," Katie said in her sternest commanding voice.

Suddenly the same man who had flipped the sign approached the door again. "Thank goodness," Josh whispered to his mom. Without a word, the man pointed to the hours posted in the picture window, then disappeared. Katie and Josh both looked at their wristwatches. It was 6:00 P.M., straight up, just when Harry's Grill closed.

"Welcome to Pardon ME Ville," Katie hissed rather than spoke. "Let's go. We'll check in real quick and find out where there's another place. Surely there's something." They got into the SUV in silence. As Katie backed out, looking behind her to merge into the stream of traffic, Josh watched the people at the counter swivel their stools back toward their plates. "Show's over," he mumbled.

"What?" Katie asked as she put it into gear.

"Nothing. Nothing, Mom. No wonder you have your own names for this place."

Katie drove around the square, veering off onto West Main Street. Within four blocks, she turned on her directional and pulled up in front of the Lamp Post. It was painted entirely in an unnatural shade of blue with a hand-made sign in the window that said UNDER NEW MANAGMENT.

"I'm not holding much hope out for computers, Mom. At least this guy obviously doesn't have a spell checker!" Again, Josh laughed at his own joke. Katie sighed, gave him a disgusted look, then opened her door and exited.

"Wait here," she said, then slammed the car door and strode with determination toward the entrance that had a hand-painted sign on it announcing RING BELL FOR SERV-ICE, to which she responded, after trying in vain to open the locked door. A young woman wearing a broad smile swiftly unlocked the door and said, "Welcome to the Lamp Post. You must be Ms. Durbin." Before Katie knew what had happened, the woman took Katie's right hand in her right hand and patted the top of it with her left. "I'm Jessica Joy. We hope to be a welcome night-light during your stay. We extend our sympathies upon the death of your aunt, ma'am, and are at your service."

Katie was stunned into inaction. She stood there one step down from the doorstep, mouth agape, staring into the sincere, soft hazel eyes of the long-haired brunette who was far from the old, dirty, crotchety person she'd expected.

"For goodness sakes, where are my manners?" Jessica said. She kept hold of Katie's hand while she led her into the little room that served as a lobby. Katie noticed, when Jessica finally let go of her hand, that she looked to be about six months pregnant behind her delicate muslin dress with blue and rose embroidered flowers around the neckline.

"How was your trip here, Ms. Durbin? You must be exhausted."

"Our trip was uneventful. And yes, I am a bit tired."

Jessica puckered up her heart-shaped mouth in a gesture of sympathy. "Well, we'll see if we can't get you settled in for the night. As you requested, I've reserved two of our deluxe rooms for you and . . ." she paused for a moment, then decided to just end her sentence with "you."

"One's for me and one's for my son, Joshua."

"Oh, I hope he's not just sitting in the car. Please invite him in."

"That's okay. He's actually quite hungry, and he's just waiting for me to reappear so we can find a place to eat. We were hoping you could help direct us."

Jessica immediately looked at her wristwatch. "Too late for Harry's."

"Yes, we found that out at exactly 6:00 P.M., when he locked us out trying to enter."

"Oh, I'm so sorry for that terrible greeting. Lester, Lester K. Biggs, is one of the nicest people you'll ever meet, and he has the biggest ol' heart. He's always got a jar out on his counter asking people to donate to whatever cause has moved him. He does have some rules that are unbendable, though, and closing time is one of them. After we get you settled in your rooms, I'll give you the name of a couple places that are close by."

Jessica moved herself behind the counter and retrieved two registration cards with Katie's name neatly written along the top line of each. "Would you like to see the rooms before you check in, Ms. Durbin?"

"No. You're the only motel in town anyway, aren't you?" Katie realized after she'd spoken this truth that she had wounded Jessica, as it showed all over her face.

"Yes, ma'am. We are. But Paul and me have worked real

hard to not take advantage of that. We don't want you to stay here unless you're happy, though. If you don't find us to your liking, the next closest one is the Ramada Inn near the mall in Hethrow, the next town over. We bought this place about eight months ago," she said, flipping the registration cards in her hands. "It was in a pretty sorry condition, but we've . . ." Her sentences were coming one right after the other in what was beginning to sound like a life's story.

"I'm sure it'll be just fine," Katie said with a tone of finality. Anything to move past this moment. "But why don't you show it to me first anyway." Katie sighed, her tone of voice relenting. She saw no cause to further humiliate someone who was obviously so fragile.

Jessica turned around and grabbed two of the keys from the twelve hooks behind her that were mounted on a piece of maple wood with scrollwork on the corners. "Follow me, Ms. Durbin." Together they walked in silence to room number eleven out of a total twelve. Jessica slipped the key into the lock and turned the knob. Katie took in the surprisingly welcome sight. The room, although somewhat crowded with two beds, was painted a very light lavender with a hand-stenciled border of green ivy. The bedspreads were a lavender-and-green floral pattern, and they flowed onto a light green carpet. Obviously a low-grade carpet, Katie thought, her Realtor's eye never at rest, but new and an excellent color with the rest of the decor.

"The bathroom is this way," Jessica said, even though it was obvious. She flipped on the light and motioned for Katie to come look. Again, it was small, but it had very pleasing colors and decorations.

Katie noticed the decorative basket on the counter containing Avon sample packets. Jessica saw Katie looking and said, "Oh, my friend sells Avon, and I thought some nice fragrances and bath samples would make it homey. I buy all my shampoo and such from her, and she always gives me a handful of samples for the rooms as long as I put her business card in the basket." Katie considered the bad business sense of someone who would give out samples to people who were only in town for a night.

"It's fine," Katie said in as warm a tone as she could muster.

"Would you like to see the other room, ma'am?"

"No, I trust it is just as nice."

"Why don't you just go ahead and take these keys. You can officially check in after dinner," Jessica said.

"No. Business first." Always, Katie thought, business first. As soon as the transaction was complete, Jessica gave Katie the names of three fairly nearby restaurants; two were chains, and the other was a smorgasbord. "Of course, there's always the snack bar at Wal-Mart just out of town," Jessica added. "I really do love their barbecue!" Katie muttered a stiff thank-you and went out to the car.

"Well?" Josh asked. "How's the rooms? And did you find a place for us to eat?"

Much to his surprise, his mother said the rooms were "quaint, clean, small but colorful." As for the food, although he didn't understand what she meant, he did understand food was soon to follow.

"Fasten your seat belt, Josh. We're heading for a culinary feast. I didn't know smorgasbords still existed. No doubt they'll have a tofu bar," she said sarcastically. And even he had to grin at that absurd possibility!

Alex my man! Yours truly checked into the Lamp Post motel in Pardon Me Ville (that's what mom calls it). Surprise surprise! I'm up and running, on-line and waiting to hear what's new in the neighborhood since I left town. Yeah, yeah. I know, it's only been a day since we talked, but HEY! You never know what blonde might appear on the scene. (Or brunette or redhead or purple-haired punker.) Of course I've got my eyes peeled here, although I'll probably have much better luck finding chickens rather than chicks.

Later Dude. Just wanted to let you know I'm available to the cosmos.

Joshmeister.

8

Arthur was sitting in his lopsided, fifteen-year-old La-Z-Boy watching TV when he saw The Tank coming up his driveway. "Oh, no. Not again!" he exclaimed to the universe.

"What? Did you say something, Arthur?" Jessie was in the kitchen slicing tomatoes she had purchased from Your Store earlier in the day. While she was busy slicing the mostly green, hard, tasteless things grown in someone's hothouse, she was daydreaming about the tomatoes they would get from their garden toward the end of summer. Fat. Blood red. Juice running down her arms as she ate them right off the vine like apples . . .

"I said, 'Oh, NO!'" Arthur bellowed. Jessie heard the leg support to the La-Z-Boy snap down at the same time she noticed the trail of dust coming up their driveway. She didn't need to ask what Arthur was talking about.

"Oh, I forgot to tell you that Dorothy said her door wasn't closing right and that she'd be coming by sometime this week."

"Glad you warned me," Arthur said as he strode up behind her to head out the door, but not before picking up a slice of tomato from the cutting board. He popped it in his mouth before she could say anything. "This tomato tastes as bad as The Tank looks," he said after two chews.

Jessie opened her mouth to respond but realized that, as odd as it might seem, this time Arthur was right. He spit out the partially chewed stuff into the garbage can near the back door, then marched across the yard toward The Tank, which had pulled up right inside his old shed turned garage turned shed. Although his face was kind of torqued up from the tomato, he was hoping Dorothy would take it as his silent commentary on The Tank's presence yet again.

The reality was, of course, quite different from what he always made it appear. Although he had long ago retired from fixing cars, that did not include The Tank. She was different. She was old, like him, and set in her ways. He was the only mechanic who'd ever worked on her, and he intended to keep things that way. Besides, today's sissy mechanics—and how they even dared call themselves mechanics he didn't know—only knew how to hook up electronic gizmos, which certainly wouldn't work on The Tank, nor would she take a liking to them. Why, there was no more to that, he used to say, than putting a thermometer in a baby's behind and thinking that would tell you what was really wrong with your child! No, The Tank needed careful consideration.

Sheba ran up to Arthur's legs, wagging her tail as fast as it would go. He gave her a head nod, which she accepted, then she ran off smelling the ground, scooting here and yonder.

Dorothy maneuvered herself out of the car door while trying to protect it from further damage in the familiarly tight quarters in the shed. She then slammed it the best she could, considering she only had about a foot and a half to work with. On cue and just as she suspected, the door didn't shut all the way. "Well," she finally said.

"Well," Arthur repeated.

"Well, I reckon, you know why I'm here, and if you don't, just take a gander at that," she said, pointing to the gap. "I've probably taken another year off the end of my life wearing myself out trying to get this door to shut right. And frankly, Arthur, I don't have that many years left!"

They traded places, and Arthur put the door through the same drill. Again, it didn't close right. Dorothy grinned like a satisfied ninny. Arthur looked at her and said, "Yup. Door doesn't close." They both just stood there looking at it for a spell until they were distracted by a chicken jutting by the door with Sheba close behind.

"Sheba! Get your naughty self over here right now!" Dorothy yelped. Sheba slunk into the shed and sat down beside Dorothy, putting her head against her leg in order to make up.

Arthur walked along the edge of the shed wall until he came to his giant rubber mallet. "It's all in the right tools," he said. Then he proceeded to bang around, first on the door above the window, then on the latch itself. Finally he tested his work and *voilà*! Slam it went, right the way it was supposed to.

"Had I known *that* was all it would take, I would have wound up and given her a few good licks myself! Probably would have helped my stress level."

"What have you got to be stressed about, Dorothy? Being on time for your next Hookers meeting?" He gave her a lopsided grin as he passed her by to hang his mallet back up.

"I imagine you'd be quite surprised to find out, Arthur. But today's not the day you're going to."

Just then Jessie appeared. "Do I have to worry about you two alone out here in the shed?" she teased.

"Not in the least," Arthur responded before Dorothy could open her mouth. "I can't get along with the one I got. Why would I make eyes at another one?"

"And don't you forget it, buster!" Jessie retorted.

"How's it going, Dorothy?" Jessie asked while rubbing her hands on her slacks. "You look tired. Everything okay?"

Dorothy sighed, picked up Sheba, gave her a few solid strokes, as though centering herself, sighed again, opened her mouth to speak, then shut it. Jessie cocked her head, but she didn't speak either. Finally Dorothy uttered, "Fine. Tired, but fine."

"Everything okay?"

"Maybe."

"Anything we can help with?"

"Nope. Just me and the Lord and a few folks in between are workin' on this one."

"Keep us posted, friend," Jessie said. "If there's anything, anything you need us for, you know we're right here."

Dorothy picked up Sheba and pointed to the rear open window of The Tank. The dog leapt out of her arms and into the backseat.

"Thanks for caring, Jessie. I imagine you'll all find out soon enough, should the Lord surprise even me." She gently opened the door and sneaked inside, having to turn somewhat sideways, the same way she had exited. Then she cranked the engine and put it in reverse.

"Look out, chickens!" Arthur hollered. "Dorothy's in reverse!" Jessie elbowed him a good one. With that, Dorothy gunned out of the shed, toppling Sheba in the process, then down the driveway they went.

"What do you make of that, Arthur?"

"I'd say she purrs like a kitten."

Jessie was about ready to give him another good elbow to the rib when it suddenly dawned on her that although she was wondering about Dorothy's peculiar behavior, he was talking about The Tank.

9

Sharon Teller sat in a deep, expensive-looking, brown, buttery-leather chair in the reception area at Craig & Craig Developers. She was waiting to meet with Colton Craig, the senior partner in his real estate monster of a machine. At least that's the way she personally looked at it. From a professional point of view as a reporter representing the *Partonville Press*, she knew she had to wear a neutral hat during the interview and writing, but it wasn't going to be easy. She detested everything about his so-called progress. All she had seen it accomplish so far was more traffic and more homes, less land, less privacy, less of everything she loved. The town of Hethrow, to the east, where most of the growth had occurred, felt like it had slithered up in the night and was poised like a python, mouth agape, ready to swallow Partonville alive, and each Craig brother was an eyeball.

She flicked a *New York Times* in front of her face in an attempt to act as if she were reading when in reality she was inner-dialoguing, mustering all the mental capabilities she could in order to live up to the press credentials she carried in her pocket. Just before she feared her head would explode from concentration and constraint, the receptionist's buzzer startled her so badly that a strange little squeaky noise escaped from her throat. *Oh, now* there's *professionalism!*

"Mr. Craig will see you now, Ms. Teller. Go through this door, and his office will be the last on your left." Without swiveling her chair, the receptionist pointed a finger over her own shoulder toward the door behind her.

"Thank you." Sharon walked past the receptionist and swung open the heavy oak door that had tiny pieces of beveled glass spelling out the name CRAIG set in the middle of what looked to be a lead glass panel. The overt decadence prickled her hide. She fingered her press card like a touchstone to keep her mental game on course. Down the long hall she walked, noticing that every door was closed. The faint smell of burning cigar wafted out from somewhere, and she hoped it wasn't from within the office she was about to enter. She stood in front of the door for a moment, took a deep breath, then knocked.

"Come in, Ms. Teller," a firm voice from behind the door announced. She snapped her head erect, threw her shoulders back and walked with determination into the office.

She was stunned at the sight before her. Colton Craig's office was nearly as big as her entire little Partonville home! He had a corner office, and both exterior walls were, from nearly floor to ceiling, glass with a slight tint of gray. He overlooked what used to be a quiet little town called Hethrow but what now, in her opinion, more closely resembled a yucky Baby Chicago. Of course, she had to admit she was personally familiar with every mall and strip mall in the entire vicinity, being the clotheshorse she was. She also enjoyed the vast selection of salons to choose from, and attending some of the new junior college's cultural events, and . . . yes, she did have those conflicts.

The room itself was austere. Nothing extra. No piles of

papers, blueprints or building models were visible. His gigantic desk had such large claw-foot legs on it that it looked like it might begin to lumber to life at any moment. It was set on the diagonal facing the windows, and his back was to her. *Pretty trusting for someone who makes so many enemies,* she thought. When she was closing the door behind her, he swiveled in his chair and said, "Leave it open, please. And welcome."

She strode across the room with steps of authority, hand extended in front of her, swallowing hard just before making contact. He had the deepest green eyes she'd ever seen and was very tan for spring, accentuating his whiter-than-white teeth. His hand was large, and the shake warm and firm. She was thrown slightly off base by his staggering good looks and feared she was blushing at her own feminine vulnerabilities.

"I'm Colton Craig, but please call me Colton," he said.

"Sharon Teller." Her voice sounded like that of a twelve-year-old rather than a twenty-five-year-old professional woman. *Get a grip!*

"Please, sit down," he said as he pointed to the over-stuffed burgundy leather couch directly in front of his desk. She noticed that the *Partonville Press* lay open in front of him. It was the only thing on the highly polished mahogany aside from his phone and an autographed baseball in a glass box.

She quickly got herself arranged, whipping out her notebook from her large handbag that also served as a briefcase. She rested it on her lap, then removed a tape recorder before setting her bag on the forest green carpet. *Looks like the color of money to me.* Before she set the tape recorder on the desk she looked up at him and asked, "Is it okay if I tape our conversation, Mr. Craig?" She was not going to take him up on his first-name-basis offer, and he raised an eyebrow at that but let it pass without acknowledgment.

"Of course. I have nothing to keep off the record, and I love being quoted verbatim. Not that I think you'd get things wrong. You're quite an excellent reporter, Ms. Teller," he said as he tapped the paper with the back of his right-hand index knuckle. "Lively writing. Passionate." There was something about the way he said "passionate."

She suddenly felt like a deer in the crosshairs of a marksman. She fumbled with the tape recorder and finally got it in place on the front of his desk, microphone facing him. By the time she'd opened her steno and taken the lid off her pen, she had collected herself, mentally pulling her own six-shooter out of its holster. She pushed the "record" button. *Fire round one!*

"Mr. Craig, word around Partonville is that your firm is seeking a land deal to the east of Partonville proper. Thus far we've been unable to verify the rumors. I'm here to collect the facts from the horse's mouth so we can either help put a stop to the rumors or substantiate them."

"Well, the horse's mouth," and he paused just a fraction of a second here, which was long enough for the left corner of his lip to curl, "says it's true that Craig & Craig Developers is always open to expand our progressive development. We believe progress and growth are good things."

"Are you talking to any Partonville farmers, Mr. Craig?"

He grinned a total teeth-showing grin and again paused for a moment, tilting his head forward toward her, as if to ricochet the answer to her via silence. After studying her blank face for a moment, he then proceeded.

"If . . ."—dramatic pause, more teeth—"if we were, Ms.

Teller, we certainly wouldn't be talking about it. And please don't read more into that answer than I've stated. I'm sure an esteemed reporter such as you understands the sensitivity of the real estate world well enough to know the drill. I do like your tenacity, though."

Truth be known, she didn't know the drill. This was her first venture into real estate waters, and she was mad at herself for being caught in her own ignorance. She was sure as shootin' gonna research it when she got back to the office! *What the heck was Harold thinking, sending me out to embarrass myself like this? He should have come himself!* Colton Craig was obviously reading her like a short book.

"So in other words . . ." she said, trying to buy herself a little time while nearly breaking a sweat trying to reveal nothing in her eyes, even though she knew it was too late.

"No, I thought we were recording my words exactly," he said, intruding into her sentence.

"Of course we are," she said politely. "But just to clarify your intentions . . ."

"Make that our *vision*, please. Just to clarify our vision," he said, again intruding into her sentence with his silky voice.

"So, your *vision* is to build a housing development where?" Her voice lifted at the end of the question.

"Our vision is to continue seeking possibilities, Ms. Teller, wherever they might present themselves. As you know, Hethrow has undergone a complete face-lift and growth spurt since our firm began development when Ford Motors announced they were bringing a plant to town a decade ago. Not only have we created more housing, but downtown businesses have flourished and grown, the new junior college is drawing from several counties, an upscale mall was established and, as a result of all that, more jobs are available, breathing further life into the community and economy. We believe we've helped improve the integrity of the entire area."

Simultaneously she noticed the dark ring around his irises and bristled at the use of the word *integrity*. *As though you have a clue what it means! More and more of everything including more money in your pockets doesn't automatically add up to integrity in anyone's stretch of the imagination. Although Partonville might be lacking in a few things, it certainly isn't lacking integrity! Why, it is oozing with integrity, from businesses to producing farms, WE ARE OOZING INTEGRITY!*

She sat there watching the tape recorder run for a moment while she leashed her emotions lest they come bursting out of her lips.

"Do you have any questions, Ms. Teller? Do you disagree with what I've said? Am I boring you?"

"I do wonder at your use of the word *integrity*, sir." *Oops.*

"You question my integrity, Ms. Teller? In what way?"

"Not *your* integrity, just your use of the word, as though more of everything equals integrity. I guess it's a matter of semantics," she said, working to bail herself out of saying what she'd already said and what she really meant.

"Yes. Semantics." For the first time since their eyeballing of one another, Colton looked a tad bristled himself.

Sharon leaned forward, shut off her tape recorder and dropped it into her bag. She folded her spiral steno so the cover was protecting the pages, ran her pen down through the spiral, catching the clip over the edge to keep it where it belonged—she had to have control over *something*—and stood up. All this without making eye contact with Mr. Craig, who, she knew, was studying her closer than she'd like to be studied at the moment.

"I thank you for your time." She pulled out a business card and tossed it on his desk. "I'd like to keep our readers abreast of any events concerning this. Please give me a call should there be any solid developments."

"I assume this means our time together is over for now, Ms. Teller?"

I will not let him pull my chain! She flung her bag over her shoulder and stretched out her hand to shake good-bye. "Yes, sir. There is no need to keep talking about nothing. When and if there is something, we'll try again."

The warmth of his parting handshake stayed with her all the way to her car.

Sharon sat in her Chevy in the Craig & Craig parking lot, reflecting on her mix of emotions. She was angry, for sure. The man was arrogant. For sure. He also had the widest shoulders she'd seen for some time and . . . *STOP IT! Go get yourself some lunch and GET A GRIP!*

Driving down the main drag, she craned her neck from side to side, taking stock of restaurants and waffling with herself and her taste buds about whether to have Mexican food, a sub sandwich, chicken or . . . *I can have whatever I want. Whatever I have a taste for, I can find it here!* As she passed by Hethrow General Hospital, she recalled reading about their new trauma unit and cutting-edge birthing facilities in one of the *Daily Courier's* editions. Of course, she usually read the syndicated paper in order to . . . um . . . keep abreast of what was happening in the world. The world, not just Partonville. The world, with ethnic diversity and research and political challenges and maybe a husband on the horizon, since Partonville seemed to nearly be fresh out of bachelors. . . .

Craig had talked about more jobs. Many of Partonville's youth had for some time been fleeing after high school to pursue higher education. More often than not, they didn't seem to be returning. Job opportunities were elsewhere. *Would it be a* bad *thing to have more jobs come to Partonville? How much more debt-free from college loans might* I *be if the junior college in Hethrow had been in place when* I *went off to college?*

Sharon snapped to attention and slammed her brakes on just in time to keep from rear-ending the car in front of her. About the twelfth car back from the red light. The red light causing a yet unknown traffic backup in quiet little Partonville. Where things weren't so crowded. Partonville, where everybody knew her name and her family. Her roots. Her life.

10

Tess Walker's funeral would take place early in the morning, and final arrangements needed to be made. Dorothy was in need of a distraction from her own thoughts and was happy to have a task at the church, especially since Nellie Ruth would be assisting. Nellie Ruth was usually humming while she worked, and since music had always been a balm to Dorothy when she was troubled, her friend's company brought many gifts.

Nellie Ruth loved being on the altar guild at United Methodist for several reasons, not the least of which was that it gave her a chance to spend more time with Dorothy. It also allowed her to spend time in this place of deep personal meaning and spiritual transformation.

Nellie Ruth had been raised in St. Louis, Missouri, where she'd learned too much about dark things at a very early age. From the time she was nine years old, her father had violated and abused her in unspeakable ways in their small apartment. When she was sixteen, her mom died of a heart ailment. Caring for her alcoholic father and putting food on the table became her lot in life. She had no worldly experiences other than the torment within her home and a job she held for three years at a local grocery. She did everything from mopping to restocking shelves to checking out customers' orders. She was happy to have a reason to be out of the house and did enjoy her job, aside from the fact that she didn't believe it would ever earn her enough to be able to strike out on her own.

She "escaped" that life when her father died. He was struck by a car in front of the tavern when he stumbled off the curb in front of the vehicle. Nellie Ruth was just eighteen years old. Without thinking things through, the red-haired girl with the oval face and sad eyes packed a suitcase, took her last two weeks' pay, filled the gas tank of the Ford and headed north until she stopped crying. It happened that was in Partonville.

Dorothy had come to town to set up the altar for Sunday's service that day when she discovered this skinny young woman sleeping in her car in the church parking lot. When she knocked on the window, it startled Nellie Ruth so badly that she awakened and began crying all over again.

Dorothy asked if she was okay, but Nellie Ruth couldn't even respond, she was heaving and sobbing so violently. Dorothy flatly stated that she wasn't leaving until Nellie Ruth came into the church, calmed down and assured her she was all right. She stood outside Nellie Ruth's locked driver's door in the pouring rain, hand on the door handle, silently praying, for nearly forty minutes.

Finally Nellie Ruth realized this woman meant what she said. She was too weak to drive a lick farther anyway. At last she dragged herself out of the car, and Dorothy led her into the church. There Nellie Ruth poured her heart out to this kind and gentle woman who held her until she had spent all her emotions. Dorothy brought her a cup of hot tea after phoning May Belle to come set up the altar for her.

Dorothy's only explanation to May Belle was that she had an important mission. May Belle knew enough about Dorothy to believe it.

When Nellie Ruth was done with her cup of tea, Dorothy invited her back to the farm, telling her she could stay in the extra bedroom until she found a job and a place of her own. For reasons unknown even to herself, that's just what Nellie Ruth did.

After three days of nothing but sleeping and eating and allowing Dorothy to nurse her back to life, Nellie Ruth was ready to face the world. Dorothy got her a job at Your Store; she was a perfect fit and a great asset. Within three weeks, thanks to Dorothy and her husband's gracious ministering, hospitality and what could be described as nothing short of the healing powers of the land on Crooked Creek Farm, she had saved enough to pay a month's advance rent at a rooming house in town and had become strong enough to tackle independence. She went on to become a head checker, a produce manager and now was assistant manager of the entire store. As in the days of her youth, she still loved working in the grocery business. She enjoyed everything about it, from the bustle of the people to the fragrance of freshly ground coffee to the orderly shelves. But especially she loved silently praying for unsuspecting people buying everything from fresh oranges to baby food to thumbtacks.

Now here these two women stood, side by side, discussing preparations for the sanctuary for Tess Walker's wake and funeral. A couple of floral arrangements had already arrived, including Katie's, whose stock sympathy card read

"Kathryn and Joshua." The altar needed to be set up according to Pastor Delbert's wishes. Back pews must be roped off so those attending would sit together. They didn't anticipate a very large crowd, and they were afraid people would scatter themselves around, making their numbers appear even smaller than they would be.

In the midst of their discussions, in walked Katie and Josh.

Before leaving Chicago, Katie had made arrangements to meet Thursday morning at nine-thirty with "please-call-me-Pastor-Delbert," as she referred to him when speaking to Josh about their appointment. Pastor Delbert Carol, Jr., had corrected her three times during their phone conversations with exactly those words after she called him Father Carol, not knowing his proper title. At 9:30 A.M. sharp, Katie walked into the sanctuary to find two women she didn't know talking about her Aunt Tess's arrangements as though they were in charge.

When Dorothy looked up and saw Katie and Josh standing there, she didn't say a word but headed right toward them with her arms outstretched. Since Katie didn't expect such an old lady to move so quickly, before she knew what had hit her, Dorothy threw her arms around her and embraced her solidly to her chest. "Why, Katie Durbin! I haven't seen you since you were a tyke, but I'd recognize you anywhere!" Her determined hug and solid back patting continued. "I'm sorry this is what's finally bringing us together after all these years. Oh, how I loved spending time with your mother and aunt when we were growing up!" Dorothy finally released Katie and backed off a bit to look at the stunned woman's face.

"Oh, honey! I didn't mean to squeeze the life out of you!" she said, patting Katie on her left shoulder with her right hand.

"And you would be?" Katie looked from Dorothy to Nellie Ruth, who had walked up behind Dorothy, then back again into Dorothy's face.

"Forgive me, child. I'm Dorothy Wetstra. Like wet straw but without the end *w*. I'm on the altar guild here at United Methodist. I was born and raised and will undoubtedly die right here in Partonville, so I reckon I know just about everybody." She noticed Katie was now looking over her shoulder, so she turned around and said, "And this here is Nellie Ruth. Nellie Ruth McGregor. She's on the altar guild too. We've been talking about your aunt's arrangements. We're so sorry about your loss, honey."

Katie hadn't been called honey by anyone since her mom had died. Although it did stir something warm within her, she also found it disturbing, considering this woman didn't really know her from a river of caffe latte.

"And who is this?" Dorothy asked, pointing and moving toward Josh, who was grinning like a hyena at his mother's obvious discomfort with the situation.

"Josh," he answered, extending his hand to ward off any possible hug attack.

"This is my son, Joshua Kinney."

"I'm sorry for your loss, too, honey," Dorothy said. Nellie Ruth hadn't opened her mouth yet; she had long ago learned that Dorothy knew how to handle strangers.

"Oh, that's okay," Josh replied almost happily. "I didn't know her anyway." Katie turned on her heels and threw Josh one of her looks that implied pending disaster should he not be more careful with his words.

"Now, can we get you a drink of coffee or water or something? You must be tired after all that driving. What on earth time did you leave this morning to get here so early?"

"We came in last night," Josh replied before his mom could open her mouth. "We stayed at the Lamp Post."

"Oh, that lovely young Jessica Joy and her husband Paul have been working so hard, adding so many nice personal touches to the place. When I come into town I see her out there in the early morning tending to those flowers, and after dinner I see him carrying a ladder or a bucket of paint from one place to another and her tagging along, hands full of whatever. Heavens, he's already put in a full day's work in the mines and her carrying that little one around inside her now. How was everything? I'm sure it was lovely. And if I'd known you were going to be in town I would have invited you out to the farm for supper. My goodness me, it's not bad enough your having to lose a relative but then to be in town with no one to talk to!"

"Actually it worked out just fine. We were tired and probably wouldn't have been good company anyway," Katie said, wondering at a woman who would invite people she didn't *really* know to have dinner in her home.

"What time did you arrive?" Nellie Ruth asked, having realized she didn't want her silence to be construed as indifference.

"About six o'clock," Josh answered, enjoying the friendliness of these two ladies.

"So you *were* here for supper then?" Dorothy asked.

Katie just nodded an affirmative.

"Did you dine at Harry's?"

"Nope. He pretty much locked us out before we could get in," Josh said, taking great delight in telling the details of the story, keeping them engaged in more conversation than he knew his mother would invite.

"Oh, my!" Dorothy remarked. "He is set in his ways. A good man but pretty unbending, I'm afraid."

"So we were told by Jessica. So we noticed ourselves," Katie said, revealing a little more edge to her voice than she would have liked.

Dorothy studied her for a moment, as though looking deep within her. It became a look so penetrating that it made Katie back up a step. Katie then inquired where she might find Pastor Delbert.

"Why, I imagine he's in his office, dear. Follow me." She was off and stepping before the phrase was out of her mouth. Nellie Ruth motioned for Katie and Josh to go ahead and told them she was going to stay and continue working. "I imagine I'll be seeing you shortly anyway," she said. "I'm sure Pastor Delbert will want to make sure we're all on the same page as he goes over things with you."

Katie and Josh followed Dorothy to the back of the sanctuary, the same way they'd come in, and then they made a right-hand turn toward a doorway at the end of the narthex. Katie fully expected to see an office when Dorothy opened the door and disappeared down a stairway. She turned around and looked at Josh, who shrugged his shoulders, then they both followed this speeding bullet of a woman. Dorothy hollered over her shoulder that the fellowship room was also "down here along with the Sunday school room, nursery and our adult Sunday school meeting place. Pastor Delbert's office is in the very back corner. He claims that since he came to us eleven years ago, following the death of his father, who had been our pastor for thirty-eight years, that he needed to have his own space and identity rather than moving into his father's office upstairs. We figure he could do whatever he wanted since he was the pastor. We long ago converted Pastor Delbert Senior's office into our library. Feel free to take a look around in there before you leave. In fact, I'll take you right to it when we're done with arrangements."

Katie listened, wrote off any need to visit a church library and considered how unusual it must be for a church to have pastors from the same family, especially ones who obviously stay around until they die. By the end of her thought they were entering Pastor's office.

Pastor Delbert Junior simultaneously stood and pushed back out of his chair, which shot like a bullet out from under him and rolled with such force that it crashed into the wall. It looked as if this chair launching was a common occurrence, as the wall behind him was dented and full of black marks. In fact, he appeared disheveled himself. His thinning hair was askew, and his glasses were slightly cockeyed. His medium stature was relaxed into bad posture. When he looked as if he might come around his desk, Katie quickly extended her hand. First surprised by Jessica's handhold, then taken off guard by Dorothy's hug, she wasn't about to let another show of affection blindside her again.

"You must be Katie Durbin. Welcome to United Methodist Church of Partonville. I'm sorry you're visiting us under such sad circumstances," Pastor said.

"Thank you. I appreciate all your help over the last few days. I can't imagine getting all the arrangements made without it." And she meant that with all that was within her. Dorothy quickly interjected something about turning this part over to them, then disappeared out of the room and back up the stairs.

"I'm happy to be of assistance. I just wish I could have known your aunt. Since I grew up in Partonville and my dad was the pastor here at United Methodist for so many years, I did get at least familiar with most of the names if not the people themselves. I knew where your aunt lived and that she had a sister in Chicago, but that was about it, I'm sorry to say. As I recall, my dad used to call on your Aunt Tess quite often when I was young, although I don't believe she actually ever attended our church. I'm not quite sure why he was so rigorous in his visits, but I do know Dad wasn't one to give up on what he considered might be a lost sheep. I understand she kept pretty much to herself these last many years."

"I wouldn't know about that, Pastor Delbert. I hadn't seen her myself for over ten years. We only corresponded once a year, and that was Christmas cards with maybe a line or two in them. She was a bit unusual." Katie figured she'd take the high road and leave it at that.

"Yes. Well, just the same, God knew her, and we're here for you now. We'd like to help you see to it that she has a good Christian sendoff. I've been talking to Eugene Casey down at Casey's, and he'll be sending your aunt's cremated remains over about two-thirty this afternoon, in time for this evening's visitation, even though you've made it clear we're not displaying the urn. It seems as though everything is pretty much in place for her next journey."

You make it sound like crazy Aunt Tess will be arriving for a bon voyage party! How can people involved in the church sound so cheery about death and so sad about people they don't know?

"There is no urn," she said flatly.

"No urn?"

"No. Mr. Casey described a few of them to me on the

phone, but I didn't see the point in having one, since I'll be disposing of her ashes anyway." She realized that sounded a bit harsh, and it was reflected on Pastor's face. But then facts were facts. She hadn't even kept her mother's ashes. Although the loss of her loving mom had deeply pierced her heart, she knew keeping that silver urn would neither help heal the wound nor give her comfort. In fact, it might even induce self-pity when she looked at it, and pity of any type wasn't acceptable.

Although Katie and her mom hadn't always seen eye to eye, they were quite close. After all, until Katie married it had pretty much been the two of them against the world, even considering the differences in their country girl heart vs. city slicker head approaches to life. Truthfully, why Clarice had ever moved that obvious country girl heart to the city to begin with was a mystery that had always puzzled Katie and died with her mom. When Aunt Tess inquired at Clarice's funeral whether Katie was going to keep or spread her mother's ashes, Katie simply asked her aunt if she'd like them, believing Partonville was where her mom belonged anyway. Aunt Tess became teary-eyed at Katie's offer, then quietly accepted the urn.

And now, no, there would be no urn for Aunt Tess.

"Please, won't you be seated." Pastor pulled up an avocado green, circa seventies chair with a frayed cushion, then retrieved the beige metal folding chair propped against his office wall. He seated himself behind his desk. Josh stepped behind the cushioned chair to push it up for his mom. She took one look at the stained and ragged fabric, another at her silk slacks, then told Josh he could have "the comfortable seat."

"All righty then, let's go over the final details," Pastor

said as Katie seated herself on the edge of the folding chair. "Dorothy and Nellie Ruth are figuring the layout for the flowers. And by the way, I hope you noticed your flowers did arrive. They're lovely. The ladies will also be tending to some of the details in the sanctuary so that we can be intimately gathered for the service. Gertrude Hands has agreed to come play the organ for us while people are filtering in and after the service."

"What else do we have to decide?" Katie asked.

"I realize you hadn't seen your aunt recently, but do you know if she had any favorite hymns or Bible verses? Or might there be any stories, funny or poignant, or things you did know about your aunt you'd like us to share?"

Katie was at a total loss. She sat staring at him, unblinking, for a moment, then realized she had nothing with which to respond. *Think. Think, Katie! Surely there's some bit of information you can share.* Try as she might, however, nothing came to mind other than her own annoyance with her aunt's peculiarities.

She tried to recall a story her mother might have shared about her sister. Again, all she could come up with was her own words, words that visibly stung her mother: "Mom, I just don't have time right now to hear about your crazy sister!" How many times had Katie brushed off her mom the last year of her life as she tried to share her concerns for her only sister? Fretted about what would happen to her after she was gone? Her mother, being a gentle soul, had never even chastised Katie. Just sighed. Yes, she remembered her mother sighing, rubbing Katie gently on the shoulder, then softly suggesting that Katie perhaps needed to get more rest.

Katie began to feel somewhat nauseated. Detached. Alone.

She realized that she had no one to call, no family to seek, no memories to mine in which to find answers to what should be an easy question. Only her responses to life, which suddenly felt like icy cold smacks to her own face.

No stories. Katie had no stories of her aunt, whose existence she'd spent more than a decade trying to deny and whom her mother had spent a lifetime loving—just as she'd loved Katie. Katie had actively refused to embrace this entire Partonville part of her mother's past, this small-town background. After all, SHE WAS A CITY GIRL! She had been filled with nothing but such distaste for this place . . . so put out with the task . . .

She became overwhelmed by the fact that her last tie to her mother was now gone, and she had never done one thing to maintain it. She was blindsided by a barrage of reality, or repressed grief, or deep sorrow, or something she couldn't name. She only knew one thing: she missed her mother, and now her last link to the woman who had borne her was gone.

Her chest became tight, and drawing a deep breath seemed necessary but impossible. She deliberately and loudly inhaled and exhaled. Her heart began racing, and her hands felt clammy. She actually thought for a moment that she might faint or become physically ill, and she turned white as a sheet. Although up to now she'd been perched with perfect posture on the edge of the folding chair, she leaned back in an attempt to ground herself.

"Mom! Are you all right?" Josh asked, rising from his chair.

Pastor's chair thunked against the wall as he launched himself. "Katie? Do you need a glass of water?" He had moved beside her and was patting her hand. She could do nothing but allow him to do so and in fact welcomed the touch of reality since her equilibrium was still swimming.

"Will you please run upstairs, Josh, and have Dorothy bring us a glass of water?"

"Sure. Just make sure she doesn't fall out of the chair, okay?" Although Josh headed toward the door he didn't leave the room until Katie spoke.

"Yes, Josh. A glass of water would be nice. I'm okay. Go ahead and find me one, please."

Josh hiked the stairs two at a time and ran into the sanctuary. Dorothy saw him bound halfway up the aisle. She was in the back corner tying off the last pew, and he didn't see her. Ran right past her. Nellie Ruth was nowhere in sight.

"Is everything okay, Josh?" Dorothy asked, nearly scaring him out of his wits.

"Mom needs a drink of water right away. She's a little dizzy or something." He wore a look of panic on his face.

"Oh, my! I'll be right there. Go ahead on back downstairs and tell them I'm on my way." Immediately she scurried to the tiny room off the library that served as a makeshift kitchen and hospitality room for Sunday morning coffee and rolls. She grabbed a plastic glass and a paper towel, ran the cold water until it actually ran cold, filled up the glass, soaked the paper towel and sped down the stairs. When she arrived, Pastor was still standing next to Katie holding her hand, and Josh stood next to Pastor. He couldn't remember his mother ever looking this vulnerable or weak, and it was scaring him.

"Here we go, honey," Dorothy said. She took Katie's left hand, the one Pastor wasn't stroking, and wrapped Katie's fingers around the glass and waited until she took a sip, then she went around behind her and held the paper towel to Katie's forehead, gently coaxing her to lean back and relax.

Katie still felt a bit light-headed . . . and there was something about Dorothy's soothing voice and the way Pastor was holding her hand that miraculously allowed her simply to be still and receive what they were giving. She downed the entire glass of water and just sat there. One of Dorothy's hands was on her forehead and the other on her shoulder. Pastor was looking up into her face as he now kneeled in front of her trying to make eye contact. Josh looked over Pastor's shoulder with tender concern. She was cocooned in care, and she could do nothing but close her eyes and be in the moment, too weak to resist.

From the depths of her, she felt a stirring. A mild stinging sensation infiltrated her nose and eyes, and tears begin to pool beneath her eyelids. She scrunched her eyelids hard together, but it was no use. Tears began to stream over her lower lids, down her cheeks, around the curve of her chin, down her neck. A quiet sob manifested in her throat and made itself known to those around her in a quick inhale and exhale.

She became aware of Dorothy's hands, now gently rubbing forward and back across the top of her shoulders, the moist paper towel having been dropped to the floor. Pastor continued to kneel and now had his eyes closed, praying, cradling both of Katie's hands in his.

Josh leaned his hips back against the desk, feeling somewhat weak himself. For the first time in his life, he saw his mother, outwardly and without holding back, begin to cry.

Katie Mabel Carol Durbin had, unbeknownst to her, in the basement of the United Methodist Church of Partonville, surrounded by those who genuinely cared and in a moment of God's grace, come home to herself. For the first time, she full-out grieved for the loss of her mother—her ballast, the one person who had loved her unconditionally, no matter how impossible she'd been.

11

"**P**ass me the sugar, will ya, Sharon?" Today's Wednesday edition of the *Partonville Press* sprawled in front of him on the counter at Harry's, Harold, the editor, red pencil in hand, was engaged in his usual routine of reading the paper from page one through the last period on the last page, ads and all. The only time he missed doing so was two years ago March, the day his daughter delivered his first grandchild. Rather than spend time on his own creation, he had examined and cuddled one of the best creations God ever plunked into his arms. His rating system for papers was how many red circles he drew, the fewer the better. Baby Carolyn got a zero-circle rating, only one he'd ever given.

Sharon passed him the sugar, watched him pour in about three teaspoons full—no stirring; always said he liked discovering the sweet spot in the bottom—then sat quietly beside him while he finished the last two pages. She knew better than to try to engage his attention until the paper was closed. She twiddled with the button on the bottom of her cardigan, then twirled the hair behind her left ear, chewed on two of her fingernails and began twisting a paper napkin. Finally, Harold folded the paper, tucked it on the stool under him, swiveled to face her and said, "Two-circle day. Okay, Sharon. What'd ya get from the Craigs' office? From your gyrations the last few minutes, I'd say either nothing or enough to fill the entire paper."

Sharon broke eye contact, swiveled toward the counter and said, to the salt and pepper, "You should have gone yourself. I can't *believe* you sent me into the lion's den so unprepared. I'm just too green for this job. You should have known better, Mr. Crabb!" By this time her eyes welled up, her nose turned red and she'd ripped the paper napkin plumb in two.

"Whoa! Whoa, girlie girl! You are the best reporter whose byline I've had the privilege to run in my papers. You have good instincts, good control and a good head on your shoulders." Sharon's entire face and neck turned a bright red, same as they did every time Mr. Crabb complimented her. "What in the world has thrown you so off base?"

"Real estate," she said, dabbing each eye with each hand holding a half of napkin, black mascara circles appearing beneath her lower lids. "I just haven't been involved in big business real estate like this, and I'm afraid I was way out of my league. You should have educated me as to how things are done. And as for Colton Craig, that arrogant, self-righteous snob, well, he caught me right up in his web of . . . of . . . ARROGANCE and made me look like a fool!"

Harold stifled a smile. He'd met the Craig brothers at a convention once, and it didn't take much looking to realize that Colton Craig was obviously a well-seasoned, good-looking ladies' man. He'd impressed Harold—who wasn't easily impressed—with his charismatic presence and smooth talking. He suspected that Sharon, who was beet red again just talking about him, had responded just as his wife and every other woman in the place had: near drooling. Now, not that he didn't fully trust Martha, knowing positively well she was a devoted wife, mom and grandmother, but being seasoned all his life as a reporter and therefore an observer, he also understood the balance of human nature.

"Here," he said, sliding Sharon's own glass into her downward sight line, leaving a trail of water across the counter. "Take a sip of water, blow your nose and tell me what happened. From the beginning." Although Lester never approached them, Harold was sure he was all ears. Earl was sitting across the U from them slurping a soda, but certainly Earl wasn't a gossip—at least not a knowing one. Good thing the place wasn't loaded, Harold thought; that's why he usually picked two-thirty for his read-through, since lunchers were gone and the evening group hadn't arrived yet.

Sharon downed a few gulps, blew her nose on one half of the napkin, wadded it up with the other and clasped it in her hands. "Well, Mr. Crabb, first off, he has the most bragging type of office! I mean, have you ever *seen* Craig & Craig's offices?"

"No, although I've met the brothers Craig, I can't say as I've been in their offices. I will say that we surely shouldn't be judging a book by its cover, though, and—" Before he could end his sentence, she jumped right in.

"His office was nearly bigger than my entire home, and it overlooks Hethrow. I looked out that window and remembered when I used to ride Molly through that beautiful countryside, and now it's one parking lot and building after another, and I just couldn't stand to think that Partonville could become a mall one day and—"

Now it was Harold's turn to jump in. "Sharon, is that what he told you? He's planning on making Partonville a mall?"

"I don't know what he's planning, but you can bet it's something. Something to make him a fatter cat at our expense."

Harold grabbed her shoulders and swiveled her to face him. "Sharon Teller, I've never known you to be so judgmental. Not good for a reporter. When you say you don't know what he's planning, did you ask? And what was his response."

"Mostly he humiliated me, realizing I had no idea how the real estate game was played. He said, of course, that he was always looking for opportunities and, of course, I understood that should there be any talk, which he didn't confirm, that it wouldn't be public knowledge up front."

"Yes."

"Yes? You mean, *of course,* you knew all this, right?"

"Right."

"THEN WHY DIDN'T YOU TELL ME I'd look dumb asking him?"

"It never hurts to let someone know we're watching, no matter what either side reveals or doesn't. And now he knows the *Partonville Press* is on full alert to his dealings, and that's a good thing."

"Gads! Has everyone turned into Martha Stewart? That's what *he* said about development!"

"What's that?"

"That it's a good thing."

"And you think it isn't?"

"And you think it is?"

"Sharon, we seem to be caught in a loop here. Let's start over. First off, we are reporters who report the news, and no matter what we think or feel or believe, we're only supposed to be gathering and reporting the facts. Did you find out any new facts?"

"No. Only that I don't know anything about real estate deals."

"Okay, then, we have no story for now. Off the record and out of curiosity," Harold said, leaning in toward Sharon, "what are your personal opinions about development? And do you believe they represent everyone's opinion in Partonville?"

"Yes. No. Well, maybe. Honestly, I'm realizing I'm not even sure what *I* think about all of it. I mean, I was born and raised in Partonville. Although my daddy wasn't a farmer, since he worked in the mines all his life, most of our friends were and continue to be. I worry about those folks if land starts to disappear. Then again, they'd probably be set for life if they sold off. I hate traffic. I wonder what will happen to *all* of us if we turn into the next Hethrow. How will the entire country survive if we keep selling farmland? See what I mean? I'm confused! And still . . . I find myself traveling to Hethrow more and more often! Am *I* a sign of the times? Am *I* the next itchy generation?"

"You ask good, sensitive questions, Sharon. That's what makes you such a fine reporter. You know, some folks are going to be stuck in their ways no matter what. Any talk of change causes them to buck and kick. Some, well, farming's the only thing they know. Some of the younger folks, they just silently move on, or away. But one thing is for sure: ready or not, one day change *will* come."

"And which side of the fence do you sit on, Mr. Crabb?"

"Ever since Ford Motors arrived in Hethrow, I've been giving this whole topic a great deal of personal thought.

Watching. Speculating. As an old reporter *and* the editor, I feel I've had to stay *on* the fence professionally, though. I love Partonville. Like you, I have mixed emotions, I guess. I'm beginning to think it's time to write an editorial, just to engage the townsfolk in a little dialogue. Stir things up a bit. Broaden the conversation. Make it bigger than Harry's. Yup, that oughta get those letters to the editor pouring in. Find out what folks are *really* thinking. Been too quiet around here lately anyway. I just know things don't stay the same, and Partonville is prime for being picked off."

"Not if *I* have anything to say about it, we're not!" Acting Mayor Gladys McKern nearly startled them both off their stools. He stared at her for a moment, wondering how long she'd been listening. *And the one thing we can be sure of is that* you will *have* plenty *to say, Ms. Mayor!*

Katie blew her nose on yet another tissue Pastor Delbert handed her from the box on his desk. She had cried uncontrollably for no less than five minutes, then spent the next five idling down between sniffs and nose blows and quiet apologies. Pastor would hand her a tissue. She'd blow. Sigh. Sniff. Dorothy would hold her hand out, Katie would place the tissue in it, and then Pastor would hand Katie another tissue as the tears once again flowed.

Nellie Ruth had peeked in once. Being highly tuned in to spiritual matters, she immediately surmised God at work, backed out around the corner, bowed her head and recalled, with clarity and a surprise gust of emotion, her own first adventure on these grounds. Prayers leapt right and left. Prayers of thankfulness for her own healing so long ago and prayers for God to be present and real in Katie's life now.

"I'm sorry," Katie uttered in a hushed tone time and again. Those around her simply listened and continued the tissue assembly line. Josh watched in awe, swallowing hard himself many times. His heart was racing as he was unsure what might follow.

"There is never a need to apologize for tears, Katie," Dorothy finally said. "It looks to me, child of His, like you've had a whole lot bottled up in there for a very long time. Crying is just what you needed to do, Lord knows."

Katie looked up at Dorothy, who had moved around next to Pastor to talk to her. The look on Katie's face was somewhat helpless yet quizzical. Dorothy gazed at Katie, searching from the top of her head to her eyes and her red nose, on down to her hands clenched around a tissue in her lap. Then back into her eyes.

"Yes. The Lord knows. And I believe you do, too. For everything there is a season, and today was crying time."

Katie's eyes darted down toward her hands that were now wringing one another. Dorothy had this way of seeing too much. More, perhaps, than Katie herself was aware of. For the first time in her life, Katie was not only unable but also disinclined to crust over and take command. She was simply too perplexed, as well as drained.

A long, motionless silence ensued.

Katie finally cleared her throat. It looked like the floods had concluded and that she was ready to move on with the task at hand. In a moment of transition, Pastor looked at his watch, then stiffly got up off his knees and offered Katie his hand to help her out of the chair.

"I think it's time we go upstairs and finish the arrangements. I imagine Nellie Ruth is wondering what happened to us!" Just then, a scuffling of feet could be heard outside the door, followed by the faint sound of footsteps running up the stairs. Dorothy grinned at Katie, an all-knowing grin. Katie was embarrassed to think that anyone else witnessed this whatever it had been.

"Yes, Pastor Delbert. We need to get things in order. Josh and I haven't even been by Aunt Tess's yet. We've got to pick up a key from the lawyer's office, and I was hoping we might settle up and dispose of her belongings in the next few days before we leave. I also need to speak with a Realtor. I'd like to get the place on the market in short order."

Pastor Delbert and Dorothy exchanged glances that didn't go unnoticed by Katie. Neither of them, however, said a word. Instead, they silently began to file out of his office, up the stairs and into the sanctuary, where Nellie Ruth fussed with some flowers she obviously had not been arranging. Within ten minutes or so, everything seemed quite in order for the evening's wake and tomorrow's funeral. At least in as good order as anything could be under such out-of-order circumstances.

Katie finally found a parking spot across the square from where Rick Lawson's second-floor office was housed, "right above Hornsby's Shoe Emporium," Nellie Ruth had told her upon leaving the church. Unfortunately, she and Josh had to walk right past Harry's to get there, and it made her bristle again. Although a bit of an inexplicable hollow longing had surfaced inside her in the church, whatever—and she did mean *whatever*—had transpired in church was now forgotten in a resurgence of the memory that she was, indeed, in Pardon Me Ville. She glared in the window as they hustled by, as if to send the gawkers a message. All she saw, however, was the reflection of her own self glaring back.

They found the doorway with RICK LAWSON, ATTORNEY AT LAW printed on it in block letters just to the left of Hornsby's Shoe Emporium. Josh pulled open the door for his mom, and they went up the creaky, narrow stairway.

Rick Lawson's secretary greeted them and took them into Mr. Lawson's office, a ten-by-ten mess. Papers and file folders sat in disheveled piles everywhere, some piles more than two feet tall, including one on his desk. File drawers were open, and files were stacked on top of them. The two green vinyl chairs in front of his desk had stacks of paper on them, and he was leaning over one holding a pile in each hand, obviously caught in the act of attempting to clear the decks for their arrival. He was quite a mess himself, wearing very worn, pin-striped, shiny wool pants a couple sizes too big held up by suspenders that were too long and that sagged across a blue-and-white striped shirt with frayed cuffs.

"Mr. Lawson?" Katie asked.

"Yes. Yes."

"Kathryn Durbin."

"Come in, please," he said as he stacked the piles in his hands, one atop the other, set that stack on top of the stack on one of the chairs, then picked the growing bundle up and set it atop the stack on the other chair. He paused, patted the ever-growing stack, then extended his arms and scooped his fingers underneath the pile. He set his chin down on top of the entire mess, picked it up, turned this way and that searching for an empty spot before finally depositing the wad on the front corner of his desk, right next to the other two-foot pile. Katie figured this is probably how the original stack had developed in the first place.

"Won't you have a seat?" he said, casually pointing toward the now empty chairs as if he and they had been ready all along.

Katie gave the chair seat a quick glance, swiped at it with her hand, then realized she was too tired to care about either her silk pants or the remaining dust bits. Josh sat beside her, and they both watched Mr. Lawson begin raking his fingers up the side of one of the stacks until swiftly, like a magician snatching a tablecloth out from under the dishes, he yanked out a folder that said "Walker" on the file tab. He sat down at his desk and set the file on top of whatever papers were already spread before him, took a deep breath, then opened the file with what seemed like rather dramatic ceremony given the mess he sat in.

"Ah, yes. You're Katie Durbin, Tess Walker's last living relative. We've already figured that out now, haven't we?"

"Yes, we certainly have." Having, within the last hour or so, just discovered the deep emotional truth of that, she quickly moved on to the business at hand. "I'm here to pick up Aunt Tess's house key, Mr. Lawson."

"So you are," he said with a tone in his voice that smacked of a Charlie Chan detective movie. "So you are." Josh actually snickered out loud, then pretended he was clearing his throat when Katie's head snapped in his direction.

Mr. Lawson flipped a few papers over in the file and produced an envelope. "Ah, here we go then. Just what we're looking for." He opened the envelope and extracted a key that was tied lanyard style to a piece of worn, dirty lace. Katie couldn't believe her eyes. "A skeleton key!" she said louder than she'd intended, especially since she didn't intend to respond out loud at all.

"Cool!" Josh uttered.

Mr. Lawson then produced a piece of folded paper from within the envelope and read a hand-scrawled note. Then he folded the paper back up, redeposited it into the envelope and said, "Just the way the Partonville police found it, Ms. Durbin. It was tied around your aunt's neck at the time of her death."

"Police?" Katie asked.

"Yes. I'm sure you know the police have to be phoned when someone is found dead in their home, and an autopsy has to be performed, just to make sure there is no foul play."

"Foul play!" Katie spat. "Someone suspected foul play? No one mentioned any such thing to me, Mr. Lawson."

"It's simply a matter of the law, Ms. Durbin. You can be sure Mac followed proper procedure to the letter of the law, ma'am."

"Mac?" Katie asked.

"Sergeant McKenzie Phillips, Ms. Durbin. Townsfolk just call him Mac."

"And I am to assume everything was found in order? The hospital told me she died of natural causes."

"Yes, of course. Everything was perfectly normal, aside from the fact she was dead."

Katie's head reared back a little, she raised her eyebrows and looked at Josh, who was clearly stifling a grin. She had to admit that this entire place seemed to be a bit of a joke. If she hadn't been so tired and stressed, she might have laughed herself.

"I am giving you this key, Ms. Durbin, not exactly in accordance with the letter of the law, as all the proper documentation hasn't been completely signed and filed. However, since your aunt was wise enough to contact me upon the death of your mother ten years ago in order to put her entire estate in a trust, and since her entire estate is worth very little, which is good because there will be nothing for probate, and"—he leaned forward at this point—"begging your pardon but we're talking reality here"—he sat back in his chair—"I rest assured, knowing you are the sole successor trustee named in her trust, that you are indeed in charge of everything located in that house on Vine Street and that everything your aunt owned is in it. And I do mean everything, Ms. Durbin."

Katie stared at him blankly, trying to sort through a sentence that seemed to have no beginning or end. For a brief moment she wondered if he looked and sounded like this in a courtroom and was glad to know she wouldn't have to find out.

"Have you seen inside your aunt's house lately, Ms. Durbin?"

"I have not been to her home since before my mother died, Mr. Lawson. But I do know at that time she was a bit of a pack rat."

"I'd say you're in for a shock then, Ms. Durbin, so you might want to get a bite of lunch before you go." With that he handed her the key. As she was about to stand up he asked her to remain seated for a moment while he got out her copy of the trust, which he immediately started tossing folders around to unearth. He said he suspected that she wouldn't be able to locate the original copy perhaps for quite some time since Tess Walker kept it in her house and, "well, that is definitely going to be a project." *Pretty funny words coming from someone whose office looks like* this, Katie mused.

Miraculously, he found the rubber-banded stack, handed her the copy and then walked them to his office door.

"I'm sorry I can't make the wake tonight. I don't mean to be disrespectful, but I've got softball practice. I'll see you at the funeral tomorrow, though," Mr. Lawson said as they parted ways.

Josh swallowed down his shock, not at the fact that the lawyer couldn't attend the wake, but softball? The guy had to be seventy-five years old if he was a day.

12

Aunt Tess's house was on Vine Street, three blocks off the square. As Katie turned onto Vine off Main, she had another flashback. She recalled always thinking that the houses on Vine Street were smaller than anywhere else in town. Today's experience was no different.

Although each home had a unique structure, color and layout, they all were wood frame with a brick chimney on one side or the other. Some had odd room additions stuck on this way and that. They each had approximately the same size yard and were decidedly sparse in terms of aesthetics. Rather sad-looking.

She crept along with the windows down, listening to the silence. She couldn't remember a time when their street in the city was so quiet. It was, in fact, somewhat unnerving, making her realize how conditioned, perhaps numbed, to the sounds of cars and sirens and televisions and conference calls and commotion she was.

Suddenly the squealing sounds of a car came around the corner behind her, knocking her out of her reverie. She looked into her rearview mirror to see the front grille of a very large white, beat-up Lincoln racing toward the backside of her SUV. Before she could turn her head to get a better look, the car and the flapping ears and windblown tongue of a funny-looking dog with its head out the window flashed by her, its driver all but running the car up on the lawns. As quickly as the car had passed her by, it zinged in front of her, pulling up toward the end of the block, then jerking to a stop in front of her.

"Take cover!" Josh hollered. "Grandma's on the loose!"

Katie hit the brakes and pulled over. She realized she was nearly in front of Aunt Tess's house anyway, so she just parked her vehicle. Before she could open her own door, out of the Lincoln popped Dorothy Wetstra. She positioned herself at her rear side window, spread her legs to steady herself, then stuck out her arms. Out the window flew the funny little dog, nearly knocking Dorothy back into the street. Josh laughed out loud. His mother sat there with her mouth agape. It was beginning to sink in that the only thing she could count on while she was in Partonville was the unexpected.

As soon as Dorothy set her on the ground, Sheba came galloping back to greet Katie, who had just swung her legs around to the ground. Up onto her slacks Sheba jumped, tongue and tail wagging, mindless of the dusty paw prints she pranced all over peach silk.

"Sheba Wetstra!" Dorothy yelped. "Why, that is no way to behave!" Katie tried to hold Sheba down while acting as if that wasn't what she was doing. "Nice Sheba," she said through her teeth while trying to grab her collar.

Josh had sprung around the car. He scooped Sheba up to his face, which Sheba immediately began to lick and lap. Katie was still dusting off her pants when Dorothy caught up to her.

"I'm sorry about that, Katie. Sheba loves everybody, and I'm afraid she just doesn't have manners when it comes to being a greeter."

"It's quite all right," Katie lied, working to be polite to this woman who had so graciously seen her through whatever it was she had gone through this morning.

"I decided you shouldn't have to go into that house alone, Katie dear. I phoned Rick and he told me you were on your way here."

"Josh is with me. I'm not alone."

"I know, but honestly, I fear you might be in for more than you expected."

Josh set Sheba down, and she took off running for the yard, where they all watched her disappear into foot-tall swaying grasses. It was the first time Katie had noticed the horrid tangle of a yard.

"Oh!" was all she could get out. Josh walked up beside his mom and said, "What next? This is turning out to be quite the day! Looks like we should have brought a machete with us, Mom!"

Katie just stood there staring. Her shoulders slumped forward. No wonder everyone had been throwing each other glances. Rick Lawson had tried his best to warn her. She was beginning to dread unlocking the door, if this was a hint of things to come.

"I'm afraid your Aunt Tess didn't handle things very well these last many years, dear, although I understand she did manage to keep her bills paid and feed herself. People just never saw her out and about. The reason they knew she was okay was because they'd see her lights go on and off at night, and she called in grocery orders to Your Store, handing them a check when they delivered. Other than that, she just kept entirely to herself. I suppose someone told you that's how they discovered her, right? She didn't answer the door when they came with her groceries. It just wasn't like

her. Eventually the sheriff was called. Her door was unlocked, thank goodness, so they didn't have to do any damage. They discovered her in her bed, where she must have
gone to lie down after phoning in her order."

Over the last couple days, Partonville residents had
pieced together a few facts, and Gladys McKern had been
eager to share with Dorothy any inside info she had gleaned
as mayor. Of course, Gladys also wanted everyone to notify
her the minute Katie Durbin gained entry to her aunt's
house. *Gladys is the last thing Katie needs right now,* Dorothy
thought.

Katie didn't say a word as she began fumbling through
her purse for the key. Once she had it in her hand, she
walked toward the rusting metal gate that swung open into
the yard, even though there was no fence. The tall grasses
had nearly covered over the cracked and heaving sidewalk.
Katie made her way toward the door, Josh right behind and
Dorothy bringing up the rear. Sheba was already facing the
door, sitting on the sloping cement front porch. Katie
stepped up behind her. Sheba didn't even look at her; she
just stood up, then began waving her backside and sticking
her nose into the space where the door meets the frame, as
though she could pry it open.

"I've heard it's quite an awful mess in there, Katie,"
Dorothy said sympathetically as Katie put the old black key
into the lock.

"There's only one way to find out," Josh said.

"One way," Katie said. She twisted the key clockwise until she heard a click, then slowly pushed open the door.
Since all the window shades were drawn tight and there was
no glass in the door, it was too dark to see. She reached her
arm around the corner in search of a light switch. Her fin-

gers fumbled over yet another memory from her past: Aunt
Tess had push-button light switches! Katie pushed the top
button and a dim overhead lightbulb came on. It had no
shade. The light cast an eerie glow around the tiny living
room. No matter what kind of awful disaster Katie might
have expected, she never could have mentally prepared for
anything quite as horrible as was revealed in this moment.
Rick Lawson's office was nothing but a bit messy compared
with this chaos.

Katie gasped aloud. She would have collapsed into a
chair had there actually been a place to sit down. Her mind
simply couldn't take in all that her eyes were trying to absorb. Josh and Dorothy were speechless themselves until
Dorothy muttered, "Lord have mercy on us all."

"Man! I've never seen such a mess," Josh finally said.
"And you think *my* room is bad, Mom!"

Katie remembered watching the news on the television
one evening. After neighbors complained, Chicago police
had discovered a woman and her five children living in conditions that they kept describing on the news as "squalor."
Although Katie wasn't sure what the word meant when she
first heard it blaring out of her surround-sound speakers,
film clips revealed the meaning. Who would have ever
guessed that real estate tycoon Kathryn Durbin would have
a relative living in those same conditions.

For a moment, Katie felt slightly light-headed again. She
reached out her arm and leaned against the wall. Thankfully, however, she slowly began to notice that although
everything was everywhere, there was no odor other than
that old smell one noticed when walking into an antiques
store. There were no moldy dishes of old food sitting
around and no piles of dirty diapers as they'd kept showing

on TV. No, Aunt Tess's squalor was just piles and piles of clothes and newspapers and books and photographs and linens and pencils and bits of jewelry and . . .

The only way, other than the front door, to get out of the living room was through a narrow passageway that was itself built up on the sides with stuff. Katie cautiously entered into what felt like a labyrinth, bypassed the kitchen, fearing it would be more than she could take, and moved through the masses until she came to Aunt Tess's bedroom. She reached around the corner and punched on the light. Again, she was met with complete disarray. Old wooden boxes and strewn clothes and yet more jewelry and books. Things were even piled on the bed, and it looked as if Aunt Tess had simply curled up in a little nest she'd built around her.

Framed photographs lined the bedroom walls. Pictures of people she didn't know. Faces that stared at her from all directions. She swiftly yet carefully moved back to the bedroom entryway, punched off the light and sidestepped her way back into the hall, where she ran smack into Josh. She let out a loud yelp, then screamed, "Joshua! You scared the life out of me!" He grabbed her arms and said, "Mom, get a grip. It's only me." Mother and son stood face to face. He realized, as he continued to hold her arms, that she was shaking.

"Mom, I'm really getting worried about you. Maybe we better just leave now, find a place to eat and go back to the Lamp Post so you can rest. This has been a . . . a . . . hard morning for all of us."

Katie drew a deep cleansing breath and announced that she would be fine, although she did acknowledge she was feeling a bit weary and edgy. They awkwardly exchanged places in the hallway so they could pass one another.

She peeked in the bathroom, sighed, then said, "I'm going to look in the kitchen before we go. Might as well face most of it so I'm not so startled when we return tomorrow after the funeral. I'll spare myself the back bedroom now—I'll save some surprises," she said sarcastically. "You are right about one thing, I need to eat something and lie down. Just give me another five minutes."

"You're gonna be real surprised when you see the kitchen, Mom."

"Swell."

Katie noticed that a glow from the kitchen light, which either Josh or Dorothy had flipped on, was infiltrating the hallway. She was glad she didn't have to reach around another unknown corner for a switch. She was also astounded at the scene before her when she entered.

Aunt Tess's kitchen was spotless! Nothing was out of place, and not a dish was unwashed. The table was completely cleared aside from three ruffly, floral cloth place mats with table settings on them, including a large, empty water glass for each. A loose bouquet of what appeared to be handpicked flowers sat drooping in the middle of the place settings, a rose-colored pillar candle that had never been lit sat on a saucer and there was a framed picture beside it. It looked as though Aunt Tess had been expecting company. Little prickles ran up the back of Katie's neck.

She picked up the photo to get a better look and froze with shock. It was the same photo of Aunt Tess and her mom standing next to a silo that she'd been viewing at her own kitchen table just days before! Tucked into the lower right-hand corner of the frame was a picture of Katie and Josh standing in Katie's kitchen. Josh looked to be about two years old. Her mother must have taken it and mailed it to Aunt Tess.

Katie stood, staring, eyes welling yet again against her will. She clutched the photo of her mom and Aunt Tess to her breast for a moment as tears streamed down her face. The longing for her mother was so intense it was nearly unbearable. She was powerless to stop the consuming ache and in fact felt strangely drawn into its depths.

Dorothy stood motionless in the doorway from the kitchen to the back porch, witnessing the moment. She stared at Katie's closed eyes and pursed lips. She watched Katie's hand cover the photo held near her heart as Katie began to sway back and forth in a rocking motion.

"Oh, Mother," she whispered. "Mother."

Dorothy couldn't help but see the faint resemblance between mother and daughter, which was most visible in the shape of Katie's face and her wide-set eyes. Clarice used to set her lips together like that when she was upset, Dorothy recalled. But most of all, Dorothy pondered, Katie looked like her tenderhearted father.

Dorothy just stood there in the shadows, not wanting to interrupt the moment, but it didn't last long. Josh bounded into the kitchen holding Sheba. He walked up behind his mom and said, "I think we ought to get a dog, Mom."

Katie spun on her heels, and Sheba quickly leaned forward toward her face and began licking away the tears. Katie was so stunned she yelled at Josh for startling her again. She set the photograph down, asked if the bedroom light was turned off and announced that it was time to go.

After she'd stormed out of the kitchen, he picked up the photograph to see what had captured her attention. It appeared as though the woman on the left could be his grand-mother, but he didn't know who the other lady was. Doro-thy noticed the look on his face and stepped forward. He held up the photograph and faced it toward her without speaking.

"Of course, the one on the left is your grandmother, Josh. The other, well, meet your Aunt Tess."

13

Dorothy had invited Josh and Katie back to her farm for lunch, but Katie declined, needing some space. Dorothy accepted Katie's refusal but insisted that everyone attending the funeral be invited back to her farm afterward. Although Katie wasn't very keen on the idea, Dorothy's argument finally became persuasive.

"Katie, honey, folks around here are used to being fed after a funeral, usually at someone's home. It's something we not only plan on but also enjoy. Obviously, child, you are not going to invite anyone back to *this* place," she said as she motioned toward Aunt Tess's now locked-up house. "Please let me serve you in this way. We'll just have Pastor make the announcement. Everybody in town knows where I live. There won't be any unnecessary explaining to do. Besides, I enjoy gathering everyone together. It would make me happy to know I helped send off an old friend."

"Come on, Mom. Sounds like a good idea to me. Besides, I've never been on a farm!"

After exploring alternatives in her head, Katie decided to follow Dorothy's suggestion rather than be stuck with a group of Partonvillers waiting like lost sheep, all looking to her for direction. And heaven forbid someone suggest they adjourn to Harry's!

"Okay. I'll take you up on the offer. But I insist I pay for the groceries."

"Deal," Dorothy said, knowing full well that she'd better stop while she was ahead. "Don't worry about a thing. I'll take care of all of it. You can either follow me out to the farm after the services or ride with me and I'll bring you back afterward. I'd love for you both to just pack up your bags and stay with me for as long as you like while you're here finishing your business, but I understand you need your privacy. Besides, I'm happy for Jessica and Paul to have the booking. I'd love to see them make a decent go of that place and reap the rewards for all the hard-work seeds they've sown."

Katie pictured trying to follow Dorothy's speeding bullet of a car. And to ride with her, well, that wasn't a choice! No one should be riding with that woman, not even her own dog! She made a mental note to have Dorothy just give her directions when the time came.

"I'll see you at the wake tonight, honey. I wouldn't expect too many to show up. It's Wednesday. Softball practice. You can count on me, though. I'm just the cheerleader." She walked to her car and flung open the back door. Sheba, who had been sitting patiently at her heels during this discussion, leapt right in. Dorothy folded herself in next, slammed the door, fired up the engine, stomped on the gas and spit roadside gravel every which direction, a few stones pelting the front of Katie's big Lexus. In a flash, she was out of sight.

Josh laughed, then summed up the entire moment in one short sentence: "Ride 'em, cowgirl!"

Katie and Josh arrived at the church at exactly 6:00 P.M., when the wake was to begin. They were surprised to find a dozen people already there, seated in the front pews. It was a bit unusual to have a wake at the church, but the *Partonville Press* and the unofficial grapevine had spread the word about the arrangements. Pastor was standing near the door to greet them.

"Good evening, Katie, Josh." Josh extended his hand, welcoming what he knew would be a hearty handshake.

"Good evening, Pastor Delbert," Katie said. "What time do you have?"

"Six o'clock, straight up," he said after giving his Timex a quick glance. "The older residents like to get to evening events early so they can get home. I'm sorry I didn't tell you. Let's go ahead and start a reception line. Nellie Ruth's had people signing the guest register. She set one out for you in the narthex. Dorothy's up front. She's been watching for you."

Katie walked up the aisle very self-consciously. At business events, she enjoyed making the grand entrance and receiving doting attention. Now, however, she simply felt conspicuous, tardy and overdressed in her green suit, heels and emerald jewelry. She wished that when she'd been packing she hadn't been so caught up in proving she wasn't one of them. Even though she really wasn't, except by bloodline, there suddenly seemed no need to prove it. As they craned their necks to watch her coming toward them—as if she were a bride coming down the aisle—she imagined that they pretty much knew that anyway. When they reached the front of the sanctuary, Dorothy sprang out of her seat to greet them. Katie could hear the murmurs at her back.

"Don't you look beautiful, Katie! You look lovely in

green, just like your mother! I do believe that was her favorite color." Dorothy had once again come through with just what Katie needed. She found herself oddly relieved to be back in the company of this most unusual, if somewhat eccentric, woman.

"And Josh! My, what a handsome rascal you are, all dressed up in a tie with your shoes shined and everything."

"Thanks, Dorothy."

"That's Mrs. Wetstra to you, Joshua," Katie corrected.

"Dorothy, for sure," Dorothy said as she grinned at the teenager before her, who was exactly her same height. "It's Dorothy, and I won't settle for anything else." She directed that statement to Katie and patted her arm. Katie was beginning to understand that there wasn't much use in taking Dorothy on.

By this time, Pastor and his wife had succeeded in ousting everyone seated in the pews and corralled them into a reception line. They were lined up to the right of Dorothy. Katie was again glad for her decision to cremate. She wouldn't have wanted people coming just to see what the town's apparently peculiar woman looked like.

Dorothy greeted people first so she could introduce them to Katie and Josh. At the head of the line stood Gladys McKern. Dorothy drew herself up as tall as she could and grabbed hold of Gladys's hand, which was at the time extended to Katie. Dorothy pulled Gladys toward herself so quickly that she nearly knocked Gladys off balance. She spoke quietly, two octaves lower than usual and with all the power and authority she'd ever claimed.

"Gladys McKern, you give this child a break. I can see the look on your face, and this is not the time for business."

"Dorothy Wetstra, I don't believe it's for you to tell me

when it is or when it isn't time for business. I am, however, annoyed you'd think I'd be so insensitive as to bring business into a wake, let alone the sanctuary!"

"Don't talk so loudly, Gladys. They're liable to hear you." Katie had glanced their way, wondering why Dorothy was holding up the line. Pastor Delbert distracted her for a spell by reiterating once again what a nice job the Floral Fling had done with her order. Katie had noticed on her way down the aisle that there were two other arrangements. She asked Pastor who they were from, and he said Dorothy and the collection pot Lester put out at Harry's. By this time, Gladys was in front of her.

"Gladys McKern, acting mayor," she said. "May I extend my sympathies on behalf of all the residents of Partonville." Gladys handed Katie a card and motioned for her to open it. "May the Lord bless and keep you in this time of sorrow," the card read on the outside. "And hold you right in the palm of his hands as you heal," it read on the inside. It was signed, "Gladys McKern, acting mayor, on behalf of all of Partonville."

"How lovely," Katie forced herself to say. Somehow this felt more like an advertisement for the mayor's office than true sympathy, but then Katie admired anyone who would seize the chance to get in a little PR.

Jessica Joy was next. "Oh, Miss Durbin, again please let me extend my sympathies about your aunt. If there's anything you need while you're here, please let me or Paul know. And this"—she turned to grab the arm of the man behind her and coax him up beside her—"is my husband, Paul. Paul, this is Kathryn Durbin and her son, Joshua."

Paul had his hands stuffed in his jeans pockets. His hair was still wet from a recent combing, his pale blue-and-white plaid shirt was crisply pressed and his eyes only glanced at Katie for a moment. He seemed uncomfortable in her presence. Then again, maybe he was uncomfortable in anyone's presence, Katie thought. She extended her hand. Paul reached for it, gave it one up-and-down shake and said, "Nice to meet you. We're sorry for your loss." He just as quickly shook Josh's hand, then stuffed his hand back in his pocket.

"I'm sorry we can't stay longer," Jessica said sincerely. "We've got to get back to the motel. We're expecting a check-in around seven, and we sure don't want to miss them. I'll see you tomorrow, although Paul has to work. The funeral is at ten, right?"

"Yes," Dorothy, Katie and Josh all responded at the same time.

Immediately Dorothy began greeting the next in line. "Katie Durbin, this is my oldest friend, May Belle Justice, and her son, Earl." Before Katie could extend her hand, May Belle pressed in and gave her a gentle hug. "I'm pleased to meet you, Katie. I wish it could be under happier circumstances. I know Dorothy and Pastor Delbert will take good care of you while you're here. If there's anything I can do to help, please let me know. I imagine you've got your hands full, having to handle all this alone."

"Thank you for your kind offer. I do have my son, Joshua, to help," she said, pointing to her side.

"Well, you're just as handsome as Dorothy told me, Joshua." May Belle turned to face Earl and said to him, "Earl Justice, say hello to Katie Durbin and her son, Joshua."

Earl's eyes never left the floor. He didn't notice either

Katie's or Josh's hands extended in greeting, but then he wouldn't have taken them anyway. A mumbled "Hello" could be heard coming out of his mouth. Katie and Josh said "Hello" back and glanced at one another.

"Earl Justice is a little shy, aren't you, Earl?" Dorothy said. "But he's one of my favorite people in the whole world." Earl looked up at his Dearest Dorothy and his eyes brightened a bit, but he didn't respond.

"Time to go, Earl. Nice to meet you," May Belle said to Katie. "We'll see you tomorrow. I'll be bringing plenty of desserts up to the farm, so please don't worry yourself about anything. You'll learn that although Dorothy isn't the best of cooks, she always makes more than enough." May Belle gave her dear friend a wink, then off they went.

Katie turned to see who was next.

"Arthur Landers," a gruff voice said. "One of Dorothy's neighbors. Didn't know your aunt, really, although we went to school together. Me and my wife both went to school with her. High school, that is," he added, as though a sudden need had come over him to clarify that. "Jessie sends her condolences and says she'll see you tomorrow. She's the captain and pitcher of the Partonville Wild Musketeers. Better than having her throw things at *me*, I guess," he said with a devilish sneer.

"Arthur Landers, now you behave yourself lest you scare our new friends," Dorothy said. "Arthur's really harmless, Josh. He just doesn't act like it. He is, however, the only human alive who can keep The Tank on the road."

"The Tank?" Josh queried.

"That white, dented wreck of a car she drives," Arthur said.

After having witnessed Dorothy and her big bomber of a car in motion, Katie understood why they called it The Tank.

"See ya tomorrow, I reckon," Arthur said. "And the first game is a week from Saturday, if you're still around. We play the Palmer Pirates. You can't miss the ballpark. It's the only thing on the hard road between here and Yorkville."

Josh, having decided that anyone over seventy who looked like they could still move must be playing softball, asked, "Why aren't you at practice, Mr. . . . um . . ."

"Landers."

"Mr. Landers."

"The first time Jessie beaned me with a softball I figured I didn't have to be very smart or dumb to let that happen again. As good an arm as she's got, having played near pro ball in her day, I knew it wasn't no accident."

Josh laughed. Katie realized she'd done the same. It was the first time in a very long time, and it felt good.

Arthur, however, hadn't even cracked a grin.

The rest of the hour-long wake went by quicker than Katie and Josh might have imagined. Pastor Delbert had warned them that an hour would be plenty. They were glad they'd listened, as the last twenty minutes brought no newcomers and nearly everyone else was gone. Dorothy had excused herself and was out of the sanctuary checking on things for the funeral when one last person literally ran in at six-fifty-five. She looked to be about Josh's age, wore dirty jeans and a baseball cap on backward. She shook Josh's and Katie's hands, didn't say who she was, expressed pat condolences, breathlessly said she'd see them tomorrow and that she was sorry she couldn't stay longer but she needed to get back before Musketeer batting practice was over. She left as abruptly as she'd entered, leaving Katie and Josh standing with their mouths agape.

"Mom, if you've got your calendar in your purse, write that ball game down. I have a feeling this could be more interesting than we think! But what's *she* doing on the team?"

"Of course I have my calendar, Josh, but I'm sure not planning on being here that long, although there is an outside possibility now that I've seen the house. I might have to come back without you so we can get you back in school by next week. Maybe I should just hire a demolition team and let them have at it, burying all that stuff in the process. That would probably be the easiest way. I doubt there's anything worth saving. I'm not sure *I'll* live long enough to go through all of it."

Josh gave his mother a peculiar look, one that she couldn't read. "What?" she said. "Why are you staring at me like that?"

"I just thought . . . I just thought . . ."

"What? What are you thinking, Joshua. Speak up!"

Josh recalled his mother's episode in this very basement, then her tears at Aunt Tess's. "I just wondered if you might, um, be glad we came."

"What on earth would make you say *that*?"

"Just a feeling I had. A feeling like maybe . . . I don't know . . . maybe there was something here for us to discover?" Now it was Katie's turn to stare. Thank goodness Dorothy, Nellie Ruth and Pastor Delbert came down the aisle and interrupted this odd conversation.

Final instructions and plans were reviewed. Katie made a mental note to arrive at nine-thirty tomorrow, a half-hour early, so she wouldn't be caught off guard again. Then it was quickly determined that they were all tired, there was a big day ahead of them and it was time to retire for the evening. Oddly enough, Katie couldn't wait to get back to the Lamp Post. Maybe she'd even draw a bath and make use of some of those Avon samples. Yes, that's just what she'd do.

14

Dorothy stood in the loft of the barn, gazing out the doors toward the west and the Landers place; their farm had been passed down through generations, too. Aside from the Landerses' farm buildings and a small grove of trees, as far as the eye could see the view was of what would soon be beautiful straight rows of corn. Dorothy considered the many years of Jessie and Arthur's friendship and wondered what their reaction might have been if she'd told them her dilemma the other day when Arthur was fixing The Tank's door.

She hadn't been able to come up with the right introduction to even a vague conversation to feel them out. Arthur and Jessie, however, would be the first to be directly affected if she sold to Craig & Craig. She hated to think that she might do *anything* to jeopardize such a long-standing and valued friendship. No, sir, the older Dorothy got, the more she valued God's gift of friends and long-lasting marriages.

Suddenly she found herself recalling an amazing story Arthur had shared with her years ago. He'd been working on The Tank in his "garage" and, as usual, they'd been gabbing about this and that while he tightened and tested, tinkered with and fretted over the obstinate "lady."

Eventually the discussion had rolled around to the price

of corn per bushel. Dorothy, never before having asked Arthur about it, queried him as to why he'd ever stopped farming his own land and gone into the automotive business. In her wildest dreams, she would never have expected the answer he delivered—about a lot of things. Obviously, Jessie had been nowhere around for this discourse. She'd have hog-tied him on the spot if she'd ever found out he'd told such a personal tale out of school.

Dorothy had never before, nor had she since, witnessed Arthur being as animated and sometimes even tickled with himself as he was during the telling.

You know I've always been a natural at fixing cars, Dorothy, tinkerin' with them for years as a hobby out in this old toolshed. Well, one day I finally admitted to Jessie—as well as myself—that I hated farming.

"Well, THAT'S just great!" she said, following me across the yard when I stomped away from her. "How do you expect we'd have eaten all these years if your dad hadn't left you this farm and all its equipment?" She was a-hoppin' mad, for sure.

I got just as mad right back at her. I worked up such a head of steam that I confessed I had always hated farming. Without thinkin', I said, "And not only did I never want to be a farmer, I never really wanted a WIFE either!" Now, keep in mind, Dorothy, it'd been ten years since that crazy night we decided to run away and get hitched!

"Well, I feel the same way about a HUSBAND!" she screamed. There we were, me stridin' toward this old shed to where I used to come just to get away from her, and her a-chasin' right behind me every stomp of the way. When we entered, screamin' like banshees, chickens went squawkin' and flappin' this way and that.

"*So NOW what?*" *she said to my back as I walked on through the shed to open the back swingin' doors. "NOW what do you have to say?"*

Well, I turned on my heels and stared at her. I put my hands on my hips and watched her begin to mimic my every twitch. There we stood, just starin' at each other from opposite ends of the shed for probably a good three or four minutes. Two stubborn, hotheaded people. I'll TELL you, we are stubborn!

I realized that although I was angry and had spoken out of turn, I finally felt free, having spoken the truth. Jessie, well she looked like she might get sick on me. Like she was thinkin' the same things I'd been thinkin' all along. We stood there actin' like a blimp blowed in between us and we were studyin' it!

Then it struck me what I needed to do. Without givin' it a lick more thought, I picked up an old piece of plywood, brushed off the dust and propped it against my workbench. Then I rummaged around 'til I found a can of black paint and a brush and I scrawled me some words. Jessie just watched. I finally had to put my hands on her arms and move her two feet to her right so I could reach my ladder. I got my old mayonnaise jar full of nails, stuck a couple between my teeth, set up the ladder right outside the shed door, climbed up carryin' the plywood and nailed my sign above the door. GARAGE, OPEN FOR BUSINESS, it said.

Jessie's eyes growed as wide as cow pies, but she didn't say a word. I climbed down the ladder, put everything away and stared at her for a few seconds. Then I said, "There. That's what I have to say. I'm gonna make a living doing what I do best and what I like most and what I already do for free. I'm gonna call Challie Carter tomorrow and lease him our land. He's been sayin' for years he'd like more farming acres. Now, woman, what do you have to say?"

"What about us, Arthur?" she asked. "What about us?" I tell you, Dorothy, her voice was steely, borderin' on a hiss. So I says, "I

reckon we're just stuck with one another, woman. Besides, I'm out of plywood to write US up a new job description."

I stomped out and began to close the shed doors to shut her inside. She raced out in the nick of time, trotted around in front of me, then threw back like she was gonna swing. Why, I just reacted, pulled back my fist, then got a grip on myself and took off again, her racin' behind me. . . . I wasn't sure where I was goin', but I knew I needed to separate myself from her. I might be an ornery old cuss, but I don't hit WOMEN! I headed toward the field, then spotted the old outhouse pappy used to sit in.

I stormed in, closed the door behind me and locked it. She began rattlin' the door and yelpin', "Arthur Landers, you get yourself out here!" I just plopped down on the seat and sat there, staring at her outline through the cracks in the wood. After a spell, she finally stomped away.

Next thing I knew there was a whap up against the side of the outhouse. It liked to scare me . . . I jumped and knocked my head against the back wall. Then Whap! Whap! I couldn't figure out what she was doin'. Then she started yellin' again.

"Arthur Landers, you listen to me." Whap! "I'm glad you're opening a garage. I'm glad you're gonna stop farming because maybe now that sour puss of yours will take on a different shine." Whap! I ducked like a boxer.

"I'm glad we finally spoke the truth to one another," she said. Whap! Whap again!

"And I agree that for better or for worse, we're just stuck with one another. But you're gonna listen to me now, and I've got plenty to say, buster!"

The peltin' stopped for a minute, and I peeked through one of the cracks. Why, that woman was throwing crabapples from her little tree! Must have been the first thing she spied for ammunition. I'll be darned if she wasn't reloading her apron pockets! I knew she still *had a pickoff arm, and I was the one she was tryin' to pick off! Why, I knew she could keep at this for hours if she was downright angry enough, and she surely was—not that I blamed her. And even as ornery a coot as she was and continues to be, I guess I'd just kinda grown used to her.*

Without thinkin', I reached in my overalls and grabbed my good ol' Hohner harmonica. Then I begun to playin' the "Dark Town Strutter's Ball" as loudly as I could, fixin' to drown out the whappin'. The more she laid out her complaints and sailed those crabapples, the faster and louder I played! I tell ya, Dorothy, it was dusk before the tree was out of apples, Jessie was too pooped to throw and I was out of wind!

Today, four decades later, they were still married, still arguing, Arthur still playing the harmonica in the outhouse and Jessie still winging whatever was at hand, including clothespins, rocks and an occasional egg a roosting chicken plunked down in her sight. The only thing that had changed was Arthur's garage. One day a few years ago he woke up and without ceremony removed the sign. It was time to retire.

Time to retire, Dorothy thought. *Arthur knew when it was time to retire. But when and how does one retire from the place they were born, even though the burden of it is beginning to wear them down? How do they know, Lord, whether it's time to fight, surrender or simply say good-bye to the past and move on with dignity while one still can? How does one suddenly put her interests above her neighbors'—or even know what her neighbors' interests are? Just as no one suspected Arthur hated farming, maybe I'm misjudging how people will react to my selling the farm.*

Or does one just stay until You call them home, letting the next generation, with their own ideas, figure it all out? Hear me, Lord?

I'm trusting You for some answers. Oh, if only Henry were here to help me understand all the details in that pile of paper. I need some help with this decision, Lord. And soon.

"Thank You, God, for loving all Your children, even those who don't make it to church on Sunday, for only You know what's truly in our hearts. And Lord, we pray for the continued healing of those who mourn Tessa Martha Walker. Amen!" Pastor Delbert boomed his grand closing finale.

He raised his bowed head and looked once again at the small gathering, his eyes settling on Gladys, who sat square in front of him. She was also eyeballing him a good one.

"Those who take the Lord seriously," she'd been heard saying on many occasions to anyone who would listen, "make their way to church on Sunday morning. And that's that."

Pastor smiled at Gladys, lifted his eyes to address the rest of the sheep and continued.

"Now, Katie Durbin, who I'm sure you all know by now is Tessa Walker's niece from Chicago, has graciously invited us all to lunch. She will be hosting us out at Dorothy's farm. Katie, would you and your son, Josh, please stand up? I believe everyone's had a chance to meet you, but in case they haven't, we want to make sure they know who to pay their condolences to."

Josh sprang out of his seat like he'd been catapulted. Katie didn't budge. Josh leaned down, gently put his hand under her elbow and pretended to be assisting her to stand. She stiffened and rose, happy she'd made the choice to skip some of her accessories today.

"Would you two please turn around so as folks can see you?" Pastor implored.

Josh swiveled right around and gave a quick wave. Katie kind of looked over her shoulder, smiled a lame smile and nodded. Quickly they both were seated.

"I believe you all know where Dorothy's place is, but just in case there is someone here who doesn't, I've prepared a simple map. Nellie Ruth will be handing out copies as you exit. We look forward to seeing you there for some good eats and fellowship."

Thank goodness there's a map! This way it'll be easier to bow out of riding with Dorothy Lead Foot. I have no earthly desire to be buried in this town! Katie lingered in the front pew, allowing those behind her to begin exiting, hoping to postpone as long as possible the engagement of further conversation.

She looked at her watch. It was barely 10:30 A.M., but she was hungry. She'd only had a salad for dinner, and her stomach just hadn't been in the mood for food when she awakened. On the way to the service Josh begged her to stop at a doughnut shop on the edge of town, where he'd pounded down a large orange juice, a small milk and three chocolate-covered doughnuts. The smell of the place gave her the chills. *How could people eat so much sugar so early in the morning,* she wondered.

Pastor finished gathering his notes from the altar, then approached Katie as she was exiting her pew. Simultaneously Dorothy hollered across the sanctuary, "Katie! Josh! You better get out here so we can beat this crowd. It's like a stampede."

"Pastor Delbert," Katie said with an imploring tone of voice, "if you would be so kind as to retrieve a map for us and explain to Dorothy we won't be riding with her. Do assure her we'll be right along."

"Sure. Wait here." He grinned as if sharing an inside joke, turned on his heels and strode over to where Dorothy stood. Josh raced off behind him without saying a word to his mom. When they reached Dorothy, Katie was assured Dorothy accepted whatever Pastor was telling her when Dorothy gave Katie a quick wave and she and Pastor disappeared around the corner.

"I'm riding with Dorothy, Mom! See ya there." Josh didn't wait for a reply, and he, too, left her sight.

By the time Katie trotted across the sanctuary and out into the parking lot, The Tank was already racing away. Sheba's head stuck out the rear window, her tongue flapping in Katie's direction as if to wave good-bye. Although Katie hadn't prayed for years, she found herself asking *someone* to keep an eye on her son.

15

Katie, concerned about Josh riding with Dorothy, was suddenly acutely aware of how much she loved him. The thought of harm coming his way prickled her clear through. Even so, she wasn't used to being with people nearly twenty-four hours a day, and Josh's ability to antagonize and embarrass her was beginning to wear thin. A little space would do her good.

She sat in the parking lot alone in her car, windows rolled down. There was only one other automobile left in the lot, and it was parked where it said PASTOR ONLY. She leaned her head back against the headrest and closed her eyes.

Did I speak to Aunt Tess again after she took Mom's ashes? What an odd thing to be wondering. Knock it off!

A vague image of Aunt Tess began to form in her mind.

What color were her eyes? The same as Mom's? And didn't she used to dye her hair some awful copper color?

"I know this is perhaps awkward timing, but I'd hate for anything to happen to your aunt. Our janitor sometimes is a little hasty about throwing things away."

Katie yelped at the startling intrusion. Right smack in her face was an eight-inch-square cardboard box Pastor Delbert held through the window. The large label aiming right at her forehead said, "Cremated remains: Tessa Martha Walker."

This isn't what I was picturing!

"I'm sorry. I didn't mean to startle you," Pastor said, withdrawing the box so Katie could catch her breath. "I'm afraid it wasn't very sensitive of me to present her right in front of your nose without warning."

Katie reached through the window with both hands, grabbed the box out of his hands and plunked it down on the seat next to her as though it were a bag of groceries.

"No need for apologies. You just startled me." She cranked over the engine. "Will I see you at Dorothy's?"

"I'm afraid not. I've got to work on my sermon, and I have two committee meetings to prepare for. You'll be in the best of hands with Dorothy. I'm sure she and May Belle have everything under control out at the farm. I do hope the service met with your approval."

"Yes. Everything was fine."

"Well, I trust your aunt is home with her Maker now."

No, she's now riding shotgun. "Yes. Yes, I'm sure she is." *Anything to end this conversation and move me one step closer to being done with this day.*

The map was a simple line drawing that served the purpose. Pastor Delbert had laughed when he handed it to her, explaining that everyone else knew where Dorothy lived but at least Katie's need for the map had validated his task. There was only one turn after you exited the church parking lot and got on "the hard road," as Dorothy and Arthur had both called it, toward Hethrow. Pastor had drawn an arrow where the Partonville sign would signal the turn. Katie got stuck driving behind a tractor and didn't see the sign until it was time to turn. She zipped around the corner, sending Aunt Tess careening into the passenger door before she could reach out and grab her.

She pulled over to the side of the road and slammed the car into park. Leaning across the seat, she ever so gently picked up the box, fearing ashes would spill out onto her leather seats. She was relieved to discover it was still tightly sealed, and felt a bit guilty she'd handled the ashes so harshly to begin with.

"That's it, though," she said rather sternly to the box. "You're still not behaving very well." She got out of the car and put Aunt Tess securely on the floor behind the driver's seat.

"Katie Mabel Carol Durbin," she addressed herself out loud, "you're starting to act like you belong in Pardon Me Ville, talking to a box like that. Snap out of it!"

After about a half mile, the road made a bend to the left. She noticed a farm in the distance. A quick check of the map noted Dorothy's as being a half mile past the first farm on the left, so she sped up a bit until pelting gravel got her attention and she backed down her speed. Dorothy'd already done enough ding damage.

Katie spied the outline of a subdivision on the horizon, perhaps a couple miles to the east. *I wonder what this'll go for an acre when progress marches down the road? There's certainly enough land here to pad someone's wallet and slam-dunk the development competition.*

Furrows of promised corn ran this way and that. The patchwork reminded her of the quilt her mom used to tuck her in with when she was little. Clarice told Katie that her grandmother had made it for her before she was born. It was hand-pieced and stitched in greens and browns with an occasional blue square. *I wonder if the quilt might have reminded Mom of this countryside. After all, she was born and raised here until she was, what? Twenty-something when she moved to Chicago? I wonder what ever happened to that old quilt?*

Katie's mom had tried to give it to her when she moved into her own place after college. "Mom, I'm not a child anymore. What do I want with that raggedy old thing?" She could still see the wounded look in her mother's eyes. Her mom had simply said, "Of course, honey. But I'll keep it just in case you ever want it for one of your own children. You might change your mind someday." Clarice had then clutched the quilt to her bosom and hugged it as if it were a child. *I don't remember running across that old quilt when I went through Mom's things.*

Suddenly Katie was well past that first farm, having lost track of how far she'd traveled. A long row of hedge apple trees met the road about a half mile in front of her. That must be the place. *Pastor said I wouldn't be able to see the farmhouse or buildings from the road because they were blocked by a row of trees that lined the driveway.*

She approached slowly, then pulled across the road up to the mailbox, which read "Wetstra." *Now I get it! Wetstra like* wet straw *but without the* w *on the end. Right.* Even though not another vehicle was in sight and she was within a foot of her turn, out of habit she flipped on her blinker.

The trees lined both sides of the long driveway, and a center row of short grass grew between the well-worn gravel tracks. It reminded her of something she'd once read in a novel years ago, back when she had time for fiction. She took her foot off the gas and just allowed the car to move forward at a slow, idle pace. She opened the moon roof, came to a complete stop and just stared up into the fluttering leaves that were growing toward their adult size for the season.

A gust of wind caused the branches to sway and dance and tousled her hair as it blew through the car. Because the graceful arms of the ancient trees on either side of the drive met, folding their fingers together across the sky, they seemed to sail up and down as one delicately knit archway when the gentle winds blew, lifting, falling, swaying. . . .

She became oddly soothed by their rhythms, cradled in their magical spell. Senses quickened, a long-forgotten time from her childhood sprang forth from her memory portfolio.

Katie stood staring at the tent she'd fashioned out of flowered sheets that she'd draped over her mom's clothesline and anchored to the ground with baseball-sized rocks. She then began creating the most dramatic doors at each end with scarves from her mother's bureau drawer, thoughtfully clothespinning each scarf along the angles of the sheets and allowing the bottom edges to trail softly on the ground. Each scarf a different color and pattern, each bright and beautiful and smelling of her mom's sachet.

Finally, when every angle and color combination was just right—and some combinations took a few tries—she lay down faceup, precisely in the middle. The winds blew through her tent, billowing the sheets so that the entire shelter ever so slightly lifted and settled back onto the line, as though they were breathing breaths of kaleidoscoping colors, scarves twirling and dancing in the wind, waving at the universe.

She opened her eyes and for another moment hid in this long tunnel of fluttering green.

What happened to the girl so in love with colors and magic? "Are you in there, Katie girl?" she said aloud. At last she sighed, blinked herself back into full reality and, with a heart that was light and at the same time heavy, slowly drove up the lane.

What she saw when the trees to the right finally ended was an old, two-story white farmhouse with a brick chimney running up the side near the driveway. A graceful, wrap-around front porch already had several folks sitting and standing on it, sipping beverages, holding plates and chatting.

The gravel drive curved around behind the house, and Katie followed it. She drove past the chaos of cars that were parked on both sides and up in the backyard. The Tank was pulled right up to the back door of the porch. The driveway veered toward the left and ran right into the lower level of a giant barn. She pulled over and parked just outside the entry to the left of the barn, unbuckled her seat belt, drew two deep breaths and exhaled loudly through her mouth, then opened her car door.

As her eyes panned down the side of the barn they locked on a tall structure. *Surely it can't be!* She stepped out of the car and backed up a bit for a larger view. The sun streaked over the roof of the barn into her eyes, nearly blinding her. She walked across the grass to get into the shade and allowed her vision to adjust. Her heart began racing and her head shook back and forth as goosebumps raced up her arms. *Oh, my!* There, like a giant looming over her, arose the very silo by which her mom and Aunt Tess stood side by side in that photo! What was it about that photo that kept inviting yet unsettling her?

"This place is really something, isn't it, Mom?" Josh said to the back of her head.

Katie screeched and involuntarily jumped back into him, trouncing on the top of his foot with her heel.

"Yow, Mom! Get a grip! You might have drilled a hole right through my Doc Martens!" he said as he hopped around on his right leg while holding his left foot in his hands.

Her heart was now racing so fast she could not get a word out. She just stood there staring at him a moment, then returned her gaze to the silo. Then back at him again. Then back at the silo. *It's as though that photo were talking to me!* Her eyes were open as wide as her lids would allow, and the color had drained from her face.

Josh finally stopped hopping around, stood behind her and looked in the direction in which she was now silently staring.

"Never seen a silo before?"

"Joshua . . . Joshua."

"Yes."

"Joshua."

"Mom! Is your record stuck?"

"Joshua," she repeated again as she turned to face him, "please show me inside."

"All right," he said, taking a moment to search his mom's face. "We were beginning to wonder if you'd gotten lost. Dorothy said she was about to send out a search party."

"When have you ever known me to get lost?" she asked as she walked behind him. "I spent half my career finding

places to which people gave me directions." Josh didn't respond; he just kept walking up the drive and around The
Tank until they reached the back entryway to the house.

He opened the old, creaking screen door for Katie. *For
goodness sake! Is that an actual spring?* Out of real estate habit
she mentally recorded it, even though her mind continued
to dwell on that framed photo displayed on Aunt Tess's set
table, appearing reverently placed next to that photo of her
and Josh. *That set table, waiting for whom?*

After taking a few steps across the small back porch enclo-
sure, she walked up four wooden steps. The door separating
the porch and the kitchen was already standing open. The
kitchen was quite large, spanning the entire back of the
house. The cabinets were painted white and had cross-
hatched glass windows in them. Not many dishes remained
in the cabinets, since most of them were stacked on the
counter. People were filing along, picking up the flower-
trimmed plates, then grabbing a packet of silverware that
had been wrapped in a napkin. How on earth Dorothy had
managed to have this buffet table ready, warmed and set up
before Katie arrived was beyond her. Katie was a wreck for
days before company, which she seldom invited for that
reason. Plates were piled high with sliced ham, sweet potatoes and green beans.

May Belle beckoned folks to continue on over to the
perpendicular counter, where she handed them a dessert
plate and asked which of the four delicacies they'd like.
"Peach cobbler, double chocolate brownies, gingersnap
cookies or tapioca pudding?"

While Katie stood taking all this in, Josh charged past her and marched over to Dorothy, who was fiddling with something at the sink.

"Hey, Dorothy! Where's my plate I asked you to save?"

"Right here, young man. I just washed it up for round two. No sense startin' with what appears to be a plate of slobbers!"

"Thanks, Dorothy!" Back into line he went.

Dorothy noticed Katie standing by the door. She tossed the dish towel over her shoulder, then wiped her hands down the front of her apron.

"Welcome to Crooked Creek, Katie, honey. You must be starved." She grabbed hold of Katie's hand and whisked her right up to the front of the line. "Pardon us, please. Our guest of honor and host has arrived, and if she waits for all of you hungry hounds, there's likely to be nothing left!" Everyone laughed at what they knew to be Dorothy's good humor, although personally Katie didn't think it was very funny. She was in fact embarrassed by the attention.

"Honestly, Dorothy, I'm not that hungry."

"Nonsense! You're nothing but skin and bones, and you've got plenty to do the next few days, so you better keep up your energy!" Before Katie could say another word, Dorothy picked up a plate, stabbed a giant slice of ham and topped it with a pineapple ring. Then she added a medium scoop of sweet potatoes and a healthy helping of green beans and handed her the laden plate. May Belle instantly flanked Katie to the left and escorted her to the dessert counter.

"I hope I've selected something you like, dear. I suspected you were a chocolate lover, and I just happened to have all the ingredients at hand for these double chocolate brownies. Of course, from the looks of me," she said while patting her own stomach with both hands, "I guess you can imagine I like all of them!"

"Now, don't be modest, May Belle," Dorothy chirped. "Go ahead and tell her that's your personal recipe for double chocolate brownies that won the blue ribbon at the county fair last year. Come to think of it, I guess you don't need to do that, since I just did."

Katie wasn't quite sure what to say, other than to admit she really did like chocolate. It just seemed that to begin explaining that she tried to stay away from it because of the caffeine would take too much energy.

"Mom, these brownies *rock*," Josh said, snatching two of them and piling them on top of his already full plate. He disappeared back into the living room as quickly as he'd zipped into the kitchen.

"I'm afraid my son is doing a poor job with his manners today," Katie sighed. It occurred to her that she'd been doing a lot of sighing the last two days.

"He's a beautiful child, Katie, such a good-looking and kind boy! You must be very proud of him." As soon as the words were out of Dorothy's mouth she rushed back over to the buffet line to slice more ham.

Katie looked at Josh through the doorway. She studied his profile as he talked to Rick Lawson, the lawyer, who appeared to be wearing the same rumpled and ill-fitting clothes he had on the other day. As she watched Josh's animated self interact with Mr. Lawson, nodding his head and talking between bites of food, she considered what a long time it had been since she'd really studied him. He was, as

Dorothy had said, a good-looking boy who looked exactly like his father. In fact, she thought as she watched him, he even had some of the same mannerisms. This might have been a good thing, had Katie not been so wounded by Bruce. She had finally crusted over, willing herself to despise the man who had betrayed her. "Kind," Dorothy had said about her son. *Hmmm. Kind.*

Katie noticed Josh suddenly looking to Mr. Lawson's left and followed his gaze. He had spotted that young girl who'd run in and out of the church so quickly last night. This morning, however, she was wearing a pair of navy slacks and a short-sleeved, light green sweater set. Her hair was very blond, shiny and straight. It draped neatly over her shoulders, aside from a few pieces that were pulled back and held in place by a petite gold barrette. When Katie looked back at Josh, she noticed he now seemed to have a difficult time keeping eye contact with Mr. Lawson.

Josh and a girl. Now, there's a new thought.

A hand whomped down on Katie's right shoulder, nearly sending her pineapple slice flying. A booming voice said, "Well, here you are. Katie Durbin, this here's my wife, Jessie Landers." Jessie extended her hand and waited for Katie to jostle her dessert plate to the counter so she could shake. She had yet to have a bite of anything. Jessie pumped her hand so vigorously it made her entire body shake.

"Pleased to meet you, Miss Durbin. I'm sorry about your loss. Can't say as I really knew your aunt, but nevertheless, I'm sure she was a fine woman."

Katie finally placed Arthur Landers and recalled his baseball tale from the night before.

"Thank you. Arthur told me you play baseball and you have quite an arm," Katie said.

Jessie shot Arthur a crooked glance, wondering what all he might have rambled on about. "I hope you'll forgive me for missing the wake, but I knew I could come meet you today and pay my respects. We've got us a big game coming up. If I miss practice, my arm just isn't what it oughta be on game day. And since this is the first of the season, we're still sorting out positions and getting back into shape."

"How long have you been playing?" Katie asked for lack of anything else to say.

"I reckon you could say all my life and not be lying," she said, then chuckled.

"Yessiree, that would be the truth, woman!" Arthur said. "Why, Jessie here played semi-professional ball in her heyday. She earned herself a golden glove in forty-two! Not only did she have the best pickoff arm of any catcher in any league—pegging off more runners trying to steal second base than any other catcher of her time—but she could catch just about anything ever throwed her way, including me."

Arthur laughed. Jessie did not. Katie just stared. The uncomfortable mix of responses didn't hamper Arthur's rambling in the least, although it did cause Katie's eyes to shift away for a moment in hopes she might spot Josh while Arthur continued to rattle on. Instead, her eyes landed on the girl who'd so fascinated Josh. She was now speaking to someone wearing one of the most preposterous outfits Katie had ever seen at a funeral.

It was Maggie Malone, and the girl was Shelby, her oldest great-grandchild. Although Shelby was about as opposite to her great-grandma as they come—a tomboy with a conservative approach to dress—she loved being with her Grammie M and shared her zest for life. Shelby wasn't afraid to tackle anything, including becoming the catcher for the Wild Musketeers.

Shelby had tried out for catcher of the high school team but didn't make it. When she found out through Maggie that the Wild Musketeers were without a catcher—no one's knees were now good enough to get them up out of the squat—she told Grammie M she'd like to catch for them. Ralph McAllister had stepped in as catcher for a season, but the Wild Musketeers got their pants licked in just about every game, since he refused to play with his glasses on and he couldn't see an entire steer without them, let alone the ball covered with its hide. By a unanimous vote he was ousted—first ever ousting on the team—and the winter season found them scouting. The year Jessie toppled over twice leaning out behind the plate was the year she hung up her catcher's mitt and traded it in for the pitcher's warm-up jacket. After all, she still had an arm, as could be proven by the outhouse pelting ritual if nothing else. In fact, Arthur'd even drawn a target on the side of his refuge, just to give her some practice when she was mad.

Maggie tried to explain that not just the team but the entire *league* was made up of oldsters, but Shelby just wouldn't take no for an answer. "Age doesn't matter, and besides you're more fun than most of my friends anyway!" was her determined response. She asked her Grammie M to find out if the "age thing" was a habit or a rule. When Maggie phoned the league coordinator and asked about any rules they might have as to what qualified a player, he answered with just what she was hoping for.

"Mags, we've never found a need to print something official since this is just a friendly competition."

Friendly my foot, she thought. This *is* softball *and reputations are on the line!* What had begun as a friendly, after-the-fish-fry habit had developed over the years into first a challenge from a neighboring fish-fry group, then another, then next thing you know there was a makeshift league. Eventually games were moved to Saturdays to accommodate travelers, records were kept, and one year people began throwing money in a John Deere cap for trophies. Just because only oldsters had signed up for the games didn't mean youngsters couldn't. And that was that. Shelby was in.

For two years she'd been one of their key players, but not without conditions. After her first appearance and a protest from most of the competition, the league, finding it had no such rule about age, took a vote and decided that although she could catch and bat, she would be required to have pinch runners. All things considered, speed needed to be equalized to, well, slow.

Katie excused herself from Arthur and Jessie and moved through the room to get a better look at Maggie's outfit, which consisted of black spandex pants with little slits at the ankles *(Is that a tattoo!),* a fluffy white sweater with a huge cowl neck, a leopard print belt, dangling earrings and a large black straw hat.

And suddenly Katie was caught staring by the person to whom her incredulous eyes were attached. She reached for her other plate, again holding a plate in each hand in order to divert her eyes and once again disengage herself from any more aggressive hug and shake attacks.

"Oh, I bet you haven't met Miss Durbin yet, have you?" Shelby asked when she noticed Maggie and Katie now staring at one another.

"Why, no, I haven't."

By this time Katie had mustered a smile. "We're very sorry for your loss," Maggie said. She then stabbed a forkful of food, green beans first and last with a bit of sweet potato sandwiched in the middle, shoveled it in through her deep mauve painted lips, gave a couple quick chews and swallowed. "And thank you for hosting such a lovely gathering. I was simply famished," she said.

Maggie turned to Shelby. "Shelby, would you please get Grammie's card case from my purse? I left it on the floor over there. I'd like to give Miss Durbin one of my business cards." While Shelby began thrashing through the giant brown leather bag with jewels dangling from the zipper, Maggie continued.

"Miss Durbin, as a token of my sincere sympathies and since I didn't send flowers, I'd like to extend to you a free wash and set at my salon. The card will have the address, but everyone in town knows where La Feminique Hair Salon & Day Spa is located. We're only a block off the square. Just phone ahead, and I'll squeeze you in. I'm pretty booked Thursdays through Saturdays, but I'll come early or stay late if I have to so I can accommodate you while you're in town."

Maggie studied Katie's hair, then plopped her fork on her plate and plucked at a couple of strands on the top of Katie's head. "It looks like you could use a good touch-up, too. I'd just charge you ten dollars for the color." Katie instinctively reared back her head. "Oh, I'm sorry to scare you like that. I imagine your nerves are about spent by now."

"You have no idea," Katie said.

Shelby had finally retrieved Maggie's card case. It appeared to be made out of sterling silver and was beautifully monogrammed with a very ornate *MM*. Shelby held it out in front of her grandmother, then, with her thumb, flipped back the lid like a Zippo lighter. Maggie fingered a card right out and extended it toward Katie, who had no hands to receive it. Shelby grabbed it and, without asking permission or indicating what she was going to do, stuck it in Katie's suit pocket. Katie was beginning to feel like a helpless mannequin being plucked at and invaded like this.

"For goodness sakes!" Dorothy said, coming up to them. "This poor child hasn't had a chance to eat a bite of her dinner, what with us all talking her ear off. Come on, honey, and follow me back into the kitchen. I'm gonna sit you down at the table."

"Really, I'm doing just fine," Katie replied. But before she knew it, Dorothy had whisked the plates out of her hands.

"Follow me, missy, and don't look left or right. Just follow." Katie felt not only at the mercy of Dorothy Wetstra but as though she were traveling in her back draft as well. Truth be known, she was happy to be rescued.

Dorothy pulled out the kitchen chair for Katie and arranged her plates in front of her, but not before getting out a ruffly place mat from one of the giant wooden drawers that lined the cabinets. Without asking, she also served her a large glass filled with water and a lemon slice. "I always take lemon in my water, I hope you don't mind. My fingers just kind of grab for the lemon without thinking."

"Thank you. I always ask for lemon in my water, too. In fact, I order it in diet colas. I can't remember who got me started on that one. I always figure a little vitamin C can't hurt." Katie took a few big gulps of the water and realized how parched she'd become.

"Josh tells me you lead a very busy life."

"Oh?"

"He liked to talk my ear off on the way out here. He said you sell homes?"

"Actually, I deal in commercial real estate, not home sales. It's been a long while since I've shown a house."

"But you used to sell homes though, right?"

"Yes. I've sold my share of properties."

Dorothy paused, waiting to see if Katie would mention her current unemployment. It didn't seem proper to bring it up herself, even though Josh seemed to feel quite free mentioning it on the ride over. In fact, Dorothy thought he almost sounded a little bit happy about Katie's recent canning. She remembered thinking how out of place his response seemed to be, considering the situation.

"So what's your plan for tomorrow? I imagine you've got quite the agenda if you're planning on settling things as quickly as possible."

"I guess Josh and I will try to scrounge up some boxes and begin plowing through all those piles. Can you tell me where might be my best chances for finding boxes?"

"Well, there's Your Store, the local grocery place just a few blocks from your aunt's house. That would probably be the best bet. Nellie Ruth's the assistant manager, and she could scout and save some for you. Or you could try Richardson's Rexall Drugs on the square. I doubt they'd have any big ones, since they deal mostly in little pills." She chuckled at her own humor. "How about I rally a few of the Hookers, and we collect the boxes and come by and help you get started? I imagine it must be overwhelming to even know where to begin."

"Hookers?" Katie nearly spilled the glass of water she was just setting down.

"Land sakes! Of course you'd wonder about THAT!" Dorothy went on to set the record straight.

Right. That's what I need. A bunch of old ladies calling themselves Happy Hookers clogging up the pathways, which are already nearly impossible to pass through.

"That's very kind of you, Dorothy, but I think Josh and I will need to tackle this by ourselves. And you saw the place—there's barely room for us, let alone extras. You could suggest some places that will accept some of that junk, however." While Dorothy pondered the possibilities, Katie said, "I told Josh maybe we should just hire a contractor to dig a big hole and shovel the whole place in it."

"Yes, he said you'd joked about that."

Joked? The idea is beginning to feel like the most inspired idea I've had in a long time.

"Well, Joshua was just a talking wonder during that drive, wasn't he?" Katie said with a bite in her voice.

"He's quite an interesting and expressive young man."

"Obviously he's been expressing more than you'd probably ever care to know."

"Goodness not. I'm always interested in what people have to say, especially young, energetic people, since they're gonna be running the country one day. I know you've got your plate pretty full right now, but should you need a break from your task and find you have a few spare moments, I'd love for you to drop by. There's something I'd like to talk to you about. I'm needing an informed outsider's opinion about a decision I need to make, and I have a feeling you're just the person who can help. In fact, I believe you might just be an answer to my prayers."

Katie wondered what in the world Dorothy was talking about, but she didn't have the energy to pursue it.

"Mom! You'll never guess what I just learned from Shelby. Dorothy, do you *really* have a computer? Are you *really* online?" Josh pulled out a chair and plunked himself down across from his mom next to Dorothy.

Josh leaned in toward Dorothy. Katie noticed how comfortable he'd become with her, how animated he became in her presence.

"Yup. And you might say I'm the fastest old lady in Partonville, since I just keep upgradin' away! I don't have enough time left in my life to spend it waiting for things to boot up and download! Would you like to see my office?"

"I sure would."

"Katie?"

"No, thank you. I think I'll just finish eating."

Dorothy and Josh bounded out of their chairs. No sooner were they out of sight than Gladys slipped into the chair across from Katie, who audibly sighed.

"It was a lovely service, dear. What did you think of Pastor Delbert's message?"

"It was fine." *And that's certainly all I'd share with you even if it weren't.*

"If, after you've been to your aunt's house, you need any assistance, please give the office a call. We'd be happy to help with any matters of business you might deem necessary."

"I have been to her house already, and I think we can manage just fine, thank you." Katie's tone of voice resonated assurance and finality.

That is, if we don't get talked to death first.

16

Guests long gone and things pretty well cleaned up, Dorothy went to check her e-mail.

Dear Dorothy, I didn't look at the piece of paper you wrote your e-mail address on until I got it out of my wallet when mom and I got back to the motel. I laughed out loud. "Outtamyway." Now that's a good one for you!

Mine's pretty boring compared to yours. Actually, I don't even like it anymore. I had to type something in when I set up the program several years ago, and it was the first thing that came to my mind. My best friend Alex Gillis started calling me that right after I met him when Mom and I moved into our brownstone. He lives next door. At this point, it just seems easier to keep it than change it. Besides, I haven't thought of a better one, so I'll just stick with Joshmeister.

Mom's taking a nap. We were going to go get boxes when we left the farm but when we got to the square, she said she'd changed her mind and we came straight here.

Thanks for sending me home with the brownies and pie. I already ate two of the brownies.

That's about it for now. I'll wait to see if I get an answer before I write any more.

Josh.

Immediately Dorothy clicked on the "Reply to Sender" icon and began typing away.

Dear Joshmeister, I think that name suits you just fine! It sounds fun and important at the same time, and by golly, we'd all do good to think of ourselves that way!

I'm glad you enjoyed those brownies. I'll tell *my* best friend, May Belle. (Of course, I'll have to phone her. She wouldn't know which end of a computer to plug in! Ha ha ha.) There's nothing she likes better than to know her cooking has been appreciated, and no one has appreciated her desserts over the years more than me! It's a good thing you took some of those brownies with you, or I'd have eaten them all myself! Goodness knows you'd have to choke down about anything I'd bake. Let's just say baking isn't my gift.

I hope your mom gets a good nap. I imagine you're both plenty tired.

Let me know if you need anything or if you'd just like to come out to the farm to visit again. I could show you the crooked creek our farm was named after.

I try to check my e-mail at least twice a day when I'm home. Of course, you can always phone, too. My number is 555-7232.

Peace and grins, Dorothy.

After two more quick e-mailing volleys, since they were both on-line, Dorothy had learned, by reading not only Josh's words but between the lines, that he didn't have very many friends and that his best friend, Alex, didn't go to his school, that he didn't like the school he attended, that he used to play soccer in grade school but wasn't that good at it since he was kind of a slow runner, and that he didn't have a girlfriend. She'd also figured out that he longed for a better relationship with his mother. But then that one she'd figured out way before the e-mails.

When Katie and Josh pulled up in front of Aunt Tess's house at 3:00 P.M., they had to park behind The Tank. Giant stacks of boxes were piled on the front porch, and Earl was in the side yard using a hand sickle, continuing to tackle what he'd already accomplished in the front yard. Dorothy and May Belle were pulling weeds from the perennial flower garden along the sidewalk; Katie hadn't even noticed that flowers were growing there, the grass had been so tall.

"Oh, no," she groaned. "Look at all these people!"

"'Oh, yes' is what we should be saying, Mom. Look what a difference they've already made in this place. And no wonder Your Store was out of boxes!"

"I do not want these people nosing into our business, Joshua."

"I wouldn't say helping is nosing, Mom. Gads. Lighten up and appreciate the help for a change." He got out of the SUV and slammed the door.

Katie watched May Belle helping Dorothy up off her knees. Josh hurried over to support Dorothy's other arm.

She patted him on the cheek after she was upright, and he just beamed.

"There's a basket in the backyard, Josh." Dorothy pointed toward the open gateway in the fence. "Would you please put this big pile of weeds in it?" Earl didn't look up when Josh said "Howdy" as he passed by him on his way to carry out her request.

"Earl, honey, that'll do for now. We best be getting home and start dinner. We can finish later. Let's let Miss Katie begin her work in peace."

"Are you coming home with us, Dearest Dorothy?" Earl asked with hope in his eyes.

"Well, I reckon I could come by for a short visit. I bet I could even be talked into staying for dinner."

By this time Katie had approached them. "Won't you and Josh please join us, too?" May Belle asked expectantly. "We probably won't be eating until six, and that'll give you a chance to get a good bit of work done here. I just live around the corner."

"I expect we'll be working late tonight. Perhaps another time." Josh glared at her from the side yard, where he was stomping the overflow of weeds into the basket.

"I understand," May Belle replied. "You do what you need to do, dear."

"We'll be running along then, Katie," Dorothy said. "Let us know if you need more boxes."

"Thank you for getting these. That was kind of you." She heard Josh sigh. "And thank you for helping with the yard." Katie perused the tiny front yard, concluding that the clearing had, indeed, helped make it appear much less depressing.

"If there's anything else . . ." Dorothy's voice trailed off. She looked as though she was considering her next words.

"And please, if you'd like a break, like I said, I'd appreciate your opinions on an urgent issue. We could share a bite to eat, and Josh can do some exploring."

May Belle studied her friend's face. Dorothy's voice had sounded a bit tight when she talked about that urgent issue. Whatever it was, May Belle hoped it would settle itself soon, since it had obviously been weighing on Dorothy for some time now.

"Would you like a ride home, you two?" Dorothy asked May Belle and Earl.

"No. Goodness me, it's only a short hike, and the exercise will do us good, right, Earl?"

Earl gave a slight nod to his mom.

Josh came bounding around the side of the house. "Where's Sheba, Dorothy?"

"She was curled up on the end of my bed when I left home and barely opened one eye when I asked her if she wanted to go for a ride. I think all the excitement around there this morning just plumb wore her out."

Finally readied to enter the house and get to work, Katie stepped up to the front door and extracted the key from her handbag. She'd left it attached to its lace ribbon. The ladies waved good-bye as she turned the latch. Josh took the basket to the backyard. The last sound she heard before entering was the squealing of Dorothy's tires and gravel pelting the front of her Lexus. *You'd think I would have learned that lesson the last time I parked behind her!*

Dorothy finished putting the last of the dishes away. Although a few of the ladies from the church had stayed a bit after the funeral dinner to gather dirty dishes and help wash things up, she'd whipped into action gathering the boxes as soon as she'd finished with Josh's e-mails. She was glad to have her counters and kitchen table finally cleared off again. She could look at dust for days, maybe even weeks, but clutter drove her to distraction.

"There's no more avoiding it," she said to Sheba. "We've got to take a good study on those papers before Mr. Craig phones us again." She opened one of the little drawers, retrieved the key and unlocked the desk. She fixed herself a large ice water with lemon, then settled down at the kitchen table, holding the binder in her left hand while opening it with her right.

Lord, please let me understand what I'm looking at. Please. Help this old child of Yours be able to figure what's fair and what's not.

Make it clear to me what I should do. I just can't take this pondering any longer. And now, since I've been getting to know Josh, I just can't help but wonder what's the best thing for the youth in Partonville. Might they all leave before change comes? What will draw them back . . . or keep them here?

Just do something to make it clear. Amen from Dorothy.

After forty-five minutes of reading and rereading, Dorothy wasn't sure she knew any more than when she first began, other than that should she decide to sell the farm, she'd have more money than she needed or would ever live long enough to spend, and no doubt more than either of her sons or her grandkids *should* have after she was gone. She believed money could be the root of evil, were it not respected and at least partially labored for. She'd been raised with the notion that each generation should earn its own keep, especially when it came to land, or money garnered from it. She closed her eyes and rested her right hand across the pages.

Oh, Caroline Ann, daughter of mine, how different things would be if you had lived. You loved this place as much as I did. You surely did.

Dorothy pictured her daughter's gentle blue eyes the color of sky. The little mole on the side of her nose. The wisps of fine blond hair she was always pushing away from her face. Her prominent cheekbones shaped exactly like her daddy's.

"Oh, how I miss you." Upon hearing Dorothy's tone of voice, Sheba uncurled herself from the floor under the table and scratched at Dorothy's leg until she set the folder down and picked her up.

More than ten years had passed since Dorothy last cupped her daughter's sweet chin in her hands.

Caroline Ann Wetstra-Blankenship breathed her last breath at 1:20 A.M. on September 23, one of the first days of fall. She was a childless widow who lived thirty-nine years, six months and twelve days before succumbing to her third bout of cancer.

Caroline had waited thirty-two years to fall in love. When she did, marriage came fast and blissfully. Kenneth and Caroline both taught at the high school in Hethrow and met during a staff poetry reading. After a six-month, whirlwind courtship, their wedding date was announced. Kenneth was very happy to be moving to Crooked Creek with his new bride and Dorothy, who had quickly become one of his favorite people. Even though Dorothy protested that a new marriage didn't need an old mother living in it, she was outvoted and in truth thrilled that yet another generation would breathe life into Crooked Creek.

Even before the ceremony took place, Caroline and Kenneth fantasized about the "pack of wild ones" they'd one day have. Kenneth had been raised a city boy and found the land enchanting, quieting, healing almost. The afternoon Caroline rolled up her pant legs, took off her shoes and socks and splashed barefoot into the cool October waters of the creek to show him how to turn rocks and go crawdad huntin', he'd fallen in love with her all over again. He'd marched into the icy waters, gym shoes and all, just to kiss his giggling betrothed.

Their bountiful love was first pierced by illness, and then an automobile accident claimed Kenneth's life. Even though Caroline's faith in the God who loved her never waned, Dorothy sometimes wondered if the cancer didn't re-attack the fragments of Caroline's shattered heart before it bolted uncontrollably through her grief-stricken body.

When, at 11:00 P.M., the hospice nurse had made it clear Caroline would not make it through the night, Dorothy phoned in what she referred to as the "choir of angels to sing her home." Pastor, Nellie Ruth, May Belle and Dorothy circled around the hospital bed that for six weeks had been set up in the living room. For nearly two hours they sang hymns, stroked Caroline's arms, kissed her cheeks and lifted her in prayer. At 1:15 A.M. she opened her eyes and without moving her head deliberately smiled at each of them, ending with her mother. Although she soon closed her eyes, the smile remained on her lips.

Dorothy cupped her daughter's bony chin in her hands, looked full in her face, then gently settled her cheek against the sparse wisps of hair now left on her daughter's head. After a few moments of silence while Dorothy, eyes closed, felt the warmth of her daughter's faltering breath against her shoulder, Dorothy began to sing quietly the words she had sung to her precious daughter when Caroline was nursing at her breast. "Jesus loves you, this I know . . ." She didn't stop singing until Pastor stepped behind Dorothy, put a hand on each of her shoulders and whispered, "It is finished, Dorothy. She's standing in front of Jesus now. He's scooping her into His arms and welcoming her home."

Tears streamed down Dorothy's face and onto page three of the document before her as she leaned over the table, cradling Sheba tightly in her arms. Sheba maneuvered until she could put one tentative paw on Dorothy's chest, then began licking away her salty tears.

"Sheba, you sure would have liked my Caroline! For someone who had one of the roughest lives imaginable, she just kept on loving the Lord. Said she couldn't imagine how people got through trials without Him. And trials she had." Sheba settled back down into Dorothy's lap. Dorothy took several long drinks of water as though trying to quench her thirst for her own flesh and blood while washing down her grief.

17

The rumble of thunder in the west prompted Katie and Josh to haul the boxes inside. After thoroughly surveying things, it was determined the only place to put them was in the kitchen near the back door, where they stacked them as high as they could go. She hated to crowd the only place in the house where she felt she had room to take a deep breath, but there was no other choice.

She and Josh smooshed together in the hallway and decided that was where they had to begin the overwhelming task before them. They'd work their way toward the living room after clearing the hall. Aunt Tess's bedroom would come next and the little back bedroom last. From what she could recall when she'd peeked in there the other day, that back room appeared to be mostly piles of furniture stacked to the ceiling.

"Mom, have we got a flashlight in the Lexus?"

"Of course. In the emergency box I keep in the back. Why?"

"I thought I'd tape one to my head. Since we're acting like coal miners, I might as well look like one." He shot her a devilish grin.

"Josh, get the two largest boxes and line them up in front of the stove. Look in the kitchen drawers, and if by some miracle you can find a felt marker, label the boxes 'Garbage' and 'Giveaway.' If you can't find a marker, let's have a rule that the garbage box is always on the left and the giveaway is on the right."

"Where will we put stuff we want to keep?"

"In one of those two boxes, Joshua. The last thing we need is any of *this* junk."

Josh started rummaging through drawers and was surprised to find them as neat as the rest of the kitchen. Not only did he find a marker, he also found a box of heavy-duty black plastic garbage bags.

"Score! I got a better idea, Mom. Let's make both boxes giveaway, and we can each drag a garbage bag around with us so we don't have to keep walking to the kitchen with everything."

"Why, Joshua Matthew Kinney, that is brilliant!"

"Really?" His eyebrows flew up in the air as if they'd been launched, and his eyes lit up.

"Don't let it go to your head."

"Right." He noticed his mom had picked fresh flowers and filled the vase on the table. It was still set exactly as it had been when they arrived, place mats, unlit candle, water glasses and all. He'd caught his mom staring at the photo more than once. And no doubt about it, the silo in that photo was Dorothy's.

Although Katie hated thinking about the possibility that anyone would come peer in the windows, it was shortly concluded that there wasn't enough light in the hallway to accomplish much of anything. She had Josh crawl over piles of things on the couch in the living room to reach the blinds on the side windows and throw them open, then stand on the bed in the bedroom to roll up the shades, at least allowing a slight bit more light to penetrate the work area. That it was cloudy outside didn't help the cause, and soon it would be dark.

"Okay, I'll start left and you go right, Josh. Let's clear the whole hall so we can get through to the kitchen when we start the other rooms."

"How will I know what's garbage and what's worth giving away?"

"If you don't know what it is or if it's broken or ripped, chuck it. We simply will never get through if we allow ourselves to begin evaluating."

"What about papers like bills and things?"

Katie sighed and thought about the question. "We'll have to start another box, I guess. Let's put any documents and correspondence in it. I can go through that later. Of course, throw newspapers and magazines and junk mail away. Keep a sharp eye out for Aunt Tess's trust papers. No doubt we'll need them one day soon."

"Mom, I wonder if they recycle here in Pardon Me Ville. Since I found out Ms. Outtamyway has a computer, who knows what else we might expect?"

"Miss who?"

"Dorothy. That's her Internet name."

"That certainly fits her."

Josh watched his mom stuff a pile of junk mail, a hairbrush, four bottles of fingernail polish and an empty coffee-filter box into her plastic bag. He concluded that, much to his surprise, his mom obviously wasn't interested in recycling even if Partonville had it. She was the one who usually hauled his pop cans and fast-food Styrofoam containers out of the trash at home, lecturing all the while. He knew better than to bring that up now, however, and decided to just follow her lead. And so the dig-out process began.

The hallway seemed to be packed mostly with personal items of clothing, years' worth of the *Partonville Press* and toiletries that didn't make their way back to the bathroom, which was the second neatest room in the house. *Thank goodness!* Katie had exclaimed when she saw it.

Katie had never seen so much polyester in her life. There were pantsuits of nearly every color folded one on top of the other. Obviously Aunt Tess hadn't been clothes shopping for decades. She picked them up by the armloads and tossed them in one of the giveaway boxes. Garbage bag after garbage bag was quickly filled, mostly with newspapers and flyers. Josh tied them with twist ties, then took them out on the back stoop, where it was now softly sprinkling and the faint rumbles of thunder were all but gone, the storm having missed Partonville.

Three large giveaway boxes were quickly topped off. Josh was stunned when his mom tossed him the keys and asked him to back the Lexus around to the gate. This was only the second time he'd ever been behind the wheel of the Cashmere Beige LX470. Katie had purchased it as a reward to herself after her last big development deal. She had boldly aced nemesis Keith Benton out of a six-hundred-acre parcel prime for the shopping center, school and housing development that now graced Kane County. Although she'd enjoyed the Mercedes SL500, it no longer packed the punch of "this mother of SUVs," as Josh liked to refer to it.

Ever so slowly and carefully, he backed up to the opening, getting out twice to see how much room was left before he'd hit the gateposts. He folded both rows of backseats to the sides and started packing in the boxes, pushing them way to the front. Then he loped back into the kitchen to do some reorganizing.

Katie came into the kitchen to retrieve a drink of water just as he was whamming the bottom of the box containing documents and mail. He'd dumped it into a bigger box, since he'd way underestimated the size box this would take. She groaned and mumbled something about probably not living long enough to sort through the "mountains of mayhem."

"'Mountains of mayhem'? That's a new one! Where'd ya get that?"

Katie stopped in her tracks for a moment to think. Where had she gotten that one? It seemed just to spring out of her mouth without her thinking about it. "Mountains of mayhem. Mountains of mayhem." She repeated it aloud like a mantra while she zoomed through her memory bank. "I have no earthly idea," she stated flatly, then she began picking through the papers, reading return addresses and postmarks aloud. "'Pierce Hospital, May 2, 1974.' 'Richardson's Rexall Drugs, December 12, 1998.' Gads." She blew loudly through her mouth, tossed them back in the box and went back to work.

The first time Katie looked at her watch it was 7:30 P.M. No sooner had she lifted her head from reading the dial than there was a loud pounding on the door, nearly scaring her out of her wits!

"Who in the world . . ." She made her way through the path in the living room to the front door, which had no window or peephole. Cautiously she opened the door. There stood the last man she either expected or wanted to see—none other than the rude man who had locked them out of Harry's Grill. He was still wearing his food-smeared apron. They stood there glaring at one another for a moment, then he spoke.

"Katie Durbin?"

"Yes." Katie set her jaw.

"Lester K. Biggs. Word around town is that you need boxes. I got a shipment of canned and boxed goods today. Usually I cut them up right away, but seeing as how there's a need, I just slit the tops and brung 'em over. I'll just leave 'em here by the door if that's all right with you." Without waiting for a response, he turned on his heels and headed for his pickup, retrieving two boxes, which he stacked right in front of her.

"That's it. Need more?"

"Probably."

"Fine. I'll drop them off as I get them." He whirled around, went back to his truck, opened the front door, reached across the front seat and strode up to Katie again, this time with a large white paper sack folded down at the top. "Brought you the rest of today's stew. Figure you had silverware." He thrust the bag at her, which she grabbed with her right hand. Again he whirled and went to his truck, only to return once more, this time carrying a jar.

"Here. I took a small collection at my place for anyone who didn't send flowers but who might wanna give a little something toward . . . whatever." He glanced at the front of her showy Lexus, which stuck out from beside the house, then back at her again. "Probably don't need this, but folks around here are generous no matter what."

Katie accepted the Miracle Whip jar. It was filled with coins and a couple of bills.

"I been good and bawled out by more than one customer. Didn't mean to be rude to you the other day. Nothin' personal. Closin' time is closin' time."

Whirl. In truck. Gone.

Mouth agape. Eat. Call it a day.

It was late Saturday evening when Josh retrieved his e-mail back at the Lamp Post. Josh popped open the lid to a can of Pepsi, set it down on the desk next to him and logged on. He was glad to learn he had two messages waiting.

> Dear Joshmeister. Tell your mom not to haul your discards to Now and Again Resale. I've got a better idea, and it's a dandy. We'll stop by after church tomorrow to tell you about it. Of course you're both welcome to attend services with us at 10:00 a.m. if you like. Dorothy and Sheba, Queen of the Mutt Dogs.

> Joshmeister! I'm glad to hear things are getting done. Well, maybe done isn't the right word but you know what I mean. I wish I could see that house. Are you sure you're not exaggerating? Any more news about that blonde baseball player you met? Melany dumped me. That's okay. She was pretty boring anyway. Mom's calling me. I didn't take out the garbage. As you can tell, nothing has changed here since you've been gone, including me. Alex.

Dorothy pulled up in front of Aunt Tess's on her way home from church Sunday, just when Katie and Josh were re-arranging the back of the Lexus, filling the last possible square inch. Sheba came bounding up to Josh, who happily picked her up and nuzzled her with his nose.

"Well, howdy do," Dorothy said with enthusiasm. "Looks like you two have been busier than two gnats on a bunch of old bananas."

"Boy, am I glad to see you, Dorothy. Mom's nearly worked my fingers to the bone."

Katie shot a quizzical look at her son, who had not complained once about their labors. Josh had, in fact, even seemed to enjoy himself while they were working, once putting a felt hat with orange feathers on his head and prancing around like a ballerina, causing Katie to laugh out loud. She learned more about events at his school than she'd ever heard him share before. He asked her probing questions about her childhood, and she found herself reminiscing about things she didn't even know she remembered. His statement to Dorothy felt oddly wounding to Katie. In fact, aside from the hard physical labor, things had been going reasonably well. May Belle stopped by once with a pot of chicken and noodles and another time with a Tupperware bowl filled with warm chocolate chip cookies. Boxes showed up on the doorstep at all hours of the day, just when they needed them. . . .

"Well," Dorothy responded, ignoring Josh's obvious teasing quip to his mother, "when there's much to be done, the best thing to do is, just do it!" Dorothy said, sounding like the Nike commercial.

"Actually, your timing is perfect. As you can see," Katie said, making a grand sweeping gesture with her arm, "we've just packed the Lexus to the gills, and I'm needing to make a run so we can load up again. What's the idea you e-mailed Josh about?"

"I can give you something even better to do with those things than haul them all the way to Yorkville, dear. I talked with the Social Concerns Committee at church this morning, and they all agreed we'd be honored to accept your donations for our fall rummage sale. As usual, I'm collecting and pricing things in my barn as they come in, with the help of the rest of the committee, of course. All the funds we raise from this event go to our Mission Support Committee. And, well," she said hesitantly, breaking eye contact, "there might just be an auction coming up, too."

"Auction? Cool. I've never been to an auction before!" Josh exclaimed. "Where and when is *that*? I hope we're still around."

Dorothy noticed movement on the neighbor's front porch. Sorry she'd mentioned it at all, and certainly not wanting to open this can of worms where a Partonville resident could get wind of it, she backpedaled a bit, saying it was all too uncertain to count on but assuring them that the rummage sale would definitely take place.

"I don't know what a mission support committee is," Katie said, "but if they're willing to accept all this stuff, they can certainly have it."

"Seeing as it's lunchtime, how about you and Josh just follow me out to the farm and have a bite with me. I've still got a mess of ham and potatoes left over from the funeral. It'll just take a minute to zap 'em."

Josh grinned at the surprising blend of old and new he continued to discover about this feisty woman. "Excellent idea, Dorothy!" he exclaimed as he slammed the back door to the Lexus closed.

Katie looked thoughtful for a moment, then agreed. "Actually, I could use a breath of fresh air myself." Josh looked surprised but beamed at his mother's response. "Go on ahead, Dorothy. We'll make sure things are locked up here, then we'll be right out."

"I imagine Outtamyway will travel faster than we can keep up with anyway." Josh looked first at his mom, then turned his head and winked at Dorothy, who laughed.

"Well, I have been accused of having a lead foot on more than one occasion, I confess. At my age, however, there's no time to waste. Like the Good Book says, my days are numbered. At eighty-seven, I imagine I'm down to my numbered breaths. I don't have time to waste going slow!

"Come on, Sheba. Time to hit the road. We've got company a-comin'."

18

Dorothy was standing by the barn when Katie and Josh arrived. She was acting like a flagman on an aircraft carrier, laughing at her own gyrations when Josh stuck his arms and head out the car window and began pretending to be signaling her back. Although Katie's breath hitched a bit at the sight of the silo, she found the tall structure had now become oddly comforting, since she'd spent so much time gazing at it in that photo on Aunt Tess's table.

Dorothy had Josh slide open the massive barn doors, which, as of the last few years and much to her disgruntlement, were more than she could manage alone anymore. Perhaps that was yet another reason to consider selling: get out before she and the place both just fell apart or Challie Carter got too old or disinclined to lease her land to farm. Under Dorothy's direction, Katie backed the Lexus right up into the loft. Josh and Katie finished unloading the boxes, stacking them next to two long banquet tables piled with miscellaneous items ranging from toasters to curling irons to old Avon bottles, which were covered with sheets of clear plastic to protect them from the elements. Dorothy said she'd be renting more tables when the time came and that their multiple deposits would be fine just stacked in place.

Josh took notice of his surroundings. The barn smelled

of hay and earth. Never in his life had he inhaled anything so heavenly. Slices of sunlight beamed in through cracks in the slatted barn walls, and dust particles danced in their light. A couple of pigeons darted from one beam to another, giving life to the stillness. The floorboards were worn by decades of tractor wheels, and a frayed rope hung from a beam. He just stood, staring, listening, inhaling deeply, taking it all in.

Dorothy noticed Josh reveling in his senses, then looked at Katie, who herself seemed to be mesmerized. Dorothy walked past them and slid open the four-by-six-foot side door, revealing a topside view of the stunning breadth of Crooked Creek Farm. She, too, drew a deep breath and leaned against the doorframe, dangling her right leg out over the ledge.

"I have lived here for eighty-seven years and never tired of this beauty. I must say, I had my fair share of travels when I was conducting and we were in competitions across the country. But nothing has captured me like this view from my own barn door."

Katie moved beside Dorothy and studied the look of peace on her face, trying to remember the last time she'd viewed something that spoke to her the way this land obviously did to Dorothy—the last time she'd felt that seemingly peaceful about *anything*. Slowly Katie panned from right to left, drinking in the vista.

Yes, there *was* something about this place. Yes.

Josh, Katie and Dorothy shared a lovely afternoon together, swapping stories, as Dorothy called it, eating leftovers and then meandering down by the creek. Dorothy said it wasn't fitting that a boy Josh's age hadn't learned how to hunt crawdads, and today was as good a day as any.

The crooked creek for which the farm was named wound its way through the property about a quarter mile back of the barn, just on the other side of the willow trees and an old cottonwood. Dorothy pointed to the trees as they passed, one after the other, referring to them as though they were people. "Meet Weeping Willy, Woodsy, Willoway . . ." Dorothy turned to face Katie and noticed her jaw had dropped. "Do you know each tree has its own personality?" Dorothy didn't wait for a response. "They display it in their leaves and bark and the stories they collect. Why, Woodsy houses the imprints of hundreds of toes that have climbed those powerful branches just to get high enough over the creek to jump in."

She led them around Woodsy to what had always been referred to as the swimmin' hole, a portion of the creek that was deeper than the rest, carved by years of water rushing around the hairpin turn. Although it wasn't quite warm enough for swimmin', Dorothy assured Josh that if she wasn't too old to crawdad hunt, neither was he. With that statement out of her mouth, she began to untie her white tennis shoes, peel back her pink socks and roll up her pant legs. Josh followed suit. When they both were barefoot and wiggling their toes, she then placed her hands on her cocked hip, looked straight at Katie and asked her what *she* was waiting for.

"I guess I'm just not the crawdad type," she said, tucking a flyaway hair behind her ear.

Dorothy considered whether to challenge her, then decided she'd best not, since she was soon going to be counting on her alliance and didn't want to do anything to alienate the hand she hoped would help guide her.

"Well, it's you and me, Joshmeister! Just do what I do and keep your eyes open." With that, she stepped into the foot-deep cool waters just north of the swimmin' hole, bent nearly in half until her face was as close to the rushing waters as her five-foot, ten-inch frame would allow, and began to stare. Remaining folded in half, she took a couple splashing steps and stared again. At the first sign of a sizable rock, she slowly sank her hand into the waters and gently picked up the edge with one hand, poising the other nearby. Like a flash, a crawdad seemed to squirt out amid the cloud of mud that swirled into the water from beneath the rock. Just as quickly, Dorothy stabbed her free hand into the waters and picked him up by the tail, waving the four-inch squirmer in the air and grinning from ear to ear.

"Now that's how it's done. Your turn."

Josh laughed out loud, then gave a loud war hoop and beat himself on the chest a couple times. "Mighty hunter go for game," he said in a guttural tone. After three tries, he, too, had his first catch of the day. Katie stood on the bank watching Dorothy's face transform into that of a twelve-year-old. No doubt about it, Dorothy Wetstra was a sight to behold.

By the time they sauntered their way back up to the farmhouse, it was late afternoon. Although Katie had forgotten Dorothy's curious statement about needing opinions and her being an answer to prayer, Dorothy certainly had not.

She was afraid if she didn't just jump right into the subject when they entered the kitchen, her courage and the opportunity would slip away. Time was running out . . . for a lot of things.

"Katie, I need to talk to you about something of dire importance. I have spent too long fretting and praying over a big decision in my life, and like I said before, I believe God has, as usual and in His perfect timing, and in the nick of time, I might add"—she looked skyward when she said those words—"provided just what I need, and that would be you. I have to trust someone."

Katie drew a deep breath and held it for a moment as she studied the look of determination that etched itself onto Dorothy's face. Long gone was the youthful exuberance inspired by bare feet and crawdads. The face she saw before her now exuded weariness, possibly even pain.

Although Josh's curiosity was piqued, he had the distinct feeling it would be better if he left them alone. After getting Dorothy's permission to crank up her computer and log on to AOL, he headed upstairs to her office.

"Please, dear, sit down," Dorothy said. Katie pulled up a chair at the kitchen table across from her and leaned on her forearms.

"Sit tight a minute," Dorothy said. "I've got to get something. And would you like a glass of water while we're chatting? I need to wet my whistle. All that walking plumb dried up my spit!"

"Yes, that would be nice." Katie studied her chipped nail polish and pondered how all the unaccustomed manual labor was taking its toll on her all-togetherness. Her hands were dry and chafed from relentless washing as she tried to keep herself at least somewhat sanitized from the years of Aunt Tess's neglect. Dorothy zipped from here to there, finally returning with two waters with lemon and a large folder she plunked down on the table between them.

"Craig & Craig Developers?" Katie was shocked, the look on her face revealing one of recognition. *Those are the guys Keith Benton invests with in this part of the country!*

"Yes, have you heard of them?"

"Of course. In fact, I've come up against them a few times."

"Come up against them?"

"Not exactly directly and not in the bad sense of the word. Just business dealings. You could say I've won a few rounds, and they've won a few more," Katie said, recalling her last losing volley with disgust. The one the Lexus still hadn't made up for.

"Well, I need to trust you, Katie. You see," she said, pausing a moment to take a deliberate couple gulps of water while she silently prayed God would help her gather her courage and thoughts in a manner that would come out right, "I am an old lady. That is obvious. And although I was born and raised on Crooked Creek Farm, and Henry and I raised three children on this spread, and lots of others have partied and healed here, there is no one in my family who wants it when I'm gone. Oh, Caroline Ann had the same heart for this place as myself, but it wasn't in God's plans for her to have it."

"Caroline Ann?"

"My daughter. My beautiful daughter."

"Where is she?"

Dorothy said the next words so quietly that it took Katie a moment to digest them. "With Jesus."

"I am so sorry. How long has she . . ."

"She died over ten years ago. She was only thirty-nine years old. She and her husband moved right in with me after their wedding. Can you imagine them wanting to do such a thing?"

Katie thought about how different this usually joyful and somewhat wild woman was from *her* mother. There always seemed to be an indefinable sadness lurking inside her mom. Although Katie'd loved her mom, no, she certainly could not imagine trying to live with her, since they were so different.

Dorothy didn't wait for an answer; she just charged right on in a near blur of words. "I have two sons. Jacob Henry is my oldest. He, like many younguns these days, couldn't wait to get out of Partonville when he got old enough to go to college. He went to Penn State and never looked back. Oh, of course he comes home for visits. He just doesn't stay long when he does. He gets antsy and impatient after a few days and usually finds a reason to leave before he originally intended.

"Now, don't misunderstand. I love that firstborn child of mine, just the way he is. I simply don't kid myself about reality." She chuckled. "In fact, he reminds me a bit of you. So much to do. So serious."

Katie wasn't sure how to take that comment. Again, Dorothy continued right on before she could file the remark.

"He never married. Came close a couple times but seemed to find something wrong with each of them just when everyone thought he'd be popping the question. He's a lawyer in Philadelphia. Mostly represents big business. He's as happy as he can manage to be, I imagine, although I do keep asking Jesus to soften him a bit.

"Partonville has begun to suffer the last many years from all the kiddos who've moved away. A town needs youth, energy, new ideas, or else it becomes stale and crotchety. Unless a child wants to farm, there's not been much around for them, other than the mines. They go out and find the rest of the world and then . . ." She was silent for a moment. "A few businesses on the square have already closed. Can't help but wonder how long some others can hang on.

"I used to think my other son, Vincent, might end up living here. After his baby sister died, he stayed here with me a couple weeks. I'd watch him disappear down toward the creek, shoulders shaking as he sobbed. He didn't want to keep falling apart in front of me." She sat quietly for a moment, refolding her hands. "He has always been so tenderhearted. It liked to kill him when Joan, his ex-wife, took Bradley and Steven and left him. Those towheaded kids are young teenagers now! They were just little guys when they came for a couple days to stay with their dad during our grieving. I'd watch Vinnie watching those kids, realizing they never had a chance to run free and wild like this, what with all the worries in the city. Oh, how Vinnie used to run like the wind through those fields!

"But it wasn't meant to be for those youngsters either. He met Joan at Southern Illinois University when they were juniors. She was from Denver, and she wanted to be near her folks after graduation. Vinnie found a solid banking job, and off they went. He maintains a very close relationship with his sons since the divorce, and he'd never move away from them. He's got him a right swell girlfriend, and they've been dating about two years now, but I think he's still working himself to the place where he can trust a woman. I pray every day for his healing to be complete so he can get on with his life and not end up alone." Her voice sounded weak at the end of her statement, and she drifted off into her own thoughts for a moment.

Katie couldn't help but notice that it appeared this spunky lady was literally shrinking on the spot. Her normal bolt-upright posture had begun rounding off in the last few minutes, as though she were melting from the weight of hard memories.

Katie studied each line in Dorothy's face. *I can't believe all of what I've heard! She's always so upbeat and funny. So spunky and ready to help. How does she manage to be so positive after having lost a daughter and been all but abandoned by her sons? How old did she say Caroline was when she died? Gads, she was younger than I am!*

Dorothy shook her head and bolted out of her chair, startling Katie. She zipped into the dining room, opened the treasured mahogany desk and pulled out a photo album, returning to the table with it. She stood next to Katie and flipped through the pages, landing on the one she was seeking, and handed the entire album over, opened to the spot.

"See? These are my children." Her arthritic finger moved and pointed at the speaking of each name. "Jacob Henry, Vincent and Caroline Ann. We had the boys so close together, they were raised more like twins. Then Caroline Ann didn't come along till quite some time later. This here is my faithful Henry. Of course, that's me."

Katie felt a rush of warmth as she perused their faces. The similarities from nose to chin to eyes filtered throughout their strong bloodline. The way they stood so close together, husband to wife and sibling to sibling. . . . Dorothy leaned in and flipped the pages again.

"Here's Vinnie with his younguns. That one there is Steven. That devilish little booger is Bradley. He'll give you a run for your money, that's for sure!" It didn't go unnoticed by Katie that the lilt was back in Dorothy's voice. "Here's Caroline Ann and Jacob the year before she died. The boys were home for Thanksgiving, too, when I snapped these." Nearly all the pictures were taken outside, different angles of the house and land framing the faces.

Katie couldn't stop staring at the photos. So drawn into the life of this woman was she that there was nearly a tug of war over the album when Dorothy said they could finish looking at it another time but that now they needed to talk business.

Katie leaned her head back against the tub and scootched down until her entire body was cocooned in the steaming water topped with bubbles that peaked like oceans of whipped cream. Closing her eyes, she tried to draw a blank, release the turmoil that had captured her earlier in the day when Dorothy entrusted her with such startling information. The swarm of thoughts, however, simply would not sink, no matter how deeply she submerged into the waters.

Craig & Craig's proposal was for the entire Crooked Creek Farm—160 acres. Dorothy seemed to think the price they were offering per acre was "gracious." Katie ran the figures in her head. Although it was more, she speculated, than most local farmers would probably be able to pay, were Dorothy to pursue *that* avenue, by no stretch of the imagination were they being "gracious"—even with the risks of such a purchase.

She did, however, understand Craig & Craig's chop licking. The lure of sweet revenge swelled within her.

Katie raced the Lexus past Dorothy's to the contingent edge of Hethrow the next morning and spent a good couple of hours poking around, also making prying phone calls without tipping her base of information or the true reason for her inquiries. Should word spread about a prime-location landholder's possible interest in selling that many acres, other commercial offers would undoubtedly spring to life and drive up the price per acre, perhaps even as much as double it. In fact, she imagined even without word spreading, other deals were ready to hit the table; there was just too much going on in Hethrow for there not to be. She spent a good while in the courthouse and library gleaning whatever she could, prowling around on the Internet as well. Luckily Hethrow was the county seat, and public information was plentiful.

She pondered the possibilities, trying to predict Craig & Craig's plans for residential development. *Yes, that's probably what it would be. Undoubtedly they could at least sell two lots per acre, maybe even three. There was already a trend set on that end of Hethrow toward mid- to upper-range homes starting at $175,000, easily topping the quarter-million or more mark. It looks like there could also be a need for new schools, should all Crooked Creek land become residential. Those Landers people next door would then become the next likely contingent target. Whew! Those prices would be through the ceiling! And surely the Craigs have an inside pulse*

of Hethrow's city planners' intentions to allow for more annexa-
tion, or they wouldn't be going after such a score. She wondered
how those in charge of Partonville might receive the challenge, but knew one day they'd have to, and probably soon.

She was alive with the hunt, captured by the opportunity and haunted by the trust of Dorothy Jean Wetstra.

19

Dear Outtamyway,

Alex says to tell you Hello. He thinks you must be one of the coolest old ladies ever. He couldn't believe I'd been crawdad hunting and that you were the one who taught me how. In fact, he didn't even know what a crawdad was until I explained it looked something like a miniature lobster but brown instead of red.

I hope you don't mind me using the term old lady. I mean, you are old. But you don't seem like it. In fact, you seem "younger" than my mom, if you know what I mean.

Speaking of mom, she's been gone all morning. I got to sleep in for a change. She slid a note under my door saying she was going to run some errands, and I didn't find it until I woke up at 9:20. Usually she's banging on my door at 7:30 or so. She said she hoped to be back at noon. She promised me yesterday that we'd have lunch today at Harry's. Can you believe it?!

Hope to see you soon. Joshmeister.

Dear Joshmeister,

I am an old lady, and that's a fact. No sense acting any other way.

Tell Alex he must be cool, too, since he's your best friend.

I'm glad you got to sleep in. I guess that hunting expedition wore you out. HA! I slept in a little myself this morning, but then Sheba and I stayed up late watching an old Joan Crawford movie on TV. I don't imagine you know who she is. I ate microwave popcorn, and I do believe there's still some kernels stuck in my upper plate.

Have fun at Harry's. I had breakfast there this morning. You'll likely meet some real characters. Oh, and you might want to wear a helmet (that ought to get you wondering ;>). Hope to see you soon. XO

Dorothy recalled her wild breakfast at Harry's that morning. Folks had been buzzing like berserk bees about Harold's provocative editorial in Sunday's *Partonville Press,* "Riding the Fence of Development." Since the grill was always closed on Sunday, Monday morning was the first chance they'd had to let their emotions run rampant, aside from church, which just wouldn't have been appropriate. Words had been flying so quickly, Dorothy nearly felt that she had to duck to keep from getting pelted with them. It was as close to chaos as she'd ever witnessed, what with heads bobbing up and down, people leaning across each other to get something repeated, shouting across the U. . . .

She'd overheard bits and pieces of Lester's coffee-pouring

talk, rambling on about a red Toyota he'd heard tell about. Gladys held court, blustering something about an interview Sharon had apparently had with Colton Craig. "Over my dead body will they. . . . ," she ranted, once even banging the counter. Arthur hollered at Lester, "Quit actin' like a girlie gossip and git my eggs a-cookin'!" Cora Davis didn't park her backside in her chair once, she was so busy flitting from person to person, passing around what she heard from each set of lips. Even Challie Carter showed up to see how folks were speculating after that editorial. He wondered if this might not be the time to stop farming all that leased land, sell *his* entire estate lock, stock and barrel, and head for retirement in Florida: "Trade in my coveralls for one of those shirts with palm trees on it."

Harold and Dorothy had been the only two who sat quietly, listening to the cacophony. She was afraid to jump into the conversation, since she was such a bad liar and something might show on her face. She occasionally nodded her head, just to let them know she was "in" on the dialogue. Of course, Dorothy was the *last* person they'd imagine was talking to someone, literally holding them all on the verge of Change with a capital *C,* and that meant progress—or did it? She wondered, if she did accept the Craigs' offer and the sale went through, what might they think of her then. Although all the development talk certainly caused her breath to hitch, she'd finally relaxed a bit, learning at least that Mr. Craig was indeed a man of his word and hadn't said anything.

Harold had studied Dorothy. Just kept tapping his pen on the counter and looking her way, seemingly drawn into her . . . silence. It caused her pretty much to gobble down her breakfast and retreat back home.

The one thing she knew for sure was that eventually progress would march its way into Partonville. For better or for worse—and she usually came down on the side of modernization—progress would come, and perhaps her last hurrah on this earth could be that of opening the door to it.

Partonville had shrunk a bit over the last decade, and she'd rather see it have to change than disappear completely. She couldn't stand to imagine what would happen to her farm if she didn't take some kind of steps. Why, what if she died without making any decisions? What would happen to her land then? No, better to take action rather than just let things happen. She hadn't been raised to be passive. Her dad would likely roll over in his grave if he thought for a moment she hadn't made some kind of plans for Crooked Creek upon her death!

Last evening, Katie had even given her hope there might be a very special way to preserve the memories of the Crooked Creek Farm for her children and her children's children, even if she were to sell it. Colton Craig had given her no idea she held the power to call a few shots. For instance, Katie said she could include in the deal that a certain number of acres be donated to the conservation district. *Crooked Creek Park. Now how would that sit with you, Mom, Dad, Henry, Caroline Ann? Think the angels would dance to the likes of that?* Or would they weep? Well, that was the one thing she could be assured wouldn't happen, since there were no tears in heaven.

Dorothy also knew progress at Aunt Tess's had been speedier than anyone expected and that Katie was eager to get Josh back in school and get herself back to the grind, as she referred to it, although any time she mentioned going home, Dorothy noticed Josh's face dull a bit. It had not gone unnoticed by Dorothy that that boy longed for his mother's attention, and somehow this trip seemed to be softening her edges. At the very least it had opened doors of communication she knew had been closed. Josh had revealed more to her in his ongoing e-mails than even he might have imagined—that he felt like an oddball in his own school and felt more at home in Partonville, that he seemed more curious about his grandmother's past than his mother did about her own mother.

Dorothy also knew she'd grown very fond of Joshmeister and, in fact, found herself praying for him nightly, along with his mother.

When Josh and Katie entered Harry's at twelve-thirty, heads snapped and tongues stopped wagging. Even though most of the folks had departed, including the early lunch crowd, and conversations had worn down, Partonvillers didn't believe in airing their laundry to strangers. Cora Davis had already come and gone—no doubt working her way from store to store and telephone line to telephone line—so Katie and Josh parked themselves at her usual table at the window.

"Dorothy was here for breakfast, Mom. Too bad we didn't come earlier! She said we might need helmets today, but I don't see anything different than we ever have. I don't know what she was talking about. At least sitting here we won't miss any of the action. We can be the Shift Two Gawkers," he said, then laughed.

"Joshua! Keep your voice down. It's bad enough I'm actually going to be subjected to all this grease," she said as she looked at the menu, "without also being shunned in the process. And how do you know Dorothy was here for breakfast? Did she phone you this morning?"

"No, we e-mailed back and forth a few times."

"E-mail? Already this morning?"

"Yes. I told you that."

"Well, I hope you . . ."—she paused for a moment to weigh her words—"know where the boundaries of friendship and private affairs begin and end."

"Oh, yes, ma'am," he said with sarcasm, then gave her a crisp salute. "How can you worry so much and talk that way about . . ."—he used his fingers to air-play quotation marks "'these people'? They've done nothing but help. Mom, even Lester Biggs has gone out of his way to bring us all the boxes and food and . . ."

"What do you want to order?" The question came without warning and with no softness around the edges. Lester spat it out before he even arrived tableside.

"Hi, Mr. Biggs. We sure appreciate all you've done for us," Josh chirped.

Lester nodded acknowledgment of the statement, then lifted his order pad.

"Do you have a special today, Mr. Biggs?" Josh asked, unaffected by Lester's curtness.

Lester didn't speak but pointed his pencil at the three-by-five index card sandwiched between the salt and paper shakers. Josh fingered the card and read it out loud to his mom. "BLT with noodle soup plus pie and coffee. I'll have that, sir," Josh said.

"Make it two," Katie added, "but keep my dessert. And do you have decaf?"

"Course," he kind of grunted, as though she was daft. Josh volunteered to eat his mom's dessert, too, and asked for a Coke rather than coffee. Lester made notations on his notepad and silently returned to the grill, collecting a couple empty coffee cups from the counter on his way.

The screen door slammed so loudly that Katie yelped aloud. Earl was returning with the empty delivery box from today's late lunchtime round.

Josh finished off the last scrap of piecrust on his second dessert. "So what was up with Dorothy yesterday? What was so important she had to talk to you?" he asked, licking the fork between words, making the *you* sound as though it astonished him.

Katie heard the squeak of stools and noticed two customers had turned to face them. "For goodness sake, lower your voice, Joshua. It wasn't anything, really." Josh noticed she didn't make eye contact with him when she answered, nor did he believe her. His mom had been wired ever since they'd left Dorothy's yesterday. She'd also evaded answering his questions as to her whereabouts all morning, muttering something he couldn't understand, then changing the subject.

Dorothy was glad she'd had Josh leave the barn doors open a crack so she could wiggle in. She stood in her favorite place in her girlish pose, foot dangling over the ledge, looking out over the farmlands.

"Dear Lord," she said aloud, causing a couple of pigeons to shift beams in the cool, dark, cavernous space. "It's me, Dorothy Jean, but then I reckon You already know that." She paused for a moment and gazed up toward the sky as though centering her attention. "I know I've been a downright pest the last week or so, but since You know everything, You already know Mr. Craig has phoned me again. He reminded me the contract offer expires in two days and that he'd like to have an official answer rather than just letting it expire. Me, too. I don't mean I'd like to expire, but that I'd like to have an answer, too. Now, although I know You want me to have patience, I have plumb run out. The weight of this decision is more than I can take. Please! Do something! Make it clear. I'm listening. Amen."

She turned to walk away from the door, then whirled back around.

"Wait! I don't know what's gonna become of this place, but it occurs to me I also don't know where I'll go if I do move. And I'm not talking about heaven yet! Be working on that, too, if You decide I'm outtahere. Okay? And give me strength and courage for . . . whatever. Whatever. Isn't that a great word, Lord? You can end just about every sentence with it. Amen again. And I mean it this time."

Katie and Josh worked until 9:30 P.M. after lunch at Harry's, stopping only once to make a run to Your Store to buy bread and sandwich meat, pop for Josh, bottled water for Katie and a giant bag of Cheetos. Even Katie uncharacteristically downed a few, then complained about her orange fingers. She was still swallowing the disappointment of not overhearing any pertinent gossip at Harry's. She was just sure she'd glean something after that editorial. She'd picked up the paper as soon as she overheard Jessica and Paul Joy talking about the editorial when she was getting in her car early that morning and they were out watering flowers. It didn't take her long to discover that Harold Crabb was one gutsy and astute guy. And he was for sure right about one thing: something was about to happen.

The next day they decided to make a run to the dump outside of town. All that hard work had produced a mound of garbage that was quite an eyesore. Katie figured Aunt Tess's neighbors had put up with enough the last few years without her creating a new reason to look away. Besides, she was also hoping things might at least begin to look marketable from the outside before contacting a local Realtor, which she hoped to do in the next couple of days. They'd already been here a week—thank goodness two of those days were teacher institute days—and Josh had to get back to school. That was that. Thank goodness at least Latin was e-mailing him assignments and he could turn in most of his papers electronically, but they had already, in a polite yet nudging e-mail to her, "certainly hoped" she'd have him back soon.

Aside from the major pieces of furniture and a few miscellaneous piles, Katie and Josh had finally nearly emptied the living room. One of the piles stacked on the gray couch was things they hoped to find the rest of, like a matching shoe or the other earring or the vacuum sweeper they speculated went with the hose. Katie would have chucked them, but Josh insisted they could bring money for Dorothy's sale, and he'd worked so hard, she gave in. There were also a couple of expensive-looking items that they had no clue about and were in hopes of perhaps finding something else that went with "it" or solved the mystery. They referred to this pile as the puzzle area.

The multiple boxes of papers caused her to moan, but she had made the decision at some point just to keep piling them up. She would go through them at her leisure when she got home. Surely the trust documents were buried somewhere among them.

After sweeping her eyes through the room, Katie decided this would be a good place to stop for the night. Tomorrow they would tackle the bedroom, which was the worst of all. The Lexus was nearly packed to the gills again, since they'd stuffed in a few extra end tables, three card tables, two footstools and a hall tree. Although Katie had been avoiding Dorothy, a run to the farm needed to be made first thing in the morning. Besides, she'd sneaked in a few phone calls, including ones to her banker, done a bit more Web browsing, studied the stock market and replayed all the possibilities. She knew it was time to make her move.

20

May Belle closed her eyes the first moment Maggie unleashed the warm stream of water on her scalp. With her husband so long-ago gone and Earl not being much of a hugger, she longed for physical touch. While Maggie chatted on about whatever, May Belle was oblivious to her words, so lost was she to the wonderful and simple sensation of warm water flowing over her head, the gentle yet thorough circular motions of Maggie's fingers as they scrubbed behind each ear and down the nape of her neck, the floral fragrance of the shampoo and then, again, the warm, flowing rinse waters. When Maggie put the towel around the back of May Belle's head and helped her sit up, she felt like she was being dragged out of a soothing cocoon.

"Don't you think?" Maggie asked.

"Don't I think what?"

"For goodness sakes, May Belle, have you heard a word I said?" Maggie patted the towel to May Belle's head, wrapped it turban style and tucked it in. She followed May Belle to the left station of the two. No need to ask; this was always the routine. Only those getting color and perms got the right chair. Since May Belle had never colored or permed her hair, let alone let anyone cut it, saying, "What's the point of paying for a cut when all I do is put it up in a knot anyway?" the routine never changed.

Maggie, of course, knew the truth about why May Belle cut her own hair; she saved costs wherever she could. Maggie sometimes wondered—and she wasn't alone in this—how May Belle and Earl managed to get by. As far as anyone knew, all the income she had was Homer's Social Security. This every-other-week routine was a necessary indulgence. Maggie had never once in all the decades she'd owned the shop upped May Belle's five-dollar ticket. Her tip always came in the form of something deliciously sweet to eat, and that was just fine with Maggie.

May Belle thunked down in the chair, and Maggie began her rhythmic pumping process to raise her to working level. Sometimes Maggie would even break out singing to the beat, although today she didn't. Maggie undid the towel and began combing through May Belle's long, white, thinning locks.

"I see you've given yourself another hatchet job." The line never changed.

"Hmmm," May Belle responded, keeping her eyes closed and her head down.

"So, what'll it be today? Spikes? Braids? Pompadour? Horse's tail?" Maggie asked as May Belle lifted her head at the end of the comb-out process. It was a ridiculous question, since May Belle always had her hair put up in a simple bun, but one Maggie always asked.

"Braids."

"*What?*"

"You heard me. Braids."

"What kind of braids?" Maggie's surprised face looked

over May Belle's shoulder as they spoke to one another in the mirror.

"The kind that look like *The Sound of Music* braids. You know, where they come up around each side of your head?"

"May Belle, are you serious?"

"Yes, I am, Maggie. It's just time for a change. I don't know another thing to say other than sometimes it's just time for a change. I used to wear my hair like that when Homer and I were courting. I've been thinking about him a lot lately, and I'm just tired of everything being the same. My hair is one thing I have control over. Of course, going back to something I wore over fifty years ago isn't exactly a change, is it?"

"Well, I'd sure say it is. It's so old it's new again! And you know how I love doing new!" Maggie parted May Belle's hair down the middle of her head. "Mind if I add a bit of a French braid touch to it?" Maggie's persona was lit up like a Christmas tree at the opportunity to do something new . . . on *anyone*! As much as she loved the hair shows and keeping her own head changing, her clientele wasn't exactly into change.

"Have at it!"

Just then the bell jingled, and Dorothy sauntered in.

"Can you believe what I just heard?" Maggie said to Dorothy.

Dorothy's heart skipped a beat. Although she hoped she could trust Katie, she had continued to feel a bit uneasy since she'd revealed her secret to anyone.

"And what would that be?" Dorothy asked hesitantly.

"May Belle here has asked for a new hairdo!"

Dorothy quick-stepped to the chair and picked up one of May Belle's wrists. "Just checking to make sure she hasn't hog-tied you in this chair, dearie. And what do you mean, a new hairdo?"

May Belle shot her head up to look at Dorothy. "It's just time for a change. Sometimes it's just time for a change."

"It must be catching," Dorothy said.

"What?" May Belle and Maggie said together.

"Change."

"Joshua Kinney. Wake up." Katie banged on his motel door at 7:15 A.M. "Get your shower. We'll have breakfast at Harry's, make a run to Dorothy's and finish our talk, then we'll get over to Aunt Tess's and begin work on the bedroom."

"Yes, ma'am." He heard his mom's departing footsteps through the door.

He tossed in bed a few times, then finally rolled out and into the bathroom. He stood under the steamy shower water, head back and eyes closed, waiting for his body to come to life. He felt achy, having moved furniture around and loading so much stuff in and out of the Lexus.

Josh knew it was peculiar that his mom wanted to eat at Harry's a second day in a row. After all, she had barely eaten a bite of her food there yesterday.

Thoughts of Dorothy and Sheba came to his mind, and he smiled. He had definitely become attached to that fun oldster and her mutt dog. Dorothy even seemed to be making a little headway into his mom's crusty hide. He was eager to be back out at the farm, if just for a little while.

Katie had to ask Josh to repeat nearly everything he said to her at Harry's. She seemed preoccupied at best and intentionally eavesdropping at worst. *Don't tell me Mom's turning into one of* them*!* He snickered to himself at the thought.

She only ate one bite of her toast, fidgeting with it, cutting it in half, spreading a wafer-thin smear of peach preserves. Doing everything but actually eating it. When Josh was just about done polishing off his "Morning Special" of two eggs, two slices of toast, hand-patted sausage patties, biscuits and gravy and a large milk, she used her cell phone to call Dorothy, even though a pay phone was right in front of her on the wall. Josh had never seen his mom use a pay phone, though she had once commented about all the germs.

"Dorothy? How are you this morning? I didn't wake you, did I? . . . Good. Josh and I were about to make a run. We're loaded up again and just wanted to make sure you were home. . . . Yes. I have thought it over and considered the details. We'll talk about it when we get there."

Squeaking stools swiveled her way. No matter how quietly she'd been talking, everyone had heard every word. *What* was *Dorothy thinking anyway, hanging around with this city slicker?* they all wondered. As far as they were concerned, she wasn't one to be trusted. No one from the city was.

Dear Lord, all I hear You saying is Trust Me. I can only assume You mean for me to trust in Katie Durbin's advice. So be it. Amen.

As usual, Dorothy was standing near the barn awaiting their arrival. Katie noticed that although Dorothy had obviously had her hair done, her face seemed drawn, as though she hadn't slept. Sheba was waiting at Josh's door before the car stopped. Katie said hello and pulled up to the giant barn doors, waiting for Josh to open them. When he did, they discovered Dorothy had dragged things around until there wasn't room to pull the Lexus in. Katie parked on the incline next to the silo and set the parking brake.

"Howdy doody, you two," Dorothy said. "I'm glad to see you this morning. Goodness me, I plumb forgot about that mess. Sorry." She walked around the car and patted Josh on the shoulder with one hand while patting Sheba's head with the other. Josh had scooped up the dog the moment he exited the car, and they were engaged in a morning hug of sorts.

Katie opened the back of the Lexus, looked inside and drew in her breath with a loud gasp.

"Joshua! Where did this come from?" She carefully pulled what looked like a large tarnished vase from between two boxes and clutched it to her chest.

"I found it behind the door in Aunt Tess's bedroom. I went to take a look in there before we left last night, trying to psych myself up for what came next. I realized something always kept the door from opening all the way. When I checked it out, there sat that vase. I think it's just full of dirt, Mom. I put it in the car before we left last night, thinking somebody might like the vase, though. Why? What's up with it?" he asked, looking at her ashen face.

She closed her eyes and ran her hand up and down the side of the urn as though stroking a soft kitty. "It's my mother's ashes."

Dorothy and Josh stood frozen, captured by the sight before them. Katie actually began to rock back and forth. When she opened her eyes, both she and Dorothy had tears streaming down their faces, such was the compassion of this older woman and the depth of Katie's moment. *Lord, heal the hurt in her heart,* Dorothy prayed to herself.

The three of them continued to stand in silence while Dorothy and Katie wiped their noses as best they could without hankies. Finally Dorothy broke into the quiet with yet another startling discovery.

"Katie, dear, perhaps this isn't the time, but somehow I feel God nudging me that it is." She walked over to the base of the silo and picked up the small square box she'd set there earlier. Katie had a quizzical look on her face until she saw the label.

"Oh, my *gosh*! Aunt Tess! I forgot all about her. Where on earth did you find *her*?"

Josh looked nothing short of dismayed.

"Well, honey, I came out here to pray yesterday, and before I went back to the house I just couldn't help but poke around a bit in some of the boxes you brought over. Imagine my surprise when I read the label on this one! I set it out here so as I wouldn't forget to give it to you. I figured it got mixed in with your boxes by accident." Both of them chuckled; Josh looked at them like they were daft, one moment crying and the next laughing. He recalled finding the box behind the driver's seat yesterday and unloading it in the barn without paying any attention.

Goosebumps raced over Katie's entire body, and her heart nearly boomed out of her chest. It struck Katie like an erupting volcano: here they were, in a manner of speaking, her mother and her mother's sister, once again reunited in front of the silo. Like the picture. Gathered with them, she and her son and the woman who had somehow brought them all together. Without a shadow of a doubt, but unable to understand or vocalize it, Katie knew this scene was meant to be. If there was a God, He had surely led her to this place, to this moment in her life.

Everything was finally unloaded but the sisters, as Josh had begun referring to them, who were now safely seat-belted into the backseat of the Lexus. Although it kind of creeped him out at first, he got used to their presence.

Finally Katie, Dorothy and Josh were gathered around Dorothy's kitchen table, each sipping water with a slice of lemon. Josh started to head up the stairs to boot up Dorothy's computer when they came inside, but Katie asked him to stay.

"Well, Katie, what have you decided? Should I accept Colton Craig's offer for the farm?"

"What?" Josh yelped. "You're thinking of selling your farm?" He looked from Dorothy to his mom, and an uneasy feeling seized him. *This is what Dorothy's been talking to Mom about? Selling her farm? This is what Mom's been up to with all her secret stuff the last couple days?* His cheeks flamed red as fear rose up within him. *So help me, Mom . . . if you've put one of your typical big-business, land-deal power plays on Dorothy and pressured her, or ripped her off in any way . . .* He could barely breathe.

"Yes. I'm afraid I have to at least think about it, dear." Dorothy's eyes shifted from Josh to Katie, then back to Josh again. "I see your mom didn't mention this to you."

"She did not!" He spat and emphasized each word.

Dorothy wondered what on earth had prompted such a strong response, but let it pass.

"Okay, I'm ready," Dorothy said. She sighed and methodically folded her hands in front of her. "Tell me what you think."

21

"I have an entirely new option for you to consider, Dorothy. I realize Craig & Craig's option contract expires tomorrow and you're down to the wire with decision making, but I hope it's one you'll at least consider."

Josh began drumming his fingers on the table and snorting loudly through his nose as though trying to contain himself. He glared at his mom, who he realized was wearing her close-the-deal face. He'd seen it hundreds of times throughout his life.

"I would like to buy the farm, Dorothy. I am prepared to pay you five percent more than the offer on the table."

"What on earth . . ." Dorothy's voice trailed off. Josh stood up out of his chair and looked down on his mother.

"I'm serious," Katie said. "I will pay you up front or spread it out—whatever works best for you. I have already spoken with my financial adviser and my banker, and I am in a sound position to make and carry out this offer with expedience. Of course, you wouldn't need to move until you were ready. There would be no hurry for that. No. No hurry. You could stay on as long as you like, and we'd work out a reasonable arrangement."

The three of them were silent for several seconds, Katie, posture erect, on the edge of her chair, while Josh stood and stared bullets at his mom. Dorothy finally spoke. "I simply do not know what to say."

"I realize this is not giving you much time for a decision, if you'd like to consider my offer against Craig's." They all looked from one to the other. "Joshua Matthew Kinney, please sit down." He simply could not.

"Oh, Lordy be," Dorothy said as she shook her head back and forth. "Lordy be and gracious me. What a mountain of mayhem this has turned out to be!"

Even in the midst of their tension, Josh and Katie shot one another an *aha!* look. "So this is who it came from!" Josh said.

"And what would that be?" Dorothy asked, happy for a distraction from her thoughts and what seemed like a release of the gripping tension between mother and son.

"Mom used that phrase the other day, and when I asked her where she'd picked that up, she couldn't remember."

"I do believe that's nearly as old as I am. No doubt you heard your mother say it, Katie, honey. Nearly everyone from Partonville used to say that." Dorothy studied this mother and son across from her, and her spirit within was suddenly stirred with a sense of hope and peace. A peace that passes all understanding.

"Yes!" Dorothy stuck her hand out across the table to shake on the deal.

"Are you talking about my offer?" Katie asked, her voice rising nearly an octave.

"Yes, ma'am. I am not only talking about your offer but also accepting it. And I am thanking God for you, His answer to my prayers. Thank you, Katie Durbin. Thank You, Jesus." Dorothy looked up toward the heavens and hollered out loud, "THANK YOU, JESUS!"

In astonishment at her own actions—not to mention in celebration of the easiest deal she'd ever closed—and fueled by an overwhelming and inexplicable sense of joy, Katie clasped Dorothy's hand in both of hers and began aggressively pumping it up and down. Dorothy pulled Katie to the middle of the kitchen and flung the slightly reluctant Katie into do-si-doing with her like a square dancer, causing Sheba to begin a fit of barking. Dorothy steered their way over to a stunned and worried Josh, caught him up in the action, and the three of them whirled and twirled away in the middle of the kitchen. He scowled the entire while.

Josh had no idea why Dorothy would ever have to think about selling her farm. He sure hoped his mother wasn't the one who tried to talk her into selling! Whatever, he suspected he knew what his mother's motives were for saying she wanted to buy it. *She better not have reeled Dorothy in, hook, line and sinker. Dorothy isn't one of her fat-cat clients! She's . . . DOROTHY!*

All he knew for sure was that at the moment, none of it seemed to make a bit of difference to Dorothy, who was thrilled. What would be the point of his trying to warn, argue with or question a woman who was so happily and wholeheartedly celebrating? He was helpless for the moment to do anything other than dance in her unbridled joy. But smile he would not. A shallow grin was the best he could muster.

Katie Mabel Carol Durbin, a self-proclaimed city girl, lay diagonally across the bedspread on her bed at the Lamp Post Motel in Pardon Me Ville, Illinois, fully clothed. She glanced at the clock; it was 2:30 A.M. She'd been staring at the ceiling for three hours, barely twitching a muscle. She couldn't ever remember feeling so physically and mentally tired, yet so regenerated and oddly relaxed and satisfied. To say she was blindsided by her own flurry of activities and choices was an understatement. To believe she now all but owned a farm was bizarre at best and ridiculous at worst. And yet . . . aside from the rest of the formalities, own a farm she did. The very thought—*regardless* of her motives, which even she herself wasn't sure about—made her grin. *Obviously, I've cracked up.*

Joshua Matthew Kinney sat slumped in his desk chair in front of his computer. He glanced at the clock: 2:30 A.M. He'd been trying to figure out what in the world to e-mail to Dorothy, if anything, for going on three hours. Feeling a need to warn Dorothy while intermittently composing e-mails to his mom, lashing out at her . . . her . . . Since, back in Dorothy's kitchen, his original fears about his mom's dealings with Dorothy had materialized and his fear had now turned to anger. He was so angry and worried that he couldn't even think straight.

Last night, while all that crazy dancing and document reading and talking about terms was going on, Josh had first gone upstairs and played games on Dorothy's computer, then retreated to the dark, quiet barn. He thought he might spontaneously erupt into flames. He was so angry on the way back to the Lamp Post that he couldn't even talk to his mom, not that she tried to initiate any conversation with him. They'd each gone to their rooms in silence.

Josh had tried to watch TV to distract himself, but he had way too many pent-up emotions and energies for that. He left the motel and jogged and walked and jogged again, all around Pardon Me Ville. He went down May Belle's street twice and circled the square several times, finally deciding to make his way back to the Lamp Post before he was picked up for suspicious behavior. He then booted up his computer and typed his fingers nearly to the bone, only to end up deleting every word of correspondence after correspondence. Finally, at three-fifteen he drifted off to sleep, at exactly the same time as did his mother.

Dorothy Jean Wetstra flopped down in bed at 9:15 P.M. after saying prayers of thanksgiving for thirty-five minutes. She slept like a log all night for the first time in a long while.

BANG! BANG! BANG! Josh pounded on his mother's motel door at 7:30 A.M. He hadn't brushed his teeth; he looked like a bear and acted like one, too. BANG! BANG! BANG!

Katie's voice was weak and distant-sounding through the door. "Who is it?"

"Your son."

"Josh, it's seven-thirty. Why on earth are *you* banging on *my* door?"

"We need to talk. Now."

"I agree we need to talk, but it's not going to be now. I've barely had any sleep, I'm barely awake and I'm not in the mood."

"No. I bet you aren't! Who could be after what you've done!"

"And what, exactly, have I done?"

Silence. Katie waited a moment, then repeated her question. Silence. She cracked open the door; Josh was gone. She heard the door next to hers slam shut. She'd deal with him later.

"Dear Outtamyway," he typed. He lifted his fingers from the keys, backed up his chair a bit, then realized he just couldn't bring himself to use a nickname that sounded like how his mother was treating Dorothy.

Dear Dorothy, We have to talk. Please e-mail me as soon as you're booted up. I'll check my e-mail every five minutes. It's 7:45 a.m. We NEED to talk.
Sincerely, Josh.

The first time he checked, she had answered.

Josh, I was up early today and happy to find a word from you. I pray you are okay, though. You sound so distressed. Phone me.

He did so immediately, explaining that he didn't want to talk over the phone.

"Have your mom bring you out, honey."

"NO! I don't want to . . . she can't."

"All right then, me and Sheba will fire up The Tank and we'll be right there."

"I'll be waiting at the curb."

Josh hopped in the car. Before he was even settled in, The Tank lurched forward, causing his head to whip back.

"You know, Dorothy, even though I totally trust your driving," he said, working to convince himself more than anyone, "I imagine you and The Tank could scare the pants off of some people."

"Reckon we have," she said flatly. "In fact, I've nearly scared them off myself a few times, especially here lately. You're not the first to mention it. I trust God will let me know when it's time to turn in my keys, however. I just hope it's not too soon. Until then . . . !" And off they went. Where they were heading, neither of them was sure, but they were on their way.

"So what has you so troubled, Josh?"

Josh remained quiet for a few moments, and Dorothy just let him. She circled round the square twice before he spoke.

"Dorothy, I need to talk to you about what my mom's done." Dorothy turned off the square, and The Tank, like a horse heading for the barn, was heading its way to a stall at Crooked Creek.

"Oh, honey! You'll just never know how much this means to me! Your mom is an angel straight from heaven! The weight of that decision has nearly plumb worn me out lately. And then in God's perfect timing, there was Katie with her kind and generous offer."

"Timing. Mom. Offer. Right. That's what we need to talk about."

"I'll tell you, I can die in peace now. Such a blessing. I just couldn't get settled within myself about that Craig & Craig offer. Seems to me they were just after my land to make a killing."

"Killing. Land. Right. That's what I want to talk to you about. Dorothy, here's the thing. You trust my mom, right?"

"Honey, I trust God, and from the peace that washed over me when your mom made me that offer, I knew it was straight from Him."

"Dorothy, do you believe in the devil?"

She glanced at him for a moment as she rounded the corner off the highway toward the farm, then said, "Yes. Yes, I do believe there is evil in the world. But what on earth caused you to ask me that now?"

Even as angry as he was with his mom, he just couldn't seem to get out exactly what he'd been thinking. It would sound too mean. Too crazy. He somehow just knew Dorothy wouldn't want to hear that kind of comparison, since she was obviously so high on this woman whom she obviously didn't know the way he did.

"Josh, what in the world is going through your head, son?"

"Dorothy, my mom is a real hardnose when it comes to business."

"Yes, I know."

"Well, I just hope she hasn't . . ."

"Hasn't what, Josh?"

He drew in a deep breath, and his shoulders nearly

touched his earlobes before he let it out, exhaling loudly through his mouth. "Hasn't ripped you off. There. I said it."

"Did you and your mom talk on the way home last night?"

"Nope. We haven't talked since we left the farm. I tried to talk to her this morning, but she said she wasn't in the mood." Sarcasm laced his tone.

"I imagine there's a lot about this you don't know, sweetheart. Things aren't always what they appear, and your mom is a softer cookie than you might imagine."

"I don't have to imagine. I live with her, remember?"

"You know, Josh, I've watched you two since you arrived in Partonville. I don't like sticking my nose in where it doesn't belong, but I believe God and Aunt Tess have brought you two to Pardon Me Ville for a bigger reason than a funeral and house cleaning."

Josh looked at Dorothy, stunned. "Where'd you learn Pardon Me Ville?"

"Your mom told me about it last night while you were outdoors."

"She told you she called it that?"

"Yes, sir. And she told me plenty else. And I'm now convinced there's plenty she hasn't told you yet, and I'm sure not gonna steal her thunder." With that, she pulled into the Landerses' driveway and turned The Tank around, pointing back toward town. She was glad she had phoned Katie before she left this morning, just to make sure she would know where Josh had gone, intuitively suspecting, from the tone in his voice, that he hadn't informed her.

"Where are we going?" Josh asked.

"To your Aunt Tess's. That's where your mom said she'd be."

"When did you talk to my mom?"

"This morning right after I talked to you. Do you think I want to be charged with kidnapping? I mean, Sheba and I might be rascals, but we're not that dangerous!"

22

Katie sat at the kitchen table at Aunt Tess's, staring at the photo of her mom and Aunt Tess. Her eyes glanced around the table, from place mat to place mat, back to the picture again, then to the rose-colored candle, then to the little picture of her and Josh tucked in the frame. It ran through her mind that the table had begun to feel like a shrine. A place of order in the midst of chaos. She couldn't help but wonder if Aunt Tess, in her own crazy way, had clung to her last remnants of sanity at this table. Waiting. But for whom and what?

She retrieved a rectangular box of kitchen matches from atop the stove and stood over the table. A sense of reverence overtook her as she struck the wooden match, quickening to the sound of the strike, smelling the essence of the puff of smoke, drinking in the sight of the flame as it flared, then settled into a slow burn. She briefly pondered how pleasurable was the simple striking of an old-fashioned kitchen match. She set the box down, picked up the candle and for the first time smelled its wax. Roses! It smelled of roses—her favorite. She put the candle back down in the saucer, straightened the wick and ignited it. Staring unblinking into the small flame, she seated herself before it, moving the photographs into its light.

Unaware of the sound of her own voice, she began

humming "Amazing Grace," the song her mother used to sing to her when she was little. The song her mother sang out loud all the days of her life.

She stared at the face of her mother, candlelight now illuminating her familiar features. Katie closed her eyes and tried to imagine what her mother would look like today, more than ten years older than when last she saw her, last heard her sing. Straining to remember the exact sound of her mother's voice, she suddenly realized *she* was singing aloud. Her throat clutched, and yet she could not stop singing the words to which she had previously paid no attention.

"Amazing grace . . ."—tears welling in her eyes—"how sweet the sound"—overflowing her lashes—"that saved a wretch like me . . ." A sob surged up from deep within her belly and interrupted the words. Even so, she didn't stop singing. "I once was lost, but now I'm found, was blind but now I see." She sniffled a bit, then very softly began speaking.

"Could it be, God, that You would use me to answer someone else's prayer? Could it be? Could it be that You *do* listen? Is it possible that I have heard YOU?"

Katie heard the front door fling open. Quickly she wiped her eyes and composed herself. Although she started to blow the candle out, she changed her mind, the fragrance of rose now filling the kitchen. She stood up just as Josh entered, Dorothy close behind.

Joshua and Katie stood staring at one another, trying to read each other's face. Katie looked at Dorothy, who nodded her head, then silently walked on through the kitchen—Josh watched, a pleading look in his eyes, but she just swept right past him, Sheba at her heels—and went out the back door into the yard, where she parked herself on the porch and began to pray.

"Sit down, Joshua. We need to talk." Katie's voice was firm yet pensive. Josh pulled out a chair, seating himself back a ways from the table, as though pulling in too close might send a wrong message.

"Joshua Matthew Kinney, I know you're angry at me." He looked away from her face and stared at the candle. "You are the one who first told Dorothy I was in real estate, remember?

"Hmph." His eyes blinked slowly and his head nodded, affirming her statement. Still he didn't look at her.

"Dorothy asked me for advice. Dorothy asked me," she said, emphasizing each word.

Josh's head snapped in her direction. "Oh, and wasn't *that* handy? She asked you. You, who care more about the color of money and landing a deal than just about *anything—* including me!" He had never so brazenly spoken his emotions like this, and right to his mother's face! Years of wounds suddenly rose up out of a buried place, the bite of his words surprising even him. It was Katie's turn to break eye contact, once again looking at the flame, her own son's hateful glare piercing her heart.

She took a deep breath, held it for a moment, then sighed, willing herself to look back into his eyes. What she discovered was the raw and revealing face of a little boy. Her child. Her son. Her baby. After having so abruptly spoken the hurt of his soul, Josh was left emotionally naked. Tears sprang into Katie's eyes. She reached her right hand forward to touch Josh's cheek. Out of reflex, he snapped his head back, blinking back his own tears.

Katie withdrew her hand, gripping it in her left, then

wringing them together. She recognized a bare longing and neediness in her son—which reflected *her* innermost self, her innermost self that had for so many years been crusted over.

"Oh, Joshua. Deals aren't the only thing I care about." Like strangers circling one another, deciding on issues of trust before moving too close, their eyes searched and darted, trying to penetrate the exterior.

"You, Joshua, you are the best deal I have ever made." Never had he heard such conviction in his mother's voice. Such tenderness. He slumped forward in his chair, elbows on his knees, fingers entwined, head hanging down so she couldn't see his eyes.

Katie rose out of her chair and knelt down in front of him, cupping her hands over his—not unlike the way Pastor had done with hers one short week ago. "You, Joshua, are the best gift I've ever been given." With her right index finger, she tilted his chin so he was looking at her, then leaned in very close and kissed his cheek. They were both full-out weeping now. Tentatively, waiting for the acceptance of her gestures, she put her hands on his shoulders. Then, still on her knees, she pressed her cheek against his and hugged him.

For a moment, he didn't respond—but he didn't reject her either. Before too long, one hand moved to her back, then the other. The embrace lasted for several moments.

While the fragrance of roses filled their senses and the light of a single candle softened their surroundings, Dorothy, still out on the back porch, just kept on a-prayin' until her spirit sensed it was time to quit.

When Dorothy entered the kitchen, she found Katie and Josh taping up a couple of boxes. She searched one face, then the next. When they both broke out in a smile, she knew God Almighty had once again "done His thing!" There was no need for her to speak a word, other than to whisper an "Amen."

The three of them simultaneously seated themselves at the table. The table that, it suddenly seemed, so long ago had been prepared for their arrival.

The conversation around the kitchen table went on an hour and a half before any of them was willing to push their chairs back and get on with life. So rooted in the moment were they that they even skipped going to breakfast. Between the three of them, they ate everything in the house—a giant bag of potato chips, the rest of the Cheetos, three candy bars and a half-gallon of orange juice. Katie said she just couldn't do "that" to her body, but she did—though, truth be told, Dorothy and Josh did most of the consuming.

Katie knew she and Josh still had a long way to go to get their relationship on a healthier track, but they were headed in the right direction, she was sure of it. And if Dorothy Jean Wetstra had anything to say about it, they would stay aimed thataway until they arrived.

Katie just listened, rather than defending herself, while Dorothy explained to Josh the evolution of the sale, how it was his *mom* who had come up with the idea of making sure there would always be a place to hunt for crawdads.

"Crooked Creek Park. Now, how does *that* suit ya?" she asked him, beaming from ear to ear herself at the very idea of it. "Why, she's even gonna help me go through the procedure with the conservation department *before* I draw up the papers with *her,* just so that land can be donated by my family, in my family's name." Dorothy placed her hand over her heart, closed her eyes and spoke a quiet "Thank You, Jesus."

Katie pursed her lips, feeling slightly guilty. Yes, that was the deal. But she also knew any land developed around a park would definitely bring a much higher price tag. Nevertheless, much to her surprise, she had been moved to give Dorothy—and every family member in her photo albums, ancient and new—that privilege and tax break, rather than closing the deal and taking the tax cut herself. She recognized her own generosity as nothing short of a miracle. Yes, perhaps there really *was* a God!

It was as though a veil had been lifted from Katie's eyes, about a lot of things. For the first time in a long time, as she studied Joshua, she saw, really saw, the essence of her son— apart from the shadow of his father. Josh caught her staring at him several times throughout the morning, and finally asked her to stop it.

"Well, anyone who's as handsome a devil as you are, Joshmeister, deserves a good gander," Dorothy said. Although he found it all a bit embarrassing, he obviously relished the attention from both these women.

"Where are you going to go, Dorothy, once you're ready to move out?" Josh asked. "And how long do you think it'll take before you're *ready* to move out?"

"Me oh my!" she exclaimed. "I haven't a clue, but I bet The Big Guy does!"

"Big guy?" Josh asked.

"Yup. The Big Guy who brought me your mother," she said, pointing heavenward. He looked at his mom, expecting her to protest. Instead, she just shrugged her shoulders and grinned.

As dew settles on the grass, it simultaneously came over

all of them that it was time to get to work. Dorothy jumped up and said she'd shake the crumbs out of the place mats while they loaded up the boxes. "These place mats are just like the ones at my house!" she exclaimed. "This is the first I noticed that!"

Katie nearly choked on the last of her orange juice. "Of COURSE!" she hollered, causing them to jump. "Why didn't I think of that before! It's so obvious!"

"Gosh, Mom. Settle down. What's so obvious?"

"Dorothy! Why don't you buy *this* place? I mean, it's in town, close to your friends, not too big. And it's soon to be available!"

Dorothy first just kind of reared her head back, then blinked a few times, appearing to Katie as though she was trying to clear her vision so her brain might jump-start.

"Of course, I'd have it good and sanitized for you. Take care of that buckling cement out front . . ."

"Well," Dorothy said hesitantly, running her finger up and down the familiar ruffle on the place mat. "Well . . . I guess I could at least entertain the notion." She stood up, cocked her hip and placed her left hand on her hip and her right hand to her cheek. She stayed in place but slowly turned in a semicircle, pursing her lips, nodding her head, occasionally shrugging her shoulders.

"We'll work a trade for a portion of the farm," Katie said. Josh warily eyed his mother, raising an eyebrow at her when she looked toward him.

"Let's take a look at the rest of the place, Sheba," Dorothy said. "See how it *feels*." Sheba jumped to attention the minute Dorothy stood, ready to move with her master.

Dorothy and Sheba walked from room to room, Katie and Josh staying their distance, but within eye range. Dorothy stood in the center of the living room, looking from window to door to back wall, trying to picture herself here . . . what her life might be like in a place this size. Actually, trying to picture herself and what her life might be like *anywhere* that wasn't the farm. It was the first time she'd truly felt the reality of her decisions. *I am going to leave the farm!* Even though she felt a bit queasy at the thought, she would never forget the absolute peace that washed through her when, out at the farm, she'd accepted Katie's deal. Yes, whenever she doubted her decision, that's what she went back to: that peace that passes all understanding, and it only came from one place.

Silently, and with her imagination fully awake, she step-by-methodical-step moved into the hall, then into the bathroom and on to the bedroom, praying her way through the entire place.

Katie noticed Dorothy staring into dirty corners and at hazy windows, up at cobwebbed ceilings and cracked tiles on the bathroom floor. Josh cleared his throat rather loudly, but didn't speak.

"Of course, I'd get the place in tip-top condition, up to building codes and all for you," Katie said, maintaining her enthusiastic tone. "I'd eat the cost of the upgrades, throw in new carpeting in the living room, if you'd like, and . . . make sure you had appropriate telephone lines for your computer! Josh and I discovered, one day when we tried to boot up from here, that Aunt Tess still had her old rotary phone lines wired right into the wall. Yes, I'd make sure issues like that are covered."

Dorothy just stared at her, first expressionless, then squinting a bit, as though sizing her up.

Eventually, like a tiny parade, the three worked their way

back into the kitchen, stopping in front of the sink. They all watched Sheba run back under the kitchen table, where she'd been before all the action, wind herself back in a little ball by the heat register—even though it wasn't turned on—sigh and instantly close her eyes to snooze.

Dorothy began to laugh, then said, "That settles it! Sheba just made us a deal!" She extended her hand toward Katie at the same time she glanced at Josh—who was scowling. Just before Katie took hold of her hand, Dorothy swiftly withdrew hers, leaving Katie reaching for air.

"And don't think I won't hold you to *all* that, missy, especially that fair-trade part for a portion of my current estate." She winked at Josh. "Why, I recall hearing somebody—who is supposedly quite the real estate wheeler-dealer—say she thought this place ought to be bulldozed into a hole!"

First Katie burst out laughing, then all of them did.

"Dorothy, you have a steel-trap mind, for sure! And I'm beginning to think you and Josh could be dangerous if you spent too much time together!"

Before Dorothy left Aunt Tess's, she stood in the living room doorway and once again scanned the living room. Actually, the thought of decorating her own place—for the very first time in her life, since she'd simply carried on her life where she'd been raised—kind of excited her!

"May Belle!" Dorothy exclaimed when May Belle opened the door. "You'll just never guess what all has happened!"

"Well, come in and close the door, dear, unless you want to keep standing on the front porch doing all that yelling." Dorothy and May Belle made their way to the kitchen.

Sheba was already standing in the middle of the floor waiting for a goodie when they arrived. May Belle went to the refrigerator, rummaged around until she produced a slice of cheese, then began feeding it to Sheba in pieces.

"Honestly, May Belle! Aren't you the least bit curious about my news?"

"Of *course* I am! I figured you'd spill the beans when you were good and ready."

"I've sold the farm!"

May Belle snapped her head in Dorothy's direction, accidentally holding the piece of cheese midair rather than tossing it. Finding it just out of her reach, Sheba began jumping up and down, yapping. May Belle tossed her the chunk without looking her way. A stunned look was plastered on her face, and her mouth was wide open.

"I don't think I heard you correctly."

"Yup. You did."

"You sold the farm? You sold Crooked Creek Farm? To whom?" May Belle thunked down in the chair, her knees feeling a bit weak.

"Katie Durbin."

"You sold the farm to Katie Durbin?"

"Yup." They sat there in silence for a moment while May Belle digested what she was hearing.

"When are you going to move? Where are you going to go? When did all this happen?"

"I sold the farm yesterday. I'll move when I'm plumb good and ready and have figured out what to do with a lifetime full of stuff. And I'm going to be moving right around the corner from you and Earl into Tess's old place, which I just purchased within the hour. Well, traded a slice of farm for. After all these years, we'll be NEIGHBORS! Won't that just be the berries?"

May Belle nodded her head. "Of course. If you say so, dear." She suddenly felt as if she were living in a fog.

"Well, I say so, but I've even got *more* to say. What do you think about that?"

"I'm not sure my poor old heart can take anymore."

"I've saved the best for last." For the next half-hour, Dorothy shared the utter joy in her heart about Crooked Creek Park. She talked about how she could picture people picnicking there and younguns running free and splashing in the creek . . . it would be a part of nature until the Good Lord decided otherwise.

Once May Belle got over the shock, she couldn't help but be relieved that her best friend in the whole world would, before long, be safely sleeping just a few doors away. For this, she was very happy, even though she knew Dorothy had a long road ahead of her.

"I've just got one worry about all of this, my Dearest Dorothy," she finally said.

"What's that?"

"That nary a cookie or cake will ever be safe on my countertop again!"

Once Katie knew the immediate pressure to sell Aunt Tess's house was removed, she didn't feel the same need to press on to finish up the house-clearing task. Although they were pretty close, there was still at least another couple days' work left on that part alone—not to mention the sanitizing and everything else she'd promised—and it was Thursday already. Like a last-hour reprieve, it came to her that they could now just lock the place up and leave it until summer break. Get both of them back into their own beds for a couple of nights before Josh headed back to school on Monday. Dorothy had already said she couldn't even think about moving until after the auction, which probably wouldn't take place until at least midsummer anyway. "And believe you me, there will be a whopper of an auction for *this* downsize!"

It was 7:00 P.M. when Josh and Katie had finished packing up the Lexus. They were on their way to Dorothy's with their last run for the day when Katie made the announcement. "Joshua, I've decided we're going to head back to Chicago tomorrow. I hope we can get on the road by nine or so and beat Friday-night rush-hour traffic around the city." She glanced at Josh, who immediately began what she predicted might come.

"Mom! We've still got lots to do, and you promised Dorothy . . ."

"Josh. I will keep *all* my promises, including promising you right now that I will keep all my promises!" She spoke in a stern tone, desiring to make known her honest intentions and keep another storm at bay. "The fact is, sooner or later, we *have* to get home, and you need to get back to school. We can come back and finish up in June when school's out. Take our time. Dorothy already told us she wasn't going to be moving until maybe even late summer. Besides, that'll give us something to look forward to."

"*You* look forward to coming back?"

Katie slowed down the moment gravel began spitting up

on the undercarriage. They drove along for a bit, just listening to the clatter-bang.

"The honest truth?" Katie asked.

"Yes."

"Yes. I must admit, I'll look forward to coming back for a visit. And I must admit that no one is more surprised about that fact than I."

Dorothy, Josh and Katie sat in the kitchen at the farm eating breakfast at 8:00 on Friday morning. The Lexus was now packed with their belongings and several boxes of paperwork, readied for the sifting. Dorothy had absolutely insisted they not leave town without Josh's having a full belly. Besides, as she'd told them the night before, "I want to give you a proper Pardon Me Ville salute on your way out." She cooked them up a huge country breakfast of scrambled eggs, bacon, fried potatoes and toast. Katie watched Josh mimic Dorothy, pouring sugar all over his lavishly buttered toast, and sighed. "Not only could you two be dangerous together, but I'm beginning to think you're two peas in a pod already!"

"Yes," said Dorothy, "I imagine Joshmeister and Outtamyway could cause a mountain of mayhem without even trying!" They all laughed and laughed, until finally their chuckling died down into silence when they realized they were done eating . . . and it was time to go.

Katie looked at her watch. Josh sighed. Dorothy sprang up from the table, announcing that they all had to do what needed to be done.

"Mom, are you sure I have to . . ."

"Yes, son." She'd never called him that before. The word

son hung in the air like Tinkerbell, flittering light and pixie dust between them.

"It's sure too bad you couldn't have stayed for the Wild Musketeers game tomorrow. *That* would surely give you something to talk about to those city folks! In fact, it should keep you entertained all weekend just imagining me wielding pom-poms!"

"I must admit, Dorothy, I am curious about that," Katie said.

"I'm more curious about your catcher," Josh said. He grinned at Dorothy.

By this time, they'd walked to the Lexus, and now they stood awkwardly looking at one another. Finally Dorothy sprang forward and threw her arms around Josh. "You better send me an e-mail the minute you two get home, Joshmeister. Don't keep me awake all night wondering if you made it."

"Yes, ma'am. I promise to send you one every day. I'll give Alex your e-mail address, too. He likes meeting new people. Maybe he can come back with us this summer and join our next hunting expedition?" He looked toward his mom, who said she didn't imagine there'd be any trouble with that. Katie also assured Dorothy she would draw up rough-draft documents for her review before completing the final version, and get them in the mail in the next couple of weeks.

Katie steadied herself, knowing that undoubtedly Dorothy was going to grab her next—which she did. "Now, you two take care of each other, hear?"

"Yes, ma'am." Katie patted Dorothy on the back. Dorothy just held tight.

Josh scooped Sheba up and hugged her. "You take care

of Dorothy, okay?" She licked his cheek several times before he set her down.

"Oh, and wait a second, Dorothy." Katie opened the back door of the Lexus. "I've got something for *you* to take care of while we're gone." Her head disappeared into the backseat area while she fumbled around for a few moments. She backed out with a box in one hand and a vase in the other—the ashes of her family.

"Since Mom and my Aunt Tess loved this place so much, and since the photo of them together in front of this silo obviously meant something to both of them, I'd like to leave their remains together here in the barn for now, if you don't mind."

Dorothy gave Katie her okay by tenderly smiling and nodding her head, then reaching out and touching Katie's left cheek with the palm of her hand.

Katie walked across the barn to Dorothy's favored spot, then set the containers next to the door. "There now, ladies, you can once again enjoy the view together."

In silence Josh and Katie got into the SUV and buckled themselves in. Katie turned over the engine. "Bye! Goodbye! *Adios! Ciao!* Bye!" Josh hollered out the window as they took off down the lane.

Katie waved over her shoulder, looking in the rearview mirror—seeing a blur of pink, waving and waving and waving back. . . .

24

Back in Chicago, Katie was struck anew by how horrid traffic was, how noisy life suddenly seemed. Although she didn't dare mention it to Joshua, the thought flew through her head that this just might be their last summer in the city. Katie Mabel Carol Durbin might actually end up to be just a little more country girl than she'd ever imagined.

Dorothy waited until she knew everyone would be settled into Harry's for breakfast before she began her drive into town. It was Saturday morning; the place would be packed. She'd determined one thing: they might as well hear the news straight from her before Cora Davis got wind of it.

As she drove down her lane toward the gravel road, she wondered how it would feel when she made this journey for the last time as a resident of Crooked Creek Farm. Acutely aware of the powerful presence the land held in her life, she also knew she couldn't go anywhere God wasn't, and that knowledge is what would sustain her—as it always had.

Her mind moved from one thought to the next as she drove slowly along, passing by the Landerses' place, wondering how they'd take the news. How their lives might or might not change. How she'd sleep in a new bedroom, only the second bedroom she'd call her own in her entire life. And yet . . . she found herself just itchin' to breathe new life back into Tess's place, maybe even paint that kitchen ceiling fire engine red! Where *that* notion had come from, she had no earthly idea. But wouldn't *that* get townsfolk to talkin'? *As though they're not going to have plenty to jaw on when I get through at Harry's this morning!*

She gazed upon the fields, knowing she'd have to make at least once-weekly trips, Lord willing, to Crooked Creek Park once it was established. No way could she survive too long without planting her feet firmly in the soil. "Crooked Creek Park," she said aloud to Sheba. She just couldn't get her fill of the idea. Made her beam every time.

Looking "down the road," as her dad used to say whenever it was time for a change, she saw the bend a quarter mile ahead and gunned it. "No sense slowing down now, huh, Sheba!" Gravel spit from behind her wheels as The Tank kicked into high gear.

"Are we there yet?" she hollered over her shoulder. Sheba, head out the window, tilted her nose to the sky, sniffed once and honest-to-goodness shook her head up and down.

Cora Davis stood up like a bolt. Her natural instincts caused her body to flip into "Full Alert Ready-to-Repeat!" mode. Dorothy Jean Wetstra had, without ceremony, stood up from her stool, asked for everyone's attention and said, in her best band-director's voice, "Listen carefully, I only want to say all this one time.

"You can put the rumors to rest. *I* have sold my farm. I have sold my farm to Katie Durbin. A portion of the land will become Crooked Creek Park, for now and forever." She paused for just a hitch, but decided to continue right on before anyone could speak. "There will be a big auction this summer. I will be moving into Tess Walker's house and most likely paint the kitchen ceiling red. Amen." *I just couldn't help myself.*

Cora Davis, like everyone else, was having trouble stringing all that together—especially since Dorothy had ended her talk with the red ceiling part and now sat down and began sipping her coffee as though nothing had happened.

A blanket of silence covered everyone. Arthur looked to Gladys, who looked to Harold, who looked to Lester, who . . . Brows were furrowed around the room as they searched to untangle this startling announcement. All eyes finally turned to Dorothy, who was happily gobbling down her sweet roll like there was no tomorrow.

As though the bell had rung on Wall Street, they all started talking at once. To one another. To Dorothy. To nobody in particular.

"Well, I'll be," Arthur said. "I'll be." Sitting next to Dorothy, he reached over and patted her on the back so hard she thought for a moment she'd been slugged. "Congratulations, Dorothy! At least somebody's got more guts than jawbone around here." He looked directly at Gladys when he spoke. Whether it was intentional or not, Gladys wasn't sure.

"*What* is Katie Durbin going to do with the place?" Gladys asked in an accusatory tone.

"I have no earthly idea," Dorothy said, speaking truth—although she had her suspicions.

"You mean to tell me you sold that land to someone who might turn it into a . . . a . . ."

"Gladys, cool your jets." She'd heard Josh use that expression, and it so tickled her she was glad to have an occasion to pass it on. Gladys huffed and bristled, tossed her money on the counter and stormed herself right out the door. She had things to look into . . . although she was already picturing herself presiding at the ribbon-cutting ceremony for Crooked Creek Park!

Arthur, having had time to digest things a bit more, said, "The only thing I'll worry about is that Miss Durbin will park that traitor Lexus where I have to look at it. Can you write something in your contract about THAT?"

Dorothy laughed. It felt very good to know that Arthur, as cantankerous as he could be, was standing beside her . . . even though he probably wasn't kidding about not wanting to look at the Lexus. "Not only that, Arthur, but I'll make sure The Tank stops by for regular visits, just so you don't get too lonesome and rusty yourself."

Harold Crabb walked up behind Dorothy and put his hands on her shoulders. "I knew it! I just *knew* it! I knew something was brewing with you. I'm happy to know my reporter's nose hasn't died. I sure don't have to wonder what story I'll be running the next few editions!"

The page one headline of Sunday's edition of the *Partonville Press* unfortunately qualified poor Harold for his next misleading headline award: "Durbin Buys the Farm."

Dorothy had granted Harold an official interview immediately following the commotion at Harry's. He reported it just as Dorothy said it: "We intend for Crooked Creek Park to be a minimum of twenty acres, including the swimmin' hole, Weeping Willy, Woodsy and Willoway. Crooked

Creek Park will be a place for picnickers and visitors, town folks and tourists, to find respite for their weary souls, drink of the land's healing powers and catch a crawdad or two.

"As for me, well, I figure I'll continue to be friends with the Happy Hookers, eat at Harry's, get my hair done by Maggie, play first clarinet and eat dessert first—same as I've always done."

A Note from the Author

I am happy to have this chance to share, since I, too, am always curious about authors. Here's what I've learned from this side of the pen: writers are no more fascinating than any reader I've ever met. The only difference is, writers never seem to run out of words!

I didn't begin writing until I was in my forties (talk about a backlog of words), and I haven't stopped writing since. Our two sons are grown and gone; my husband, George, faithfully cheers me on, and leaves me alone when necessary. I once left him a note on the kitchen table that said, "I'm not here, not even when you see me." Yes, he's used to me by now.

I love what I do, which is to write (and speak) about life. One thing that never changes is the power of story. I believe God speaks to us through stories—ours, others', fiction; good, bad, dubious—and that each moment of each day delivers the potential for us to listen, learn and grow through them. As with my fictional characters, in real life, we don't always get it right, but God is always there to shine a light on a better path while loving us all the while.

'Tis that sovereign presence and graciousness of God, Dear Readers, that keeps me writing.

–Charlene Ann Baumbich
www.welcometopartonville.com

PENGUIN BOOKS

DEAREST DOROTHY, SLOW DOWN, YOU'RE WEARING US OUT!

Charlene Ann Baumbich is a popular speaker, journalist, and author. Her stories, essays, and columns have appeared in numerous magazines and newspapers, including the *Chicago Tribune,* the *Chicago Sun-Times,* and *Today's Christian Woman.* She is also the author of the first book in the Partonville series, *Dearest Dorothy, Are We There Yet?,* and six books of nonfiction. She lives in Glen Ellyn, Illinois. Learn more about Charlene at www.welcometopartonville.com.

Dearest Dorothy,

Slow Down,
You're Wearing Us Out!

Charlene Ann Baumbich

PENGUIN BOOKS

PENGUIN BOOKS
Published by the Penguin Group
Penguin Group (USA) Inc., 375 Hudson Street
New York, New York 10014, U.S.A.
Penguin Books Ltd, 80 Strand, London WC2R 0RL, England
Penguin Books Australia Ltd, 250 Camberwell Road,
Camberwell, Victoria 3124, Australia
Penguin Books Canada Ltd, 10 Alcorn Ave, Toronto, Canada M4V 3B2
Penguin Books India (P) Ltd, 11 Community Centre,
Panchsheel Park, New Delhi – 110 017, India
Penguin Books (N.Z.) Ltd, Cnr Rosedale and Airborne Roads,
Albany, Auckland, New Zealand
Penguin Books (South Africa) (Pty) Ltd, 24 Sturdee Avenue,
Rosebank, Johannesburg 2196, South Africa

Penguin Books Ltd, Registered Offices:
80 Strand, London WC2R 0RL, England

First published in the United States of America by Guideposts Books 2002
Published in Penguin Books 2004

PUBLISHER'S NOTE
This is a work of fiction. Names, characters, places, and incidents either are the product
of the author's imagination or are used fictitiously, and any resemblance to actual persons,
living or dead, business establishments, events, or locales is entirely coincidental.

ISBN 0-7394-4324-0

Printed in the United States of America
Set in Berthold Garamond
Designed by Sabrina Bowers

Dedicated to the real *Oldster Characters*
in my life who inspired creativity;
taught sensitivity; modeled kindness,
acceptance and wahoo fun;
were unabashedly thier own True Selves;
and cheered me on—all the way from heaven.
Especially my Dearest Dorothy.

Acknowledgments

How do I begin to thank everyone who helped wing these books to life? I mean, the cast of characters (real ones) is huge! Although I have already written my dedication page to the Masters of My Inspiration, there are OH! so many more friends, family and just plain good folks who helped knit these books together. Their range of contributions is nothing short of astounding: inspiration ("I know you can, I know you can"); education (teaching me details about stuff I know nothing about so that my fiction doesn't get too many "I don't think so!" responses from you astute readers); cheerleading ("Great chapter!"); shrink duty ("Yes, sometimes 'reality' is slippery, Charlene"); hysteria stopping ("Snap out of it!"); listening to me whine (yes, I do my fair share). And a WAHOO! thanks for friends who never gave up on me, even when I was impossible; who provided laughs when I needed them, breaks when I needed them, tolerance when I needed it, mercy when I needed it and a kick in the butt when I needed it.

Without Terri Castillo, there would be no *Dearest Dorothy* books. Her verbalized question became the materialized project. She asked; I knew; it was. (Okay, there were years of hard work and creative flying in the midst of this, but the short and True Birthing Miracle version is this: She asked; I knew; it was.) As I type, I pray blessings upon her journey. She has gently launched me with full spiritual sails into the delicious waters of Story.

Regina Hersey, my editor, was a constant bellows to the all of my all (and she'll probably tell me "'the all of my all' doesn't make sense," but I'm writing these acknowledgments and she'll just have to live with it—HA!). Again, without Regina, no *Dearest Dorothy* books. Simple as that. From the very first e-mail forwarded to me after she read my first draft, to the very last conversation I've had with her (which was probably yesterday, since she's become my True Friend), she has been nothing short of a pure-gold gift. I have no doubt that our synergy was God designed, and 'twas the genius of Terri Castillo who matched us up. Even though I sometimes quake at Regina's ability to be a self-ordained Grammar Nazi who always has "just a few little things" for me to address in my manuscripts, she is, without exception, grace upon grace in my life.

Oftentimes we need a mentor who has honorably journeyed down the road before us. Novelist Terri Blackstock graciously gave me ninety minutes of her time during one frantic, out-of-the-blue phone call. It was ninety minutes' worth of genuine, literal, literary and Big Picture guidance. My journey became instantly lighter and wiser.

Between *Are We There Yet?* and *Slow Down, You're Wearing Us Out!* the following are people who fell into that "education" category I mentioned before, going above and beyond the call of duty to help guide a stranger through the back roads of things like commercial real estate development, long-haul moving, heart conditions, auto repair, demolition derby and a host of other details: Steve Gibson, Larry Alexander, Thomas Wood, Harold Benware, Dave Thompson, Bruce Bradley, Mary S., Donna Manley, Robin

Webb, Joanne Boppart and Gregory Baumbich, who, against his Chevy heart but for the love of family, talked to me about a Ford product. My apologies to anyone I left out before this rolled to press. Your exclusion implies no less importance but speaks to my fuzzy, midlife brain cells.

The folks at Guideposts Books and Inspirational Media Division, especially Elizabeth Kramer Gold and her snappy sense of humor, were definitely guideposts. I thank them for their courage and their ministry.

The first time I met Carolyn Carlson, both my professional and personal life brightened. Her enthusiasm for the first two books in the Partonville series, and her sensitivities to what *really* matters in *all* of life—which is the same message in the novels—made for a rousing combination. When it became official that Penguin Books would be bringing the books into book stores, a shout of joy erupted from my soul (once I stopped freaking out), which has yet to stop twirling with delight.

And to my husband, George, I give my utmost thanks for standing watch at the door to Our World. He has countless times stood there alone, staring down the road (or up the stairs to my office, or into my eyes), waiting for me to return from Partonville. I love you, my Honey Bunny.

Introduction

ⴰⵖⵄ ⴰⵖⵄ ⴰⵖⵄ

To be seventy years young is sometimes far more cheerful and
hopeful than to be forty years old.
—Oliver Wendell Holmes

And now, welcome to Partonville, a circle-the-square town
in the northern part of southern Illinois, where oldsters are
young, trees have names and characters are just that.

Dearest Dorothy,

·=·=·=·

Slow Down,
You're Wearing Us Out!

1

Dorothy leaned against the doorframe, her keen brown, eighty-seven-year-old eyes slowly casting back and forth across the horizon. From her favorite and sacred spot in the barn, all her senses—her very soul—drank in the June glory of the tiny rows of corn marching across a bountiful earth. She delighted in knowing these young, green stalks would yield pure gold come October. Distant trees separated earth from sky, and varying twilight shades of amber lavishly swirled the firmament like a ball gown flared to its fullest billow.

Dorothy turned and gazed into the barn, willing herself to memorize the whole, and each detail, of what spread around and before her: a familiar, safe and cavernous space lined by sturdy wooden floor slats and beams, powerful and centuries-old, honed and built by her father's father's sweat.

In silence, she made a slow, 360-degree turn and drank deeply of the familiar. It was then she knew God was whispering, *Remember well all you see, for these splendid images will sustain you in the days to come.* Within a blink, a sharp pressure, a clenching claw, seized her chest, and she slumped to the floor where she remained until she could draw a deep, trouble-free breath. Once the pain subsided, she slowly up-righted herself, brushed the dust off and went about her day—her life—neither fretting a moment nor telling a soul.

Four of the five-strong Social Concerns Committee were seated around the old wooden table in the hospitality area of United Methodist Church, awaiting Jessica Joy's arrival. It was twenty minutes past their "seven o'clock sharp, the third Wednesday of each month" starting time, as it was stated in the bylaws. When Partonville's acting mayor, Gladys McKern, dramatically raised her wrist and stared at her watch, Dorothy Jean Wetstra, one of the few in Partonville brave enough to spar with Ms. Mayor, jumped in before Gladys could utter a disgruntled word.

"My, how I remember those first few months of new motherhood. Nothing, I mean nothing, could get my Jacob Henry to settle down when I was trying to get out the door! I was so tired I thought I'd plumb lose my sanity about once a day. Vincent and Caroline Ann were much better babies, but oh that Jacob Henry gave me a run for my mind."

May Belle, too, had spied Gladys's chastising windup. She brushed a wispy strand of silver-white hair back up toward her bun and chimed in. "Well, Earl was just the opposite. That boy could hardly be roused to eat, even when it was well past feeding time. Homer and I would try to wake him by pulling the cozy flannel blankets away from his little body in hopes the chill would do it. When that didn't work, and it usually didn't, we'd talk louder and louder. Why, we had to practically take to shouting, and you know my dear Homer wasn't one for raising his voice, so that took quite an uncomfortable effort. Finally, Earl would open his sleepy eyes, peeking at us, one eyeball at a time." She giggled at her own silly expression and memory, and then out of habit covered her mouth with her hand. "Quick as a toad hops, I'd start nursing him before he could fall back to sleep.

"When I think back, it seems like just yesterday I held that sweet, soft bundle in my arms." May Belle closed her eyes and continued speaking. "I can still feel my thumb bumping across the top of each of his tiny toes . . . his soft breath against my cheek as he drifted back to sleep, propped on my shoulder. . . ."

The women sat in stillness, each lost in her own moments of memory. Finally May Belle's eyes flew open and she broke the silence. "I can't believe Earl's already forty-five years old!" She paused, then added, "Nor can I believe I'm eighty-six!"

"Well, he is, and you are, and you can also believe this," Gladys belted out. "My Caleb was a cranky, colicky little pistol, and I was glad to get away from him when I had the chance, and *especially* when I had an outside responsibility." With that, she once again held her wrist high in the air, tapped her oversized watch face three times with her short, thick index finger, threw back her shoulders and stated, "Children are children, not excuses for tardiness. We have a big agenda this evening, and I have an early meeting in the morning and goodness knows I don't need to be held up because of . . ."

"I am so sorry!" Jessica said as she burst through the door and into the room. Having been startled into action, Sheba, Queen of the Mutt Dogs, sprang up from sleeping beneath Dorothy's feet and began barking. The moment Dorothy said "Hush!" Sheba stopped barking and trotted back to resume her slumber.

Jessica's shiny, straight, brunette hair, which normally

danced atop her shoulders, was haphazardly pulled back into a ponytail not quite centered on the back of her head. Faded jeans and a bleach-stained sweatshirt replaced her usual delicate, hand-embroidered clothing. The bags under her beautiful hazel eyes were so dark that they all but clouded out the sparkle in her irises.

What Dorothy, and nearly anyone who'd raised a newborn, had suspected was of course true. In Jessica's case, it was double the stress, since not only did her husband, Paul, work long hours in the coal mines of southern Illinois, but together they also ran the Lamp Post Motel. What with Sarah Sue and late check-ins keeping her up all hours of the night, and motel clients occasionally checking out early in the morning, she was worn to a frazzle.

Jessica had spent the last hour trying to get her firstborn to concentrate and finish nursing her evening meal. Of course, the more anxiety Jessica felt as she watched the clock, the more Sarah Sue sensed that tension and fussed. When she finally handed the sleeping babe—with a heart-shaped mouth exactly like her own—to Paul, it was then she remembered she hadn't typed up the minutes from last month's meeting. This kind and highly organized young woman couldn't even remember where the file was, and it hurled her into a thus far stifled crying fit unlike any other her husband had ever witnessed.

"Honey," Paul had said quietly as he embraced his daughter to his chest with one lean arm while reaching out with the other to draw his wife close, "you're worrying me. You're just trying to do too many things." His gentle voice, often mistaken for shyness, washed over her as she looked up into his dark green eyes that seemed to lighten a shade when their eyes met. "The ladies will understand. Just go, tell them the truth, get some time in with your friends, eat you some good desserts, then come home and go to bed. Sarah Sue and I will be just fine. If she gets hungry before you get back, I'll try giving her that bottle again. Doc said it would be okay." Jessica tilted her head forward and rested it on Paul's chest, close to where Sarah Sue's head was snuggled. As their family threesome stood sacredly bonded, a quietness had enveloped her. Finally she sighed, grinned at her husband, kissed his cheek, put her finger to her mouth to indicate silence and scurried off to the meeting where she'd just made her entrance.

Nellie Ruth McGregor launched from her seat, ran over to Jessica and threw her arms around her, as if to shield her from the angry-faced Gladys. Even though sixty-two-year-old Nellie Ruth had never married or had children, Gladys's grumbling had galvanized the rest of the women into a mighty force of protection for this fragile beauty. Nellie Ruth's short-cropped, fading red Irish hair framed her pretty oval face, and her wide-set eyes sparkled with compassion.

"Oh, honey! You look absolutely tuckered out! But I am so glad to see you! So glad you're here. Come on and sit down by me, I've saved you a seat." She guided Jessica to the folding chair next to hers. Dorothy and May Belle, being lifelong, fast friends and of a like mind, both headed for the coffee pot to pour Jessica a steaming cup of decaf. May Belle yielded the task to Dorothy and instead plopped a couple of her homemade snickerdoodle cookies on a paper napkin. The bustling ladies soon flanked Jessica with goodies. Gladys, her stout frame as stiff as a board, just sternly eyeballed her across the table as Dorothy and May Belle pampered one of their favorite dears. The moment Jessica looked up at Gladys's intimidating face, she burst into tears.

"I don't have the minutes!" she wailed in a full-out confession, once again breaking into heaves of crying. "Not only do I not have them, I don't even know where they are!" Her voice sounded nothing like the sweet, melodic one that belonged to her. She buried her face in her hands, her elbows crunching into the pile of cookies.

"Now, honey, that's just fine," Dorothy said as she patted Jessica's shoulders. "I reckon we all remember what we said last month anyway." She paused a moment to shoot Gladys a threatening glance. "What's important is that you're here and that God has graced the world with our precious Sarah Sue. Why, I'll take the minutes for you this evening. You just drink some coffee and eat some of May Belle's healing cookies while we tend to business." Dorothy's touch and affirming words helped calm Jessica. She sank back in her chair, took a sip of coffee and, through dwindling sniffles, began to chow down on a cookie, first retrieving the broken bits stuck to her elbow and popping them into her mouth. It suddenly occurred to her she had not eaten dinner and she was famished.

Gladys, the chair of the committee for the year, made her way back to her seat, picked up the gavel, banged the table a little too loudly and called the meeting to order. Although Sheba didn't arise, she did raise her head and give one swift, halfhearted bark.

"We can begin by making note that the entire committee is *finally* present, that we are coming to order at 7:30 P.M., and state that the minutes to our last meeting *cannot* be read because we don't have them." She turned toward Dorothy, raised an eyebrow and waited to see that she was properly taking notes. Dorothy stiffened her stately five-ten frame in her chair, stared right back at her and said, "Yes, Gladys, I wrote that all down."

When Gladys called for the treasurer's report, Dorothy had to put down her pink pen, pick up her worn pink backpack from the floor next to her and retrieve the folder. In the shuffling to help Jessica relax, and then preparing to take minutes, she'd forgotten to get ready for her own report. Gladys tapped her pen on the table through the entire wait. May Belle grinned, knowing her otherwise quick-moving friend well enough to realize she was proceeding in intentional slow motion. Dorothy could still be the defiant, rebellious kid when she wanted to, and somehow that always tickled May Belle. Luckily, for the most part, Dorothy, via God's grace and design and the tutelage of her patient parents, had learned to aim her stubborn energies, using them for the good. But every once in a while, the devilish girl within sprang out of her like pent-up waters blowing through a dam.

Finally, the totals were read. Dorothy reported, with very slow and deliberate words, that there was "exactly $107.52 left in the treasury after last month's twenty-five-dollar-monetary donation to the nursing home for candies to be distributed to those without family, and another twenty-five dollars was given to Lester K. Biggs's collection jar at Harry's Grill for the DeKalb family in Yorkville, whose father had recently undergone a kidney transplant."

"Well, then, if there are no additions or corrections to the treasurer's report," and Gladys paused a moment to defy anyone to open their traps, "we'll be moving right to old business, which is, of course, our annual Fall Rummage Sale, held in the barn at Crooked Creek Farm," which was

Dorothy's place, although Gladys wasn't about to say that, since naming the farm sounded so much more official—not to mention appropriately stinging to Dorothy. Although the sale actually took place on Labor Day weekend, which wasn't fall at all, it had, upon its inception, been recorded in the minutes as the Fall Rummage Sale and always advertised as the Fall Rummage Sale. Since nobody questioned the matter or complained about the inaccuracy, the Fall Rummage Sale it remained.

Ever since Dorothy had stunned the citizens of Partonville by announcing several weeks ago that she'd sold her farm to Katie Durbin, a city slicker from Chicago—and most in Partonville knew you couldn't trust one of *them*—and that Dorothy would be moving into town and into Tess Walker's old place (also owned by the city slicker but traded in the deal with Dorothy), she and Gladys had been openly at odds. Gladys didn't like surprises. Anyone selling Partonville land that was contingent to Hethrow and ripe for development without first consulting *her* would have a price to pay. It didn't matter that a portion of the land was earmarked for a park, and it didn't matter that Gladys was already salivating, picturing herself one day cutting the ribbon at the park's grand opening, newscasters surrounding her. No, what mattered was that Dorothy Jean Wetstra seemed to think the only people she ever had to answer to were God and herself! It had been the same ever since high school, when people talked about "Dorothy the Dear" and "Gladys the Gladiator." *Well,* now *Dorothy'd see who held the cards,* Gladys often thought since she'd been proclaimed mayor after her "husband the mayor" died in office, thus the "acting" part of her title. Of course, Gladys had no doubt she'd be officially elected come the next balloting period. Then folks could quit buzzing about her backdoor reign.

"As you know," Gladys stated with authority, "this is our biggest fund-raiser of the year, and this year it looks to be bigger than ever due to the donations from the Walker estate."

Dorothy jumped in. "And it was mighty generous of Katie Durbin to donate her aunt's estate goods, I might add. And I'm adding the words 'generous donation by Katie Durbin' to the minutes," Dorothy said with determination as she wrote in deliberate and large letters. She was rather enjoying the official recording power she suddenly wielded.

Jessica, uncomfortable around conflict, rose from her seat and said, "I believe I'm okay now to go ahead and take the minutes."

"Never you mind, child," Dorothy said as she waved her back down in her chair. "We've got everything under control. You just take advantage of having nothing to do for an hour but take care of yourself and let us oldsters pamper you."

"Speak for yourself," Gladys said. Even though Gladys was in her eighties, one could be sure *oldster* was not part of *her* identity! No sir, with dyed hair, an ever-present long-line girdle and too-thick makeup base to cover the age spots, Gladys worked hard at holding herself together—any way possible.

Dorothy turned a deaf ear toward Gladys and continued. "And May Belle, why don't you get that child a couple more cookies?" Dorothy understood, from the returning tension on Jessica's face, that she'd pushed things with Gladys as far as—perhaps further than—they should go. She concluded that Gladys had been put in her place and that it was time to halt the sparring. She looked straight at Gladys and announced that she would from here on in be taking careful notes and would do her best to not interrupt again. "Of course, this old hand can't do near as good a job or write as poetically as that youngun's over there," she said, nodding and winking at Jessica, "but it'll do as good as it can." Gladys was so stunned at Dorothy's obvious back-pedaling that she had to clear her throat before she could continue.

"As you also know, Dorothy is having an auction at the farm the same day as our rummage sale, so not only do we have more donations than usual, but we'll undoubtedly have the highest attendance ever. Nellie Ruth, you're in charge of refreshments. Have you talked to your boss to find out if Your Store is going to set up a hot dog stand for us?"

"Yes, Gladys. Yes, I have."

"For goodness sakes, Nellie Ruth! What did Wilbur say?"

"He said Your Store would be proud and honored to be a part of the day and that he would contribute ten percent of the sales to the Social Concerns Committee!" Her voice was as enthusiastic as it was high-pitched. Everyone applauded. Everyone but Gladys.

"Ten percent? That's the best he could do?" Gladys huffed as she threw her hands up over her head in a dramatic gesture. When she raised her arms, the fastened top button of her blue blazer sidled up over her ample bosom and stayed there. She yanked on the blazer's hemline, pulling the jacket into its proper position, and without missing a beat said, "I imagine he'll make quite the pretty penny." She smoothed her hand across her ever-present bronze name tag etched in black stating, "Gladys McKern, Acting Mayor," just to make sure it was riding proudly exactly where it belonged.

"Wilbur wanted us to know," Nellie Ruth said rather pointedly, "that he will absorb the costs for hauling all his equipment out to the farm, including tables and condiments—which he's donating—and hot trays, as well as pay extra staff out of his own pocket so we can save committee members to work the actual sale. He also wanted us, especially you, Gladys, to know that he'd be glad to give a full accounting of his books at the close of the day, if you requested one."

"Humph" was all Gladys said in response. Dorothy opened her mouth to say how lovely and fair and accountable she thought Wilbur's offer was, but her conscience was pricked when she recalled that she had, within the last few moments, volunteered to keep her mouth shut.

"Dorothy," Gladys said, "you volunteered to be in charge of parking. What do you have to report to us about that?"

"Nothing." As soon as the word was out of her mouth, she wrote on her minute-taking paper, *"N-O-T-H-I-N-G."*

"Nothing?"

"Nothing."

"When do you think you might have *something*?" Gladys spat.

"By the next meeting. I have a couple ideas up my sleeve, including talking to the Boy Scouts. I thought it might be they could all earn some kind of badge working on an all-day project like that."

"And it might be," Gladys responded, "that we could all

earn our own badges of courage trying to untangle ourselves from the nightmare of having allowed a wild pack of
boys to direct us as to where and how to park!"

"Why, Gladys McKern!" Dorothy nearly shouted. "Isn't
your very own grandson a Scout? Isn't your very own
brother the pack leader? I imagine he'll know whether the
boys can handle it or not. And like I said, I'll have a report
at the next meeting. The Scouts are just one of the options
I'm exploring."

"I move we move on to the next order of business," Nellie Ruth said, hoping to halt the once again escalating duo.

"And what would you suggest that be?" asked Gladys,
turning her sour tone of voice toward Nellie Ruth.

"Pricing. Let's hear from May Belle about pricing and
the bake sale."

Before being acknowledged by the chair—a rule suddenly
no one was abiding by—May Belle announced that plans
for the bake sale were under way and that as the date grew
nearer, sign-up sheets would go out in the narthex. She said
she thought that if they put them out too soon, nobody
would remember they had signed up. The committee quite
agreed. She also shared that she'd like to plan a trip to
Hethrow to check out price tags at the new discount office
supply store someone had told her about. Although in previous years they'd used rolls of masking tape and just ripped
off pieces, writing prices on them with marking pens, she
thought this year that would be too time-consuming, what
with all the extra goods. Gladys, in an unusual but genuine
gesture, gave verbal applause to May Belle's "forward and
progressive thinking."

Although there was a bit of discussion about new business, all agreed that the old business was going to fill their

time for the next several months. At precisely 8:10 P.M., the meeting was adjourned.

Gladys hustled out of the building without so much as a good-bye to anyone. Nellie Ruth went into the sanctuary to check communion setup for Sunday. Dorothy and May Belle cleared the debris and began to rinse out the coffeepot, taking their time so Jessica could relax a bit longer. Jessica sat at the table, pounding down the remaining cookies May Belle had stacked in front of her, then she swigged the last few dribbles of coffee in her ample mug, which displayed a line drawing of the church with the words "United Methodist Church celebrates 100 years" right above it. At 8:25 P.M., she sighed so loudly it caused Dorothy and May Belle to wink at each other; she'd eaten an even one dozen cookies.

At last, four of the five Social Concerns Committee members shared a good laugh and a group hug in the parking lot before bidding one another a good night.

Dorothy waited until she saw that the ladies were all safely on their way home before firing up her rusty-and-white, battle-scarred 1976 Lincoln Continental, known and referred to by everyone in Partonville as The Tank. Although she had to crank it over twice and gun it a good one before it actually kept running—something she'd have to see Arthur Landers about before long—Dorothy was convinced The Tank was as evergreen as she was, even though they were both taking a little longer to start these days and they each had their peculiarities. She rolled down all the windows and revved her up, delighting in the sound of power. She was sure they just didn't make V-8s like the one in The

Tank anymore. Most in Partonville would agree that they sadly didn't make them like Dorothy anymore either.

Foot on the accelerator, Sheba's head sticking out the driver's-side back window, Dorothy zipped The Tank across the blacktop parking lot, turned onto Main Street to head for the farm, then suddenly turned onto Vine Street, deciding to cruise by Tess Walker's old place, soon to be *her* new home. Slowly, almost as if she were sneaking up on her own emotions, she pulled up in front of the little frame house.

She turned off the headlights and let The Tank idle as she stared, trying to imagine what it might be like to park right here for the night rather than making that delicious, calming drive through the country and up the lane to the farm. She wondered what it would be like to have that streetlight, which she'd never noticed before, outside her front window rather than nothing but the awesome, dark night of twinkling sky. She pondered what type of sounds this house might make when the wind blew, compared with those familiar creaks and groans, hums and whistles, of the home in which she'd been born, and where she'd lived her entire life.

"Lord," Dorothy said aloud, "I know You're with me no matter where I go, whether it's to the familiar or the new . . . I *know* it. Just help me *remember* what I know. Amen." With that, she turned on her headlights, gunned the engine a time or two and sped off into the night, into the country, into her own uncertainty. Nearly instantly she remembered that God had once given her an unmistakable peace about this decision, and she claimed it—whether she felt it right now or not.

"Now, that was fast!" she said to the heavens. "Thank you. Thank you. Thank you."

As she turned off the hard road near the WELCOME TO PARTONVILLE sign and onto the gravel road that would lead to her lane, at the top of her lungs she loudly finished singing the last chorus of "Great Is Thy Faithfulness." Sheba howled once, sending up her own doggy praise.

2

Dorothy prowled through her refrigerator, trying to decide what to heat up for lunch. It was a warm and sunny Thursday afternoon, and she was thankful to feel rested and ready for action after last night's testy meeting. On the spur of the moment, she phoned to invite May Belle and Earl over for lunch, announcing that it was "Smorgasbord Time!" May Belle understood this meant Dorothy had lots of leftovers in her refrigerator to clear out before they turned bad.

May Belle readily accepted the offer and packed up a goodie bag of her homemade sweets for Dorothy. Earl, May Belle and Homer's only child, was nearly beside himself with enthusiasm when his mother told him Dorothy would soon be there to pick them up. Although Earl was challenged by mental slowness, most folks around Partonville had always loved and accepted him just the way he was, and that was that.

May Belle never had found it necessary to learn how to drive, what with Homer's steady and capable ability to do so, and the fact that they lived in town right off the square. When Homer died, it just didn't seem like the time to start. Although Dorothy's lead-footed driving behind the wheel of The Tank often admittedly made the slow-moving May Belle a bit nervous, she would never let her nerves keep her from accepting the opportunity to spend time with her best friend. On their drive out to the farm, they rehashed the meeting, talking a mile a minute. They both hoped Jessica had gotten some sleep and hadn't suffered a stomachache from all the cookies. They giggled, wondering if it was even possible for her sugared mother's milk to make that precious baby sweeter than she already was.

Sheba stood on the back seat, head sticking out the window, tongue flapping in the breeze. Earl sat silently next to her, hanging on to the bill of his baseball cap with both hands just to keep the wild winds from scalping it off his head. He'd never forgotten that on one of their rides out to the farm, Dorothy had had to back The Tank down the road and he'd had to jump out and race toward the field to retrieve his cap, luckily stomping on it just before it rolled into the muddy ditch. Sometimes he even held on to the bill of his cap with both hands when the windows were rolled up, just in case.

While Dorothy finished off the last of the desserts, she and May Belle got to talking about the sale, deciding to work off some of their calories by doing a little preliminary work out in the barn. Besides, it was a perfect day to open up the big barn doors and Dorothy's favorite little back-wall door to take advantage of the cross breeze that would set their sails for work and allow the sun to shine in on the otherwise dimly lit space. Dorothy, now physically a little too weak to manage those massive, heavy sliding doors, knew Earl's brute strength—just like his dad's—could handle them with ease, and nothing made Earl happier than being around his Dearest Dorothy and being helpful.

After opening things up and taking a few minutes simply to enjoy the day, the ladies engaged in a bit of finger-pointing discussion about how to proceed. When Katie Durbin and her fifteen-year-old son, Josh, had begun clearing out Tess's house six weeks ago, they'd delivered so many loads of things to the barn that Dorothy had told them to just pile them any old way. They had needed to spend their limited time in town dealing with the funeral and chipping away at the overwhelming cleaning project before heading back to Chicago to return Josh to school. It was discovered, upon Tess's death, that every room in her home, aside from the pristine kitchen, was stacked high with clothing, newspapers and just about everything else anyone could think of. She'd been a recluse for many of her last years, and this was the first anyone had learned of the magnitude of the disheveled state of her home . . . her life.

Yes, piles in the barn had been fine for then, but now, now they had to begin to initiate a plan of order for the big event before things got too out of control in the barn, causing them all quadruple work.

With Earl's capable help, May Belle and Dorothy began by moving Tess Walker's things around a bit, trying to arrange a better floor plan to allow for more white-elephant donations that townsfolk would be dropping off in the coming months, and to make room for the auction items Dorothy would be clearing out of her home. Finally, a plan was put in order and the task begun.

As the ladies peeked and prodded, slid and arranged, Sheba ran from one box to the next, trying to stick her nose in them, hoping to find something to nibble. Dorothy had already lamented to May Belle over lunch that only about one-twentieth, if that much, of her lifelong possessions would fit in her new dwelling place. "I have to figure out how to turn a mountain of mayhem into a molehill of order," she'd said. "Now, that's gonna take not only some doing, but some ruthless decision making as well—not to mention a miracle!"

For the first time that day, a shadow of grief flickered across Dorothy's face. Even though she knew she'd made the right decision, the task before her felt heavy. She knew sorting through a lifetime of accumulation would be an emotional ride, each item sparking its own memory. Some of the process would undoubtedly be gut-wrenching, especially when she came to the boxes containing her only daughter's memorabilia from school days, college, career and marriage. Caroline Ann had lost her husband in an accident before losing her own battle with breast cancer at age thirty-nine. Dorothy blinked a few times, willing herself to keep her mind on the task at hand. *One step at a time, Lord. Don't let me get ahead of myself,* she silently prayed.

"Goodness me!" May Belle exclaimed as she held up a dented metal bedpan stuffed with plastic poinsettias. She was blowing at the dust on the now more brown than red plastic flowers. "Where in the world do you think Tess put *this* for a Christmas decoration?" Many in Partonville wondered what Tess Walker had done with her life, but especially they sadly wondered why they hadn't gotten more involved with it. "Or do you suppose she just one day stuffed the flowers in here to store them? You know how we do when we're in a hurry."

"I wish I knew," Dorothy said thoughtfully, bent over a box, rifling through its contents. "I surely wish I knew." When she straightened herself, a chest pain accompanied by a slight rush of light-headedness caused her to stumble back a couple of steps for balance. She willed herself not to draw her hands to her chest and cause any undue concern.

"Dorothy! Are you all right, dear?" May Belle dropped the bedpan to the floor and moved toward her friend. Earl, who'd begun unstacking and rearranging a couple of bales of hay—for no reason other than he liked doing so—immediately moved to Dorothy's side at the sound of his mother's alarm. He braced Dorothy in his strong arms, eyes filled with fear that anything would happen to his Dearest Dorothy.

"Earl, help Dorothy over to that hay bale so she can sit for a spell," his mother said, pointing to the bale he'd just unknowingly, but perhaps divinely, positioned to within a couple of feet of where Dorothy would suddenly need to sit down. Earl did as he was told, gingerly bracing his arm around Dorothy's back. Dorothy protested she was just fine and that they didn't need to be making such a fuss over her, but neither of them listened. After Earl got her seated, he began to pace back and forth in front of her, wringing his hands, staring at her. Sheba jumped right up in Dorothy's lap and began licking her face.

"Earl," Dorothy said in her most tender and assuring tone of voice, "I'm just fine, honey. See, Sheba's helping me, aren't you, girl?" Dorothy stroked Sheba's head with one hand and then the other. "I was just too quick for my own good. Really, Earl, I just stood up too fast." He stopped pacing and stared at her, then looked to his mom, who smiled and nodded her head. Although that helped him to stop pacing, he didn't stop wringing his hands and staring.

"I'll sit here with Dorothy a moment, honey. Why don't you go to the house and get her a glass of water?" Although she didn't really believe Dorothy needed water, May Belle knew Earl needed to be doing *something*. As soon as he left the barn, May Belle asked Dorothy if she was *really* okay, remembering she'd recently seen Doc Streator to get her heart medications refilled. "Now, Dorothy, you don't be hiding things from me, okay? Tell me true blue and swear on a stack of Bibles, are you okay?"

Dorothy chuckled at May Belle's resurrection of their childhood expression. Not to tell the truth after that personal-pact challenge would surely invite trouble. Besides, not to tell the truth *anyway* would also cause her immediate repentance in order to get things right with The Big Guy, as she often referred to God, such was the sensitivity of her spiritual self.

"Okay, true blue," Dorothy said. She raised one hand in the air and pretended to put the other on a stack of Bibles. "I am fine . . . although Doc says my old ticker's probably slowing down a bit. What the heck, though, it's been banging away in there for eighty-seven years!"

"Dorothy Jean Wetstra! When were you planning on letting your oldest friend know THAT?"

"May Belle, it's just not important. I'm not giving it another thought."

"What on *earth* do you mean, it's not important?" May Belle yelped more than asked. "And you out here dragging stuff around in the barn! It's time you slow down, Dorothy Jean Wetstra!"

"Now you tell *me* true blue and swear on a stack of Bibles," Dorothy said. She paused for a moment until she and May Belle were locked in eye contact. "Do you think for one moment I'm going to let that little bit of health information slow me down? Truly? Do you believe I even *have* another gear? Do you *honestly* believe that anything either one of us could do would change God's plan for my life anyway?"

The two friends silently sat next to one another, the

refreshing breeze swirling around Dorothy's pink sweat suit and May Belle's faded green housedress while the glorious fragrance of hay and history wafted up their noses. When they heard Earl's footsteps thumping on the gravel outside the barn, May Belle quietly said, with a tone of surrender, "No. No, I don't reckon you do have a slower gear, and I guess you're right about our days being numbered. Anyway, you'd probably plumb explode before you'd idle down. I imagine when it's your time, the good Lord will have to hog-tie you to get you to go!"

"Right," Dorothy responded as she laughed and patted May Belle's hand. They each put an arm behind the other's back and rested their heads together, soft hair fluttering around their faces. They were peacefully grinning, resting in the security of their faith, when Earl ran in. He froze in the doorway for a moment, staring at them. Then he broke out in a smile. He handed Dorothy the giant iced tea glass clutched in his hand. Most of the water had splashed out as he'd run back to the barn. What remained was the perfect amount to wet her whistle before getting back to work. It wasn't long, however, before May Belle insisted they needed to call it a day so she could return home—although for what, she couldn't exactly remember.

When Dorothy returned to the farm after dropping May Belle and Earl off in town, even though she was bone-tired and ready for a nap, she was eager to retrieve her e-mail. She was hoping to find her daily installment from Katie Durbin's son, her new and solid friend Joshua Matthew Kinney, a.k.a. the Joshmeister, as he called himself in the land of electronic mailing. Since they'd met, around the time of his aunt's funeral, he'd become one of her favorite people in the universe, and he'd taken to Dorothy as a blank piece of paper receives its first splash of true color. Although Josh and his mom loved each other, Dorothy had quickly discerned that their relationship was a strained one. "Sometimes divorce leaves more in its wake than anyone imagines," Dorothy'd said to her own grieving son Vincent soon after his divorce from the mother of his sons.

Making her way up the steep stairs, Sheba close on her heels, Dorothy had to stop twice and catch her breath. Finally, she made it to the smallest bedroom, which she jokingly referred to as her office, since she said it's where she mostly did monkey business. The ancient and massive mahogany desk in the dining room was where she kept her important documents and paid bills.

While she booted up her computer, Sheba curled up beneath her desk next to Dorothy's feet. After retrieving her e-mail, she was delighted to discover Josh's familiar greeting, which began with the screen name she used with everyone who wasn't a blood relative. To Josh, the name not only made him laugh out loud the first time he saw it, but it summed up the way he viewed her *and* her driving.

∘⁂∘

Dear Outtamyway,
   I can hardly STAND it! We're gonna be THERE in THREE DAYS! Coming back to Pardon Me Ville is even more exciting than school getting out for the summer! Finally you and Alex, my two best friends, are going to get to meet! (My English teacher would say I'm using too many exclamation marks. But she's not reading this!!!)

Your last e-mail about the committee meeting
was so funny that I forwarded it to Alex. I hope
you don't mind. He needed a good laugh since he
was grounded. (He got a D on his Spanish final.)
"Forward and progressive thinking," you say, huh? I
only kind of remember meeting the mayor at the
dinner at the farm after the funeral. As I recall,
she didn't seem nearly as much fun as you, and
obviously she isn't. But then who IS, aside from
Alex?

And speaking of Alex, he had a super idea! (There
I go again with the exclamations!) He said you
should buy some pages of small computer labels
and print up a bunch of price tags. That way you
could just slap them on the stuff. You know, like
bunches of nickel and dime and dollar tags, or
whatever you'd need the most of. Think that would
work?

I was glad to learn that the Wild Musketeers are
still playing ball. I'm anxious to watch the oldsters
(that's what *you* call them, but mom doesn't like it
when *I* do, which is okay since she's not reading
this either!!!) round those bases. Alex said he can't
believe you're a cheerleader and wants to know if
you have your own pom-poms. (Do you?) Of course
ever since I met that catcher at the dinner, I've been
especially anxious to see her in action. Maybe she'll
want to catch ME, think? (Hey, a guy can dream,
can't he?) She is exactly my age, right? I mean she's
not seventy-five and just looks really, really young
for her age, right? (Not that there's anything wrong
with being seventy-five--or eighty-seven! ;>))

Gotta go. Mom's standing in the kitchen yelling for me to take out the garbage, which I already did two hours ago! I think it will be good for her to get back to the country again, even though she CLAIMS she hates it. She's been acting weird again, staring into space a lot lately, making secret-type phone calls. Feels like something's up.

Joshmeister! King of EXCLAMATIONS!!!!!

Dear Joshmeister! King of EXCLAMATIONS!!!!!
I, too, have been counting the days until your return! I remember when I was a kid, we used to make those paper chains at Christmas, using leftover newspapers since we couldn't afford pretty construction paper the years crops were poor. December 1, we'd break off the first of the chain of twenty-five, removing another each day until Christmas Day finally arrived! (I guess exclamations are catching!) That's just what it will feel like when you and your mom come up my lane: Christmas Day!

Of *course* I don't mind if you shared my letter with Alex, although I imagine he was pretty bored by the ramblings of an old lady carrying on about her band of United Methodist Church Committee Ladies. HA!

And speaking of committee things, Earl and May Belle and I worked in the barn a bit today, rearranging some of the piles into different piles. But first we cleared the leftovers out of my refrigerator (Smorgasbord Time!). I'm no dummy; I knew if I invited May Belle, she'd bring dessert! She packed up a couple of her award-winning double chocolate brownies. Remember *those* from the dinner? I made a plumb pig of myself and didn't even share them. Good for me!

By the way, do you happen to remember where at your aunt's house you found the bedpan with the plastic flowers in it? We were just wondering . . .

Tell Alex I DO have pom-poms. One red and one black, although they're looking pretty ragged. I bought them about three years ago at the Now and Again Resale Shop in Yorkville. Couldn't resist. Tell him I can't do split jumps, though. In fact, I can't jump high enough to clear the cracks in the sidewalk lately. That's okay, though. It's the next generation's turn (make that a couple next generations) to be jumping anyway.

Sorry to be so short but I need a nap. See what a little work does for me?

Tell your mother hello and tell her I said she should drive carefully on the way down here. If it takes you less time than I remember it should, I'll know your mom goes as fast as I do! HA HA!

Bye for now. SEE YOU SOONER THAN LATER!

Outtamyway XO

As soon as she pushed the "send" button, she turned off her computer and slowly shuffled down the hall to her bedroom, where she flopped down on her bed. Sheba snuggled up beside her, and within minutes they were both snoring.

3

❧ ❧ ❧

Alex tossed Josh his duffel bag, the last of the items to be packed. Josh put the bag on top of the cooler his mom had filled with yogurt, carrot sticks, energy bars, granola and soy milk. He slammed the rear tailgate door to the cashmere beige Lexus LX470 SUV, then both boys bounded back toward Josh and Katie's Chicago brownstone, leaving Katie sitting behind the wheel.

"Hey! Where do you two think you're going?" Katie hollered after them, leaning out her door. "I'm ready to hit the road!"

"I gotta send Dorothy a quick e-mail. I told her I'd let her know what time we're leaving."

"What on earth for?"

"So she doesn't worry we're late arriving when we really just left later than we thought." As soon as the door slammed behind them, Josh said to Alex, "And so Dorothy can find out how fast *Mom* really drives." They both laughed as they leaped up the stairs two at a time.

Katie's distant voice followed behind them: "You two be back out here and buckled up in five minutes, you hear me?"

"Okay!" they responded in unison.

Josh had left his computer on so he could just bang off a short note. All it said was "Dear Outtamyway, we're outtahere at 10:30 A.M. We might stop for lunch. Will phone when we arrive at the Lamp Post. Joshmeister." Josh sent the e-mail, turned off his computer and whirled around to find his mom standing right behind him. Before he could change his momentum, he'd plowed right into her.

"Joshua Matthew! You nearly knocked me over!"

"Gads, Mom! What are you doing sneaking up on me like that?"

"I had to come in and make sure you locked things up before we leave. You know there's been a few robberies around our neighborhood, and I don't want to leave the door open, just inviting burglars in for the next week or so." Josh thought they were only going to be in Partonville for five days, but he'd be thrilled if it lasted longer.

"Mom, I think I'm old enough to know to lock the door behind me," he said, shaking his head back and forth. He kept from making eye contact with Alex, since it embarrassed him when his mom treated him like a baby. Alex just stood back, uncomfortable in the tensions that often hung in the air between these two. The only time it seemed to dissipate, at least for a spell, was when they'd last returned from Partonville. Yes, for a while they'd just been friendlier to each other.

Sometimes Alex wondered what it would be like if Josh's mom and dad had stayed married. Josh almost never talked about his dad, other than to say, after occasional visits, that his dad seemed to care more about his new "daily kids," as Josh referred to them, than he did about him. Alex remembered Josh once saying, "I feel like Invisible Boy when I'm there, aside from questions about how I'm doing in school."

"Let's go, Alex," Josh said. Alex stepped in behind Josh

as they brushed by Katie, then scurried back to the car, allowing Katie to do her thing. In a few minutes they were on the road. When Katie turned up the volume on her ever-present National Public Radio station, Josh turned to Alex, made a cross-eyed face and dragged out his headset. Alex followed suit. All three lost in their own sounds and thoughts, they headed south.

Dorothy looked at the clock, figuring Josh and his mom might call from the Lamp Post in a little under an hour and a half, by the time they checked in and caught their breath a bit. When it occurred to her that they might just accept an invitation to dinner, if they got to town in time—especially knowing Katie's dislike for Lester K. Biggs's hometown, greasy-spoon cooking at Harry's Grill—she decided to do last-minute grocery shopping.

The Tank's bucking and coughing behavior had steadily become worse the last few days; the entire journey to town and back was a rough one. Sheba, whose head normally rode outside The Tank in good weather, had settled herself in the middle of the backseat halfway home from Your Store after getting tossed to the floor twice during the herky-jerky journey. Even though there were frozen foods and milk in the trunk, The Tank just seemed to turn *herself* toward her personal hospital, as Arthur had often referred to his toolshed, once his official AUTO REPAIR, as said the worn sign that was propped up along an outside wall.

Arthur and Jessie Landers owned the adjacent farm, townside to Dorothy's, and rather than pass by, up their drive The Tank went, coughing and bucking all the while. As if announcing her arrival, she backfired shortly before

Dorothy pulled straight into the shed like she owned it and shut off the engine. Since the day The Tank was brand-new, Arthur was the only mechanic who'd ever been allowed to work on her. Sometimes Jessie believed her husband had as much of a personal relationship with The Tank as he did with her—and that was close to being the truth, what with the cantankerous decades of bickering the Landerses had seemingly learned to coexist on. Arthur, who had nodded off in his recliner for a mid-morning nap, sprang to wakefulness at the sound of the backfire.

"The Tank's here," Jessie hollered from the kitchen. She had seen Dorothy pull up the drive and disappear into the shed.

"Yup," Arthur replied. "So I heard."

"How'd you know it was The Tank?"

"Cuz Dorothy's been a-ridin' her lame for a few days now. I've heard her sputterin' up and down the road. I figured she'd be here sooner or later. I'm just glad she made it before it was *too* late and she got herself stranded somewheres. And of course you just *know* who'd she'd call for help when *that* happened! I guess I better get out there before Dorothy comes a-bellowin' to the door." As much as Arthur always let on that he was put out when The Tank arrived, truth was, he always enjoyed the challenge, as well as the opportunity to jaw some with Dorothy. For that matter, Arthur liked jawing with just about anybody.

"Arthur Landers!" Dorothy called out as she flung the screen door open without knocking. "Did you hear THAT?"

"Yup," Arthur said as he rounded the corner into the kitchen. "I reckon the whole county heard it and has done took cover."

"Howdy doody," Dorothy said to Jessie, ignoring Arthur's wisecrack. Jessie flung the kitchen towel over her shoulder, rubbed her hands down the front of her jeans and extended a hand to her friend. Jessie, having been a tomboy her entire life, wasn't into that hugging stuff like Dorothy and the rest of her friends. The two women shook hands like a couple of truck drivers as Jessie cast her eyes to Dorothy's ankles, looking for Sheba.

"She's undoubtedly out there chasing chickens," Dorothy said. It seemed there were always a few squawking friends hanging around the shed for Sheba to torment. "Well," Dorothy said, turning to Arthur, "The Tank's been—"

"Yup. I know," he said, cutting her off.

"Arthur Landers, you don't even know what I was going to say!"

"You don't have to tell me, woman. The Tank's been complainin' about it for a few days now," he said as he walked past her and out the door. "I could hear her clear out in the back forty!" Dorothy spun on her heels and followed close behind.

"Arthur Landers!" Jessie yelped after them. "You haven't been to the back forty since you quit farming and leased our land to Challie. And you two behave yourselves out there in that shed, now," she said. It had been their standard joke for years.

Sheba came running from the field, cockleburs stuck in her scraggly tail. "Well, I do declare!" Dorothy said. "Now you surely do look like the Queen of the Mutt Dogs!" Sheba cast her eyes toward the ground as she approached Dorothy, understanding that the tone in her master's voice—although some wondered who mastered whom—wasn't a happy one.

As though circling The Tank to corral her, Arthur went around to the front of the corncrib turned auto repair shop and opened the single sliding door. Dorothy entered through the back, sidling her way past the rear of The Tank and through the narrow passageway up to the front door of the car. She slid behind the wheel, already knowing what Arthur was going to say after he raised The Tank's giant hood.

"Fire her up, Dorothy." Dorothy cranked a time or two. The Tank didn't fire but instead ground away, sounding more like a growling bear than a V-8. Dorothy turned the key off, waited a moment, pumped on the gas a time or two, then began cranking again. Just when it sounded like The Tank might turn over, she backfired, sending Sheba scampering toward the house.

Dorothy patted the dashboard and said, "Come on, honey! You can do it!" She cranked and pumped a time or two more, the smell of gasoline wafting up her nose. Just as she was ready to give up, The Tank sputtered to life, kicking a bit, but nevertheless working her way into running roughly.

"I'll tell you, Arthur, The Tank's acting just like I've been acting lately!" She could see the top of Arthur's hat through the gap between the dashboard and the lifted hood. He was, as he had been during the entire procedure, fast at work, touching, lifting, listening, swiping and wiping, moving his burly hands from here to there . . . considering . . . gently pouring liquids down her throat as a mother administers medicine. . . .

"Shut her down, Dorothy. Wait a second, then fire her up again, but don't stomp on the gas unless ya just have a hankerin' to drown her like a cinder block throwed to the bottom of the creek!" His tone of voice sounded like he might snap Dorothy's head off, but Dorothy understood that when The Tank was ailing, so was Arthur. In fact, it was the same with her. The three of them seemed to have made an unspoken vow long ago that they would each of them last as long as the other. Again, Dorothy turned the key and lightly tapped on the gas pedal, holding her breath as The Tank kicked into rumbling a bit more quickly and smoothly than she did on the last go around.

"Sounds better," Dorothy said.

"Don't tell me how she sounds! I got my head stuck right in her mouth. I guess I can hear her stomach growl from here, wouldn't ya say?"

"I reckon," Dorothy said to the top of Arthur's hat, squishing herself down a tad, trying to get a peek at his eyes so she could tell what he was thinking. The tone of his voice didn't sound good. A chill ran up the back of her neck, even though the temperature was nearly balmy.

"What do you think, Arthur?" Dorothy said as chipper as she could. "Think she'll live?" A forced chuckle escaped her throat.

"Turn her off and don't fire her up again 'til I tell ya," Arthur said flatly. Dorothy turned off the engine and began squeezing the steering wheel, then letting go, then squeezing, as though she were trying to pump lifeblood through the steering column. "Come on, honey," she whispered. "Come on."

"Quit your mumbling in there and start the engine!" Arthur hollered. "Ya act like you're deaf or something!" Again Dorothy cranked, this time holding her breath. Without protest, The Tank began to run somewhat more smoothly.

"Thank you, sweetie," Dorothy said as she patted the steering wheel. "Thank you, Lord!" she said as she looked up toward the heavens and instead spotted the faded blue fabric over her head that was starting to sag a bit. "We get more alike every day, don't we, dearie?"

"Back 'er out!" Arthur yelped. "Back 'er out and run 'er up and down the lane a few times to see if she's gonna have herself another hissy fit." Dorothy never needed encouragement to see how quickly The Tank would move across the countryside. Since with every passing day Dorothy's neck was harder to turn more than forty-five degrees, she looked in the rearview mirror, slowly backed out of the shed and into the ninety-degree gravel turnaround. She put her into drive and tromped on the gas so quickly that it caused gravel to spew out from under the tires. As The Tank roared toward the end of Arthur's driveway, Sheba followed in fast pursuit, her short legs nothing more than a blur. Dorothy grinned as she got a peek of Arthur in her rearview mirror, waving his fist in the air. With barely a rolling stop at the end of the drive, she pulled out onto the gravel road toward her house, where she planned to turn around in her driveway before heading back.

"MOM! LOOK OUT!" Josh screamed from the backseat. He and Alex had been gazing across the fields, talking about how far you could see. Josh had looked up just in time to see The Tank barreling down the Landerses' driveway. If things stayed on their immediate course, The Tank would plow right into his door. Since he was sitting behind his mom, he quickly noticed she, too, was staring off to the horizon rather than looking in front of her. That's when he screamed.

Katie looked up and slammed on her brakes, skidding

on the gravel as the anti-lock mechanism tried to pump into controlling a situation it wasn't used to. Out of citified instinct, she raised her hand to lay on the horn before realizing it would take both hands to try to hold the Lexus steady. They fishtailed back and forth a few times before finally coming to a stop, right front tire in the shallow ditch. Thankfully they'd slowed down enough that the SUV didn't roll, nor were they too badly jolted when they stopped. But they were definitely on a physical tilt and emotionally shaken.

Katie's face was as red as a beet as she unbuckled her seat belt and spun around 180 degrees to look at her son. Even though she was rattled to her bones, a look of relief spread across her face after the boys assured her they were fine.

Josh looked down the road at the trail of dust flying behind The Tank as she headed toward Dorothy's driveway. "Well, I have just two things to say: Mom, nice piece of Evel Knievel driving! And Alex, my man, you've just received your unofficial introduction to Miss Outtamyway!" Simultaneously, Josh and Alex broke out in peals of laughter while Katie slipped the SUV into four-wheel drive and put it in reverse.

"Joshua Matthew Kinney!" she said into the rearview mirror, her teeth clenched and her volume at full pitch. "There is nothing funny about nearly being killed!" Slowly and with the sound of power, they backed out of the ditch and onto the road while Katie mumbled something under her breath about having been thankfully seasoned by years of dealing with Chicago's crazy drivers. When Katie had straightened the wheel, she looked up to see The Tank barreling back toward them.

"They're HERE!" Dorothy said aloud when she recognized the Lexus, for certainly there wasn't another vehicle like that hanging around in Partonville! "Thank you, Lord, for their safe arrival!" Dorothy stuck her arm out the window, waving them to pull over, unaware they were already at a complete stop—her depth perception not being quite what it used to be. She pulled up next to them across from Katie's open window and hollered, "Howdy doody! Howdy doody! I see you made it here in one piece!"

"You could have killed us!" Katie yelled back. Her face was flushed and her voice cracked.

"Mom, lighten up. We're fine," Josh said, tapping her on the shoulder and waving at Dorothy through his open window.

"You pulled right out in front of us!" Katie screamed, totally out of control. "You could have killed us ALL!" The enthusiasm on Dorothy's face melted as her mind groped to understand what in the world Katie was talking about. Just then Arthur loped up between the cars to find out if everyone was all right. He'd chugged his stiff body all the way down the driveway when he saw the Lexus career into the ditch.

"Is everyone okay?" he asked, looking into Katie's vehicle.

"Sure. We're fine," Josh answered.

"*Luckily,* we're okay," Katie spat. The redness had nearly left her face, but her neck was still crimson, and her heart was hammering away.

"Would *someone* please tell me what on earth happened?" Dorothy said.

"Woman," Arthur responded, "you mean to tell me you don't even *know* you ran these folks plumb off the road?"

"What in the world . . ." Dorothy tried to think how on

earth she could have done such a thing. Surely she'd looked down the road before she turned . . . she remembered seeing Arthur in her rearview mirror and . . .

"Oh, MY!" she shouted. "Don't tell me I pulled right out in front of you!" she exclaimed.

"Yes, you did," Katie said flatly.

"Lord, THANK YOU for Your grace!" Dorothy boisterously proclaimed.

"I'd say you can thank ME," Katie barked, "for veering us into the ditch rather than broadsiding you, or vice versa!"

"The DITCH! You mean to tell me you had to run yourself off the road to keep from hitting me?"

"Yes, Dorothy. I am telling you exactly that."

"Please forgive me, Katie. Is everyone really okay? Oh, *please* forgive me!"

"Thankfully we were all wearing our seat belts, and thankfully I didn't lose control, and thankfully my four-wheel drive got us back on the road, and yes, we are all right, aren't we, boys?" She asked once again, more to reassure herself than to impart any information.

"Mom wasn't exactly looking where she was going either," Josh said out the window. He'd held his tongue long enough. He drew in his breath, waiting for his mom's fiery retort.

Katie started to respond, but like Dorothy, when challenged to think about it, the last thing she recalled before hitting her brakes was Josh screaming, and then . . . she'd been looking at the fields, and . . . She stared blankly at Dorothy, eyebrows scrunched together, while the incident played like a filmstrip in her mind. There was no denying it: she had been watching the fields rather than the road. But she *certainly* had the right of way, and Dorothy was going too fast, and—

Katie focused her stare. "Oh, *please* forgive me!" Katie heard ringing in her ears once again. Dorothy's sorry and apologetic face stopped the harsh words right in Katie's throat. What *was* it about this woman that always seemed to burrow into her? Until this moment, she had nearly forgotten how Dorothy seemed capable of looking clear into her being.

"Josh is right, Dorothy," Katie said quietly. Josh's eyebrows flew up and he turned his head to look at Alex. Alex, too, seemed surprised at Katie's response. "Joshua is exactly right. I was looking at the fields rather than watching the road and . . ."

"Never you mind, child," Dorothy said. "You certainly had the right of way . . . and who *wouldn't* be looking at this beautiful land?" she asked, her eyes panning the horizon through her windshield.

"While you two hens are a-sittin' here decidin' whose fault things is and how beautiful things is, you'll both like to cause an accident if you don't git yourselves out of the road," Arthur grumbled.

"Yes. Yes, we better all be getting back to my place, have us a big glass of iced water with lemon and calm ourselves down."

"Well, I don't need to calm down. I need to get back to my nap," Arthur said.

"Have you two already checked in?" Dorothy asked. "I mean you three?" She bobbed her head to look past Josh and get a peek at Alex.

"No, Dorothy," Josh said. "I talked Mom into coming straight to the farm so we could surprise you. I guess we surprised each other, huh? And by the way, Dorothy, this is Alex."

"Well, howdy do, Alex," Dorothy said, waving her hand at the boy, who was waving back.

"Pleased to meet you," he said.

"And this here is . . ." Dorothy turned to introduce Alex to Sheba, who was usually riding either shotgun or in the backseat. She was nowhere to be found.

"Sheba!" Dorothy recalled last seeing her chasing The Tank down the Landerses' driveway. She cranked her body around, looking every which way. "Oh, MY! You didn't hit Sheba, did you?"

Alex unbuckled his seat belt and hopped out of the Lexus. Katie followed suit, as did Alex. Just then Jessie appeared at the parking lot in the middle of the road, announcing she was happy finally to figure out where everybody had gone.

"We're looking for Sheba," Dorothy said in a flurry of words as Alex, Josh, Katie and Arthur all began running toward the ditch.

"Well, you don't have to look far," Jessie said. She held her hand over her eyebrows and looked down the road toward Dorothy's place. Here came Sheba, legs flying, tongue wagging, galloping as fast as she could go. Apparently, she was still trying to catch up with The Tank after it had made the turn in Dorothy's driveway.

4

Harry's had just opened, and as usual Arthur was among the first to seat himself at the U-shaped counter. Of course, he sat on "his" swivel stool, just as the rest of the regulars were seated on theirs. Lester K. Biggs, sole proprietor, cook and waiter of Harry's, thunked Arthur's coffee mug in front of him, sending spews of coffee from the filled-to-nearly-overflowing mug onto the counter. Arthur stared at the splashes of coffee, then reached toward the chrome napkin holder in front of him. Deliberately, he pulled out a wad of napkins and with a dramatic flair swiped at the counter, then set his coffee mug on top of the soiled napkins.

Although Lester had seen Arthur's performance, he didn't acknowledge it until he was facing the grill flipping bacon, his back toward Arthur. "Think I'm made of money that I got napkins to waste like that?" he said. "You act like a princess or something. Like you might melt if you had a drip of coffee get on you."

"Well, it sounds like *somebody* got up on the wrong side of bed," Harold Crabb, editor of the *Partonville Press*, said to Lester. "Did that howling wind keep you awake last night?"

"The only thing that keeps me awake at night," Lester answered, swiping his hands on his apron and turning his head ninety degrees to stare at Harold, who sat at one of the ends of the U that, like bookends, surrounded the grill area, "is worrying I might go broke buying paper supplies—as if the cost of *bacon* isn't enough to make me cinch my belt buckle a notch."

"Is that why I only got three strips instead of four last week?"Arthur asked Lester while winking at Harold. Arthur relished stirring up the pot a bit, getting Lester—or just about anyone, for that matter—going.

Lester, who also enjoyed their ongoing sparring—even though forty years ago it hadn't started out so friendly when Arthur stole Jessie away from him—whirled around on his heels, put his hands on the counter on either side of Arthur and got right in his face. "You know for a fact I've never served you less than four strips of bacon in all the decades I've been having to put up with you first thing in the morning. In fact, I do believe there have been several instances when you've had an extra strip or two, and I never once heard you complain about *that*! Come to think about it, I also never heard you thank me, either."

Arthur broke out in a wide grin, and, performing a very bad imitation of Marilyn Monroe, slowly sang, "Well, thank you, Mr. Bi-iggs and Happy Birth-day to you." It was such a hysterical scene that Lester couldn't help but break out in laughter, just like everyone else in the place—all twelve of them. Even the ever-appropriate Acting Mayor Gladys Mc-Kern nearly snorted coffee right out her nose. Cora Davis, Partonville's unofficial town crier, who was sitting at her usual table by the door so as not to miss anything, said, "Well, Arthur Landers! I do declare that I didn't think you had that in you. Does your wife know you can sing like a sick cow?"

"I feel a news bulletin coming on," Harold said. He grabbed his reporter's steno from his inside jacket pocket—

Harold always wore a suit on working days—and pretended to take notes. "Headline: Arthur Landers Finally Cracks," he said aloud as his hand went through the writing motions, although ink never touched the page.

"I'll tell you what you ought to be writing about instead of an old geezer like me," Arthur said. "That city slicker is back in town again." He knew just how to get Cora going, too.

"She surely is," Cora said. "I saw her big fancy vehicle go around the square a couple times lately, and I've noticed it parked at the Lamp Post. Sure enough, it was parked at Tess Walker's place, too. Of course, I understand they're not even done clearing that mess out yet."

"She and her boy was out visitin' Dorothy the other day." Arthur halted himself, deciding not to go into the near accident, what with Cora's ears wide open. Next thing he'd know, everyone in town would be talking about the calamity that took three people to the hospital, she had such a way of bending and exaggerating things.

"Is she figuring on finishing things up this trip?" Cora asked, actually leaving her chair and walking over to Arthur, just smelling that he knew more than he was telling. "I mean, have we even learned yet if she's going to move into that farm, or is she just going to have it torn down and turned into a shopping center? You know, I heard she was a big shot in real estate up there in Chicago."

"I have no idea, Cora," Arthur said, staring into his mug. "Why don't you ask her yourself, since you seem to know where she is at any given moment?" Cora snorted at Arthur's usual rudeness and went back to her seat.

"I just hope Dorothy isn't getting too caught up with her," Gladys said. "I wouldn't trust her as far as I could throw her. There's just something fishy about a woman like her buying a place like Dorothy's. What ever possessed Dorothy to sell to an outsider is beyond me. In fact, what ever possessed Dorothy to sell in the first place is *still* something I can't get over."

"I reckon Dorothy knows what she's a-doin', Gladys," Arthur said flatly. Arthur was one of the few people, aside from May Belle, who had actually gone so far as to be happy for Dorothy when she made her announcement. "Don't get your knickers in a knot over something that ain't none of yer business, Miss Mayor."

"Arthur Landers, as the mayor of this town, I reckon just about everything *anybody* does that might affect our lives *is* my business. And that's all there is to THAT!" She wadded up her paper napkin, tossed it down on top of the smear of egg left on her plate and asked Lester for her bill.

"Same as every day, Gladys. Two poached eggs, rye toast and coffee. Two dollars and seventy-five cents."

"Well, at least *some* things never change," she said in a huff as she threw down three singles and stormed out.

"Yeah," Lester said under his breath, "like my quarter tip from *you.*"

"You think that woman ever just walks out of anywhere like a normal person?" Arthur asked Harold, already knowing the answer to the question.

The Tank roared up and parked on the street behind the Lexus. This was the first time Dorothy would be back inside Tess's since Katie and Josh were here six weeks ago. *This will be* my *house, after the late-summer closing,* she kept telling herself.

Katie had phoned Dorothy from the Lamp Post the night before and asked her if she wanted to come over to the little house on Vine Street the next morning to see if she might want to keep any of the furniture before they hauled it out to the farm for the sale. It occurred to Katie that most of Dorothy's massive furniture would hardly fit in this house. Once she and Josh had finally cleared out all the extras and were now down to the bare bones, and they'd mopped up a bit, Katie thought it would be worth Dorothy's time to come see the possibilities.

As Dorothy approached the front door, she once again tried to imagine her upcoming life in this place. What would it be like to get her mail out of the rusty box—first time she'd noticed it, and she made a mental note to replace it—mounted to the right of the front door rather than going down the lane with Sheba on their afternoon "constitutional stroll" to the gravel road to retrieve it, or pulling up to the mailbox in The Tank on their way home from here or there?

It did flash through her mind as a good thing that she'd no longer have to depend on, or wait for, Challie or Arthur and their tractors to plow her out in the winter. Everything she'd need would be within walking distance, although she never once thought about getting rid of her car. No, giving up driving this side of heaven was not in her plans, although she had to admit she was still troubled about nearly ramming into people she cared so much about. In fact, she'd had nightmares the last two nights about car wrecks. No amount of prayer could seem to move her past her sense of horror.

Katie, Josh and Alex had spent their entire second full day back in the house working from morning until night.

Every time they thought they were about to find the end of the piles, they'd discover one more closet or crawl space, attic or missed drawer, and the sorting, tossing, setting-aside process would begin again. For such a tiny house, it seemed to have no end of places for "stuff" to be stuffed. Katie made a mental note that when she got home, she was going to clean out every "nook and cranny," as her mother used to say. Even though she was definitely not a sentimental saver, she was sure there were some things that could go. And she vowed to Joshua never, ever to keep one single empty cottage cheese container. Aunt Tess had more than a hundred of them taking up one entire cabinet. In fact, she'd even stored them in her oven.

After Katie and the boys greeted Dorothy, before getting to the task at hand, Dorothy extended a meal invitation from May Belle for them all to join her and Earl for an early dinner. May Belle lived just around the corner, and everyone heartily accepted. In fact, Josh had been pouting because they hadn't spent much time with Dorothy since they'd arrived, other than the short while they'd visited over sandwiches right after The Incident, as they'd come to refer to it. Other than a short run to show Alex the barn on their arrival evening, the boys hadn't even gotten down to the creek yet, something Alex had heard a lot about. After all, there were crawdads to catch, and they sure had never seen *them* lurking around a Chicago brownstone! From the moment Dorothy'd taken Josh on his first crawdad hunt, he'd longed to go on another.

Formalities and invitations behind them, Dorothy took her first look around. She was blindsided by just how stark and sad the little home looked.

"How easily removed are traces of someone's life after

they're gone," she said solemnly, not even realizing she'd spoken aloud. "What we leave behind, Lord, surely needs to be of spiritual value, for my oh my, how quickly the rest of it can vanish."

Katie stared at this woman, who just *talked*, out *loud*, to . . . God! Then again, Katie had a look on her face as though she might have been wondering if Dorothy was trying to send *her* some kind of message.

Dorothy put her hand over her heart, wishing once again she'd worked a little harder to break into Tess's seclusion. She was somewhat haunted by the reminder before her that life was fleeting and that chances to help others were fleeting as well.

"You know, Katie," she said, looking into the face of the woman whose mouth was hanging open, "we better be living the life we want to live and not wasting our numbered days on what doesn't matter. Like my father used to say, 'Life is for the living!'" With that, she sighed and took a good study of the room, then she asked Josh to move a somewhat rickety side chair from where it was sitting, against the back wall, over next to the window. Then she looked up at the ceiling.

"You know, it crossed my mind to paint the ceiling fire engine red. I think I just might actually do it."

5

❀❀❀ ❀❀❀ ❀❀❀

Dorothy sat at the head of May Belle's dining room table and Katie at the foot. Josh and Alex were seated next to each other along one side. Although May Belle hadn't plopped down yet, she would sit next to Earl, who was seated across from Josh. She would have preferred to flank Dorothy with the boys, but she knew Earl would be too uncomfortable sitting next to someone he didn't really know, and she wanted him to have a chance to get more comfortable in their presence without becoming intimidated.

The seating took place according to the handmade place cards with which May Belle always graced her dinner tables, and her guests. She kept greeting cards people sent her, cut out the pretty pictures and punched holes in them to attach to the curly ribbon that secured one of her Saran-wrapped cookies or brownies. Of course, she always served one of her yummy desserts after the main course, but this way each guest had a little something sweet to take home. She meticulously wrote the names on the place tags in her best cursive. Handling them as reverently as if they were holy and sacred objects, she positioned them next to her Fostoria water goblets.

At last, after the chicken and homemade noodles, cooked baby carrots with a pinch of dried dill, lima beans canned from her last year's garden, kidney bean salad made Southern style with mayonnaise, boiled eggs and pickle relish, *and* her pickled beets and famous slaw were settled on the table, May Belle seated herself.

"Dorothy, would you please give thanks?"

"Of course, dear." Dorothy and May Belle each reached out a hand to take Earl's, then extended their other hand toward the person seated next to them, May Belle taking Katie's and Dorothy, Josh's. The boys glanced at each other, then clasped their hands together as well. As close friends as they were, *this* would be a first!

"Lord, THANK YOU!" Dorothy shouted in her loudest voice, actually startling Earl a bit. "Thank You for this gathering of old and new friends. Thank You for the fine cooking talents You've given May Belle; for the sturdy and strong hands and heart of Earl, who takes such good care of his mother and me; for the Joshmeister, who has kept me such good company the last weeks with his lively e-mail; for his friend Alex, who looks to be as fine a friend to him as May Belle is to me; and for that dear Katie, who was Your vessel and answer to my prayers, and who I just know is going to become my good friend, too. And thank You, Lord, for creating me. For surrounding me with not only folks who matter a great deal to me, but new possibilities as well.

"Thank You again, Lord, for protecting us from my careless driving, for supplying us this great food and for the smell of cooked chicken and the song of the red-winged blackbirds I heard this morning and the circle of love I feel such a part of at this very moment. May we learn to notice and appreciate every blessing, Lord, and lead the lives that not only help others, but make us happy as well. Amen."

Katie never closed her eyes throughout the entire prayer. As Dorothy mentioned each name, Katie looked from one bowed head to the other, noticing the smile that beamed across their faces as Dorothy spoke about them. Her own son, lively and thoughtful, spending time e-mailing someone so much older than himself. May Belle, Dorothy's lifelong friend. What good friends did *she* have? Her heart ached at the void. And Earl, well, he was retarded, as far as she could figure, and here Dorothy was thanking God for *his* strength and care for *them* . . .

". . . that dear Katie . . . vessel . . . answer to prayer . . ." Katie's eyes welled up. She wondered if God could, *would* really use somebody who never talked to Him. Just about the time she felt brave enough to ask God that question, she heard the "Amen."

La Feminique Hair Salon & Day Spa was bustling. The two-chair salon had both chairs in use at the same time only when someone was sitting with perm rods or color in her hair in one chair, and someone else was getting cut or styled in the other—since there was only one operator, and that was the owner, Maggie Malone. This was a two-chair moment. Gladys was sitting in the color chair, hair flattened to her head by a bottle of Brunette Brown hair dye, her color since 1963; Dorothy was being readied in the other to get "her pink scalp and few hairs rearranged," as she was fond of saying.

Usually these two weren't there at the same time. Gladys had been waiting outside the door when Maggie opened, saying she had a "very important meeting" to attend tomorrow, and it "just won't *do* to have myself looking like *this*," she said as she parted her hair so Maggie could get a close look at her inch-long, snow-white roots. Of course, everyone knew her "very important meeting" was probably just the monthly gathering of the Happy Hookers, Partonville's decades-old group of ladies who used to meet to hook rugs together but had long ago quit rugs and turned to playing bunco. In fact, the gathering was at Maggie's house, but she kept herself from asking if that was the meeting Gladys was talking about. If it was in the realm of possibility, it was usually easier simply to accommodate Gladys rather than to antagonize her and then have to listen to the fallout. And so Maggie had sighed and gotten her started and situated with the color before Dorothy arrived.

Maggie washed Dorothy's fine hair, blew it dry—which only took a few seconds on low—and was preparing to give it a couple of crimps with the curling iron when Gladys finally acknowledged Dorothy. Until Sheba had barked at the blow-dryer, Gladys had acted as if she hadn't even realized Dorothy was there, keeping her head buried in a magazine. Then it occurred to Gladys that Dorothy might have some information she wanted.

"Getting your hair done for the ball game this evening, Dorothy?" Gladys asked as soon as Maggie turned off the blow-dryer.

"Nope. I'm getting it done while I still can. At the rate my hair is disappearing, I figure it won't be long before I can just do my entire head with a washcloth!"

"How's Miss Durbin doing, getting that Walker estate cleared out? Do you think I'll need to get the health inspector out there before she leaves town? And do you know when that might be, exactly? I'd like to have a few words with her before she disappears again."

Maggie crimped the curling iron around a row of Dorothy's hair and held it there with one hand while she patted Dorothy on the shoulder with the other, as though to calm her.

"Which question do you want answered first, Gladys?" Dorothy asked, looking at Gladys in the mirror.

"There is no need to use that tone of voice, Dorothy. After what I heard the paramedics describe as *squalor* when they removed Tess's body from her house, I just want to make sure I'm not allowing a health risk of any kind to go unattended."

"I was in that home yesterday, Gladys, and I can assure you there is no *squalor*."

Gladys raised an eyebrow upon learning Dorothy really *had* been hanging around with that Durbin woman again. Evidently, Cora was telling the truth.

"There never was *squalor*, Gladys. There was plenty of chaos and piles of stuff everywhere, like one might imagine accumulates when a poor soul is kind of lost in her own world, but there was never garbage or anything unhealthy in the piles. In fact, her kitchen was probably every bit as neat and tidy as yours. Besides, about all that's left now is furniture. Katie Durbin and her son have worked very hard to clear out that place quicker than I imagine most folks could get the job done, as well as to ready it for me, in case you've forgotten. They're even going to redo the wiring and repair a few things. Don't worry, we'll have a proper building inspection before the closing.

"And as for her 'disappearing,'" Dorothy went on, using her fingers to draw quotation marks in the air around the word *disappearing*, and talking so fast that Gladys didn't have a chance to respond, "she has never disappeared. She simply returned to her home in Chicago to get her son back in school. She has returned to Partonville to finish what she started. She will go back home when she wants to—and I'm sure you have your ways of finding out exactly where that is anyway."

"Time to get you shampooed," Maggie said, spinning Gladys's chair around and stepping on the hydraulic bar, lowering Gladys in one swift and surprising move.

Dorothy sprang out of her chair, Maggie having finished up her "do" while Dorothy was speaking, and announced to Maggie that she'd left her money by the brushes and assured her she'd be back at the same time next week. Before Gladys could respond, even though her mouth had been open to do so for some time now, Dorothy had bustled out the door, Sheba at her heels, leaving a grinning Maggie. It didn't escape either Dorothy or Maggie that someone had actually beat Gladys to a dramatic exit.

The Tank backfired once upon startup, as though to put an exclamation point on the entire event.

6

Jessie Landers stood on the pitcher's mound, arms down in front of her, hands clasped around the softball. She glanced at the first baseman, who was staring at the runner for the Palmer Pirates, who was acting as if he was going to try to steal second. What Jessie knew was that he couldn't run fast enough to make it to second by Tuesday, so she didn't give him another thought. Instead, she stared an evil eye at the batter, winked at her young, blonde catcher, then gave her windup and lobbed the ball home. Even though Jessie could still "zing 'em into the breadbasket," this was relatively slow-pitch ball since most of the players were over sixty and that's just how they'd unofficially decided to go about things.

"Stee-rike three!" the umpire bellowed, nearly before the ball thunked into Shelby's hands. The batter had gone down looking, just as Jessie'd known he would.

"Nice catch," Alex shouted from the stands behind the backstop, hands cupped around his mouth. He was hoping Shelby would glance in their direction on her way to the bench so he could appropriately embarrass Josh. Like Arthur and Lester, Alex and Josh enjoyed teasing each other, given the opportunity. Josh poked him a good one in the ribs with his elbow, which was all the action Alex got out of his antics. Shelby didn't pay a bit of attention to anyone other than her Partonville Musketeers teammates, who were engaged in a flurry of high-fiving Jessie. Although Josh was hoping to make eye contact with Shelby—or at the very least he hoped she'd noticed he'd arrived—he was also watching to see if Dorothy was going to give a cheer.

Since he and Alex and his mom had arrived five minutes late, they'd missed the Welcome Cheer, as Dorothy referred to it. Of course, there hadn't been a soul on the field or in the bleachers who had missed the tardy and awkward arrival of the city slickers.

Dorothy had walked over, waving her pom-poms, to greet them after they'd gotten seated in the stands, apologizing for having to give her Welcome Cheer before they arrived. She'd explained she probably wouldn't have the wind to do another cheer for a couple of innings. But now Jessie's last strikeout had put them into the bottom of the third, and they usually only played five innings. It was time to give it another go. She waited just a moment until May Belle and Earl got done selling little ribboned and Saran-wrapped packages of three cookies for a quarter. They did this every week as a fund-raiser for the Musketeers, who occasionally needed to buy a new softball and always gave the umpire a couple of bucks.

Dorothy stood in front of the bleachers, where fans of both teams sat intermingled. Most knew one another after all the years they'd played, and they enjoyed the weekly gab sessions, often joking about being Bleacher Bun Buddies. Although the rivalry could occasionally be felt, no one was too serious about it, other than Jessie. Having traveled around the country playing semi-pro fast-pitch softball in her heyday, she found it impossible to enjoy losing. Although she'd been a golden glove catcher in her prime and had the deadliest pickoff arm in the tri-state area, several years ago it became too difficult for her to get up out of the squat. She was a natural for a pitcher, though, and she loved the fact that Shelby—the only one under fifty-five on either team—was the catcher, because unlike most of the other players, Shelby could actually catch the ball.

Dorothy signaled the fans by raising her pom-poms above her head. They all immediately stood up—aside from the city slicker group, who drew attention to themselves once again by the omission of their behavior—for even the opposing team's fans stood when Dorothy cheered. Dorothy gave Katie and her crew a moment to catch on, then as soon as they, too, were standing, she began. The cheer was given in the cadence of a drill sergeant who was marching his troops. To the beat, she alternated thrusting her red and black pom-poms out in front of her. Having been a band director all her working days, of course the beat was of utmost importance. Sheba barked and ran around her in circles all the while.

Howdy, folks, let's do some cheers
for the hometown Musketeers.
Hit and run and catch the ball.
Huff and puff, try not to fall.
Sound off.

"One, Two!" yelled the crowd.
"Sound off."
"Three, Four!"
Then they all finished in unison: "One, two, three, four—LET'S GO!"
Dorothy held her pom-poms high above her head, jig-

gling them and grinning. The people in the stands laughed, applauded and whooped it up, all at the same time.

Dorothy ended her cheering session by abruptly spinning around and sitting down on the front bleacher, nearly plopping herself onto Arthur's lap. Although she didn't let on, once again she felt a light pain in her chest.

After the game, The Tank bucked and coughed all the way home. It was all Dorothy could do to get herself up the stairs and into bed. She didn't even wash her face.

"Lord," she said before drifting off, "I know heaven is going to be a mighty swell place. It's just that I'd rather not go there right now. I've still got a few things to do."

"Dorothy," Doc Streator said when he handed her the new prescription, "it would be good if you could slow down a bit. Now, it was wonderful to see you cheering for the Musketeers last night, but Dorothy, it's time you put down your pom-poms." He saw Dorothy open her mouth to respond, but he put his finger to his lips, then picked up her hands, one in each of his, and continued. "There's just not a whole lot *more* we can do to help you. I believe this medication *might* help a little, but no promises. And you be sure to put one of those nitroglycerin tablets I gave you last visit under your tongue the moment you feel a hint of pain." He studied her face and noticed she looked away when he talked about the nitro.

"Dorothy Jean Wetstra, have you been keeping those handy and using them like I told you?" She didn't answer. She just continued studying the bountiful age spots that decorated his strong, aged hands, which were so gently holding hers. As Arthur had been The Tank's only physician, so

Doc Streator had been hers since the day he came to Partonville right out of medical school. He had seen her kids through fevers, chicken pox and bronchitis. He'd been with her when her husband, Henry, died and helped her daughter, Caroline Ann, get a few more years out of her life before succumbing to cancer. He had attended her youngest son's wedding and been a good friend to Dorothy when that same son went through his divorce. He was a regular attending member of the United Methodist Church of Partonville, and he could read her like a book. He sighed and shook his head. "What am I going to do with you, Dorothy?"

"Watch me live until I die," she replied matter-of-factly. "Continue being the good friend you have been since your first day in practice. Don't preach to me—that's Pastor's job. And Doc, never stop holding my hand. It's the closest I get these days to sparking!"

They both shared a good laugh, then Doc gave her a long and genuine hug. He spoke softly in her ear as he was hugging her. "Dorothy, the good Lord helps us through much, and one of the ways He does that is through medicine. Promise me you won't be too stubborn and too proud to know His answer to prayer when it's staring you in the face—or hiding in a little pill bottle in your handbag or pocket, okay?"

Dorothy gave the doc a sweet peck on the cheek. "Thank you," she said softly. "Thank you for caring." Then she stood, whirled on her heels and departed, leaving not even a hint of a promise in the air.

7

It was the height of the lunch business at Harry's when Katie, Josh and Alex entered. The swivel chairs creaked in unison and heads nearly screwed themselves off their necks as the regulars strained to get a gander at the city slickers. Most had now seen at least two of them—at the *very* least, had them pointed out in one place or another—during their last visit while attending either the wake, funeral or dinner afterward, or at the recent ball game. Those who hadn't actually met them or viewed their whereabouts had certainly heard the buzz, if not about the slickers themselves, then at the very least about their showy vehicle.

How Katie had ever let Josh talk her into coming back to this greasy spoon of a café was momentarily beyond her. With discomfort, she noticed that the few tables were filled. Before she could open her mouth to tell the boys they'd wait outside for a table to open up rather than be stared at the entire time, Josh and Alex had eagerly bellied right up to the counter, where there were three stools available together at one bookend of the U, which was unusual for this time of day. Her choices were to stand in the doorway by herself, leave or join them. Although she had endured Harry's before, this distasteful predicament went far beyond both her comfort zone *and* the call of motherhood. At least during the last venture she'd been seated at a *table*.

Kathryn Durbin, as she was known in Chicagoland commercial real estate development circles, wasn't a counter sitter. No, she was used to "Good evening, Ms. Durbin. We have your table ready." She was used to having her chair pulled out, linen and complete tableware for five courses, not perching herself at worn Formica in front of a chrome napkin dispenser. This entire happening was so foreign to her that she actually found herself unsure of how to properly *seat* herself on a stool. Did one plant one's backside first and then swivel toward the counter? How did one get on the stool without looking as if one was mounting a horse, since the stools were so tall?

With wide eyes, Josh watched his all-together mom become paralyzed by a stool. The moment she made eye contact with him, he pointed to his foot, which was resting on the elevated, running footrest near the base of the counter. He tapped his pointed toe, as though this delivered a clue for her dilemma. After a brief frozen moment, she awkwardly slid one foot onto the runner and finally—albeit hideously—positioned herself on the stool.

Immediately, however, she faced a new dilemma: where should she put her rather large Gucci handbag? Certainly she couldn't just drop it to the floor, which was too far down for her to lean over to reach without falling off the stool. When she tried to rest it in her lap, it instantly began to slide off since her knees were lower than her hips. She lurched on the stool to make a grab for it. She glanced down at the footrest, thinking she'd set it in front of her legs, but chalked off that idea since the footrest was black, and she wasn't sure why . . . but she suspected something gross. Finally, she put the straps over her shoulder and hugged the handbag to her side with her arm.

Cora Davis, now seated on the edge of her chair at the table by the window, studied Katie's every move. Acting Mayor Gladys McKern readied herself to seize her chance to talk to the horse's mouth without Dorothy running interference. Arthur, Harold and Lester had watched Katie's uncomfortable procedure with fascination, glancing from Cora to Gladys, then winking at one another. Alex, always bolder than Josh, had witnessed their winking. When they looked Alex's way, he grinned and winked right back at each of them, one after the other.

Katie stared at the menu, which didn't contain a semblance of a healthy-heart meal. "What'll it be, folks?" Lester asked them as he plunked down a knife, fork and spoon at each of their settings, causing Katie to rear back a bit.

"I'll have the special today," Josh said. How could he pass up a Double High Burger, as it said on the index card that was paper-clipped to the menu propped up between the salt and pepper shakers? "And it's nice to see you again, Mr. Biggs." Lester looked surprised Josh remembered his name.

"I'll have the special, too," Alex said. "And it's nice to meet you."

Lester took mental note of how popular his special had been today. Usually Wednesday was liver-and-onions day, but he'd made a last-minute change when the liver hadn't arrived. "I imagine you boys want colas to drink," Lester said rather than asked, writing it down before they could reply.

"Yes, please," they said in unison.

Lester stood staring at Katie, who was still staring at the menu, trying to find one thing that didn't smack of a gastrointestinal attack and flabby thighs. Her eyes rested on the side dishes. "I'll have a baked potato and green beans," she said without looking up.

"Don't have baked today," he said flatly. "Fries or smashed taters, if you want spuds today."

"Mashed potatoes and green beans would be fine," Katie said. "You don't serve the potatoes with gravy on them, do you?" she asked, crunching her face up.

"Not to you," he said. Katie couldn't decide if Lester was smiling or scowling. He stifled himself from saying that his white chicken gravy was the best in the tri-county area, according to May Belle. And if May Belle said something about your cookin', then it was so.

"I'll just have water to drink . . . please."

"I figured," he said.

Katie and Lester locked stares for a moment before Lester turned back toward the grill area, right after the left corner of his mouth tilted upward a bit. Katie decided he *was* being friendly, in his own odd little way. Even though Lester was gruff, she remembered his kindness at bringing a meal by the house for them when they were last in Partonville. She also remembered how he'd delivered the collection jar. It had been filled with change and a few dollar bills. He said he'd kept the jar in the restaurant so folks who didn't go in on flowers could donate toward her loss and pay their respects. She noticed the jar now sitting by the register had a sign on it that said DEKALB FAMILY.

A sudden tap on the shoulder caused her to gasp. She swiveled to see who had tapped her, and the awful squeak of her chair startled her nearly as much as the tap. She discovered an outstretched hand, right at her midriff.

"Cora Davis," Cora said, lit up like a Christmas tree at this one-on-one, face-to-face opportunity. "I wanted to reintroduce myself, since I imagine you don't remember me from the funeral, what with all the new faces." Oddly,

Katie did not remember meeting Cora, and usually she was very good with names and faces.

"How are things coming along at your aunt's house? I understand it's been quite a job. I saw Dorothy's car there the other day. How good of her to help you. But then I suppose, since she'll be moving in, she has a personal interest in the process."

Katie was instantly wary of Cora Davis, who seemed a little too fast-talking, friendly . . . and curious. "Things are going just as they should be," she said, withholding any information about Dorothy, feeling oddly protective. Cora stood, waiting for Katie to continue. When it became clear that she wasn't going to, Cora gave it her full press.

"I imagine you and Dorothy have worked out all the details as to when she'll be moving in, which will be . . ." Cora's voice lifted at the end, implying the dangling question.

"When she's ready," Katie said without emotion. Josh looked on with interest while Alex stared at Arthur, who was staring at him. Gladys noticed all the impolite staring Alex was doing and threw her head back in disgust, dabbing at the corners of her mouth with her napkin.

"If you need anything, just look me up in the phone book. We're the only Davis in Partonville." Cora then spelled Davis, just to make sure Katie understood. No sooner had Cora dejectedly stepped away than Gladys sidled up to Katie before she had a chance to swivel back toward the counter. It was nothing short of tag-team interference.

"Acting Mayor Gladys McKern," she said, thrusting her hand in front of Katie.

"Yes, I remember," Katie said. The two shook hands, Gladys delivering her practiced, mayoral shake of two firm up and downs, then separation. Like a ventriloquist whose lips didn't move, Josh mumbled to Alex, "forward and progressive." The two of them snickered, causing Gladys to stiffen a bit at their rudeness, even though she hadn't heard what passed between them.

"How are your plans coming along for the Crooked Creek estate?" Gladys asked. Like Cora, she wasted no time.

"And what plans would you be referring to?" Katie asked, playing dumb.

"Why, whatever plans you might have, of course," Gladys said, not easily dissuaded from her mission to find out what, exactly, Miss City Slicker Durbin might have up her sleeve.

"No plans are final. Many plans are being considered. The only thing for sure is that a portion of the land will become Crooked Creek Park."

"Of course, you don't plan on moving to the farm, right?"

"I don't recall saying that," Katie said nonchalantly. Josh's eyes got as big as full moons. He'd never heard his mother even entertain the idea of moving to the farm herself.

"Oh," Gladys said, "so you *do* plan on moving to the farm."

"I don't recall saying that," Katie said, now grinning at this cat and mouse game. Everyone in Harry's had by now stopped talking and tuned in to the entertaining verbal sparring, hoping to learn something themselves.

Gladys yanked on the bottom of her blazer, eyes flashing fire. "I guess you really haven't said much of anything, have you?" Katie stiffened a bit and raised a threatening left eyebrow. Gladys immediately realized the tone of her own voice wouldn't help her glean anything, so she friendlied up the presentation of her next statement. "As the acting mayor of Partonville, I just want to make sure that you feel welcome, should you become one of our residents. And, of course, I'm always looking out for the good of the people of Partonville, what with Hethrow perched at our doorstep and Crooked Creek being the path that leads to the door."

The women sized each other up for a bit, Katie finding herself mildly admiring Gladys's tenacity, yet unwilling to give an inch—partially because it did not seem any of Gladys's business, and partially because her own plans were not yet cemented. She nodded her head up and down in acceptance of Gladys's statement, but she didn't speak. You could have heard a pin drop in the restaurant until the slam of the screen door caused everyone's heart to skip a beat.

"Mr. Lester," Earl said, "I finished my deliveries."

For decades Earl had foot-delivered call-in lunch orders to local businesses. Lester was glad for the help—the only help he "hired"—and Earl was proud to have a job.

"Thank you, Earl," Lester said. "Just put the basket back where it belongs, and I'll see you tomorrow."

"Yes, sir, Mr. Lester. See you tomorrow."

Josh waved at Earl, who almost grinned before flashing his eyes to the ground and moving toward the door. Immediately after the screen door banged shut, Lester announced, "Food's up." He set the boys' burgers down, stating, "Two specials." Then he retrieved Katie's order, one small bowl in each hand. "Green beans and smashed taters, hold the juice. Better eat it while it's hot," he said in a loud and stern tone as he slid the order in front of her, seemingly intentionally intervening in the ladies' standoff.

"Thank you, Mr. Biggs," Katie said, turning to face him. "Yes, I do hate eating cold hot dishes." This time without a shadow of a doubt, the left corner of Lester's lip curled up.

His eyes even sparkled at her a bit. Without spoken collaboration, he had entered into battle, taking sides with Katie Mabel Carol Durbin, a city slicker worth her salt.

When they were done with their meal, Katie left an ample yet unpretentious tip, deftly slid off the stool, marched directly to the cash register, paid her bill with a smile, then put the change in the jar for the DEKALB FAMILY, whoever they were. Lester gave her an approving nod before the three of them marched out the door.

Gladys and Cora sat at their posts, looking rather like deflated frogs.

Dorothy had elected to keep an old rocker of Aunt Tess's, a charming floor lamp with faded purple fringe around the lampshade, which was similar to the one she'd always admired at May Belle's, a mahogany wooden end table with a pocket at one end for books or magazines or whatever one might want to keep close at hand, and the kitchen table, chairs and ruffle-trimmed place mats that matched some of her own.

When Katie had first entered Aunt Tess's home after her death, the entire house was in shambles, aside from the kitchen, which had been kept in perfect and readied tidiness as though Tess had expected guests. Indeed, the table setting presented itself as an oasis in the midst of chaos. Centered on the table there had been a vase filled with wilted wildflowers from her tangled yard—obviously freshly picked before her death—and three perfectly set place mats and water goblets. Next to the flowers, Aunt Tess had kept a framed photo of herself at thirty or so with younger sister Clarice, Katie's mom, standing next to a silo. Katie learned that it was Dorothy's silo and that the three had been friends way back when. The photo had been taken before Clarice suddenly decided to move to Chicago, leaving Tess, who had nearly raised Clarice after their parents' death, heartbroken and alone. Tucked into the frame was a photo of Josh when he was a baby, obviously one Katie's mom had sent to her sister, since Katie had no recollection of doing so.

The day after Katie'd arrived this trip, she'd stopped by the Floral Fling and picked up a bouquet of daisies, her mother's favorite, for the vase. The kitchen table had grown to feel like the comfort zone, "a sacred place to be honored," Dorothy had said when she'd announced she'd like to keep the table as it was. Although Katie would never have come to that phrasing on her own, she certainly knew truth when she heard it. Dorothy just figured Aunt Tess and the house wanted the table to stay, and so it would be—although Katie'd made it clear *she* was going to keep the vase for a memento.

Katie, Josh and Alex worked at the Vine Street house the rest of the day, dropping off the last load at the farm before returning for the final sweep-out and mop-up. At 8:00 P.M., the threesome finally plopped down at the table. Katie announced that the next order of business was to call in some contractors to deal with the electricity and a few other minor repairs. "Tomorrow's project will be the hunt for skilled labor," she said, running her finger over the petals of one of the bright daisies. "Maybe you boys can finally get to your baby-crab hunt at Dorothy's while I spend the day working on that task."

"Mom, it's crawdads. Crawdads. Somehow I don't think we're going to find crabs in Crooked Creek."

"Right. Crawdads." Mindlessly, Katie lifted the daisy from the bouquet and held it up close to her face, studying it for a moment.

"I should," she said after plucking the first petal, "I shouldn't" after plucking the second. She continued doing this until only one "should" petal remained. She hesitated, grinned, then plucked the "should" petal from its stalk, which she then laid on the table next to the tiny pile of petals.

"I thought when girls did that they said, 'He loves me, he loves me not,'" Alex said.

"I didn't think *my* mom did that at *all*," Josh said, revealing his obvious shock that his own mother would actually engage in a childish game like this to begin with.

"She who plays the game can make up her own rules," Katie said with a mock tone of defiance in her voice. "All of life's major decisions do *not* have to involve MEN!"

"Okay, Miss D," Alex said, using the name he often used to address her. "We get it. You pluck the petals, you call the rules." It was a rare moment of silliness between Katie and *anyone*, and Alex was totally into it.

"Yeah, Mom," Josh said with sarcasm and a hint of anger in his voice, "we get it now. You don't need men." Brusquely he pushed back from the table. "I'll walk to the motel," he said, and stormed out the door. Alex shrugged at Katie, then raced to follow his best buddy—into the street, into the night, into whatever had suddenly grabbed hold of him.

❧

Katie sat at the kitchen table for an hour, mulling over the sudden and odd turn of events after what had been a productive, positive day—even including the fiasco at Harry's. For the life of her, she could not figure out what had so riled her son. At 9:00 P.M., she decided just to head back to the Lamp Post, draw a bath and deal with . . . *whatever* tomorrow. She recalled Dorothy once saying, "*Whatever.* Isn't that a good word? You can end nearly every sentence with it." Yes. "*Whatever,*" she said aloud before turning off the light in the kitchen, locking the place up and getting into her SUV. She'd just leave the boys alone, since they thankfully had their own room, and soak in a steaming-hot tub until she turned into a raisin. While she had once questioned the business head of someone who, hoping to drum up repeat business, would leave Avon samples in a motel room, she now simply felt appreciation and anticipation of the pleasure.

She drove the few blocks to the Lamp Post and turned into the parking lot, her headlights flashing across a slender figure sitting in one of the white wicker rocking chairs on the front porch. The NO VACANCY sign was lit, which was odd, since the lot was not even half full; the front porch light was off; and Jessica sat in the darkness, a small, blanket-wrapped bundle nestled to her chest. Katie parked in front of her room, which was the farthest from the front porch. When she went to put her key in the keyhole, a near desperate sense of loneliness struck her, and she sighed. She suddenly dreaded entering her empty room. Although she could hear muffled voices coming from her son's room next door, their recent episode of *whatever* kept her from knocking. Quite to her own surprise, she found herself walking toward the front porch.

When she reached the end of the building, before making the turn onto the porch, she stopped, wondering if Jessica would even want company. Besides that, she wondered what on earth the two of them might even have to talk about. They barely knew each other.

Just then she heard someone opening a motel door and realized she didn't want to be caught looking like a lurker, so around the corner and onto the porch she went. It was just dark enough that she couldn't see Jessica's face.

"Hello," Katie said, her own voice sounding strange to her as she stared hard toward the shadowy figure.

"Katie? Is that you?"

"Yes. How could you tell in this blackness?"

"I recognized your vehicle when you pulled in. Then I heard the door close and your footsteps coming up the sidewalk."

"Oh." A long silence followed.

"Did you need something?" Jessica asked.

"Oh, no. I was just . . . I mean I . . ." Katie couldn't believe this was *her* behaving like some backward, bashful or guilty person. "I mean, I thought you might like some company," she finally got out.

"I would *love* some company," Jessica said. "Please, sit down. Can you see the chair right there by you? I can turn on the porch light if you like."

"NO!" Katie hollered, realizing she sounded harsher than she meant. Lowering her voice to a near whisper, she said, "Please, just stay put. This is much more relaxing." She welcomed the dark of night as a respite from Partonville's magnifying glass, which seemed to be constantly over them.

"Honestly," Jessica said, "you are like an answer to prayer. Although I am enjoying the feel of this *finally* sleeping baby in my arms, I was just thinking how lonesome I am for the company of . . . another mother."

"I'm not sure I would qualify this evening." The words escaped Katie's mouth before she'd thought them through. She was still nearly dumbfounded by the second person in Partonville who had told her she was an answer to a prayer! "I mean . . . I don't feel like a very *good* mother tonight," she continued, shocked at her own confession, words just tumbling out of her mouth.

Again a silence hung in the air. Then Katie heard Jessica sniffling. "Are you all right, Jessica?"

"I am just so glad to hear another mother say they didn't feel like a good one! You cannot *know* how that blesses me!" Her voice sounded as forlorn as it was appreciative. Katie found herself swallowing hard. Then she, too, began to sniffle. "Are *you* all right?" Jessica asked, grabbing the corner of Sarah Sue's blanket and wiping her own nose.

"Yes. I mean, no. I mean . . . *whatever!*" Instantly, the two women began to chuckle at each other and themselves. Sarah Sue wriggled at the noise, causing Jessica's breath to catch. She just did not think she could take one more bout of crying *or* nursing. She already felt like a wrung-out dairy cow. Thankfully, Sarah Sue melted back into the soundness of sleep.

"You know," Jessica said softly, "wouldn't it be wonderful if a mom could just turn on her *personal* NO VACANCY sign when she needed simply to go off duty for a spell?"

"Just wait until Sarah Sue gets to be a teenager," Katie said. "Teenagers have the ability to make you feel like all you have in your entire head *is* vacancy!" Jessica actually snorted through her nose while trying to stifle a possibly awakening burst of laughter.

"Oh, Katie! I had no idea you were so funny!"

"Neither does my son," she said somberly. This time they both burst into uncontrollable laughter; there was just no holding it back. The two ladies laughed so hard in the darkness that Sarah Sue finally started squawking—which only made them laugh all the more.

8

✿ ✿ ✿

Dorothy had continued to fret about the condition of The Tank as well as The Incident at the end of Arthur's lane. As many times as she'd tried to turn it over to God, her feeling of unsettledness just wouldn't go away. She had begun to wonder if, with every cough and buck of The Tank, God wasn't trying to send her some kind of sign about her driving, her health . . . her *life*. She'd spent a restless several hours, from 2:00 A.M. to nearly 5:00, praying on and off, then listening. Praising God, yet again, for keeping her from having done harm to anyone. Pleading with God to give her good sense. She just couldn't move past the niggling feeling that there was something she was supposed to "get."

"Lord," she finally said at 4:45, after having crawled out of bed to sit in her prayer chair by the window, "You *know* I can be a pigheaded old coot when I set my mind to it. You *know* what The Tank means to me. You *know* . . . everything.

"So many changes, Jesus. Things to think about. Moving, for one. Lord, I have just *got* to get busy sorting through all these pieces of my life stored here in this house. The longer I hesitate to begin the process, the more difficult it will be. I mean, You and I both know it isn't going to get easier! Help me set the course and stick to it. And while You're at it, give me the strength to do what I need to do before I can no longer do it. I mean, doesn't that just seem obvious?

"Okay, now, that's enough whining. I have *got* to get some sleep. Please give it to me, now. Please.

"Your child, Dorothy. Amen." She crawled into bed, and the next thing she knew, it was 9:00 A.M. Josh and Alex would be knocking at her door within twenty minutes.

Alex stood in the chilly, foot-deep water of the briskly running creek. Clouds of dark swirls oozed from around his feet and wildly raced downstream toward the unknown as he squished his bare toes deeper into the mud. He reached into the water and tilted a football-sized, slippery, moss-covered rock, fighting to hang on to it, hoping one of the thus-far elusive crawdads would squirt its way from underneath. When it didn't, he lifted the rock completely from the water, the moss coating it like hair on a head when one quickly surfaces from the bottom of a swimming pool. He stood inspecting the silky green strands in the warming beams of sunlight, mining for any organisms that might be lurking there. Alex loved anything to do with science. While others groaned and complained about dissections, lab experiments and chemistry terms, Alex took to them like a mosquito takes to skin: ready to drink. Of course, languages—even his own—were another matter. But biology, now that was fascinating.

Finally squirting through his hands, the rock plunked back into the creek, splashing him clean up to his nose. He deemed this cause suddenly to kick water at his friend. Soon both boys were kicking and scooping handfuls of water and launching mud, simply wallowing in the freedom to act like children and explore what interested them, rather than having facts and factoids, as Alex referred to them, crammed down their throats around every corner. Josh most often felt as if his private school were choking him rather than educating him. He had yet to find his niche, his passion or an ounce of enthusiasm for the stuffy place. He never stopped wishing his mom would let him attend the public school that Alex attended.

When the boys tired of frolicking, they once again resumed the business of hunting. Josh removed his sopping-wet T-shirt and tied it around his head, wearing the knot to the right side, and declared that this was the CC Tribe's official tribesman uniform, CC being short for Crooked Creek. Alex followed suit. Even though they were soon chilled nearly to the bone, neither would be the first to admit it.

"GOT ONE!" Josh yelped as he held the wriggling brown crawdad in the air. He walked it closer to Alex for an official inspection, passing off the critter while trying to make sure its snappers didn't get to his fingers—even though they would hardly do any damage. "Dorothy would be proud at the size of *this* conquest," Josh said. Although he'd been really disappointed when Dorothy opted not to come on the hunt, stating she believed Josh had been fully enough trained during his last visit to be officially a chief hunting trainer himself now, Josh wondered if she wasn't just tired. She looked like she hadn't slept much, and that worried him. She was the closest thing to a real grandmother he'd ever had, at least that he could remember. She'd said she was going to fix them up some lunch for whenever they returned, as no doubt crawdad hunts made one hungry. She'd also said she needed to start making a plan to tackle sorting through all the things in her house. He hoped that was really all there was to it.

Katie opted just to ignore Josh's peculiar behavior last night and follow his lead today. Although he still acted a bit cool toward her this morning, he was otherwise civil and openly eager to get to the farm. She'd already eaten her yogurt, read two magazines, watched forty minutes of CNN, browsed through the *Partonville Press* and studied the *Daily Courier,* Hethrow's paper—which she was surprised to find at the gas station just off Partonville's square—by the time the boys finally knocked on her door at 9:00 A.M. On the way out to Crooked Creek, she'd stopped at Your Store and picked up some doughnuts for the boys, grabbing a couple of extras for Dorothy.

Jessica was weeding flowers when Katie returned to the Lamp Post after having dropped off Alex and Josh and said a quick hello to Dorothy. Katie noticed that Jessica looked relaxed and happy in her labor. How *anyone* could seem actually to enjoy getting his or her fingernails clogged with dirt was beyond her, but . . . *whatever.* . . . "Yes, it is a good word," she mumbled aloud to no one in the car.

Jessica stood up, a handful of weeds grasped in each hand. "Good morning, Katie!" she said when Katie exited her vehicle.

"Good morning to you, too."

"I'm feeling much better this morning," Jessica chirped. "Again, thank you so much for last night. It made all the difference in the world. Helped give me a little perspective, you know? Sometimes we think we're the only one with struggles. How's things on your front this morning?"

"Acceptable," Katie replied without hesitating. "Let me upgrade that to *better,* I guess. I just dropped the boys off at Dorothy's. They were so excited about crab . . . crawl . . . looking for slimy things in the creek that it seemed to overshadow last night's bump in the road."

"Were the boys going crawdad hunting?"

"Yes! *That's* it! Crawdads! I do not know why I cannot seem to retain that bit of information."

"I imagine a strong, independent, single-mom businesswoman such as yourself has enough information to retain. Honestly, I just don't think I could handle it. How *do* you do it? And now the loss of your aunt and all the responsibility involved with clearing out her place. I couldn't make it without Paul to lean on and comfort me. He's just the best thing that has ever happened in my life. And now Sarah Sue . . . I thank God every day for my family and friends . . . their support and putting up with *me!*"

Just like Dorothy's prayer at May Belle's, Jessica's words had quickened something in Katie. It seemed as if ever since she'd returned to Partonville a quiet ache brewed within. For what, she wasn't exactly sure, but the words *blessed* and *friends* and *family* swirled around her. Tugged, prodded, beckoned.

"Oh, I'm so sorry," Jessica said, noticing the look that settled on Katie's face. "I'm afraid I've offended you, and that is the last thing I would want to do. Please *forgive* me for whatever I might have said that was inappropriate or crossed a line! Certainly I didn't mean to be intrusive. . . . Oh! Sometimes I just talk too much!"

Forgive me. Another two words that continued to haunt Katie since Dorothy'd spoken them after The Incident. Katie finally spoke to Jessica, whose fretting yet sincere face loomed before her. "You've done nothing wrong, Jessica.

I've been so busy with life, I just never really thought about myself in all those terms, and to tell you the truth, it kind of stopped me for a moment. I don't recall ever once, with intention, thinking about myself as strong, or as a single mother"—and she spoke the phrase *single mother* as if it was genuinely startling to her—"and whatever else you said. I just know that after Bruce left me for another woman, I've had to survive. Oh, not that I haven't always been a head-strong and relatively self-sufficient person, but that day I had to learn how to lean on nobody but me. Period." As much as Katie was shocked to find herself sharing these pieces of her life with Jessica, she found it a relief to let them out . . . take them in.

Jessica tossed the weeds down, brushed off her hands and moved toward Katie with open arms. Rather than back away or stiffen, which would be her normal instinct, Katie stood and received this gentle woman's hug. Before she knew it, she was soon hugging her back, tears once again welling in her eyes.

Jessica stepped back from Katie, her soft hazel eyes pooling, revealing her emotions. "Katie, I am no expert, Lord knows. But I do know life is always better with friends, whether they're husbands, relatives, kids or others God brings to us. And if I had forgotten that fact, I would certainly be remembering it right *now*, because I just know *you* are already my friend. My new friend. And that feels very good."

My new friend. The words played in Katie's ears. In Dorothy's prayer, she had referred to Katie as a new friend, too. In this sun-brightened instant, a burst of joy erupted in her heart.

"I'll tell you what," Dorothy said to Katie through the receiver, "give Arthur a call. I reckon he knows everybody who can fix everything and fix it right proper. I've just had no use for an electrician for a good long spell now. The last person who did any electrical work for me was buried about fifteen years ago. There was a man . . . oh, just ask Arthur."

Katie hung up and dialed Arthur's number.

"Yup," Arthur said when he picked up the phone.

"Is this Arthur Landers?"

"What other man do ya reckon might be a-pickin' up the phone in my house?"

"Arthur, this is Katie Durbin. Dorothy said you might be able to recommend an electrician. I need someone to completely rewire my aunt's home. Someone who can bring the place to strict code."

"Strict code, ya say? Is there any other kind of code? I reckon I wouldn't wanna be livin' in a house that followed it, if there was!"

"Right," Katie said, ignoring his supposed wit. "So do you know anyone who might be available?"

"Edward Showalter. Lives in Yorkville. You'd have to look up his number in the tel-eee-phone book," Arthur said, seemingly exaggerating his dialect just for her. "Edward Showalter *might* be available. Last I heard tell some few years back, Edward Showalter got religion and got sober for good. He was always the best with wires, when he was sober."

"Might you know anyone else, since Mr. Showalter sounds like he could be a bit unreliable?"

"I might. But I wouldn't recommend 'em none. No, I'd say Edward Showalter's the man for the job."

"And you think he's sober?"

"Miss Durbin," Arthur said, sucking through his teeth, "what I said was that I heard tell he got sober for good, *g-o-o-d*. That means for good, not for o-ccasionally."

"Thank you, Arthur."

"Let me know if you git ahold of him. I'd like to git ahold of him myself, since he still owes me for a lube job I gave his Chevy about twenty years ago—nah, never mind," he said, interrupting himself. "Be more trouble than it's worth, and he probably wouldn't remember it anyways, since he was on a three-day bender when he finally came back to git it. Slept in my barn one night and in his car the next. I found two empty bottles of . . . Never mind all that. Just tell him I said hello and that I'm the one who passed along his name. Tell him Arthur Landers said hello." He said it as though Katie had forgotten whom she'd called.

It just so happened that, like Arthur, Edward Showalter was retired, but he was also available for a look-see, as he called it, and he sounded sober. He would meet her at the house on Vine Street at 10:30 A.M. "I know just where that is, *and*," he said with emphasis, "I know just what you look like. You'll know it's me when I get there," he said, and he hung up before she could ask how either of those could be possible.

At precisely 10:30, a van showed up in the driveway painted in multicolors of green, creating an outrageously bold camouflage pattern. Big black lettering declared "Edward Showalter, Electrician. Affordable. Dependable. Sober. Jesus Loves You. Even if you don't SEE Him coming again, HE IS!"

By 11:25, Katie had worked up a deal with Edward Showalter—for some reason everyone, including him, always said both his names as though they were one—to completely rewire the house. Since Edward Showalter also did a bit of this-and-that handyman projects, she'd gone ahead and set the deal for him to make a few other repairs too. She became convinced not only that he knew exactly what he was doing, but that he would do all of *whatever* it was within a very reasonable amount of time, "given any unforeseen circumstances, like termites or other vermin," he'd added as his only disclaimer.

Katie figured once Edward Showalter was done with his portion of work, all that would remain to get things in order for Dorothy would be for the phone company to get everything updated and wired up for her phone and modem lines. Although Katie would never have believed anyone still had a rotary phone and no snap-in phone jacks, Aunt Tess had proved her wrong. For two women in their eighties, Aunt Tess and Outtamyway Dorothy were about as polarized as you could get when it came to modern-day living.

9

✿ ✿ ✿

Maggie Malone bustled around in her bountiful family room. Ben had built the spacious sixteen-by-twenty-foot addition onto the back of their home decades ago, after the arrival of their sixth child and before their seventh. Maggie was arranging and rearranging all her piles of colorful throw pillows until she got them in just the right order to please herself—or at least until she rearranged them all again. It was her turn to have the Happy Hookers over for bunco, and Maggie adored entertaining. This wasn't the regularly scheduled meeting night. On *that* evening she and Ben and every other club member—as well as many other Partonville folks—had sadly ended up attending the wake of Joseph DeKalb.

Maggie was as vibrant and exotic in her decorating as she was in her clothes, her hair, her life. Currently sporting somewhat chestnut-colored locks pulled severely back into a knot, she'd wrapped a couple of beaded bangle bracelets around it, and they clattered when she bobbed her head. She wore tight stretch-denim slacks and a highly patterned, short-sleeved cotton top and was barefoot, every other toenail painted either blue or violet. Referring to herself as a bit of a gypsy at heart, at seventy-two Maggie continued to be a real corker, as she'd always been.

The ladies loved coming to Maggie's, because they never knew what to expect. For dessert this evening, they would be served herbal ginger iced tea; strawberry-licorice sticks happily sprouting out of a crackled-glass goblet; Maggie's personal blend of salted Spanish peanuts, Oreo cookie bits and frosted pretzels; and homemade caramels with pecans that she'd purchased special for the occasion from her two o'clock appointment last Saturday. Of course, bridge mix was always on everyone's playing table.

Even Maggie's dice were unusual. She'd found them in a novelty shop in Chicago one year after the hair convention. Each pair was a different pastel color. Although Gladys always complained vehemently that the dots were difficult to see with the color—and truly, they were—everyone else would have been disappointed not to find them on Maggie's table. Even the evening's individual score pads set themselves apart. She'd decorated Post-it Notes with sparkling star stickers one of her great-grandchildren had given her for Mother's Day. She'd saved them for just such a special occasion.

At precisely 7:00 P.M. the doorbell rang. Acting Mayor Gladys McKern, who was still wearing her name tag from the day's activities, Nellie Ruth and May Belle all arrived at the same time and stood chatting outside the screen door. Ben came to the door, bowed from the waist—one hand at his belly, the other at his back—and greeted them. "Enter. Enter," he said, as he swept his arm inward. "Maggie's in the family room beating the stuffing out of her pillows. Perhaps you ladies can rescue them before she completely tears them apart."

"Oh, Ben!" Nellie Ruth said. "You tickle me."

"You going to fill in for us tonight?" May Belle teased.

"Certainly not. But thanks for asking. I'm on my way to Lester's this evening. He said he's got him a couple fine cigars, and we're going to sit out on his back porch and smoke them, away from any women who find it necessary to tell us how bad they smell and how bad they are for our health."

"And how bad *you'll* smell when you're done with them," Gladys said, waving her hand in front of her nose, as if the very mention of a cigar had caused smoke to waft up her nostrils. Ben just smiled and headed out the door after the ladies had passed by. He shouted from the front porch that they should tell Maggie he'd gone, and that he'd be back when he reckoned *they* were gone ("Nothing personal, ladies")–whether Maggie wanted him to return or not. They all laughed. Jessie was just pulling up to the curb when he rounded the corner. He stopped a moment to say hello to her, encouraging her just to go ahead on in since most of the ladies would be back in the family room by now. Jessie was surprised she didn't see The Tank in front of May Belle's when she passed by, since usually Dorothy stayed in at May Belle's on Hooker nights. She must have been running late, too.

When the ladies entered Maggie's family room, Gladys stopped dead in her tracks at the sight of the two card tables with four score pads at each table. Although bunco clubs usually had four players at each table, after the long-ago deaths of two of their regulars, they had just learned to play their own peculiar version with six.

"Margaret!" Gladys exclaimed. "What on *earth* are you doing with eight places?"

"It's a surprise," Maggie said with a look of mischief on her face.

"Well, I don't like surprises," Gladys said. "I've had enough surprises the last two days."

"Well, you're in for another one anyway," Dorothy said, stepping into the room behind her. "Ladies, please welcome our guests for the evening. I believe you all know Jessica Joy. I just figured it was time Jessica learned what *real* women do at these meetings. Besides, she could surely use a night out now and again." Jessica looked from face to face, her own turning a bright crimson when it landed on Gladys. "And I do believe you've all met Katie Durbin," Dorothy said, stepping back a bit so Katie could move forward. "She has been working herself to a near frazzle making sure my new house on Vine Street will be in tip-top shape for me, and I just thought it was time she had some *real* Partonville fun." Katie, too, scoped the room, wondering how in the world she'd ever let Dorothy talk her into *this.*

Maggie broke the pregnant pause. "When Dorothy phoned the shop today to ask me if it was all right to bring a couple visitors to the meeting tonight, I was not only happy about it but honored to be hosting such fine ladies. And I just knew you'd all be as excited as I am to be able to play two full tables for a change!" With that, she broke out in a thunderous, one-woman applause, her hair beads clacking as she swung her head from Katie to Jessica to the rest of the ladies.

May Belle and Nellie Ruth scooted over and gave the visitors each a proper welcome, as did Jessie. Rather than end up feeling like an outcast herself, Gladys decided to fall in line with the greeters, whether she actually did welcome them or not.

After a bit of conversation, Maggie announced that they should each take their first seat for the evening. She figured that it had been so long since they'd played the *right* way, they'd better get started on time, since all the proper rounds, all twenty-five of them, might take longer than they remembered. As soon as everyone was seated, she scurried into the kitchen and retrieved the handsome, hand-painted serving tray she had readied, then gently placed it atop her Egyptian-pattern, ceramic-inlaid coffee table. Using her candy-apple-red acrylic ice tongs, she plunked a couple of ice cubes into each cobalt blue iced tea glass. Then she began to pour the herbal ginger iced tea from her giant pitcher, which was decorated with an encircling underwater scene. One by one, she set a glass next to each lady. One by one, they sipped the refreshing new experience, all seeming to enjoy it—aside from Gladys, who took a pass, saying she'd wait for the coffee, thank you.

At last, Maggie settled down at the table with May Belle, Katie and Nellie Ruth. Then she picked up one of the dice, shook it in her hand and tossed it, rolling a three. Each of the others then rolled. The one with the highest number would begin play for her table; the woman seated across from her would be her partner for this round. Nellie Ruth was the only one to roll a six at her table, which had become designated as the head table. She would be Katie's partner this round. The way Dorothy and Jessie had seated themselves at their table had left Gladys and Jessica matched up as partners for the first round. Gladys suspected that Dorothy had cleverly and intentionally gotten away with it before Gladys knew what had hit her. Jessie rolled a six, so she rolled first for her and Dorothy's team.

The game began with the ladies shaking three dice at once. During round one, the object was to shake as many ones as you could (the next round was for twos, the next for threes), accumulating one point for each. You kept rolling (always all three dice at one time) until none of your dice contained a one, then you passed the dice to the woman on your right and recorded your accumulated score for your current team. If, in one roll of the dice, you got three of any number other than the number you were currently shooting for, that was worth five points and your turn continued. If you rolled, in one roll, three of whatever number you were currently rolling for, that was a bunco. You loudly proclaimed "BUNCO!" and play immediately stopped at both tables. If no one rolled a bunco, bunco was declared when a team had scored twenty-three points. Then each lady recorded her win or loss on her score sheet with an X or an O, with a special notation made for a one-roll bunco. The two losing ladies from the head table moved to the second table, each joining with a new partner. The two winning ladies from the second table moved to the head table, following the same pattern. Prizes at the end of the evening were given for the most wins, second most wins and third most wins, as well as the most buncos, and there was a booby prize.

Although Jessica was familiar with the game, it took her a while to become comfortable in the setting. Getting invited to the Happy Hookers meeting was like being inducted into Partonville's private Hall of Fame, even if it was only a one-evening visit. Katie felt like a fish out of water, finding herself just picking up the dice and plunking them to the table rather than shaking them—which would have made her feel *completely* silly. She was used to intense games of bridge. Thinking. Strategizing. Memorizing. Somehow just picking up the dice and rolling them seemed a bit mindless at best and senseless at worst.

Even so, by the third round of the second set, everyone

had found her rhythm and loosened up a bit, including the two visitors. In fact, Katie's competitive nature betrayed her own stoic posture, and she began uncontrollably yahooing a bit when she'd find herself on a roll. Although Gladys and Jessica had lost the first round they played together, they'd been teamed up once since, and Jessica had actually rolled a bunco during their play. Gladys couldn't help but let out a little cheer, finding it exhilarating to mark yet another win on her card—even if Jessica was the one responsible for giving it to her.

By the end of the evening, Gladys had won the most buncos, Jessie took most wins, May Belle took second and Katie took third. "Not too bad for a rookie of a city slicker," Dorothy said with a chuckle. No one could believe she'd called her that to her face, or that Katie had actually laughed out loud when she heard it. When the ladies were filing out for the evening, Jessie was surprised to learn that Katie had not only driven Jessica to the meeting, but she'd picked up Dorothy, too.

The boys had stayed out at Dorothy's to watch videos—she had a major collection—and shoot some hoops in the barn. Alex never traveled anywhere without his basketball. Henry Wetstra had mounted the now rusty backboard to a support beam after Santa Claus brought it for Vincent, Dorothy and Henry's younger son, one Christmas when the boys were just little guys. Although the net had long ago rotted away, the backboard was as secure as the day Henry lovingly brought that bit of exercise, camaraderie and brotherly fun to the barn. Dorothy still carried moments of that Christmas Day in her memory portfolio. Henry nearly froze his fingers off working to get it set up. But her sweet Henry would never once have thought about making his sons wait for their joy. Besides that, he loved shooting hoops himself.

It was a sunny and clear yet bitter cold winter day, and you could see your breath inside the barn. The boys wrestled around with each other in the hay bales, stopping every once in a while to ask, "Is it ready yet? Huh? Is it READY?" Henry would occasionally send them running through the snow to the toolshed for a square, bolt or level, more to burn off some of their energy than out of any real need. He'd ask their opinions about this and that, and, of course, as was customary with Henry, he followed the instructions to the letter.

Finally the task was complete. Henry drew a quarter out of his pocket. He tossed it high in the air and asked Jacob to make the call quickly as to who got to throw the first ball. "HEADS!" Jacob shouted, but alas, it was tails. Vincent got the privilege, which only seemed fair anyway, since Santa had brought the hoop to him.

Vincent bounced the ball a couple of times, then with all his might he hurled it up toward the net. It didn't get within three feet of the bottom! It was then that Henry realized he'd have to lower it for a few years, and the mounting process began all over. By 1:30 P.M., they were all finally playing, the thought of food nowhere in their minds. Try as Dorothy might to keep those boys and her husband bundled up, there was just no way they could play basketball for two hours straight without occasionally peeling off a layer or two.

Eventually, Dorothy packed a late lunch in a big basket and hauled it and baby Caroline Ann out to the barn. Sitting on bales of hay at the base of the backboard, together they prayed, then ate, then played some more until the sun went down and they were all simply too pooped to bounce, pass or shoot.

After the Hookers' meeting, Katie dropped Jessica off at the Lamp Post before she ran Dorothy home, knowing Jessica was anxious to see how Sarah Sue and her husband were getting along. Jessica imagined that Paul would have called if Sarah Sue got out of control, but just the same, she would be glad to get back—even though she'd had a wonderful time. Paul needed to get a good night's sleep for his very early start at the mine, and Jessica wanted to make sure he got just that. He had been so tender and caring to both of his "ladies," as he'd taken to calling them. Besides, her breasts were full, and whether Sarah Sue needed her at the moment or not, Jessica would soon need to relieve herself. Although she hadn't yet braved trying the breast-pumping machine she purchased at the Wal-Mart, she knew it was soon going to be time—and maybe that time was now. Then again, maybe not. The entire idea made her cringe.

Katie made the drive back to Crooked Creek slowly that night, allowing the fresh air to fill her up. The night sky was absolutely amazing. She and Dorothy rode in silence, craning their necks toward the heavens. Not since Katie had been skiing in Aspen had she noticed so many stars. What with all the city lights around Chicago, even a clear night sky usually appeared like nothing more than a moon and a few starry twinkles.

When she finally pulled up the lane and turned off the engine, they could hear through the open doors of the barn the thump, thump, thump of the basketball bouncing against the wooden floor. The yard light was shining bright, as were all the lights in the barn.

"Oh, how it makes my heart sing to hear the sounds of young life in that barn again," Dorothy said. "I just wish it could stay forever." Katie leaned her head back against the headrest, sighed and closed her eyes. "I almost said I wish *I* could stay, too," Dorothy continued in a reverent voice, "but I've fully realized within the last few weeks that I am ready to go."

"Dorothy! You're not talking about *dying,* are you?"

"Goodness no, child. I'm just talking about moving."

"You scared me there for a moment!"

"Well, the task of moving itself is kind of scary. But even so, the notion of just being able to stay in town tonight began to feel safe and right. Yes, it's time to move on."

"So it is," Katie said. "So it is. And Dorothy, I'm going to tell you something now before I change my mind. I'm going to say it right now while *I* know it's true: it is time for me to move on, too. Yes, although the task is daunting, not to mention completely SHOCKING for me," and she said the word *shocking* so loudly that it caused Dorothy to bolt a bit in her seat, "I realized when I saw my son covered with mud and grinning from ear to ear today that staying in the city is no longer the right thing. He hates his school, he hates our house, he hates his life, I fear. Staying is not the right thing for Joshua, and it is not the right thing for me. It is not the right thing for *us.* It is time to try to let go of some wounds I didn't even know I was carrying until I came to the country and learned to breathe again."

Dorothy sat as still as a post, her spirit quickened. Could it be that God had answered her prayers for *this* precious child of His *and* her son? *Lord, keep my lip zipped until she runs out of words.*

"I'm not exactly sure what I'm even getting myself into, or how it will work out in the end," Katie said, "but I realized for the first time last evening how lonesome I've been for a very long time. Thanks to you and Jessica and all your other kind friends, I am beginning to understand *why* friends are important, and how much I've missed by keeping too busy to have them. I soaked in the tub last night and thought, *Katie, if you don't make some changes now, you're one day going to die an old, miserable, lonesome woman.* Honestly, I think it's one of the most profound moments I've ever experienced. Then today when I saw Joshua covered with mud and again tonight when I heard so many of the stories the Hookers have accumulated . . . and I hear you speak of young life . . . That's it!" Katie said as she pounded the steering wheel with the palm of her hand. "We're moving to the farm! I'm sure I can find challenging work in Hethrow . . . I hope Josh will like the school . . . You know, Dorothy, when one keeps going too fast, one doesn't take heed of what *really* matters. Although I never thought I'd hear myself say this, sometimes it's just time to slow down."

Goose bumps flashed across Dorothy's entire being. Dorothy knew she had heard the voice of God, and it was speaking directly to her about her *own* life.

10

❦ ❦ ❦

Edward Showalter was a man true to his word. Katie walked from room to room flipping light switches on and off, marveling at the swiftness with which he had single-handedly—aside from a half-day of assistance from Josh and Alex, when together they pulled wire through conduit—rewired the entire house, including the installation of a circuit breaker box. Not only had he reengineered and rewired, but he'd done so in five days, and there wasn't a mess to be found. He'd even swept the floor where he'd drilled. And thankfully for everyone involved, not a single specimen of "vermin" had dared to show its face.

"Edward Showalter," Katie said, curious at her ability to easily call someone by both names, "you would be in high demand if you were in the Chicago area." Having spent her entire professional career involved in one way or another with real estate, Katie had had hundreds of occasions to deal with electricians and handymen. Never in her experience had she dealt with one so honest, thorough, swift *and* neat, not to mention affordable. Katie made up her mind on the spot that there would be a bonus waiting for Edward Showalter at the end of the refurbishments.

"I'll tell you what, Miss Durbin, you wouldn't have said that had you known me in my drunken days. No sir, I mean ma'am. You would not have been saying *that.* You would have been saying, 'Now, *there's* a man who needs JESUS!' "

"Oh, I doubt I would have said *that,*" Katie said aloud, although she hadn't really meant to.

Edward Showalter studied her for a moment, wiping the knuckle of his left index finger across his lips as though to zip them shut. After a few awkward moments, he shook his head up and down, obviously having made his final determination about something.

"You say you're good friends with Dorothy Wetstra, Miss Durbin?"

"I'd say we're getting to be very good friends."

"That's good."

"Why do you ask?"

"Oh, just glad you know such a fine woman of God. Why, Dorothy has one of the most excellent reputations in the entire area. I'm also glad she's got someone like you who's looking out for *her* well-being by hiring the best in the business to wire what will soon become her house," he said, winking at her while grinning from ear to ear.

Although Katie felt there was more to his statements than he was revealing, she didn't pursue it. Instead, she moved right on to the next order of business.

"Would you like me to pay you for the electrical work now, or wait to give you a final payment for time and materials after you've seen to the other repairs?"

"Shouldn't take me over a couple days to finish up, unless you suddenly add quite a bit to my agenda." He paused a moment, then repeated the word *agenda,* using it as its own sentence. "Strong word, isn't it? My *agenda* for the day. My *agenda* for the week. My *agenda* for my life." He pursed his lips, then got back to the topic at hand. "I reckon it would just be easiest to give me one lump sum when I'm done." He reached into his back pocket and extracted the large leather wallet attached to his belt by a chain, then leaned against the wall as he flipped open the bill compartment and retrieved a small collection of papers. He then handed them to Katie. "Here's my expenses so far, minus, of course, my labor. I figure we're about right on the quoted fee, timewise, especially since those two fine young men gave me such good assistance. Now that the electricity is done and I can actually plug in my power tools without worrying I'm going to short something out and burn down the place, I'll have the rest of your list taken care of in no time.

"I've been inspecting the bathroom real good," he went on, allowing his body to slide down the wall until he sat on the floor, "and aside from replacing a few cracked floor tiles, it really doesn't *need* much more than a few new washers and a toilet float. No *need* for all new fixtures—you could get by with just those few fixes and a new toilet seat. Of course, a new toilet and sink *would* make it right nice."

"Yes, go ahead and get those," Katie said without a moment of hesitation.

"Of course, now you'll have to let Dorothy establish if she prefers a roundie or oblongie toilet and seat." He laughed out loud at his own observation. "I'll tell you, some folks have to come to quite the compromise over *that* one!" Katie smiled a dull smile, realizing he'd gone off on a tangent—something that came naturally to Edward Showalter—that was far more entertaining to him than to Katie Durbin.

"One thing is for sure: the whole house could use some new vents. The furnace still seems to be working fine and doesn't appear to be more than fifteen years old, but I think I'll have my friend Melvin Jack stop by to give it a once-over. And never you mind about paying Melvin—he owes me one. Of course, if there's work to be done, that would be another financial story."

"You know," Katie said, looking down at Edward Showalter, who rested his forearms on his drawn-up knees, "how about you take a day or two off? You look like you're exhausted. Besides, it will give me a chance to go over some final details with Dorothy concerning her decisions about carpet and ceiling fans . . . and toilet shapes and such."

"Miss Durbin, that sounds like a great idea to me," he said, removing his camouflage hat with "Jesus Saves" printed across the front and wiping his brow and lips with the white handkerchief he pulled from his shirt pocket. He briefly studied the dirty smears the handkerchief had captured before stuffing it back into his shirt pocket. "Let's see, this here is Friday . . . how about you phone me at home Sunday afternoon and we'll go over the list. I'll be here first thing Monday morning, then, unless I need to get me to Hethrow first for supplies. Yes, Sunday afternoon would be perfect. That way we'll both have a chance to get to church, get to lunch, then think about getting back to work on Monday."

"Right," Katie said, beginning to believe that Edward Showalter had an *agenda* for *her* on his mind, and that it had nothing to do with home repairs.

❦

Although the City Slicker Crew, as they'd come to refer to themselves, had been in town more than a week already, Alex had no trouble clearing another week or so away from home. His mom loved hearing the lilt in his voice and was happy for her son to have a "real country experience." She said, "Just bring us back a batch of fresh air when you come." Josh, of course, was thrilled. And at the very least, they'd now get to attend another ball game. Although he'd kept his eyes peeled at all times for a Wild Musketeers Catcher Sighting off the field, he had done so to no avail.

Katie had busied herself the last few days working with lawyer Rick Lawson on Aunt Tess's final trust documents. Thankfully, she'd unearthed the originals from the bottom of one of the huge boxes of paperwork—and there were still two more to sort through—they'd hauled back to Chicago after their first trip. Although most of the papers were junk mail and decades-old bills, she was thankful to discover that Aunt Tess had kept all the legal documents together, even though she'd stored them in a shipping envelope in which she'd received catalog items from JCPenney.

Between Katie's large legal firm in Chicago and the peculiar, somewhat hokey, disorganized, yet oddly thorough and cooperative Rick Lawson here in Partonville (Dorothy had been his saxophone teacher in high school, and he was now her one and only lawyer), final sale papers on both properties and land trusts for the Crooked Creek Park were at last all in order. Katie had held her breath while Jacob Henry, Dorothy's older son, who was a lawyer in Philadelphia, went over all the faxed documents. Katie got the feeling he was worried that his mom was being taken advantage of. Actually, Katie was glad Dorothy's sons would find out how fair she *was* being.

Closing would take place in one week, after final walk-throughs at each piece of real estate. Katie had drawn up farm papers stating that she would accept all conditions "as is" and postpone possession until whenever the farm became available; a clause had been added to the Vine Street sale guaranteeing something to the effect that any and all discovered problems would be remedied prior to the closing, with a ninety-day follow-up period after Dorothy moved in—whenever that would be—to repair any thus-far unknown inadequacies. It was the most liberal and unusual set of terms Katie had ever agreed to, and yet it was she who wanted to cover all the bases, including her own. Although she had surprised herself by determining to move to the farm, at least for the time being, she didn't want to risk any unforeseen circumstances stopping this sale, what with Crooked Creek Farm being the most prime development property contingent to Hethrow. In fact, she had concluded it was undoubtedly the jewel of the county.

The last thing she had to do was break the news to Joshua that they would be moving. Although it appeared clear that he was blossoming here, one could apparently never be sure about the reaction of a fifteen-year-old. And then it hit her: Josh's sixteenth birthday was tomorrow!

The Partonville troops were activated! Once word among Dorothy's best friends had spread about the small surprise party, people insisted on their particular roles, saying it was a great chance to use their gifts—although Arthur surely never used that term. Setting: Dorothy's front porch. Decorations: Maggie and Jessica. Birthday cake and all other sweets: May Belle. Property setup: Earl. Extra lawn chairs: Jessie and Arthur. Hot dogs and chips all around: Lester K. Biggs. Games: Alex. Nellie Ruth said she'd pray for nice weather. Katie instructed each of them to bring their receipts, since she wanted to be hosting the party, although she had nothing to do physically to prepare but come up with a gift.

It was determined that the birthday party would immediately follow the ball game. And it would be a surprise . . . sort of. Although in front of Josh everyone would be talking about the spontaneous picnic after the game, everyone but him would know the real reason. Katie made them all promise there'd be no gifts lest someone think the City Slicker was pulling a fast one just to take home some booty.

"Stee-rike three!" the umpire yelled, causing Jessie to whirl on her heels in disbelief. "Raymond Ringwald! You know for a FACT that was low and away! You better get you some new glasses."

"Now, Jessie. If it's true my strike zone has expanded a bit today, you can be sure when you're pitching, it will be exactly the same size. I bet I won't hear you complaining then."

Jessie shot him a fiery eyeball, tossed the bat to the ground, stomped to the bench, slammed a couple of gulps of water from her sports bottle, grabbed her mitt and headed toward the mound. "Get ready, Shelby," she said. "Three up, three down. I feel it in my bones."

"Right," Shelby said, then swatted Jessie on the rump with the back of her hand. "Let's get 'em!" Just before Shelby went into her squat for warm-up, she looked into the bleachers. Josh couldn't believe it: she smiled at him. Directly at him. Having witnessed the event, Alex poked him so hard in the ribs that it caused Josh to grab his stomach. Nothing like appearing like a wimp. Unbeknownst to

Josh, Dorothy had told Maggie, who had told Shelby, that Josh had been on the lookout for her ever since he'd arrived back in town. And truth be told, she thought he was pretty cute, too.

❦

Josh leaned forward in the backseat as far as the seat belt would allow, trying to comb his hair in his mom's rearview mirror. It had taken all the courage he could muster after the game to ask Shelby if she'd like to come to the picnic. Oddly, she already seemed to know about it. He figured her exotic "Grammie M," as Shelby referred to her, must have told her. And yes, she would certainly be there—smile, smile. Why on earth Mom needed to stop at Your Store after the game, then disappear into her motel room for twenty minutes to "freshen up" for a picnic, was beyond Josh. All he knew was that he wanted to get there, and now he felt late. Alex just grinned and shook his head, watching his friend try to redo his hair time after time.

"Give it up, Joshmeister. Your hair just has a life of its own today."

Once they pulled up close to the front of the farmhouse, Josh couldn't believe how organized everything already looked. And what was that banner strung across the front porch? He began to read the bold-lettered, multicolored, spatter-painted words out loud: HAPPY 16TH BIRTHDAY JOSH-MEISTER! Then he noticed streamers hanging from tree limbs, chairs with colorful throw pillows arranged in a circle and Sarah Sue sleeping soundly in a basket under a tree, Sheba curled up next to the basket. "HAPPY BIRTHDAY TO ME?" Josh asked in full voice.

Alex burst out laughing. "Boy, we got you good, didn't we?"

Josh was stunned; he'd thought no one had remembered his birthday. Before Katie had even stopped the Lexus, everyone ran under the banner. Dorothy, ever the music instructor, lifted her hand high in the air and gave the downbeat, then everyone began singing "Happy Birthday." Everyone including Shelby, who stood right in the front. Although she still wore her Wild Musketeers T-shirt and had dirt streaks up her leg from sliding into third, she had let down her ponytail, and her golden hair actually appeared illuminated by the sun. Earl stood toward the back, eyes mostly downward but lips occasionally moving to the "Happy Birthday" song.

Josh got out of the Lexus, face as red as a beet, reluctant to move toward the gang. Alex jogged up behind him and started pushing him toward the little crowd of people. "Okay, can we EAT now?" Alex asked loudly. "I'm starving! Enough with the Birthday Boy stuff already."

"Dogs are almost ready," Lester said as he poked at the red-hots on the barbecue grill.

"Sodas are in the Landerses' giant cooler over there," Dorothy said as she strolled toward Josh. He stood frozen, just taking it all in. Dorothy, dressed in pink from her head to her shoelaces, threw her arms around him and gave him a big hug, then a kiss on the cheek. "Sweet sixteen! Remember this moment, Josh, because the next thing you know, you'll be an oldster like me!"

"Dorothy, if I can be like you when I'm an oldster, I'm not worried."

Katie stood off to the side, watching and listening to this exchange. It occurred to her that she spent way too much time worrying about aging. It occurred to her that her son was very handsome and that she was, at this moment, feeling happier than she'd felt in a very long time. When Jessica Joy walked up beside her and put her arm around her waist, then whispered, "Behold, your baby," it occurred to Katie that life was too short to stay locked in anger over ex-husbands and days gone by, and that new friends were priceless.

It also suddenly occurred to her that Dorothy had given only one cheer at the game. When Dorothy finished smooching Josh on the cheek and giving him one last hug, Katie watched her slowly walk over to the porch and plop herself down on the swing, reach into her pocket and, with a look of concern on her face, slip something into her mouth.

The hairs on the back of Katie's neck stood up, and an odd thought flashed into her mind: she was glad Dorothy's sons and grandchildren would, in the not too distant future, be arriving to help with the sorting/sifting/selling/auction/moving process. Dorothy was such a spunky character that it was easy to forget she *was* eighty-seven years old.

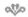

The sun was beginning to sink into the horizon by the time it was Shelby's turn to play the one and only game Alex had come up with. She was last to try her hand at Pin the Grin on the Joshmeister. Out of poster board, Alex had made a caricature outline—something he was very good at—of Josh's face, including everything but the mouth. They'd taped the face to the side of the barn with duct tape. Of course, Alex drew Josh's detached mouth with a ridiculous, wide-open grin, one tooth missing in the front. One by one, folks were blindfolded, turned around, then headed in the direction of Josh's poster-board head. People got hysterical, seeing the grin land between his eyes, on his chin, next to his ear. Earl stood back under a tree and watched; blindfolds weren't for him. But he did smile on occasion at the silliness. Much to everyone's surprise, even Arthur and Lester each took a turn.

But now it was Shelby's turn. Alex blindfolded her, handed her the grin—upside down, of course—then spun her around. Rather than facing her toward the head on the barn, however, he aimed her right at the living Josh. Everyone laughed as she headed toward him, his ridiculous paper grin extended in front of her. Although Josh was embarrassed, somehow the idea of Shelby coming straight toward him kept him from letting her in on the trick.

Suddenly, her hand reached his chest and she drew back when she realized she had touched fabric rather than poster board and that everyone was hysterical with laughter. She ripped the blindfold off and discovered what they'd all been up to. Without batting an eye, she took the paper grin and taped it right over Josh's mouth. Everyone broke out in wild applause as the two of them also erupted in peals of laughter. Although you couldn't actually see Josh's *real* smile behind the poster board one, his eyes twinkled just about the merriest his mom had ever seen.

By the time the laughter wound down and people started making noises about heading home, Katie announced she'd first like for Josh to open his gift from her. She ran to the Lexus and withdrew a plain brown box about as big as a basketball, then handed it to Josh, giving him a motherly peck on the cheek, something she hadn't done since he'd turned six years old. "I hope you like this," she said with sincerity. Josh walked over to the food table, cleared a spot and set the box down. Cautiously, he opened the lid. A puzzled look settled on his face as he reached down in the box and withdrew a metal colander and a fishnet such as you'd find in a pet store. Quizzically, he held them up, shrugged his shoulders and looked at his mom.

"I figure anyone who lives on a farm ought to have the appropriate crab-catching paraphernalia," she said.

"Crawdad-hunting paraphernalia," Dorothy and Jessica, to whom Katie had revealed her intentions, shouted at the same time.

"Crawdad," Katie said slowly. "Maybe after five years of living here myself, I'll get it right."

Josh stared at his mom, trying to make sense of what he was hearing. He looked at Dorothy, then at Alex. They were both beaming, obviously in on whatever was happening. *Lives on a farm . . . five years of living here. . . .* He heard those words ringing in his ears as he struggled to make sense of them. Then the light finally dawned. "Mom! Do you mean to tell me we're moving to this farm?" His face revealed no evidence of what was going on inside of him.

Katie's heart felt as if it skipped a beat as she realized that this could possibly turn out to be the worst moment of her life. "Yes," she said, in a tone just above a whisper. She moved close to him and looked him straight in the eyes, trying to create an intimate space of privacy in the midst of the now gawking gathering. "Yes. As soon as Dorothy's safe in the house on Vine Street and we've closed up things in Chicago, we're moving right to *this* place in Pardon Me Ville."

"Mom, are you kidding me?" Josh asked with a hesitant tone in his voice.

"No, son, I am not kidding you." The silence throughout the entire party was deafening as many took in this news for the first time and others were holding their breath.

Suddenly, Alex began applauding. Then Lester joined in, as did Dorothy and Jessica. Then May Belle and . . . everyone, including Earl, was applauding. Everyone but Josh and Katie, who stood wide-eyed, staring at each other.

Then, in a sudden, fluid move, Joshua Matthew Kinney stepped forward and picked his mom up clear off the ground. "Yahoo!" he screeched in her ear. "YAHOO!"

"Joshua, I can't breathe," she finally said. Josh set her down in front of him, then backed off to look into her eyes, which welled with tears. "I take it you're happy about this, then?" she asked, somewhat hesitantly.

"Happy? HAPPY? I'M THRILLED!" And the next thing they knew, they were being hugged by everyone, including Shelby. It was just about the most wonderful moment of Josh's life.

11

⊶⊷ ⊶⊷ ⊶⊷

Josh and Katie had been back in Chicago for two weeks. Katie had always kept their brownstone in top shape, living a nearly compulsively neat life—much to her son's disgruntlement. And properties in their neighborhood usually sold before listings were in print, often going for more than the asking price after bidding wars ensued, so from that standpoint things looked good.

But the mental game of preparing for such a drastic lifestyle change was what seized her in her rocky moments. As she walked to the ethnic deli or contemplated the bountiful luxuries of spas and libraries, museums and cultural events . . . when she engaged in conversations with businesswomen or picked up a *New York Times* or *Atlantic Monthly* at the corner newsstand . . . No, she wasn't worried about leaving; it was the thought of what she would be *missing* that occasionally caused her to become nearly overwrought with anxiety. When she was in Partonville, things seemed simpler and very clear. When she was in Chicago, things seemed . . . well, they seemed like what she'd been used to all her life, and the familiar always delivered a certain sense of security—even at its worst.

One thing was for sure, she'd simply have to return to Chicago for her hair appointments. No way was that outrageous Maggie Malone getting her hands on Katie's perfectly colored and styled tresses. Yes, a good dose of the city every six weeks or so would be in order. After all, it was only a half-day away.

Back in Partonville, the little Vine Street home was all safe and up to code in every possible way. Now complete with ceiling fans and white carpeting in the living room and a new sink and roundie toilet, it patiently awaited Dorothy's arrival. "There's no turning back now, Lord!" Dorothy had announced to the heavens when she set down the pen after signing the final paper. "Yes," Katie had added somewhat pensively, "there's no turning back now."

Dorothy had been extremely lonesome for the city slickers since they departed, even though she and Josh were continuing their daily, sometimes twice-daily, e-mailing and she and Katie spoke about once a week on the phone. Dorothy even received an occasional cheery greeting from Alex. Although Josh and Katie had promised they would return before school began, even if they needed to set up camp once again at the Lamp Post should Dorothy not be quite out of the farm yet, their arrival still seemed a long way off. Truth was, her heart had embraced them as family, and it was as though her own children were once again moving away—at least for a spell.

Dorothy was, however, very eager for her sons and grandchildren to arrive, which they'd be doing within days now. It had been far too long since they'd *all* been together. Jacob Henry hadn't even made it home for Christmas last year. Dorothy feared that his absence, due to the excuse that he just had too much work, had not only wounded his brother, but further widened an awkward gap that had grown between her adult sons. The difference in appearances, priorities and lifestyles of offspring produced by the same parents never ceased to amaze her. Vinnie, as family members often called him, was spontaneous, outwardly emotional, fun-loving and a divorced father of two sons living in the suburbs of Colorado. He was about her height, had sandy hair and had always been a tad on the chunky side. Jacob was a stoic, single, well-to-do lawyer living on the East Coast who, the last few years, often seemed buried in his work. He was dark complexioned, more than six feet tall and solid as a rock, working out at a health club nearly daily.

Nevertheless, the brothers had been equally stunned at what seemed like their mother's sudden decision to sell Crooked Creek. And the grandsons were deeply saddened at the thought that they might no longer get to visit their grandma at the farm. But in their own way, they were all relieved she'd be in town, closer to friends. Vinnie especially had been vocal about his mom's being isolated so far out in the country at her age, and he worried about her driving. The last time he'd been home and she'd driven them into town was almost scary. He wished things in his life could have worked out differently so that he could have taken over the farm and kept it in the family. As fate would have it, however, marriage, divorce, job security and young children whose mother had moved them to Colorado—and no way would he be separated from them—had made that impossible.

Everyone knew if Caroline Ann, who was closer to Vinnie in personality and who loved the land as powerfully as her mother, had lived, there wouldn't be any question that Crooked Creek Farm would continue to flourish and be loved under her passionate care. But as his father used to say, "Sometimes it's just time to let go. And once you do, never look back." Wise, and also easier said than done.

Dorothy began spending a bit of time each day perusing the house and occasionally putting a few items in a box she kept on the back porch for the sale. She figured she'd have Earl take it to the barn next time he visited. She started taping stickers to items she wondered if one son or the other might want, as well as cataloguing them in a notebook so she wouldn't forget their whereabouts, knowing her time with her sons would fly by and that they would need to make the most of it. She wasn't sure if they'd both get to come back for the auction or not, and she surely didn't want to let go of any sentimental items that would grieve one of her sons later.

Some items simply wouldn't fit in her new home. Others were family treasures that Dorothy decided were best passed on now, while she could still remember and talk about their stories. She recalled how sad it was for her after her parents were gone, the day she realized that with them had gone so many of the stories. "After all," her mother used to say, "how would we even define ourselves if it weren't for our stories?" Dorothy had thought she'd always remember the details her mom so often repeated about this and that, but alas, she did not.

Dorothy wandered over to the hutch and picked up the beautiful hand-painted bowl with the marking "Prussia" on the bottom. Her mother had received it from a friend. What friend and why, Dorothy couldn't recall. She only knew that her mother spoke about it with reverence and a soft heart. "Things like this ought to have dates and stories attached to them, Sheba." Sheba rose from her slumber and trotted over to where Dorothy stood, fully expecting Dorothy at least to toss her a treat for her trouble. When she didn't, Sheba actually made a groaning sound when she yawned before resetting herself and entering back into her slumber. "Sometimes we just don't get what we expect, do we, dearie?" Dorothy said to her lazy dog, contemplating the deep truth in her own statement.

Suddenly she was overwhelmed again with all that was before her. She decided to head upstairs early and check her e-mail one last time before retiring. Once she sat down at her computer, however, she couldn't help but open a new file she had named "Family Stories." She determined right then and there that in her spare time—as much for cathartic release as for the recording of family history—she would write up all the details she could remember about life on the farm . . . this person and that . . . family events. . . . She would begin tomorrow by writing up the story about the basketball backboard. She knew the boys would appreciate that. The boys and their boys and . . .

She wandered into the spare bedroom that she used as a guest room and opened the lid on the old wooden trunk filled with photographs. Picking up a small handful, she began to label the backs of the photos of those people she could identify. Then she stood for a long while studying an ancient tin photo. "Land's sakes, Sheba! I have no idea who one single person in this photo is!" The thought made her feel so sad, she tossed all the pictures back into the trunk and let the lid slam down, rather than gently snapping it into place the way she usually did.

"Lord, it's just too much for an old woman. Too much to let go of. Too much to remember. Too much!"

By the time she took off her clothes, put on her pj's and swiped her face with a warm washcloth, she was plumb worn out. She tossed her partial plate into the container and didn't even bother to fill it with water and drop in a tablet. She'd do that in the morning. She lowered herself into her prayer chair, turned on the small lamp, tossed a blanket over her legs and picked up her Bible. There was only one cure for this type of loneliness, sorrowful and overwhelming, and that was her evening moment with The Big Guy. Psalms, it would be. No doubt about it. Flipping open her Bible, immediately she spotted words she'd highlighted in bright yellow during a previous quiet moment. They were the closing words to the Nineteenth Psalm: "Let the words of my mouth and the meditation of my heart be acceptable in Thy sight, O Lord, my rock and my redeemer." She reread the passage three times, then closed her Bible and her eyes.

"Oh, Lord, how I complain. And they're all good things I complain about! Parents who loved me, worldly goods that have helped make my life a comfort, my own children coming to see me, the chance to move to the security of a nice small house near my good friend May Belle, not a financial care in the world . . .

"Lord, forgive my complaining self and let the words of my mouth not be ones of more complaint. But thanks for listening to my complaints anyway, and for loving me even when complaining is what I'm doing. Amen."

"Jessica, it's Katie!"

"Katie! I was just thinking about you, thinking about how much I miss you! Honestly, I was out pulling weeds around the front porch, remembering our conversation about parenting that evening, and . . . then the phone rang . . . and it's YOU! Oh, it's YOU!"

Katie took in how wonderful it felt to be so happily acknowledged. "You know, I've thought about that night many times myself. You might have a hard time believing this, but that was one of the first times in my life I had ever shared such a vulnerable piece of myself with anyone, let alone someone I barely knew."

"Well, you were definitely *my* angel. Up until that very moment I thought I was the only mom in the world who didn't instinctively and automatically know everything."

"Listen to us! We sound like the mutual admiration society in full bloom," Katie said, then they both laughed.

"Did you need something?" Jessica asked when their laughter subsided.

"Yes." A long pause ensued. "Just to hear your voice." The statement was received with silence on the other end, and finally Katie asked Jessica if she was still there.

"Yes," Jessica said right after she sniffled. "You have no idea how timely your call is. It's been one of *those* days. For the first time I tried to use the breast pump. I've never felt so ridiculous in my life. Did you ever use one of those things?"

"Heavens, no!" Katie was even a bit embarrassed at the question. "To be honest with you, I just didn't think I'd be very good at nursing. I found the entire idea intimidating. Bottles all the way. I know that sounds silly, but that's exactly how I felt. I have to admit that I've always been a little envious of those women like yourself who just seem more comfortable with their own skin and womanhood."

"And I've always felt a little envious of women who are more independent than me."

"Oh, Jessica, I watch you and Paul and Sarah Sue together and . . . why is it we always think we need what we don't have?" The unanswerable question hung in the air for a moment.

"When do you think you'll be coming back to Partonville, Katie?"

"We're both hoping to find an excuse to head that way again real soon, although we've certainly got our hands full, what with the move and all. I've been making lots of phone calls, getting school records transferred, tasks like that. Josh is so happy to be leaving Latin that he doesn't much care *where* he goes, as long as it isn't there again. I imagine this will be a bit more difficult than he's picturing, but we'll just take it one step at a time."

"I hate to cut this off, Katie, but Sarah Sue is beginning to squeak, and I better get to her before she winds herself up into full-blown hysteria. I am just *so* glad you called! You know your rooms will be waiting when it's time for your return, if Dorothy isn't out of the farm yet. Not only are you my friend, but you're my best client!"

"I'll keep in touch, and you do the same. I'm sure my home number is in your records."

"This is a bit embarrassing, Katie, but we're having to watch our pennies since Sarah Sue arrived, so I probably won't be phoning very often, which doesn't mean I won't be thinking about you!"

"Jessica, I'm so glad you mentioned that. I have an 800 number. Let me give it to you." By the time Jessica had written it down, Sarah Sue was at full volume, and the women said their good-byes over the desperate cries of a heart-shaped mouth.

"The meeting will come to order," Gladys said, pounding the gavel on the table. "The meeting WILL come to order! It is seven-thirty-four already!" One thing was for sure, it wasn't Jessica's fault they were tardy, because after last month's fiasco she'd made it a point to arrive five minutes early. No, it wasn't Jessica's fault. It was all the conversation about Dorothy and her impending move. *Dorothy this and Dorothy that,* Gladys thought. Enough was enough.

"It can be noted that everyone is present. The secretary will now read the minutes from last month's meeting."

Quickly Dorothy handed the typed-up notes to Jessica. Although Jessica wished she'd had a chance to read through the minutes privately before she had to read them aloud, she started right in without hesitation, desiring to please Gladys—if that was humanly possible. There were a few snickers choked back as Jessica read the ongoing commentaries Dorothy had interjected into that near-hostile last meeting, but nevertheless, the minutes were approved as read.

Dorothy then read the treasurer's report, letting everyone know that flowers had been sent on behalf of the Social Concerns Committee to the DeKalb family upon the passing of their father. Other than that, there had been no income and no further expenses.

"Moving right on to old business, then," Gladys said. Dorothy's hand shot up in the air before the statement was all the way out of Gladys's mouth.

"Yes, Dorothy. You have something to report?"

"Actually, I have something to ask. Something highly unusual, I know, but urgent and important. I'm wondering if it might be possible to have our Fall Rummage Sale a week early this year, that last weekend in August before the holiday weekend."

"Did you just listen to yourself, Dorothy?" Gladys asked. "Fall sale in August? That doesn't even make sense. Fall does not begin until September."

Dorothy decided that rather than taking on the issue of fall versus Labor Day—which is when the sale was but which also wasn't fall—she'd just stick with the matter at hand. "As you know," she said, casting her eyes toward the other committee members, "I'm going to be moving into town. Not only that, but Katie Durbin will likely move into the farm as soon as I'm out. Although she is not pushing me in the least, even though she now officially owns Crooked Creek, it would be wonderful if she could get herself and her son settled before school starts and not have to deal with all *this* commotion on the heels of taking possession."

"I do not believe an out-of-towner getting settled before school starts is *our* problem, Dorothy. And frankly, I'm surprised you'd even bring up such a request."

"She is no longer an out-of-towner, Gladys. She is now officially a property owner right here in our community, which officially makes her one of *us*." May Belle nodded her head in agreement, as did Jessica. Nellie Ruth's face was neutral, since she was pondering the possible ramifications of changing the date of something that was so well known and established throughout the area to take place on Labor Day weekend.

"Dorothy, you need to bring this up as a motion before we pursue further discussion," said May Belle, this year's sergeant at arms.

"I move we move our Fall Rummage Sale to mid-August," Dorothy said. Jessica seconded the motion.

"Any discussion?" Gladys asked.

Nellie Ruth raised her hand, and the chair recognized her.

"I am wondering if it might not work against us to tamper with the date. I mean, folks around here have been coming to our sale Labor Day weekend for years. Why, I imagine some of them already have their calendars marked."

"I quite agree," Gladys said, yanking on the bottom of her jacket. A silence hung in the air as the ladies contemplated the situation. All that could be heard was Jessica, crunching on one of May Belle's pecan crispies.

"I agree, too," Dorothy said, stunning everyone. "Nellie Ruth makes a good point. We *don't* want to jeopardize the strength of the sale by messing with a date people are familiar with." Dorothy had heard the faint whisper of *slow down* in her head. "Besides, as I consider it now, I don't think we can be properly ready if we lose a week of planning at this stage in the game. I can go ahead and begin moving into town, and Katie can go ahead and move into the farm if she wants to. She's been so good to me thus far that I can't imagine she won't be totally understanding about *whatever* it is we have to do. After all, much of what we're selling is from her aunt's home anyway. Yes, I imagine it will be all right. Madam President," Dorothy said, looking Gladys square in the eye, "I withdraw my motion."

"So do I even write all that down, then?" Jessica mumbled through her mouthful of cookie.

Gladys sighed and rolled her eyes. "Of COURSE you write all that down, Jessica! It happened, didn't it?"

"Sometimes it's hard to tell *what* exactly happens in these meetings, Gladys." That coming from the mouth of the ever-gentle Nellie Ruth!

12

⚜ ⚜ ⚜

Although Dorothy hadn't been driving The Tank much lately, realizing that she somewhat unnerved herself when she did, the car still behaved badly. The intermittent troubles continued to cause bucking and kicking, backfiring and cranking. She phoned Arthur before leaving for her hair appointment, hoping she could stop by early and have him take another look. Unfortunately, the Landerses weren't home, leaving her, Sheba and The Tank simply to endure the herky-jerky ride into town.

As Dorothy was merging onto the square, a giant blue garbage truck groaned onto it at the same time, one 90-degree turn ahead of her. When Dorothy was readying for her turnoff to La Feminique Hair Salon & Day Spa, The Tank suddenly developed a bad case of sputtering and coughing, sounding as if it was threatening a death rattle. Dorothy stomped harder on the accelerator when the car nearly died out, hoping to gun enough fuel or whatever into *whatever* to keep her from dying.

"Come on, sweetie! Come ON!" Dorothy coaxed as she gripped the wheel, neck lunging forward and backward as The Tank hopped along, backfiring once between lunges. Sheba had long since jumped down to the floor, where she remained. "Just get me to—"

BLAMMO! Just when Dorothy once again stepped heavily on the pedal to keep The Tank running, she decided to run momentarily on her own, causing Dorothy to accelerate so quickly that she nose-dived The Tank right into the back of the garbage truck. The Lincoln was such an old, heavy car that the truck driver, upon feeling the solid impact, slammed on his brakes, causing The Tank's bumper to hook onto the back apparatus. It looked like she had bitten the truck in its hindquarters and simply wouldn't let go. Dorothy was shaken and becoming breathless, the ache in her chest beginning to form. Her purse, containing the nitroglycerin tablets, had slid onto the floor upon impact and was just out of her reach with her seat belt on. Somehow she couldn't seem to collect herself to unbuckle it.

The incident took place right in front of Harry's. Regulars, already alerted by the backfiring that The Tank was on the square, witnessed the entire episode. Stools and tables were cleared immediately as everyone came running out to the street. The driver of the garbage truck opened Dorothy's door and inquired if she was okay. Although she couldn't recall his name, she recognized him as someone who'd long ago played tuba in the grammar school band.

Arthur arrived at Dorothy's passenger side door and flung it open. Dorothy, speaking in a weak voice, said, "Oh, Arthur! Would you please hand me my handbag?" Although he thought Dorothy must be delirious—for certainly no one was thinking about theft at *this* moment—he did as he was asked. Dorothy stuck her arm deep into her giant pink bag and began to thrash around its contents until her hand landed on the now familiar pill bottle. While everyone who had gathered around the car watched,

Dorothy opened the bottle, retrieved one of the little pills and put it under her tongue. She leaned her head back onto the headrest and closed her eyes.

"Call 911!" Jessie hollered. Although Dorothy quietly protested, no one was paying any attention to her "I'm fine." They wanted her to get to a hospital and *now*! They also wondered what on earth she'd popped into her mouth.

By the time the ambulance arrived, her dizzy spell, sometimes caused by the nitroglycerin, had begun to pass and Dorothy's coloring had returned. Doc Streator arrived at the same time as the ambulance.

"Oh, Doc, call off the hounds. I'm not dead. Not yet," she said, mustering a feeble grin.

"Just stay still, Dorothy. Let the paramedics have their fun, okay? It's been a while since they've had a drill with a real live person. They've about worn that dummy out for lack of real victims." When he picked up her hand to take her pulse, he noticed her fingers were still clutched around the prescription bottle, and he gave her an approving wink and nod.

"Why, Doc," Dorothy said as she studied his eyes for a sign of the seriousness of her condition, "are you calling me a dummy?"

"Of course not, Dorothy. I'm calling you a real live person," he said as he gently set her hand in her lap after taking note of her pulse. "And I suspect you're going to remain that way for a spell yet." He knew she was examining him, trying to glean his opinion as to how she *really* was. Thankfully, he had spoken what he believed to be the absolute truth of that moment, barring any internal injuries that had not yet revealed themselves. Although she was shaken, she otherwise appeared to be fine. He did suspect, however, that she'd have a bruised chest from the yank of the seat belt upon impact.

As Dorothy was taken off to the hospital in the back of the ambulance, Jessie at her side, The Tank was dragged off behind the garbage truck so the square could be opened up to the traffic that had accumulated, like tentacles on an octopus, sprawling out from the head of the square. The police were already trying to make sense of what had happened, gathering reports from all the eyewitnesses, who were not only plentiful but all talking at the same time.

"Well, it was just a matter of time," Cora Davis snapped to Arthur, who was standing next to her, watching The Tank disappear around the corner. "That woman has been asking for it for years, the way she drives."

"That *woman*," Arthur said with not an ounce of kindness in his voice, "is Dorothy Jean Wetstra. And that *woman* has never asked for a thing in her life. She's one of the most givin' women I have ever been rightly honored to know!" With that, he spat on the ground, spun on his heels, picked up Sheba, hopped in his truck and headed for the hospital. Although Cora Davis might—*might*—have spoken the truth about Dorothy's driving, Arthur wasn't about to give her an ounce of satisfaction by affirming her mean-spirited and poorly timed comment.

"Katie," Jessica said. "I'm phoning with some disturbing news . . . although I want you to know before I tell you anything else that she's basically all right."

"Who? Dorothy?"

"Yes."

"NO! What's happened to DOROTHY?" Katie screeched,

surprised at the intensity of her own reaction upon learning *something* had happened to her.

"She was in an accident on the square. From what I've heard, her car ran into the back of a garbage truck. Although she was taken to the hospital for observation, word is that other than being a bit shaken and probably bruised from the seat belt, she'll be released tomorrow."

"Released? Are they *sure* she's okay?"

"Honestly, the way Dorothy is loved by everyone in this town, I am sure they wouldn't release her unless they believed it was okay to do so."

"She's not going back out to the farm by herself, is she?"

"No. Although that's what she wanted to do, she reluctantly agreed to stay in town at May Belle's for at least a night so May Belle and Earl can keep an eye on her. Besides, it's not clear to me if The Tank is drivable or not. Apparently something's been wrong with it anyway, and that had something to do with the accident. Word is, it was tangled and attached to the back of the garbage truck and simply hauled off somewhere. If I know Dorothy, though, she'll be back out to the farm in short order."

"When is her family arriving?" Katie asked.

"You know, I'm not sure. But I'll find out and call you back. I'll also let you know if anything changes, okay? Promise."

Katie's breath caught in her throat. To think that something might change with Dorothy was more than she could stand. It occurred to her that Dorothy was beginning to feel more like a mother than a friend, and fear gripped her heart.

"The prayer tree at church has already been notified," Jessica said. "We're all praying for her complete and swift recovery and that she will feel God's presence as she heals. And that she will take good care of herself!"

Although Katie wasn't sure what a prayer tree even was, it somehow gave her a sense of peace to know people were praying. Prayer had never seemed to do much for *her* life, but perhaps it would for a godly woman like Dorothy, as Edward Showalter had referred to her. But without even giving it further thought, Katie found that deep within herself, she was already saying, *God, watch over my dearest Dorothy.*

Katie didn't relish having to give Josh this information, knowing he'd be very upset at the news. Within five minutes of telling him, they agreed that they would be heading back to Partonville quicker than they had thought, at least for a short visit. When Josh said, "Oh, Mom! We *have* to go see for ourselves," Katie knew they did.

Dorothy learned that Katie and Josh would be arriving in Partonville for a visit the day after tomorrow, the same day as her family. She was beside herself with joy that they'd all get to meet! She invited Katie and Josh to stay out at the farm with her, but Katie insisted she'd already have a full house. Katie also suspected that were she and Josh to stay at the farm, their presence might appear to Dorothy's sons to be invasive at best and way too pushy at worst. Besides, Katie was happy to be able to spend more time with Jessica, and she just wasn't mentally ready yet to be sleeping at the farm—although, barring any unforeseen circumstances, it wouldn't be long now until she must, night after night after night. Her brownstone was already sold—*definitely no turning*

back now—and the closing was scheduled for the last Tuesday in August, right before the Labor Day weekend.

When Katie agreed to that date, it was under the assumption that school wouldn't begin in Hethrow until *after* the holiday and that the Fall Rummage Sale was in the fall, giving them plenty of time at least to get their beds set up at the farm and a skeleton of order put in place before the school year began, and also enough time *before* the sale to rope things off from the public. But now she learned the sale would be on her farm—*my farm, what an odd ring*—the Saturday of the *holiday* weekend! Not only that, but when Josh's high school registration papers arrived, she learned that, rather than starting after the holiday, school began the day before. *Obviously no parent was on* that *planning committee!* Definitely a Plan B for all these untimely conversions of big events would have to be established, not the least of which would be to deal with the moving company.

When she got to thinking about her timeline, however, what irked her most about the entire transition was that undoubtedly many people would show up at the sale just to get a gander at her and any possible changes to the place. Do some snooping. See what they could learn about the city slickers.

She wondered if they would always be known as the city slickers. She wondered if she would always feel like one. Yes, she wondered . . .

Both Arthur and Dorothy found it unbearable to think The Tank was sitting at the dump, so Arthur had hooked up his tow bar and hauled her back to his shed. He had to find out what was wrong with her—although he predicted the worst, what with his suspicions from their last visit, which he'd kept to himself. He simply could not let her disappear into the heap of other dead metal soldiers without at least a proper diagnostic burial. Then again, like a phoenix rising from the ashes, The Tank always seemed to find another life. Surely things wouldn't be different this time.

Truth be told, Arthur carried a bit of guilt over the accident. "What kind of mechanic sends a car out onto the streets acting like *that*?" he asked Jessie at the dinner table the night of the accident. Before she could assure him that no one had ever cared more thoroughly for a vehicle than Arthur had for The Tank over the decades, he stormed away from the table, dinner only half eaten, stuck his head into the mouth of The Tank and kept it there until 11:00 P.M., working like a diligent surgeon performing microsurgery by the light of a single bare bulb.

13

❧ ❧ ❧

"**G**randma, we're going on a crawdad hunt," announced Bradley, the older of Dorothy's two teenage grandsons.

"Boys, you haven't been at Grandma's for more than thirty minutes! How about you stay and visit at least a *bit* longer before you run off," their dad said rather than asked.

"Oh, Vinnie, let them go," Dorothy said. "In fact, maybe you ought to go with them! It's not like we don't have the next several days to spend together. When was the last time *you* had yourself a good crawdad hunt?"

"How about we all go on a hunt, then?" Vinnie asked her.

"How about just the men do their manly thing this trip?" Dorothy asked, looking from her grandsons to Vinnie, then to Jacob. "I'd just slow you down."

Vinnie sat there studying his mom. It seemed she'd aged since Christmas, or maybe just gotten frailer, or . . . maybe the wreck had temporarily knocked the energy out of her. Of course, with all this moving stuff and . . .

Vinnie had always been extremely sensitive and intuitive about emotional things, especially concerning his mom. He immediately discerned that it might fret her to think he felt he had to be clinging to her every moment, as though she were going to die on the spot or something. He also figured she was already reading *his* face.

"You know, I think I *could* use a good hunt," he said enthusiastically. "Great suggestion! Wait a minute, boys. Let me change into my shorts. Come on, Jacob, roll up your pant legs."

"Think I'll just sit this one out with Mom. I'm a little travel weary myself, what with trying to tie up all the loose ends at the office before heading out."

"Oh, go ahead on down there, boys," Vinnie said cheerfully. "Just don't start without me, okay? And do not get wet! I repeat, do not get wet." It was, of course, a standing joke of a line. No one ever returned from the creek dry. To do so would be to violate some kind of unspoken law and certainly prove there was no longer fun in the world.

As soon as Vinnie was out of the house, leaving Jacob and his mom alone, Jacob's face turned dead serious. Thus far he'd been pretty quiet. "Mom, are you sure you're going to be up to all this moving? I mean, maybe you should just put it off until—"

Dorothy jumped into the middle of his sentence. "Until when? Until I die and then you boys have to deal with everything? Or I'm drooling and a hundred times as forgetful as I am now? I should say *not*! Besides, I'm ready to move on. Oh, sure, the task sometimes feels a bit overwhelming, but God shores me up when I need it. And now that you boys are here to help me sort through things, truth is, I'm finding the notion of being in town a welcome one. I'm surprised at my own anticipation. And think about it—I've never once had a chance to decorate from scratch. I was born into my mother's home, and my mother's home, in many ways, it has remained." Jacob's eyes revealed his dismay at this thought. "It's time to PLAY HOUSE!" Dorothy's gusto and hand slamming on the table caused him to reel back a bit. "I'm even thinking of painting a ceiling fire engine red!"

"Mom, tell me you're not thinking about getting up on ladders or . . ."

"Good heavens no, Jacob! I know of a right dandy handyman who will do anything I ask for a very fair fee. Why, he's already gussied the place up and brought everything up to code. I can't wait for you to see my little dollhouse. The good Lord has watched over me all these years here at the farm, and I reckon He'll continue to do just as good of a job in the next place. Besides, May Belle will only be a few doors away. Imagine getting to move nearly next door to your lifelong best friend! Why, I bet you won't even recognize me by Christmas, I'll be so fat. I won't even have to drive *anyplace* to get my sweet treats—I can just hobble over to her house in a flash. Like a little piggy!"

"Mom, I'm serious."

"Jacob Henry, you are *always* serious! Just like that Katie Durbin. I mean to tell you, the two of you would probably tie in a contest to see who can be the most serious."

"And that's another thing, Mom. You seem to be getting awfully close with this woman you hardly know. I get the feeling she's been pressuring you." His mom opened her mouth to speak, but Jacob beat her to what he was sure was her next statement. "Now, I know the documents were all in order, but I can't help but wonder if you're not being taken for some kind of ride."

"Jacob Henry Wetstra! I will *not* have you talking about my friend like that. I simply will *not*." Dorothy launched up out of her chair, then with determination, lowered her voice and continued. "God brought Katie Durbin into my life when I most needed answers. Somehow I just could not trust that the Craig & Craig Developers' land offer was fair, not to mention the decision itself. I was nearly beside myself fretting about whether to sell or stay . . . considering the fact that progress will one day come to Partonville, ready or not.

"Son, don't you know I've prayed long and hard about all this? And there, by the power of God's grace and His almighty ability to have something good come out of the death of Tess Walker, came Katie Durbin to my rescue. And don't you think for a *moment* God isn't doing a mighty work in *her* life, too, not to mention His healing balm I see being spread between her and her son, Josh!"

Her voice had escalated in urgency, volume and pitch. She once again regrouped herself and reached across the table for her son's hand. "Jacob, I know you sometimes wonder about God. But let me tell you something, God never has to wonder about you. He *knows*, son. He KNOWS!"

Jacob's serious eyes began to flick around from his mom's eyes to her forehead to the kitchen cabinets, then out the window. Dorothy knew it was time to change the subject. Never did she want to be one of those people who made others uncomfortable by diatribing about her Lord and turning them off rather than simply letting her light shine all over them, beckoning them to draw nearer.

"Speaking of May Belle," she said, circling back into her own conversation, "she's invited the entire lot of us over for dinner tomorrow evening—you, me, Vinnie and the boys, and Katie and Josh. I imagine the boys will surely get along swell!"

"I thought Miss Durbin and her son were back in Chicago," he said flatly.

"Well, they're coming back tomorrow for a little visit. Once Jessica Joy phoned Katie about my accident, she and her son, well, they just wanted to come give me a hug, is how they put it. And I've surely never been one to deny anyone the opportunity to do *that*! Anyway, I'm so glad you'll all have a chance to meet them. Get to know them a bit. Maybe, *maybe* even get to like them," Dorothy said, with a wink. "Don't you want to meet the people who will soon be caring for Crooked Creek Farm?" She didn't wait for an answer.

"May Belle said an early dinner would be waiting for us around five-thirty, so I told her that's just when we'd arrive. Do you reckon we can all squeeze into your rental car?"

"I guess," he said flatly. "It's a roomy SUV like the one I drive at home."

"Sounds like Katie . . ." Dorothy cut herself off, realizing she needed to back down for the time being from mentioning her name every other sentence.

"Right," Jacob said with sarcasm in his voice. "Sounds like we could be twins."

"Oh, child of mine. Give yourself a chance to be happy, son. Happy feels so good."

Jacob headed down to the creek to find his brother and nephews, leaving Dorothy alone in the house. About forty-five minutes after his departure there was a sturdy, three-bang knock on her kitchen door. Dorothy figured it was the gang returning, so she just hollered, "For goodness sakes! Just come on in!" Arthur appeared and stood before her, just inside her kitchen door. He was twiddling his thumbs out of nervous habit. "Dorothy, what I have to tell you is not going to make you happy. No, not one bit." The air crackled with doom. Dorothy could count on one hand the number of times Arthur had stopped by her house unannounced. Surely she was about to hear something truly horrible.

"I'm afraid The Tank's sick. Terminal-like sick."

"No," Dorothy said in a hushed whisper.

"Yes," Arthur replied, matching his voice to her tone. A moment of staring passed between them as Dorothy searched Arthur's face, hoping he'd break into laughter at any moment.

"It can't *be!*" she finally said, realizing Arthur wasn't kidding.

"Well, it is."

"You mean to tell me I broke her for good with my latest trick?" Dorothy's heart felt as if it were jumping into her throat. She had to think a minute whether she might need a nitroglycerin tablet, then she realized she was just nervous, not dying—although with *this* kind of news, one could hardly tell the difference.

"Dorothy, ya know better than to think a little accident with a garbage truck could kill The Tank. If *that* was the case, you'd have plumb done her in about three wrecks ago. No, I don't mean to tell ya that. I mean to tell ya all that buckin' and kickin' she's been a-doin' was more than the need for spark plug cleanin' and wire adjustin'. I mean to tell ya she's got herself what I feared most when I saw the little puddle in the dirt after ya left the last time, and that's a cracked engine block. Sometimes those two can act alike, but eventually the sad truth reveals itself." Arthur had removed his hat and was holding it in both hands, which hung down in front of him, as though he was paying his last respects.

"And you can't replace a cracked whatever? I mean, you can't weld it or something?"

"I mean, although she ain't plumb seized up yet, she's close to it. I ain't gonna lie to you, Dorothy, she's gaspin' for breath, and there's just not much more that can be done. And you know if there was, I'd be a-doin' it!"

A long pause ensued, during which time they each stared at their own hands.

"You say she's gasping but not dead? You reckon I could squeeze just a couple more years out of her, Arthur?" A hopeful tone had welled up from within her.

"I reckon you—and especially *you*, Dorothy—couldn't squeeze but a couple more miles out of her before she froze up quick as a warm tongue on an ice-cold bumper."

Again the atmosphere crackled with tension as voices slipped away into the deep recesses of foreboding silence and worried imaginations, wherein one's worst fears play out. After a long while they heard the happy voices of hunters coming up from behind the barn toward the house. Dorothy straightened herself to her full five-foot, ten-inch frame, reared her shoulders back and said, "We'll figure what to do later, Arthur. Goodness me, with all the changes I'm going through, I might just get me a shiny new SUV! Now, not a word of this to my family, Arthur. I don't want to spoil their first day here fretting them with my latest dilemma. For now, let's just keep this to ourselves. The boys will be driving me around anyway while they're here."

"You want me to tow The Tank out to the junkyard, Dorothy?" It almost looked like Arthur was about to cry. He asked the question with such reverence that it broke both their hearts. Dorothy's eyes misted up a bit, but she swallowed down her rising vulnerabilities. The boys were almost to the back door.

"Goodness me no, Arthur! I haven't had a chance to pay my final respects. Just leave her in the shed for the time being, if that's okay."

"Yup, I reckon that'll be just fine . . . for now. We'll talk later." He turned to head for her front door, so as not to have to speak to anyone right now. Dorothy understood the soft heart behind this gruff man and didn't even ask if he wouldn't like to stay and say hello to everyone. She knew they'd have a chance to chat later. But not now. Now was the time for Arthur to be allowed to grieve in privacy, for after all, one of his very own, oldest, best and most personal patients was gasping for breath.

14

Jessica couldn't remember ever having been this excited about the arrival of a motel guest. Coincidentally, her artistic side was finally beginning to reblossom, and a creative vision to add a few unique touches to what had now become known as Katie's Room ignited in her muse. For the first time since Sarah Sue had been born, Jessica found herself with the motivation *and* the courage to take a mother-daughter excursion—without Paul's assistance.

A few weeks before she delivered her baby, she saw some wonderful baskets in the Now and Again Resale Shop in Yorkville. Even if they were no longer there, she would still enjoy the exploratory prowling, as she liked to call it. "Feels like mining for gold when I dig through the piles in resale shops," she once told Paul, who had, of course, just stared at her in amazement that she could be so easily entertained. Her enthusiasm was one of the things he most loved about her.

Sarah Sue screamed the entire time Jessica was buckling the squirmy little bugger, as her daddy often referred to her, into her car seat. It almost caused Jessica to bail on the entire idea. But she was spurred on by her vision of what she was going to do with those baskets. The moment she pulled out of the motel parking lot, Sarah Sue nodded off. Jessica wondered why it had taken her so long to test this tried-

and-true mother's trick she'd heard so much about. She'd also once heard a mother say that she put her baby on top of a running dryer to calm her down, whether she had clothes to dry or not. Jessica used to wrinkle her brow at moms who talked like that, but that was before *she* had become a sleep-deprived mother of a screaming baby. It now crystallized in her mind that she would try any and all suggestions given to her by mothers who had run the course.

Once parked in front of Now and Again, Jessica attempted another first. She boldly began to strap on the baby gift she'd been given by Nellie Ruth at the church baby shower. The contraption held your infant to your chest or your back, depending upon how you rigged the thing. After several failed attempts to get it facing in the right direction and the straps adjusted to the right lengths, she finally nestled Sarah Sue to her chest. Although the wriggly babe looked a bit puzzled by it all, she made not a peep while her mommy began her prowling.

Within minutes, Jessica had retrieved quite the pile from the Crafters' Corner of the shop: three baskets of varying sizes; two half-rolls of grosgrain ribbon, one red and one brown; one bolt of jute; two packages of brown pipe cleaners; and a swatch of fabric with barns on it. She had no idea how, but her artist's eye had always had a way of pulling things together in the most pleasing ways. It crossed her mind that flying by instinct would be a wonderful attribute to have as a mother. Perhaps she would have to learn to approach parenting more like art. Perhaps.

Katie and Josh arrived in Partonville three hours later than they'd thought they would. There had been a multi-vehicle traffic accident on the Chicago outskirts, and they had sat at a complete stop for nearly an hour before their portion of the five-mile backup even began to move—and this after a late start. Katie just had not been able to get off the phone with one wheeler-dealer in commercial real estate development after another, each wondering if she was soliciting or accepting partners in her latest adventure. Mac Downs, who had been offering her a premium partnership for some time now, was relentlessly tickling her business prowess, phoning her at least once a week in his admitted attempt to wear her down, one time even sending her four dozen roses with a card saying, "Whatever it takes . . . name your price." Once word had gotten out about her impending move, gossip quickly spread about her "land killing" in southern Illinois. Playing her cards close to her chest—and also, in her weakest moments, still occasionally waffling about her ability to live in the country, not to mention the never-ending lure of the Big Deal conquest—she neither confirmed nor denied her intentions about development. The only thing that was for sure beyond anyone's belief was that Kathryn Durbin would be moving to the country for any reason other than money. She had, after all, spent the last decade cultivating and validating her reputation. Nobody believed for a moment she had helped some old lady donate— *donate*—land to a conservation district for a park because she felt sorry for her.

One thing was clear to her, however, and that was that she truly *had* found herself worrying about Dorothy and missing her open conversations with Jessica. For the first time in her life, she sighed with relief when she saw the WEL-COME TO PARTONVILLE sign flash by. When they pulled into the Lamp Post lot, Jessica, with Sarah Sue strapped to her chest, literally bounded out the office door to greet them. Within a minute, Katie had exited her SUV, Jessica had run up, arms outstretched, to hug her and they had learned in a wink of a moment how to hug around a baby strapped to one of their midriffs. "Might as well be pregnant again!" Jessica said. Immediately, they both rippled with the familiar and knowing laughter of motherhood friends.

Dorothy and her sons and grandsons began the arduous project of sifting through their heritage. They were at it by 8:30 A.M., having gone to bed early the night before, after the traditional Wetstra bonfire. Just behind the barn was a fire pit encircled with field rocks and decades-old, hand-hewn benches made of log rounds with giant split branches laid across them. By the time the major constellations were identified—always a must on clear nights—and the last roasted marshmallow was down the hatch, everyone was yawning.

The plan of action established at a kitchen-table meeting over breakfast was to begin upstairs in the spare bedroom, since it had the most available floor space. As Katie and Josh had done when beginning to clear Aunt Tess's place, so had the Wetstras tapped Your Store for boxes, each writing his name in Magic Marker across the top of his designated box.

Items that no one wanted would be moved to the hay wagon they had hooked up to the old John Deere and parked near the front porch for easy staging. When the wagon got full, they would haul it up into the barn—one grandchild hanging over each tractor fender—and unload. Since it had been determined that Katie now wasn't moving in until after the auction, large furniture items earmarked for it could be left in place in the house. Undoubtedly, furniture displayed best in place and perspective anyway. Vincent thought up the idea of designating them as auction items by applying large yellow Post-it Notes with a bold *A* drawn on them; things Dorothy would be moving to her new home on Vine would have a blue Post-it with a *V*. In order to accommodate the masses of people who would be entering the farmhouse, however, all that could be hauled out to the barn would be.

The men in Dorothy's life, as she took to calling the working band, were at first reluctant to stake claim to items and move them out of what often felt like sacred territory and into a box, feeling that they were picking clean the bones of their mother's life while she was still among them. Dorothy finally convinced them that it gave her great joy and a true sense of peace to witness her heritage moving on to where it rightfully next belonged. "And don't worry," she'd told them with a tone of finality and authority, "if you've got your eyes set on something I still want to call my own, I won't be shy about telling you so! Going about the business of life—and preparing for the day when the good Lord calls me home—in *this* manner sure beats a family having to go through what poor Katie Durbin endured after her aunt died and left all that chaos."

"Gads, Mom," Vinnie exclaimed, "is that what you've got us doing here? Preparing for the day you . . . you . . ."

"Die," Dorothy said matter-of-factly. "Yes, and no, son. Yes, of course I'm going to die. We're *all* going to die. But I'm also plumb ready to move on to what comes next before I do." With that, she picked up the pad of Post-it Notes, drew a big *A* on it, ripped off the sheet and slapped it on the white headboard of what was now the guest bed, but which long ago used to be her daughter's. "It's time the energy of another little girl brought new life to this old wood."

"Grandma, we'll need a bed to sleep in when we come visit again," Steven protested.

"Don't you worry, honey. Grandma will have a place for you. I might just get me one of those phooey-tons. Isn't that what you younguns like nowadays?" She didn't wait for an answer. "Or maybe I'll just get me a new couch with a hideaway bed, or an air mattress that blows itself up like I've seen on TV or . . . who knows *what* I might just go and do!" She whirled on her heels and moved to the items across the room. "Next!" she yelped without batting an eye.

"You mean futon, don't you, Grandma?" Bradley asked, after snickering under his breath.

"Of course I mean futon," Dorothy said. "I just wanted to see if you were paying attention."

When the first wagon-load was hauled behind the chugging green John Deere into the barn, Dorothy played boss lady, assigning and directing which items she wished to be donated to the guild sale and which were to be set at the opposite side of the barn for her personal estate auction. Although her sons noticed she often sat down for this bossing process, neither mentioned to the other or to their mother that they'd noticed toward the end of the day that she'd been doing more sitting than standing.

"Jessica! You MADE THESE?" Katie held the baskets, one in each hand, high up in the air and turned them this way and that as she marveled at the craftsmanship.

"Yes, ma'am. All by my lonesome. Of course, Sarah Sue contributed her bits of drool here and there, didn't you, Muffin?" she asked her awake yet content baby strapped to her chest as she stroked the top of her fine, slick blonde hair toward her forehead.

"Where in the world did you get such lovely baskets?"

"Now and Again Resale."

"A *resale store?*"

"Yes, ma'am. And the fabric and the pipe cleaners and the ribbons and . . . everything but the twigs. The twigs I got along the roadside on my way back from Yorkville." She had spent the entire afternoon after her arrival home arranging and rearranging, lost in the timeless bliss of creativity. Nearly as soon as one basket was all set she would begin the other, often scalping items from the first, envisioning how they'd better enhance and intertwine, blend and bend, perfect the lines.

"And how much did it cost you total to make these?"

"Let's see, including the free sticks from nature and the goods I have left over, my total bill, as best I can recall, was about seven dollars."

"For both of them?"

"Yes. Oh, wait, the buttons I attached were already in my sewing kit."

"The buttons," Katie said. She set the baskets down, then picked up the larger of the two so she could explore it with both hands. That was the first she noticed that the few strategically and perfectly placed dangles hanging from the bounty of arching twigs were made out of buttons. "Jessica, you never told me you were an artist!"

"Oh, goodness no, I'm not an artist. I just enjoy doing crafts."

"No. You are an *artist*," Katie said with a definitive tone that left no room for backtalk, especially not from an artist.

"You know," Jessica said while tearing up, "my mom used to call me her little artist every once in a while." She leaned down and kissed the top of Sarah Sue's head as tenderly as if it were the most fragile of hand-blown glass. "And you? You, my little wiggle worm, what will I one day call you?" She closed her eyes and rested her cheek atop her warm baby's head while she maneuvered her forefinger into her daughter's tiny fingers until they nestled round her own.

"Your mother was certainly right to call you that," Katie said reverently. One thought after another began to fly through her head. *Gift of grace. I remember Mom sometimes calling me her blessed gift of grace when I was a child.* She bit her lower lip as she recalled the warm tone in her mother's voice and the way her eyes seemed to cloud over when she would bend down, tilt her daughter's chin upward and utter those words. Then she would swoop Katie up in her arms and hug her tightly. Katie never did quite understand why her mom called her that or what it really meant.

"What do you call Joshua?" Jessica queried between tiny kisses to her child's silky angel hair.

A long silence followed the question. Katie was now chewing on her bottom lip, aghast at her own truth: she had never called him anything other than Josh, Joshua or Joshua Matthew when she was angry. Her son had never heard a sweet, mother's affirmation. Tears started pouring down her cheeks.

"Katie! What is it, honey?" Jessica reached over and took Katie's hand.

"What is it about the two of us being together that causes us to flit so easily between laughter and tears?"

"Hormones," Jessica immediately replied. "Hormones."
Through her tears, Katie began to laugh. She laughed so
long and hard that her laughter spilled over into full-blown
weeping, which of course sent Jessica down the same path.
Before they knew it, they were both heading toward the
bathroom to grab some toilet paper with which to blow
their noses.

15

❧ ❧ ❧

Katie gave an audible sigh of relief when Dorothy, Earl right by her side, greeted her on May Belle's front porch. She was elated to see for herself that Dorothy wasn't bruised from head to toe and that she was quite ambulatory and spunky, albeit a bit slower. Elation was short-lived, however, for as soon as they entered the living room where Dorothy's men were seated, an emotional chill blasted Katie.

Although Vincent had been friendly enough during their introduction, extending his hand in welcome to both Katie and Josh, when it was Jacob's turn to meet the city slickers, he simply glared and nodded his head, leaving Katie's hand awkwardly dangling in front of her. To say he was openly hostile was no exaggeration. Josh, witnessing the overt shunning, quickly stuffed his hands into the front pockets of his blue jeans when it came time for his introduction.

The fact that Dorothy had entered the living room with her arm around Josh's waist and his around hers had unexpectedly tilted her grandsons toward a jealous edge. Although they both shook hands with Josh, the exchange was limp at best. It was obvious they were giving him a careful looking over. He wished Alex had been able to make this trip so he wouldn't feel outnumbered in the teen depart-

142   *Charlene Ann Baumbich*

ment. Dorothy pulled Josh a little closer to her side during the eyeballing interlude, clearly sending a physical message to her grandsons about Josh's being welcome. Sensitive to her grandsons' emotional needs, however, when she finally let go of Josh and after her grandsons reseated themselves, she marched straight across the room to the couch where they had plunked themselves and playfully wiggled her way between them, draping one arm over each of their shoulders.

May Belle appeared from the kitchen, first wiping her hands down the front of her gingham apron, then tucking flyaway hairs behind her ears with her index fingers. She opened wide her stocky arms and greeted Katie and Josh with genuine warmth and welcome, then asked Earl to move a couple of dining room chairs into the living room so the new guests could be seated until it was time for dinner.

"Help yourselves to the snacks there," she said, pointing toward the sectioned, clear-glass food tray carefully arranged atop two flowered napkins. "There's mild Colby cheese and Ritz crackers. The celery sticks are stuffed with cream cheese and a bit of freshly diced chives from my garden. And what can I get you to drink? I made some fresh lemonade, if that sounds all right. Otherwise I've always got iced tea available this time of year. But I tell you, Your Store's lemons were just as ripe and juicy as I have ever seen them!"

"Sold!" Josh said. "Sold on the lemonade."

"Make that two," Katie added.

"You won't be sorry, I guarantee," Dorothy said with gusto, downing a gulp herself. "So how was your trip down, aside from long?" she asked while Josh and Katie seated themselves side by side on the chairs Earl had dutifully pulled into the room—although he had disappeared immediately following.

After a debriefing about the tardy start and the traffic snarl they'd endured, Katie switched the topic to Dorothy's accident. "I am just so relieved to see for myself you're up and about, Dorothy."

"Yeah, I guess the garbage truck driver didn't know Miss Outtamyway was following him, huh?" Josh laughed at his own statement, as did Dorothy. In fact, the two of them got to laughing harder and harder, apparently lost in their own private jokes. Dorothy's men simply looked at both of them as though they were daft.

"Miss out of my way?" Steven finally asked when the laughter died down, looking at his grandmother.

"Oh, that's just the screen name I use for my e-mails with everyone who isn't a blood relative, and the Joshmeister here seems to think that's funny!"

"Joshmeister?" Steven asked again, this time raising his eyebrows and making a face that indicated he thought this all a bit hokey.

For whatever reason, Josh felt compelled to explain. "My buddy Alex started calling me that, and I just ended up keeping it as my e-mail name, for lack of the ability to come up with something more clever." He paused a moment, then added, "And so your grandmother uses that name, too."

Silence. The boys stared at one another, Josh shifting his eyes from Steven to Bradley, then back to Steven again, hoping he'd see some sign of understanding or acceptance cross their faces—which he didn't.

"So, Dorothy," Josh said, breaking the uncomfortable silence, "I didn't know you even had another screen name. What is it?"

"GrandmaDW," she replied. "Doesn't sound as zippy, but it's who I'm proud to be!" She winked at her grandsons, who broke out in grins.

"Mother tells me you're in real estate, Miss Durbin," Jacob said, looking at Katie across the room and over the top of his glasses. "What type of real estate?"

Katie, now venturing into *her* waters, felt her security slip back into place. "Commercial development," she said without apology, "although you might say I'm currently unemployed." *Let him chew on* that *one awhile!*

"Unemployed?"

"Yes." She offered no more, but smiled her most pleasant of smiles.

"Dinner is just about ready," May Belle said, appearing once again in the doorway.

"Can I help you with anything?" Katie asked, rising from her chair, hoping to leave her last statement dangling in the air.

May Belle waved for her to sit back down. "Goodness me no! Why, I've got Earl as busy as a bee in here, and I'm sure he wouldn't want anyone taking over his job. You folks just continue visiting, and I'll be calling you shortly." In a flash, she disappeared back into the kitchen. Soon her happy music of spoons clanking against pans and bowls could be heard loudly rat-a-tatting its way into the living room.

"Did you find you could quit your job *after* securing my mother's estate?" Jacob asked, the tone in his voice accusatory.

Katie opened her mouth to respond, but Dorothy jumped in first. "Jacob Henry," she began, holding the line in her voice from verging into one of chastisement, knowing her son's dander was already raised and that it would only further antagonize and rile him to embarrass him by using her motherly tone, "I do recall telling you, honey, that Katie was not acting in her professional capacity when she purchased the farm. I imagine that just slipped your mind. She bought it as a private citizen who, after years of good investments, is blessed enough by God to have the money to do so, and I continue to be grateful to God for His divine timing."

Jacob looked at his mom, aware of exactly what she was doing: trying to avoid conflict. He swallowed, twice, as though driving down his own words. After all, the deal *was* struck and there was nothing he could do about it. Of *course* he remembered every word his mother had told him about Miss Katie Durbin. Every ongoing word. In fact, it seemed his mother just could not stop talking about her. And like it or not, dinner was now being served to their entire gathering, according to May Belle's announcement. They were each to find their place cards and be seated.

Dorothy and May Belle were seated close together at the head and corner of the ample, ancient table; Jacob was at the foot. Vincent and his sons were along one side; Earl sat next to May Belle and Josh beside him, leaving Katie to fill out the other side—and sitting next to Jacob.

Dorothy gave the blessing, as usual expressing her gratefulness for, and mentioning something unique about, each member seated at the table. Three times throughout her prayer, she repeated the use of the words "My family gathered around me." The third time, Katie's eyes couldn't help but flutter open as she peeked toward Jacob—who was staring straight at her.

"So, has Arthur got The Tank running yet, Dorothy?" Josh queried while scraping the last bits of cherry pie filling off his plate with his dessert fork.

"Yeah, Gram. Good question," Bradley added.

Dorothy slowly wiped her mouth with her napkin, folded it back into a perfect square and set it on the table before she answered. "No. No, he hasn't."

"You know, Mom, I'm surprised *you* haven't mentioned The Tank yet," Vinnie said. "So what's up with her?"

"How long do you think it will be before you've got your wheels back?" Steven asked.

"What's up with The Tank?" Dorothy asked, as though she had to repeat the question to take it in. "I'd say not much."

"What's that supposed to mean, Mom?" Jacob asked, cutting himself another piece of pie, which gave Josh the same idea. Josh quietly asked his mom to please pass him the pie plate when Jacob finished serving himself.

"Just that. No more, no less," Dorothy said.

"So when *will* you have her back?" Josh asked without making eye contact, since he was busy picking up piecrust crumbs that had fallen from his last serving onto May Belle's powder blue tablecloth.

Dorothy watched her own hand nervously play with the edge of her folded napkin, her silence and obvious avoidance in answering eventually commanding everyone's attention. At last she looked up at the staring group and spoke in a voice that was barely audible. "Well, now," she said, drawing a deep breath, "Arthur seems to believe The Tank has given us her last ride."

After a brief pause, Vinnie spoke. "Mom, I'm not sure I understand what you're saying. You mean The Tank is wrecked beyond repair?"

"No, son. I mean The Tank was already having some technical difficulties before the accident, and this just seems to have been her last straw."

"Technical difficulties?" Bradley asked.

"Cracked engine block," Dorothy said, shaking her head back and forth, again staring at her napkin.

May Belle's eyes were as round and nearly as wide open as her favorite pie plate. "Dorothy! You never told me that!"

"I haven't told anyone. I just couldn't bear to hear *myself* say it."

"So now what, Mom?" Jacob asked. Before she could respond, he added, "Surely you're not going to get another car, are you?" Although everyone was thinking that, in Katie's opinion, nobody should be rude enough to ask it!

"Of course Grandma will get another car, Uncle Jacob!" Steven said. "Won't you, Grandma?"

"To tell you the absolute truth, I haven't quite made up my mind *what* I'm going to do, honey. But never you mind, because me and the Lord will work it all out."

"Mother, to get another car at your age seems like a vast waste of money. And after all, you'll be moving into town soon anyway. What on earth would you need a car for?" Jacob's tone of voice came out a bit harsher than he'd meant.

Katie had had it. "So she can visit whomever she likes

whenever she wants!" she snapped. Even though she didn't really think Dorothy should be driving, it was not a *man's* place to tell her when she had to stop!

Jacob's head reared back. "Well, nearly all of her friends live in town, Miss Durbin," he said sarcastically.

"Well, *we* won't. *We* won't live in town. And neither do Arthur and Jessie Landers."

"No. Of course you won't live in town," Jacob tersely said. "You'll be living at Crooked Creek Farm. Or will you? I imagine you could make quite the killing just turning that place over to one of your conglomerates." Jacob pushed himself back in his chair, abruptly stood up and threw his napkin down onto his empty plate, somewhat hovering over Katie, who immediately stood her full height—albeit a good eight or nine inches shorter than Jacob—and tossed her shoulders back.

"Mr. Wetstra. I have every intention of moving onto that farm. AND, with all good will, I even helped your mother donate a portion of that estate to be designated as a park. Not to mention that what I do is none of your business! In fact, it doesn't seem like what your mother does has been much of *your* business lately, either! Maybe that's why she was looking for outside help!"

"NOW, THAT IS ENOUGH!" Dorothy yelled, briskly standing. "That is just enough from *both* of you. Goodness me, I can't remember when I've seen two adults make more of a mountain of mayhem out of a molehill. You'd think I was ten years old, or at the very least as deaf as a post, since you're both talking like I'm not even here!"

Suddenly Dorothy stooped over a bit, leaning on her chair. Before anyone else could react, Earl was out of his chair and behind Dorothy, steadying her in his strong arms.

"Sit down, Dearest Dorothy," he said softly. "Please sit down. Please sit down and be all right." He'd never heard her yell in his life. Although raised voices always sent him scurrying, there was no way he would leave her now.

With May Belle's and Josh's assistance, they pulled out Dorothy's chair and helped get her seated. Earl ran to the kitchen for a glass of water, since that's what he'd been asked to do the last time Dorothy was in distress. Dorothy leaned over in her chair and began fumbling under the table.

"What do you need, Dorothy?" May Belle asked. "Please sit still and just tell me what you need."

"My handbag. Did you see where I put my handbag?"

"I believe it's over there on the couch," May Belle said, glancing that way and then nodding her head with affirmation. "Yes, there it is. You just sit still, dear."

"Get it for me, quick, please," Dorothy said weakly. She raised her hand to her chest. Before May Belle had barely moved, Jacob was back at the table handing the purse to his mother. Dorothy immediately began rifling through it until her hand felt the familiar little bottle. She popped off the lid, removed a tiny pill and slid it under her tongue. "I'll be fine in a minute. Really, I'm fine. Everyone sit down and relax." She smiled faintly, then rested her head on the palm of her hand, her elbow propped on the table.

"What are you taking, Mom?" Vinnie asked.

"Just a little nitroglycerin," Dorothy said. "I'll be better in a jiffy." She lifted her head and broadly smiled at her younger son, trying to reassure him. Earl tapped Dorothy on the shoulder and handed her the giant glass of water he'd retrieved, then he began wringing his hands. Dorothy reached over and rested her hand atop his. "Earl, your Dearest Dorothy is going to be just fine, honey. Thank you so much for the water." She looked at everyone at the table. They were all still standing. "Please sit down. I'm not dead or dying . . . just yet," she said, then she began to laugh. Although they did cautiously sit down, glancing nervously from one to the other, no one else joined her in the laughter.

"Mom, how long have you been using nitroglycerin?" Vinnie asked.

"Oh, just for a while now. Look how quickly it works. It's like a miracle, really. The pain is nearly gone already. I just need to sit here a bit longer, since sometimes the pill makes me kind of woozy—when I don't make myself that way!" Again, she smiled a hearty smile.

"What's wrong with you, exactly, that you need to be taking nitroglycerin?" Jacob asked, trying to hold a soft and reassuring tone to his voice when in fact he was scared and still reeling from Katie's barb—which, although he'd surely never let *her* know it, had pierced his conscience.

"The old ticker's just wearing down a bit. Me and The Tank are just heading toward the end of the road, I reckon."

"Mom! That is not funny!" Vinnie said emphatically.

"Now is not the time for you to lose your sense of humor, Vincent Wetstra. But in fact, I didn't mean for that to be funny. Just honest. And now you know another of the reasons I'm so glad to be moving into town. In fact, it wasn't until this moment that I realized I should not be driving. I imagine since I didn't have the good sense to quit driving on my own, the Lord has just figured out His own way to help me in that decision. Why, I wouldn't put it past Him a bit to be able to put a crack in an engine block, whatever that is!"

"Dorothy!" Josh exclaimed. "You mean you really are going to quit driving?"

Dorothy reached down and picked up Sheba, who was standing on her hind legs and leaning her front paws in Dorothy's lap. "I reckon it's time we two ladies settled down a bit anyway. Since that day I ran you and your mom and Alex off the road, well . . ."

"You WHAT?" Jacob asked.

"It was nothing," Katie said. "It was really nothing. I wasn't looking where I was going either and . . . well, it really was nothing." Josh's mouth flew open.

"No, Katie," Dorothy said. "It *was* something. I have had nightmares about what could have happened had you not driven your vehicle into the ditch to miss me. And me not even knowing what I'd done! I tell you, I have had nightmares. Yes, it's time I turned in my keys before something worse happens."

Nobody said a word. Finally May Belle got up and began clearing the dessert dishes. Josh jumped up to help, but May Belle waved him back down. "Earl, you know what comes next," she said. After May Belle made the round picking up the plates, Earl gathered all the silverware. Still, nobody spoke a word.

"My goodness me!" Dorothy finally exclaimed. "You'd think you were all attending a funeral or something. It's only a car. It's only driving. It's not like I'm turning in my pom-poms—although they'll probably be next."

"Pom-poms?" Jacob asked. "Pom-poms? I don't think I even want to know about them!"

16

❧ ❧ ❧

"**W**here in the *world* does time go?" Dorothy asked Sheba, who simply stared back at her without a single helpful response. They were seated in the kitchen, Dorothy at the table, Sheba curled at her feet. Dorothy was sorting through piles of her ancient, mismatched everyday tableware. She'd concluded she was going to put all her oddball pieces in the sale and buy herself a new service for four. She'd seen them in Wal-Mart for next to nothing and wondered why she hadn't replaced her everyday stuff years ago. "If not now, when?" she asked Sheba, who still had no reply.

It was the second week in August, and it was nearly two weeks already since all her men had returned to their homes, of course promising her they'd be back to help with the auction and sale, as well as to say their final, official good-byes to the farm. Even though Katie assured them before she left that they'd always be welcome in the place where they were raised and that crawdad-hunting opportunities would *never* disappear since Crooked Creek Park would carry on, they simply looked at her as though she'd somehow missed the point. Although Jacob had pursed his lips, he refrained from saying what was on his mind.

During the week-plus that Dorothy's men had been at the farm, they managed to sift through everything that mattered, each packing a box or two and taking it to UPS. There were only a few items mentioned that Dorothy wasn't ready to part with, one being the massive mahogany desk that had been her father's. She wasn't sure yet whether it would fit appropriately in her new home or not, but the thought of leaving it behind or shipping it out was more than she could take, at least at the time. Of course, one day it would go to Jacob, the elder son. But that day wasn't here yet.

Vinnie had mentioned liking the pocket watch she kept displayed in a nine-inch-tall, glass-domed case set atop the dining room bureau. It used to be her mother's father's watch, and even though it hadn't worked for decades, it somehow gave her comfort to know that it was the very same face and hands that had marked her ancestors' days, and the very same twelve-karat, rose-gold casing they'd held in their fingers that now sat within *her* gaze. On rare and moody occasions, she removed it from its domed home and held it curled safely in the palm of her hand like a crystal ball, imagining what they might have been waiting for as one or the other asked the time and her grandfather pressed the button, flipped opened the front cover and pronounced it, *exactly*. Yes, she recalled how he used to report it: "Why, sweetie pie, it's ten minutes and twelve seconds after two o'clock," he'd say. He died when Dorothy was only fifteen years old, but she would never forget the twinkle in his eyes and the way he all but sang the syllables when he called her sweetie pie, which is what he always called her, even when he was perturbed with her occasional stubborn behavior.

Steven mentioned liking a pocketknife with a bone handle he found in one of the junk drawers. Dorothy didn't know where Henry had procured it, but every time she opened that drawer and thrashed through it for one thing or another, it made her smile to discover once again its presence in her life. No, it, too, needed to stay for now.

Vinnie studied an outdoor photo of her and Henry taken shortly after they were married. She kept it in a small oval frame near her bed, and it had been there as long as he could remember. "Not yet, son. No, you can't have that yet. I still need to wake up and see us the way we used to be. Oh, we were so in love!" She picked it up and held it to her chest like a sleeping baby, then gently kissed the glass before setting it back in its sacred spot.

Katie had been good enough to let the guys use her Lexus to take a couple loads of piddly stuff, as Dorothy referred to it, over to the house on Vine. Two SUVs lessened the number of trips they had to make. They hauled items like an end table, some small kitchen appliances, a couple sets of sheets for her bed—which she was certainly taking, she'd decided—extra towels, an old iron doorstop shaped like a bulldog, a fairly new halogen lamp that would probably light up her entire new home, a dresser, a filing cabinet, a couple of paintings and a few other odds and ends. She didn't want to move any large furniture items until she'd made up her mind for sure about paint colors and such. "I'm just gonna sneak up on the place bit by bit," she teased.

As far as Dorothy knew, Katie and Jacob never again had entered into verbal battle, probably worrying they'd kill her with their bickering, what with her chest pains following their last bout. She tickled May Belle during a phone conversation in which she shared her "death by verbal sparring" theory. "Oh, Dorothy! You're such a corker!" May Belle had said. Mostly, Dorothy told May Belle, Katie and Jacob had ignored each other after that, speaking only when they had to, and being very polite at that.

Katie and Vinnie had actually entered into some lively conversations, Dorothy explained during her continuing recap to May Belle, seeming to hit it off by the time she and Josh headed back to Chicago a few days before the men left. And once the boys all went crawdad hunting together, their uneasiness with one another completely disappeared. "I guess once a fellow squishes his toes in the same rushing waters as another and they come up the hill together with their pant legs rolled up, they are bonded for good." The entire, lengthy phone conversation had caused the two women to begin reminiscing about some of their own best hunts, making fun of themselves along the way for telling "fish tales" about crawdads!

After she and May Belle had hung up—when the silence of the farm seemed to ring very loudly in the shadow of their giggling conversation—Dorothy thought how odd it was not to be able to jump into The Tank and retrieve May Belle and Earl for a smorgasbord night. The emotional pangs that raced through her when she thought about taking a ride, then realized yet *again* that it was now impossible, were sometimes so intense that they felt nothing short of a physical wound, or what she imagined one suffering withdrawal symptoms from drugs might experience, such was the intensity of her longing.

Although Arthur had once even volunteered to come pick her up so she could "just pet The Tank," she'd declined, realizing she couldn't bear to see such a faithful old friend parked for good. Not yet, at least. Arthur had asked what she wanted him to do with her, but the best Dorothy could do was to tell him she'd let him know later. Yes, later.

In the meantime, she had to put her lipstick on and ready the treasurer's report for the evening's Social Concerns Committee meeting, which seemed to have rolled around again quicker than a flash. Then again, they had moved it up a week, feeling that time was running out before the rummage sale. Jessica volunteered to come pick her up, saying she could certainly use an excuse to leave the house a bit early and return home a bit late since Sarah Sue had been so cranky lately. Dorothy accepted Jessica's gracious invitation, realizing it would probably do them both a world of good. It occurred to her that even after she moved, she'd have to find a ride when community band practice began again in the fall, since it was out at the park district building near the edge of town—allowing that she had enough breath left by then to play her clarinet.

Dear Joshmeister,

Well, our meeting was pretty uneventful, aside from Acting Mayor Gladys McKern, who is still having fits about the Boy Scouts directing traffic at the auction, which I cannot believe is only a couple weeks away! That woman can stay rankled about something longer than anyone I KNOW, and no amount of facts can persuade her to change her mind. Nevertheless, we voted and she lost. End of story. HA!

I can hardly believe you talked your mother into private driving lessons! What? You don't trust Hethrow High drivers' education to train you proper? Too bad The Tank isn't still up and running; I could teach you how to drive. (Did your stomach just do a flip-flop?) HAHAHA! So, do you think you'll have your license before you move down here?

LOOK OUT, PARTONVILLE! A JOSHMEISTER ON THE
LOOSE! And they all thought *I* was something!

I finally did IT today: I phoned Edward Showalter
and told him to paint my kitchen ceiling fire engine
red! He called me back in the afternoon and said
the only true fire engine paint he could find was
enamel, and he asked me if I knew what I was
doing. Did I really want a shiny red ceiling in my
kitchen? I assured him that I might be old but that
I wasn't daft—at least not too daft—and that I
wouldn't have it any other way. I'm leaving everything else white. Who knows what I might do once
I get in there and start playing. I just might draw
flowers on the walls with Magic Markers!

When I asked if he knew of any movers he might
recommend, he told me that he and a couple of his
AA buddies can move me since they've done that
type of thing before. (Is there anything Edward
Showalter DOESN'T do?) Your mom bragged on him
so much that I just went ahead and gave him that
job, too. I'll soon be moving into my New Home for
GOOD; my bed will be the last thing to get moved in.
I've come to terms with the fact that I don't want to
actually be living at Crooked Creek during the auction.
No sir, I want to feel like I've already moved on.

Last I talked to your mom, your moving company
was hopefully now set to get your stuff down here a
week after the auction, which she figured would
give Edward Showalter time to do whatever she
might want done beforehand—which she didn't
think would be much. I imagine it's costing her a

pretty penny to have all your fine furniture moved. I surely do wish I could see your fancy townhouse before you leave it, but so goes life. It does give me pleasure, though, to think my old "office" will now become your room. Yes, new life in old places is what I like to picture. I reckon you'll be sitting nearly where I am now, just typing away on YOUR computer!

I'm going to bed. And YES, I've been taking good care of myself and not working too hard. I sit like a queen in the barn and just boss people around when they come to drop things off or price them for the sale. I think I've finally found my calling! HA!

Peace and grins,

Outtamyway (although it doesn't exactly fit anymore) & Sheba

P.S. Looks like the Wild Musketeers will win the league, as usual. I don't think anybody can catch them now unless the Palmer Pirates win every game for the rest of the season. Fat chance of THAT!

"I tell you, I just can't *believe* it!" Lester said as he poured Arthur his fifth cup of coffee, if he'd been keeping track correctly. "And if you have another refill, I'm gonna have to think about charging you double!" Arthur just stared Lester a good one, ignoring his familiar and hollow threat.

"Well, you *can* believe it, I tell ya! And it came direct from Dorothy's mouth. The Tank is nearly dead as a doornail, and she's parked in my ol' shed where I towed her after the wreck. Dorothy hasn't even been by to see her, and like I'm a-tellin' ya, she's claimin' her drivin' days is over."

"I can't believe it. I *tell* you, I just can't *believe it!*" Lester said again, shaking his head while staring out the window. "Now, I can't say I'm not a bit relieved to know that old car won't be racing around anymore, but I just wonder how Dorothy is going to handle this. I mean really. I mean, I know she's moving into town soon, but . . . I just can't imagine giving up driving myself."

"I know what ya mean," Arthur said empathetically. "I try to imagine myself what that might be like. Nope. I can't even imagine it. No siree, Bob. I cannot imagine not drivin'. Why, when that woman of mine gets to naggin' for too long a spell, sometimes my good ol' Ford truck just kidnaps me down the lane. Know what I mean?"

"You say The Tank is *nearly* as dead as a doornail. Does that mean she's got at least a lick of life left in her?"

"I'd say about one good slurp would be it."

"I declare. I just never thought I'd see the day."

"What day is that?" Cora Davis asked as she entered Harry's.

"The day Dorothy Jean Wetstra stopped driving," Lester said.

"What?" Cora bypassed her table in the window and bustled right up to the counter for this bit of information. "Surely you're not telling the truth!"

"Well, surely he *is* tellin' the truth," Arthur grunted. "Said she's givin' up drivin' for good. The Tank is rightly sick, and Dorothy figures it's time." As before, Arthur didn't go into what had scared Dorothy, figuring she had a right to her own stories without Cora muckin' them up with her exaggerations.

"How will she get around?" Cora asked.

"I reckon the same way May Belle has done all these

years since Homer died. After all, she won't have far to go
for nothin' once she moves onto Vine," Arthur replied.

"And she's going to do that *when?*" Cora asked Arthur.
She spun her stool toward Lester and all but ordered him
just to serve her coffee at the counter today, then quickly
spun back to face Arthur.

"I reckon when she's good and ready. Beans, Cora! I
don't keep a collar on Dorothy. But I reckon she'll be
movin' before the sale so as Swifty don't auction her furniture right out from under her." Swifty Forester, the county's
premier auctioneer, had once been accused of doing just
that. Word had it the owner had to buy his very own couch
back from the highest bidder since Swifty said he never
went back on a sale.

"And when is that Katie person moving in? Or is she?"

Arthur tossed his money on the counter, told Lester to
keep the change, stood up off the stool, hiked up his pants,
then turned to Cora. "Cora Davis. You have always done
asked too many questions of too many folks about too
many things. And this time ya ain't gittin' an answer." And
then he was gone. Here The Tank was, gaspin' for breath in
his garage, and all Cora Davis could think about was that
city slicker. Wasn't it bad enough he was soon gonna have
to endure a foreign car parked right on the farm next to his?
What was the world a-comin' to?

17

◦✿◦ ◦✿◦ ◦✿◦

Katie walked from room to room in their brownstone, thinking about how Dorothy's sons were preparing themselves to say good-bye to the farm. Try as she might, she could not muster one hint of emotional attachment to the brownstone. *Surely there's something.* . . . She meandered from the spacious dining room, with its oversized black lacquer table and hutch and its African décor, to the kitchen, which was mostly white and serene, to her bedroom, which had no clutter or extras other than the multiple bottles of French perfume she displayed on top of her bird's-eye maple dresser. *Nothing. I feel nothing.*

Then she wandered into Josh's bedroom. Although she'd always nagged him to get that place in order and un-clutter the mess, she had never actually taken stock of what the mess consisted of, other than occasional building mounds of dirty clothes piled on the floor. Since the house-keeper actually cleaned his room, for the most part Katie never entered.

Right inside the door next to the wall switch was a poster of Bruce Springsteen. Alex had seen him in concert a year ago and bought Josh the poster for a souvenir. Katie hadn't allowed Joshua to attend the concert, believing the influence of fans would not be a good one. Josh had been angry with her for two weeks, repeating again and again that many of the *parents* were going—*had gone*—to the concert. "Well, I'm not *them*," she'd said.

"Well, *that's* for sure," he'd replied.

After hearing a few of her business associates talk about how much they'd enjoyed it and how multigenerational the crowd had been, she'd been somewhat sorry she hadn't let Josh attend, although she never admitted that to him.

Next to the Springsteen poster was a small shelf about a foot long where Josh kept a plastic model of a ship he'd built when he was about ten. It wasn't very well done—paint drips here and there, things not quite matched up correctly before the glue had dried—so why he kept it was a mystery to her. But there it was, a piece of his past perched in the air. To the left of that was a curled-up piece of paper about five inches square, secured to the wall across the top by a piece of masking tape. She gently ran her index finger from top to bottom to uncurl it so she could decipher what it said: "Thank you for bringing your lovely boat for show-and-tell, Josh. I could see by your enthusiasm that you really enjoyed the project and that you obviously love the water. Perhaps one day you'll own your own boat! Mrs. Sharper."

Katie's heart began to pound. *All these years . . . a note from his teacher . . . I never heard him talk about boats or the water. Then again, when have I really asked him what he likes?*

On the long shelf against the next wall were ribbons, two small trophies and a pinewood derby car from his Scouting days. Propped in the midst of those were a six-inch-high figure of Tony the Tiger and a blue square of chalk, the kind used to chalk the end of a pool cue. *Where in the world did that come from? I have no earthly idea. Maybe during a visit with his dad?*

The next wall was completely covered by his desk, computer equipment and shelving to hold all the manuals. A notebook sat next to the keyboard, a three-hole punch beside it. She flipped open the notebook and discovered it was completely filled with printed copies of e-mails from Outtamyway!

"Dear Joshmeister, Just a note to let you know I'm still alive and kicking this fine Wednesday morning. I loved hearing all the gory details about your science project, even though Alex seemed to like dissecting much more than you. HA!" Note after note, Katie was drawn into the web of learning details about her son's life she'd never known existed.

Suddenly her face flushed when she thought she heard Josh returning home, fearing she'd be caught red-handed in his personal business. Although nothing intimate had been revealed and Josh had in fact *not* returned, she felt guilty enough to close the notebook and scurry toward the door to leave his room. But not before stopping in the doorway and taking one last look at these fragments of her son's life, mentally moving them into shape as though trying to fit pieces of an important puzzle together to reveal the whole of something . . . someone.

"Josh," she said aloud. "The only thing I would miss about this place would be you, if you weren't coming with me. You, a son I hardly know." Tears began to stream down her cheeks. "It's time that changed." She gingerly stepped toward the plastic model ship and lifted it into her hands. "Okay, so we're not moving next to the ocean and we won't have a boat, but it's a creek with running water and . . . clams. NO! Crabs. NO NO NO! CRAWDADS!" she shouted triumphantly.

❧

Dorothy was reclining, feet up and her head resting in the shampoo bowl, relishing the feel of Maggie's hands heartily scrubbing her scalp. When it came to hair, Maggie knew just what every woman liked, and for Dorothy, it was a good, hard scrub. "You just can't get too rowdy with my pink scalp," she used to say. Not so for May Belle. May Belle enjoyed the slow feel of trickling warm water and a gentle massage. Jessica, although she'd come only a few times because of a lack of funds, nearly became euphoric sniffing the fragrances of Maggie's small collection of aromatherapy products—very cutting edge—while Gladys worried that "all that smelly stuff" would do something to her sinuses.

Although Maggie always set up an official index card in her jeweled box for new clients, she never needed to look at it again. She knew. And although she loved what she did, basking in the feel of hair slipping through her fingers—whether it was wet or dry—it was always a regret that no one in Partonville was brave enough to try any of the new, exotic styles she learned at the hair convention each year. No amount of persuading, cajoling and even bribing with "free product" could move them out of their boring ruts—other than that one time when May Belle, out of the clear blue, had stunned her by asking for a braided updo like she used to wear when she was courted by Homer.

Maggie began chattering to Dorothy as she towel-dried her thin white locks. "I wouldn't have believed it until I saw Jessie drop you off! You really are not driving, then?"

"Nope. The Lord has made it clear to me that it's time to stop before I hurt somebody. Besides, what fun could I *really* have behind the wheel of a vehicle that wasn't The Tank?"

"True enough. Although I can envision you driving one of those big old SUVs like Miss Durbin bombs around in."

"Funny you should say that, since it did cross my mind. But then I thought better. I tell you, it's quite the adjustment to have to depend on others to make your way from here to there. It has made the idea of moving into town even a little sweeter, though. Having to walk for my dinner will keep me up and moving."

"Well, just be sure you're not moving too swiftly, Dorothy! Now that everyone in town knows about your nitroglycerin tablets, you're likely to have them being stuffed down your throat every time a sneeze comes over you!" The women broke into peals of laughter, realizing that probably wasn't far from the truth. When they settled down, Maggie began the blow-drying process, which interrupted the conversation and caused Sheba to scurry out from under Maggie's station. As soon as she turned the dryer off, conversation resumed, but Sheba stayed put near the back room.

"I heard Arthur's got The Tank at his place. What are you planning to do with her, Dorothy? Maybe we ought to have a town burial, think?" Maggie combed Dorothy's hair this way and that, knowing there was only one way it would end up and that it was too thin to do much of anything with.

"Maybe I ought to put her in my auction. Think I could get a dollar?"

"I'm afraid my answer might incriminate me, so I'll keep it to myself," Maggie said, grinning mischievously.

"It did cross my mind that one year at the county fair

they had an old wrecker car they let people hit with a sledgehammer for a few coins. I think the Rotary did that for a fund-raiser. Maybe Social Concerns could earn a few bucks from something like that—say, set The Tank out in the square or something."

"I know!" Maggie said to Dorothy as she spun her around in the chair so she could talk directly to her rather than via the mirror. "How about you put her in one of the demolition derbies out at the fairgrounds! Now, *that* would be the perfect ending!" Maggie threw her head back and chuckled at the mere thought of such a crazy idea.

"The way Arthur talked, I'm not sure The Tank's got enough life left to even *get* to the fairgrounds, to be honest with you."

"Spray today?" Maggie asked as she patted at Dorothy's wispy, round hairdo.

"Just give me a squirt or two. Don't imagine it will change the look of my pink scalp one way or the other, but I do like the way it smells."

"You and Jessica and your fragrances."

"Has she been in?"

"Not for some time now. But she does love fragrance. In fact, even though I almost never sell a lick from my aromatherapy display, it's worth keeping it out—aside from my own pleasure, of course—just to watch her delight in inhaling a lungful from each bottle."

Dorothy squinted as she thought, then said, "If I recollect correctly, her birthday's coming up." Maggie unfastened the plastic drape from around Dorothy's neck. "I tell you what, I'm gonna leave you whatever it costs for a cut, wash, set and bottle of fragrance for her, but don't tell her who did it, okay? You call her and tell her an angel passed through and left her a do, then surprise her by giving her the bottle of the fragrance she most likes. You've got all this grandbaby stuff and playpens and what-not in the shop anyway, so she wouldn't even have to worry about getting a sitter!"

"Done deal," Maggie said. While Dorothy was paying, she was blessedly reminded how wonderful it felt to give, especially to someone as hardworking as that Jessica Joy.

Dorothy walked out the door of La Feminique Hair Salon & Day Spa, yet again surprised to find The Tank missing from its usual parking spot in front of the shop. Sheba sat down on the curb and just stared at her mistress with a look on her face that said, what are we supposed to do now? About that time, Jessie pulled up and tooted her horn, sending Sheba into a barking fit until Dorothy opened the door and she jumped right in next to Jessie.

"You look beautiful as ever, dearie," Jessie said to Dorothy once she was belted in.

"Looks, schmooks," Dorothy said. "Wait until Arthur hears what I've finally decided to do with The Tank! Maggie Malone is not only a dear friend and a great beautician, she's an inspired genius as well!"

"Now hear this!" Gladys belted out to the Happy Hookers, causing everyone in the room to stop their chattering and snap to attention. "Since the last two members have finally arrived and since they're the only ones who haven't asked me yet—only because I didn't give them a chance—let me make this an official announcement so we can get on with the game. Miss Durbin is not even in town, so obviously I didn't invite her, and no, I did not invite Jessica Joy either.

Why? you ask. Well, for one, Miss Durbin's absence speaks for itself. For two, I didn't know that just because one of us decided to invite special guests for an evening of bunco it meant that the *rest* of us had to do the same thing! How could we play with seven anyway?"

"I reckon the same way we learned to play our own special brand with six all these years," Jessie said, taking the words right out of everyone else's mouths.

Gladys yanked down the back end of her blazer and rested her knuckles on the table in front of which she was standing. "And why, pray tell, after all these years of playing with six would we need to change *that*?"

"Well," Nellie Ruth said a bit hesitantly, "perhaps because we finally figured out we *have* more players and that it's more fun with two complete tables? And because we *liked* our guests?" Somehow it had come out as more of a question than the statement she was wishing to make.

"Humph," Gladys said in response.

It was now Maggie's turn to get in her two cents' worth. "Well, I for one quite agree with Nellie Ruth. Yes, I'm the one who invited them last month. And truthfully, I didn't think about it being permanent until about halfway through the evening and I thought to myself, why not?"

"For one thing, we barely know Katie Durbin," Gladys immediately responded.

"Maybe some of you barely know Katie, but I know her very well, and so does Jessica," Dorothy said. "And as for Jessica, my goodness *me*! She's *already* one of us. She's fun and I'm sure she'd love to be a member."

"She's tardy." Gladys's mouth spoke before she herself even knew it had opened.

"For goodness *sakes*, Gladys!" Dorothy nearly shouted.

"Give a new mother a break! One time tardy does not make her anything other than one time tardy!"

"I think Jessica would make a fine addition to our club, as would Katie—if she's interested in joining," May Belle said.

"And after all," Dorothy said without a gap after May Belle's statement, "if we don't get some new blood in here pretty soon, this club will die—one at a time and literally. We're none of us getting any younger, you know." Everyone but Gladys broke into laughter. "So I'd say it's unanimous—almost. Who's got the next meeting? We'll leave it up to them to do the official invite."

"Me," Nellie Ruth said. "I think I'll send them written invitations so they understand they are being invited into the club, not just for the evening."

"And if either of them declines, then what?" Gladys asked.

"Then they will have declined," Dorothy said. "Amen and pass the dice!"

18

❧ ❧ ❧

It was quite the parade. A large orange U-Haul truck led the way, followed by a green Chevy truck, a tangle of items and boxes held in the bed with miscellaneous straps and bungee cords, followed by two overflowing station wagons, tailgates open. The caboose was Edward Showalter's camouflage van with "Jesus Loves You" written across the side—Dorothy riding shotgun, Sheba in her lap. Arthur stood at the end of his lane, having just picked up his mail, shaking his head as he watched them go by. He held his mouth shut so as not to be swallowing the dust kicking up from the gravel. Although he waved at Dorothy, she didn't seem to see him.

Dorothy was bone-tired, hot, thirsty and feeling disoriented. Edward Showalter had talked at the top of his lungs the entire time his crew was packing up, then he'd hurried her into the van so they wouldn't "miss the parade!" Her moments alone to say her good-byes to the empty bedroom where she'd been born, her anticipated farewell to the kitchen table at which she'd sat for most of her life, her final moments in the barn . . . each vanished in a flurry of hurry and blather. She felt as though she'd been punched in the stomach, her umbilical cord to the land severed without warning.

"If I'd rented a U-Haul just one inch shorter, that bedroom set and big old desk would not have fit! That desk must weigh a ton. Me and the boys have never lifted anything that heavy. It took prayer and an act of God to get that thing to budge an inch. What is that made of, anyway?"

A long silence followed.

"Dorothy?"

"Yes."

"Dorothy, I asked you what that desk was made of."

"Tradition," she said. "Memories. Heartache. Business deals. . . . Memories and . . . more memories. . . ."

Edward Showalter looked her way for a moment, then decided just to leave her be. This was the first it had occurred to him just *how* difficult this transition was for her. She'd been so chipper and happy when they'd talked about things for the Vine Street house, it had never before struck him the impact it must have to leave a lifelong dwelling place. With his shaky background, including the fact that his dad had also been a drinker—although he'd never quit until he died—Edward Showalter had never had a chance to grow the same kind of roots that obviously tied Dorothy to her farm.

Dorothy thought for a moment that she might throw up, she felt so ill. *Lord,* she prayed to herself, *hold me close. Hold on to me, Jesus. I know I'm doing the right thing, I just didn't realize it would be so hard to drive away.* She closed her eyes and let her head fall back against the headrest. If Edward Showalter hadn't seen her hand stroking Sheba's head, he might have thought she'd passed out.

Lord, it's not like I'm never coming back. Why, I'll be back here tomorrow, helping price things for the sale. And I'll only live a few miles away. . . .

Maybe it's best I didn't have a chance to walk around saying too many good-byes alone, probably working myself into full blubbering. Maybe, just like with The Tank, you're really helping me, and to tell the truth, after all the praying I've been doing over this, I just know you are.

Jesus, I need to move through this. Lordy, Lordy, help shore me up. Amen.

By the time the little parade pulled up in front of the house on Vine, Dorothy felt that she had at least caught her breath, although she neither opened her eyes nor lifted her head off the headrest until she heard all the car and truck doors slamming around her, calling her out of her reverie.

Edward Showalter had walked around to Dorothy's side of the van to open the door for her. Before he knew what hit him, Sheba had bounded through the window and into his arms. "I tell you what, Missy," he said to her as he set her down, "it's a darn good thing I've been off the hooch as many years as I have, or you'd be nothing but a splatter on the sidewalk!"

"Oh *my!*" Dorothy said, realizing what Sheba had done. "She's spent her entire life leaping out The Tank's window and into my arms. I guess old habits die hard, or so they say."

"Yes, ma'am. I guess they do." The truth of those words didn't escape them, and it hung heavily in the air for a moment, especially in light of the current situation.

"Welcome to your new home, Dorothy," he finally said as he opened the creaky van door for her. "May I escort you? Now, if you were my bride, I'd be carrying you over the threshold!" Although Edward Showalter was doing what he could to try to lighten the moment, Dorothy didn't seem to catch his humor. She in fact still looked somewhat glazed over as she stared at the front porch, toward which they were now walking elbow in elbow.

"What in the world?" Dorothy stood stunned as she looked at the beautifully painted mailbox now mounted where the old rusty one had been. Delicate multicolored blossoms, some painted on swaying stems, covered the entire box. Every color of the rainbow was represented, and it was just about the happiest "bouquet" one could imagine! A grapevine wreath was mounted in a large circle around the mailbox, as though it had been framed, and Dorothy's house numbers were hand-painted between the wreath and the box. "Who in the world . . ."

"You mean, you didn't know about this?" Edward Showalter asked. "Why, that woman worked for hours. . . ." Suddenly he stopped talking, realizing he was about to give away what had obviously, unbeknownst to him, been done in secret.

From around her neck, Dorothy removed the old skeleton key, which Katie never had detached from Aunt Tess's original lace. Although Katie had apologized for the odd, makeshift key chain when she presented it to Dorothy at the closing, Dorothy couldn't imagine letting go of the fingerprints of the one who had passed through this door before her. Katie even offered to have Edward Showalter install new door hardware with a dead bolt, but Dorothy had fervently declined. "There's something about the feel of a skeleton key that assures me the past really did happen," she said. When Edward Showalter had handed the key to Dorothy, having had it in his possession for all the painting and such, he had joked about how the lace didn't match his camouflage and therefore he couldn't keep it.

But to Dorothy it was no joke; the combination of lace and worn key was a poignant mark of Tess's life.

After Edward Showalter heard the lock click, he pushed the door open for Dorothy. Strung across the entire living room was a banner hand-printed on shelf paper. WELCOME HOME DOROTHY! it read. Again, beautiful flowers—obviously painted by the same artist who'd done the mailbox—were painted inside each of the *O*s.

"If you think this is all something," Edward Showalter said, "wait until you see the kitchen! And *that*, Miss Wetstra, was *your* doing!"

Dorothy rounded the corner into the kitchen and was immediately captured by the fire engine red that blazed across her ceiling. "Don't blame it on me," Edward Showalter said. "I tried to warn you!" She stood looking upward for quite a spell, then she backed out of the room into the doorway so she could get a good gander at it in perspective to the room. It was then she noticed the tiny band of flowers that had been hand-painted mid-wall around the kitchen, creating a delicate border. The miniature flower bouquets were about a foot apart, each joined by a hand-painted, fire engine red ribbon, which perfectly matched the color of her ceiling paint. In fact, she was sure it *was* her kitchen paint.

"Well?" Edward Showalter stood, shaking his head, waiting for the explosion.

"It's absolutely the most glorious thing I've ever seen! Why, I can almost see my own pink scalp reflected up there! And to think that someone actually painted flowers on the wall . . . I do believe God has been eavesdropping and spreading around my most secret desires!"

Edward removed his painter's cap and scratched his head. "To each his own. I better get the boys busy moving before they all fall asleep out there. Where, *exactly*, do you want that desk, since we're not going to be moving *it* around any more than we have to. And which bedroom do you want the bed and dresser in? I'm assuming the largest one toward the front of the house, right?"

"Right. And didn't you load the bed last?"

"Yup."

"Well, why don't you go ahead and move that in as well as the rest of the stuff, and I'll figure about the desk." The minute he was out of her sight, she sat down at the kitchen table and simply marveled.

Dorothy, wearing her pink pj's, housecoat and fluffy slippers, turned off the front porch light, then slowly shuffled her way through the living room toward the kitchen. The house was now lit only by the overhead hall light. May Belle, Earl, Nellie Ruth, Jessie and Jessica had all dropped by an hour after the movers had left and stayed until about an hour ago, helping Dorothy move things from here to there. May Belle said she'd waited until she saw the trucks pull away to call the girls, figuring there was enough chaos in the small house at one time already.

May Belle, with Earl's help, of course, had packed a giant container of sweets in a new Tupperware container, which was their housewarming gift to Dorothy. Jessie brought a big pot of beef stew and stuck it in the fridge, figuring Dorothy could chow on it for a few days until she got her kitchen duly in order, adding, "not that you do much cookin' anyways!" Nellie Ruth presented her with a metal cart for groceries that pulled on two wheels. "Something to bring your supplies home from town in," she said. She had attached a child's bicycle horn, saying if Dorothy drove the cart the way she drove The Tank, she figured she'd need a horn. Of course, that tickled everyone. Jessica gave Dorothy a giant decorative basket she had purchased at Wal-Mart, having found none large enough at the resale shop. She'd decorated it, color-coordinating it with the bright florals that had been painted on the walls. She was sporting a new short-and-sassy hairdo that swung this way and that when she turned her head, and she radiated the delicious fragrance of soothing lavender.

Although none would admit to the painting, Dorothy noticed Jessica's eyes light up when she let it be known how much she delighted in the kitchen—not to mention the fact that Jessica's gym shoes were spattered with fire-engine red paint. When Dorothy pointed that out, Jessica assured her that an angel must have spattered her shoes the last time she flew through Partonville. "I've heard there are *lots* of angels flying around here lately," she said. She then winked at Dorothy, kissed the top of Sarah Sue's head—who was suspended in yellow and fast asleep at her mother's chest—then gave Dorothy a quick peck on the cheek, too.

Jessica told Dorothy that it was Katie who had purchased the mailbox during her last trip, then asked Jessica to decorate it. "Katie said although you hadn't mentioned that old rusty thing, she'd certainly noticed it. She said it felt downright depressing, since it was the first thing you saw when you came to the front door."

"How sweet of her," Dorothy said. "How sweet of *all* of you!"

But now Dorothy was alone, standing near the kitchen table in the dim light from the hall. At night, the fire engine red paint appeared as a deep, rich, warm glow. Smelling of fresh paint and embraced by flowers, the kitchen was more wonderful than any Dorothy could imagine. She moved toward the Tupperware bowl sitting on the counter, reached in and grabbed the first cookie her fingers touched, then re-sealed the bowl. Taking a large, delicious bite, she discovered it was a snickerdoodle. "Perfect," she said to Sheba, who had rushed to her ankles just waiting for a morsel to hit the floor. "Absolutely perfect."

By the time she reached the bathroom, she'd polished off the cookie. She flicked on the bathroom light before turning off the hall light, then fumbled around a bit trying to locate her plate container. "Where in the world do you think that thing is?" she asked Sheba, who continued to hover at her ankles, obviously unclear as to where they were heading for the night in this unfamiliar place. Finally Dorothy gave up her search, brushed her teeth, then put the new stopper in the sink and filled it with water, plunking in her partial plate. "That'll have to do for now." She then turned on her bedroom light before turning off the hall light.

She stood at the foot of the bed, staring into the room that now, especially compared with the kitchen, felt bare without decoration. Definitely she needed new curtains. Darker ones to help block out the light from that street light outside. And color. Yes, color. She loved her kitchen so much that she'd already decided the rest of the house needed to be just as cheery.

She moved to her prayer chair, which she had instructed the men to place in the corner, and turned on the familiar little lamp on her nightstand. As soon as she picked up her

Bible and plopped into the chair, Sheba jumped up on the bed and rolled into her usual little ball at the foot, sensing that this was the place. Dorothy picked up the favored picture of her and Henry and spoke directly into his eyes. "Well, what do you think about *this*? Could you ever imagine me not living out at Crooked Creek? I can hardly believe it myself." She set the photo back down on the nightstand and just sat quietly for a moment, her hands folded on top of the Bible resting in her lap.

"It's wonderful to know you're everywhere, Lord," she said aloud. "And it's especially wonderful to meet You in this familiar chair this evening." Although she was aching with tiredness, it just wouldn't be right to spend her first night in her new home without reading something from the Psalms. She put her fingers on the braided bookmark and peeled open the pages. Her previously highlighted words at the end of Psalm 29 caught her eye: "The Lord will give strength to His people; The Lord will bless His people with peace."

"THANK YOU, Jesus!" she said aloud in a strong voice. "That about does it. Amen."

She set her Bible back on the nightstand, stiffly rose and walked to the wall switch and flipped off the overhead, removed her robe and slippers, peeled back the covers, slipped into her familiar bed, turned off her familiar bed lamp on her familiar nightstand next to her familiar prayer chair by her familiar Bible and photograph, and snuggled under the familiar blankets. She could have been anywhere.

"Good night, John Boy," she said. "Good night, Sheba. Good night, Crooked Creek . . . Good night, moon."

By 6:30 A.M., Dorothy had finally located her plate container and given the teeth—both in and out of her mouth—a good scrubbing. She had taken a sponge bath, rearranged two dresser drawers and fussed with a few knickknacks in the living room. Although she hadn't slept well—waking several times, each time spending a quarter hour first remembering where she was, then listening to the new sounds of unfamiliar creaks and occasional traffic passing by—she finally determined at 5:30 that she would not go back to sleep for fear she wouldn't awaken until noon, when Maggie, who was working only a half-day, was coming to pick her up for pricing out at the farm. Although Maggie wasn't on the Social Concerns Committee, she was one of more than a dozen people who had volunteered to help with the pricing. Everybody wanted a sneak peek, and this was one sure way to get it—although absolutely no presales were allowed.

It was time for breakfast, and nearly past the time Dorothy should have taken her heart medication. She had finally promised herself, her family, Katie and Josh and May Belle and nearly everyone else in the world, it seemed—including the doc, who occasionally called to check up on her—that she would be careful about things like that. And yes, although she was tired, she was, now in the daylight, somewhat exhilarated by her new surroundings. "Ta dah!" she said to Sheba as they entered the kitchen and she flipped on the light. "Isn't this just the most *wonderful* thing you've ever *seen?*"

She got her pill bottles out of the kitchen cabinet, lined them up on the counter, then opened the refrigerator door to get some milk. Inside the fridge she was surprised to discover a foot-square box with a giant ribbon tied around it and a note that said, "Open carefully!" Withdrawing it from the fridge with two hands, even though it was surprisingly light, she slid the pill bottles aside with her arm and carefully set the box on the counter. She grabbed hold of one end of the navy blue ribbon to untie the bow and discovered it was tied in a knot. After rummaging through four drawers before she remembered where she'd put her new set of tableware, she finally found a knife and cut the ribbon in two places, since it was wound so tightly in both directions around the box. And then she opened the lid.

Six eyeballs were looking straight at her! Three crawdads wiggled and squirmed and crawled over one another, apparently responding to the light that had suddenly invaded their darkness. They were rollicking in an empty ice-cream carton filled with a small bit of water and a few pebbles. A piece of paper was folded and tucked between the box and the ice-cream container. Unfolding it, she read aloud so Sheba wouldn't miss a word.

Hello! Our names are Clam, Lobster and Crawfish. A humanoid named Katie asked another humanoid named Jessie to pick us up (literally and by the tail) from our home and give us a ride to Vine Street, where we thought we'd spend a cool afternoon. A humanoid named Joshmeister translated our words from Crawdaddie to English, which is why we're able to talk to you.

We are your Official Welcoming Party, just in case you found yourself a tad bit (which is different than a tadpole) lonesome for the country. Although we'd love to stay, we'll be hitching a ride back with you and Maggie today since we don't like snickerdoodle cookies and we figured that's all you'd have to eat.

Please come and visit us any time you like. You know our slogan: Our creek is for your feet.

Love, Clam, Lobster and Crawfish.

Dorothy was laughing so hard she thought she might wet her pants. Every time she thought she had finally recuperated, fits of laughter would wash over her once again, one time causing her to fold nearly clear in half. When she finally pulled herself together and got the family safely tucked back into the fridge, she phoned May Belle.

"How in the *world* did you guys get those little buggers into my refrigerator without me knowing it?"

"You mean to tell me you just found them this morning?" May Belle couldn't believe it. "I couldn't imagine why you didn't phone me last night, and now I know why! We were all just bursting last night, hoping you'd discover them while we were still there, but we didn't want to spoil your surprise. We just wanted you to come across them on your own."

"Well, I guar-an-tee you I was surprised! Whose idea was this, anyway?"

"Katie and Jessica got to talking on the phone—I guess they do that pretty regularly—and believe it or not, Katie's the one who thought it up. She told Jessica, who phoned Jessie, and the plan was on. Josh wrote the letter, then faxed it to the drugstore. They phoned Earl to come pick it up and take it to your house while Edward Showalter was finishing up yesterday. Jessie said she could have brought them in when we came to visit, but she thought you might get too nosy before we got them in the fridge. No, we wanted you to discover them on your own."

"Well, now, that was quite the team effort!"

"Believe you me, it was. But what fun we had!"

"Oh, May Belle, you cannot imagine how good that laughter felt. Honestly, I think the gift of laughter is one of the best gifts God has ever given us!"

"And you, Dear Dorothy, are one of the best gifts God's ever given to me!"

19

✥ ✥ ✥

Ever since Dorothy had e-mailed Josh that, much to her total shock, the Wild Musketeers were indeed going to have to have a playoff game with the Palmer Pirates, he had been afraid he would have to miss it, especially since it was going to be held the weekend before the brownstone closing. But now his mom had promised they'd be there to cheer. Even though she was up to her freshly colored red roots in things to do and still wrangling over the marathon of upcoming events, she just didn't have the heart to say no. *What kind of mush pot am I turning into?*

"Too bad I don't quite have my license yet, Mom, so you could buy me a car and I could just drive myself down there!"

"Right." She rolled her eyes so swiftly that Josh thought they might actually launch out of her eye sockets.

Katie put on her full business press with the moving company, trying to alter their original contract. Since there was now no way they could get moved in before the first day of school, she'd decided they might as well give themselves plenty of time to get things squared away, allowing Edward Showalter to do his thing after the auction and allowing them to have a more thoughtful, organized transition rather than practically having to be "dumped off" at the farm. Dorothy quite agreed with this plan when told about it. Katie determined to let the moving company do as much accurate placement of furniture as possible, sparing her and Josh more physical labor than they cared to endure. They were used to nearly living at the Lamp Post now anyway, so that wouldn't be a problem. Katie figured she could just drive Josh to school until they got settled into the farm and onto the bus route. Although she did get the moving company to bend a bit, van storage for more than two weeks was out of the question. If she wanted her items packed up but not delivered for more than two weeks, she'd have to have it all offloaded and put in a storage crate, then reloaded since no company was willing to tie up a trailer for that long, especially at this time of year. To have her unique and spendy items handled—possibly manhandled—four times rather than two was out of the question.

So now the plan boiled down to this: they'd travel to Partonville for the Saturday playoff game, head back to Chicago immediately afterward for the final packing and closing, then return to Partonville two days later, the night before school started. That would also get them there two days before the auction. Although auctions were really not her cup of tea, Katie's proprietary mode had kicked into high gear since Crooked Creek was now officially her property, and it would be filled with strangers. More than once she'd fretted about liability issues. Dorothy told her the church's umbrella policy covered off-site, official church events, but she wondered.

Edward Showalter had, as promised, reserved the entire week after the auction and before their moving in for any and all odd jobs. Katie decided to try to stop fretting about what might have to be left undone at that point, suspecting that the public would probably take a toll on the property anyway. And after all, until she found a job—her financial situation was strong enough that she never really *had* to do that, but she truly did miss the energy and pace—what else did she have to do if not to spend her leisurely days transforming an old farmhouse into the dwelling place of a city slicker! Perhaps she would have her decorator come visit for a weekend after they got moved in.

The one thing she couldn't stop fretting about, however, was how Josh would make the transition. She knew he would probably have to be patient about making new friends. Although Hethrow High was undoubtedly now more urban than rural, because of the town's progressive years of growth since auto manufacturing had recently come to Hethrow, nevertheless, he would still be the new kid on the block, or in the country, or from the farm—depending upon how one wanted to look at it.

In the meantime, Katie had double-dutied her appointments with her stylist, her massage therapist, her manicurist, the woman who gave her facials and her yoga instructor. Although she would never have thought it possible, she was on the verge of overprimping before she remembered she'd already determined somewhere along the line to come to the city once a month or so anyway after she moved. Get her city fix. And if she dropped her standing appointment with Jeffrey, her colorist, she would probably *never* be able to get an appointment, such was his reputation, loyalty base and schedule. A friend of hers had once worn a turban on her head for five weeks! Her roots were so long by the time he could fit her in, she decided just to let it all go gray, cut it severely short and save her money for Maui.

❧

Josh had been spending so much time at Alex's that Katie felt a bit isolated. Only her daily long-distance calls with Jessica filled in the solitude. Since she hadn't been full-fledged working around the clock, which had been her habit for so many years, she realized how little time Josh spent around the house—or how often he must have been home alone. But she was now shockingly aware of how completely uncultivated her own social life was. It wasn't until she had recently started to slip out of the loop that she became aware of how business breakfasts, lunches, dinners and after-hours meetings had *become* her life. The perpetual competition and deal cutting made it difficult to be able to trust anyone as a true friend. From that standpoint, the upcoming and drastic changes in her life felt welcome, when they didn't unnerve her to pieces.

Katie agreed that Alex could come along for the ball game trip. Not only was he easy company and Josh's best friend, but she had also realized during their last journey home together that listening to the two of them chatter—when she wasn't buried in public radio and they weren't hiding behind headphones—was a good way to glean some information.

When Josh told her that Alex had suggested they *all* take pom-poms to the game, Katie swiftly and thoroughly rejected the idea. "I mean, *really*," she said. But after she mentioned it to Jessica, who went wild with enthusiasm, the idea finally began to capture Katie. Next thing she knew, she was dialing Alex's number.

"Hello, Mrs. Durbin. Just a minute. I'll get him. He's in the den."

"ALEX! WAIT! I want to talk to *you*!"

"Me? You want to talk to me?"

"Yes. You know, I heard about your pom-pom idea."

"So Josh told me," he said dejectedly.

"At first I didn't think it was a good idea, but now I do. Where were you planning on getting pom-poms?" Alex couldn't have been more stunned if he'd been blindsided by a flying lizard.

"I'll probably be able to borrow them from a few of my cheerleader friends." Josh came around the corner just then, and Alex cupped his hand over the handset and laughed. He mouthed to Josh that it was his mom. "*My* mom?" Josh mouthed back. Alex nodded his head up and down, then continued. "Since I can't get a date with them, the least they can do is lend me their pom-poms. And, hey! I figured if Josh was making a fool out of himself, Shelby would for *sure* notice him *then!*"

Right after he hung up, Alex began hurling himself around the room, whooping and hollering, telling Josh what had just transpired. Josh's mouth stayed agape so long that Alex finally chided him for looking like the world's biggest geek. "The only thing I can think of to make you possibly look geekier, my man, is pom-poms, and they're all but on their way!"

Even though nine people had worked all afternoon sorting and pricing, it seemed that they had barely made a dent in the mounds of sale items. Since Dorothy had moved off the farm and the ads seeking donations were still running in the newspapers, people seemed to feel free to drop off truckloads—such was the price of growth in the surrounding area, they figured. Gladys decided she didn't want to give the sale a bad name by putting out all that "junk mixed in with solid resale items." No matter how Dorothy and Nellie Ruth argued that there was a buyer for everything, Gladys replied, "I cannot believe anyone would stoop *this* low!" while twirling a metal bedpan filled with plastic poinsettias over her head. Before Dorothy or May Belle could open their mouths, Gladys had tossed the bedpan to the floor with a clank and departed to procure a Dumpster.

Gladys phoned the four garbage and refuse hauling companies in the county and harshly explained to each of them why, if they cared anything about Partonville, its beautification or its sanitary conditions, they would surely donate the use of a Dumpster. They, however, either didn't care, or didn't care for the way she talked to them. In the end, the best she could negotiate was a fifteen percent "charitable discount" (to which Gladys responded, "Well, not *very!*") for a seven-day rental.

When Gladys returned to the barn looking frazzled, disappointed, angry and more determined than ever to have them all work two more hours, the committee decided the Dumpster shouldn't arrive until four days before the sale; they would just pile rejects up until then. Then they would have the day of the sale to keep garbage containers from the food service area emptied and a couple of days afterward for easy cleanup. They all ended up agreeing a Dumpster was, indeed, a very good idea. Gladys gloated throughout their next hour of labor, at which time everyone quit, whether she liked it or not.

The moment Gladys was gone, Dorothy and May Belle made sure that Aunt Tess's old bedpan and its poinsettias were appropriately hidden in the "keeper pile." Had it not been for the Absolutely No Presales law of the committee, Dorothy would have paid good money right on the spot the moment Gladys began twirling it, just to save it from the rubbish. It had, without reason, become a comforting symbol of something, although she wasn't sure exactly what.

Delbert Carol, pastor of United Methodist Church, walked from behind the pulpit, his forefinger and thumb rubbing his chin. Everyone knew that when Pastor moved from behind the pulpit, something either personal or not in the bulletin was about to spring from his mouth.

"I know I ran a little long with my sermon today, but nevertheless I'd like to take an extra moment for announcements before we dismiss. What with the sale out at Dorothy's place, I mean Crooked Creek . . . um, Katie Durbin's farm. Oh, heck, you know what I'm talking about. What with that sale just around the corner and it being our biggest fund-raiser of the year, I do believe it's worth a special moment of notation, prayer and blessing."

He rubbed his hands together, then ran one through his reddish-brown, thinning hair, which most in the congregation thought would look much better were his wife to stop cutting it. Although he always looked slightly disheveled when he spoke, nobody noticed since his heartfelt care for his flock simply erased anyone's thoughts about appearances.

"I know many of you have already worked long and hard hours, with many more to come. Everyone from grandmothers to the Boy Scouts have already put in days of planning, sorting, pricing, not to mention a few hours of quarreling about logistics—and word *always* has a way of getting back to pastors about disgruntlement." He paused long enough for everyone to "get" his joke. Finally a few chuckles wafted through the pews—although none from Gladys, who responded with her usual nasal grunt.

"I'd like to take this moment to thank each and every one of you *before* the sale. It's nothing short of a God-given spirit of servanthood that moves busy people like yourselves to take on such a grand endeavor." Gladys poked her brother, the Scoutmaster in charge of parking, and whispered, in her condemning voice, "or the bribe of a badge!" Pastor tilted his head toward her, smiled and raised a friendly eyebrow, as he was wont to do when Gladys sat in the front pew and felt a need to interrupt, which was nearly every week.

"As I'm sure you've seen by all the posters around church and town, a majority of this year's funds are earmarked for the new county rape prevention and crisis center and the tri-city shelter for the abused. As people of faith, we can feel very good about our hand in helping those who are suppressed in any way since the Good Book encourages that time and again. I know it's difficult for some of you to believe that even right here in Partonville, abuse leaves its mark, but believe me, as a pastor I've heard the unspeakable uttered on more than one occasion." He noticed eyes suddenly flicking this way and that, some wondering if they *really* knew their neighbors.

"Let's just bow our heads a moment and say a prayer not only for those who suffer from abuses and hard times, but for all the people who are helping them with the proceeds from this sale and through other forms of volunteerism." The rustle of people shifting in their seats could be heard as parishioners brought their minds, hearts and bodies to attention for prayer.

"God, we come before You as a humbled people, desiring to please You—knowing You still love us, even when we don't behave very kindly toward one another. May all our efforts come from our true hearts, and may the funds we raise lift Your children from their desperation and despair, as well as keep some from having to deal with it.

"Lord God Almighty, we ask Your protection for everyone attending the sale and the auction, that none might stumble. We ask for safety, and if we might be so bold, good weather to boot.

"I also ask a special blessing for all the fine people who have given of their time and talents and who will continue to do so until the sale is over and packed up. May our labors please You, Lord, and may we be good stewards of all the gifts You supply.

"And Lord, if it's Your will, how about a win for the Musketeers! Amen."

He lifted his bowed head, then looked up and dismissed them. "Go in peace. SERVE THE LORD!" A spontaneous and thunderous applause erupted that could undoubtedly be heard throughout the entire square block.

"Arthur," Dorothy said into the mouthpiece of her telephone, "I'd like for you to stop by tomorrow morning on your way home from Harry's. Any time will be fine—I'll be here. After all, I can't go too far away now anyway, can I?"

"Nope. I don't reckon ya can! But are ya needin' something, Dorothy? I can surely pick it up for ya and drop it off."

"What I am needing is to talk to you in private, Arthur."

"I won't tell Jessie!"

"Oh, Arthur, you know better than *that*. It's about The Tank."

"I don't imagine there's much to say about her, Dorothy, other than may she rest in peace. Maybe you're really just wantin' to show off that red ceiling I've been a-hearin' 'bout. Why, I heard I could probably shave myself in the reflections and believe I cut myself to pieces with all that red paint."

"Well, folks say lots of things, don't they, Arthur? Some of them are true and some of them aren't, wouldn't you say now?"

"Yes, ma'am. I'd say ya've got that right. But I'll see ya in the morning so as I can make up my own mind as to what folks is sayin' 'bout this one."

20

◆◈◆ ◆◈◆ ◆◈◆

"Scoot down!" Arthur had tried to settle his backside into a space at the end of the third row that was too small but that appeared to be the only one available in the entire bleachers. No amount of wiggling and prying would allow his posterior to fit unless people scrunched together. "SCOOT DOWN, I TELL YOU!" The bleachers were mobbed, and there were still ten minutes left before the first pitch.

The only other option was a lawn chair, if he only had remembered to bring his along. Dozens of them lined both baselines nearly clear to the stakes, three deep in some places, and people were still coming. May Belle and Earl had sold out of sweets within their first five minutes. There had been so much hype about this game in the papers and on local radio and at fish fries—not to mention beauty shops, barbershops, street corners, phone lines, bars and grills—that the otherwise calm rivalry had percolated into a full-blown brouhaha. Some even heard there'd been bad blood spreading here and there, although most didn't believe it was for real. The opening pitch would now be thrown at 6:00 P.M. Lester, for the first time that anyone could remember, had closed Harry's fifteen minutes early. It was unheard of.

"Ladies and gentlemen," the announcer said over the

loudspeaker, which was a battery-operated karaoke machine, "will those of you in the bleachers please all move toward the middle? Let's see if we can't make room for a couple more fans, okay? I know it's a hotter-than-tar day, but get to know your neighbor. Go ahead, don't be shy. Snuggle right up to one another. Who knows, maybe you'll *like* it—or them!" People laughed, but not many made very serious attempts to move, aside from those who would either have to make way for Arthur or have him sitting in their laps.

The announcer—first ever at a Musketeers game—was none other than Harold Crabb. As the hype had grown, Harold had decided to run a small feature in Wednesday's edition of the *Partonville Press*. He interviewed the pitchers of each team, a few fans and the sponsoring fish fry establishments. Jessie talked with the confidence of someone who knew she'd win, but Reggie McDermott, pitcher for the Palmer Pirates, had been on a hot streak, and the Pirates' bats had suddenly come alive. Jokes about illegal doses of Geritol started running their course, and pundits took note that the rumors regarding such matters were never denied—by either team. Harold reported the jolly suspicions, allegations and accusations in his lively and humorous story. It was the first chance in quite a spell he'd had to resurrect his journalism skills and his long-lost dream to be a sportswriter. He pulled out all the stops and let the words fly.

He dug up clips from Jessie's heyday as a catcher in the semi-pro, fast-pitch softball leagues and published some of her record-breaking stats. No doubt about it, Mugsy Landers, as everyone called her back then, was a champion among champions with a "bullet-force pickoff arm and nerves of steel." But now she was the pitcher, putting that pickoff arm to a different use. Of course, in his story, Harold couldn't help but stir up the pitching duel between the sexes. "No matter how wicked a hot streak Reggie's been on lately, Mugsy Landers doesn't fear the heat. Town against town, woman against man, men and women on the same team. It should prove to be a game worth much more than the price of admission," which surely got people to talking, since there wasn't any. But then getting them talking about his story and the event was his goal.

After reading Harold's story, the Thursday morning regulars at the grill cast a vote and decided that Harold ought to announce the game, since his color commentating would obviously liven things up. "By golly," he said at the suggestion, "I just believe I will. All I need is a microphone." Although he'd been joking, within an hour the karaoke machine showed up at his office.

The city slickers were right in the thick of things. Having arrived early, they had plopped themselves down in the center of the bleachers, the bag of pom-poms clutched between Alex's feet. They hadn't told Dorothy about them, figuring they would wait until she started waving hers, then they'd quickly pass them out and do their thing.

As usual, Musketeer and Pirate fans—or about any fans in the area, for that matter—were mingled with one another. Harold Crabb announced the lineups for each team. Although a few friendly jeers could be heard now and again, for the most part, everyone clapped for everyone as each player waved at the reading of his or her name.

As soon as he was done with introductions, Dorothy realized the Musketeers were taking the field. She rose from her lawn chair, which was parked dead center right behind the backstop, turned to face the crowd and held her pom-poms high over her head, which was the usual signal for everyone to stand up for the Welcome Cheer. Alex rifled the pom-poms to everyone. "Go!" he shouted while Dorothy's arms were still uplifted.

Up in the air their arms flew as their pom-poms thrashed this way and that. "Woohoooo!" they yelled. They made such a commotion that Shelby actually turned around to take a look-see, as did everyone at the ballpark. Dorothy's mouth flew open, and for a moment she was speechless. Then she broke out in the biggest grin Katie had ever seen on her face. As Dorothy had promised to everyone who cared about her, she then quickly sat down in her chair to lead her cheer. "And if you don't, I'll come and personally hog-tie you, hear me? And don't think I won't!" Doc had warned.

It was the most raucous Welcome Cheer that anyone had ever heard, proving it's not how high you can jump, but how much enthusiasm you can muster! When it was over, Harold Crabb, who was laughing into the microphone, said, "Let's hear it for our head cheerleader, Dorothy Jean Wetstra, and her band of merry pom-pomers!" The cheering began all over again. By the time everyone got settled down, play was about to begin and the anticipation peaked. But suddenly, unannounced, the national anthem came blasting out of the karaoke box and everyone had to stand back up again.

At long last, the umpire called, "Play ball!"

Jessie left the mound where she'd been warming up and began walking toward Shelby, who immediately stood and flipped up her catcher's mask. They met halfway between the pitcher's mound and home plate.

"Looking into your young eyes reminds me of my youth," Jessie said. "Sometimes if I didn't look into the mirror, I could forget I'm old. This is one of those times. It's you and me today, kiddo. You and me. Show me the target, and I'll give you the pitch, right into the old breadbasket."

"You got it, Jessie!" Shelby nodded. Jessie whirled on her heels and headed back toward the mound, but not before Shelby patted her on the behind, just like in the big leagues.

Arthur couldn't believe what he saw next. He hadn't seen his wife spit on the mound since probably 1945, but sure enough, spit she did, and right over her left shoulder. "By golly if it ain't just like the old days, woman!" he said to no one in particular. "This is gonna be good!"

"Well, folks, we're already heading into the top of the final inning and the score is tied, zero to zero. If I can trust my statistician here"—he looked toward Lester and his chaotic statistician's sheet, which Lester was keeping on the back of a sandwich wrapper they'd found in the garbage can, since no one had thought to bring paper—"and I do believe I *can* trust him, it looks like . . . hold on a minute . . ." He put his hand over the microphone and conferred with Lester as they both tried to decipher the somewhat confusing scrawl. "It looks like although somewhere between seven and nine men and women have made it on base, none has been able to cross the plate—which is the only stat we're *really* sure about." A chuckle rippled over the loudspeaker and spread amongst the crowd. "It's been a pitching duel all the way!"

Arthur had long ago abandoned his seat in the bleachers, unable to sit still. Gol' darn if his cantankerous wife wasn't pitching one of the finest games he'd ever seen! Although he hadn't given the rivalry much consideration, he had now determined that he didn't want his *wife* to lose, no matter whose team she was on. He paced up and down the first-base line behind the people on folding chairs as if he had ants in his pants. As Jessie took the mound and began tossing warm-up pitches, out of nervous habit Arthur retrieved his ever-present harmonica from his top middle coveralls pocket and began to play "You Are My Sunshine." The moment Jessie heard the music, she knew from whence it came.

"ARTHUR LANDERS," she yelled, looking his way, "SHUT THAT THING UP!" Nearly everyone in the ballpark heard her; but Arthur, whose hearing *un*admittedly wasn't what it used to be, was playing faster and faster. "ARTHUR! ARTHUR LANDERS!" She stood on the mound, ball in her right hand, which was settled on her hip, posing in a stance exhibiting her disgust. Everyone was now staring at Arthur, a few actually beginning to sing along to his playing. After one last ignored yelp, Jessie brought the ball to her waist in her pitcher's stance, then gave it a swift counterclockwise whirl around and lobbed it high into the air in Arthur's direction. Like a homing pigeon, the ball arched its way toward Arthur, the crowd's heads moving in the same arc. Just as a sharpshooter of old would zing the cigarette out of his lovely assistant's mouth, so the ball came down on Arthur's hands, flipping the harmonica right out of his mouth, stopping the tune between "skies" and "are gray."

For a stunned moment, he had no idea what had happened, other than that he was no longer playing the harmonica. Then he looked down and saw his harmonica on the ground, next to the softball. He glanced toward Jessie, who had already started walking toward the umpire.

"BALL!" she hollered. "I NEED ANOTHER BALL!"

Neither she nor Arthur had noticed that everyone was on their feet cheering. If the game had ended right then and there, it would forever go down as one of Partonville's most repeated stories. No, nobody would have cared if the game ended—except Jessie, who had fire in her eyes and determination in her pursed lips.

"GET READY!" she bellowed to Shelby. "This one's coming down the pike!" She pitched six strikes in a row, both batters going down swinging. The next batter hit a blooper to right field that should have been an easy out, but the right fielder was still recovering from a knee replacement and couldn't make it to the ball in time to make the play. Jessie spit, for the fourth time in the game.

Arthur was now sitting on the ground next to Dorothy. He figured, as mad as Jessie undoubtedly was at him, if he could remain anywhere within her vision, she'd *really* fire 'em in there. Although he was clearly embarrassed and a bit angry, he was *more* proud of his wife's aim and much better natured about the incident than anyone expected him to be.

With the runner on first base, Jessie fired one in there, all right, but it was close to being a wild pitch. The batter reached way out and tipped it, laying it down just inside the first-base line for a fair ball. Shelby tossed her mask over her head and scrambled to retrieve it, accidentally kicking the ball forward instead. By the time she picked it up, the runner had made it to first and the first-base runner to second. She strode out to the pitcher's mound, hoping to settle both of them down.

"Okay, kiddo," Jessie said. "We got that out of our system. Now let's get the batter out. And don't let him scare you. He's big, but he's blind as a bat. He'll swing at anything," which is just what he did. In three pitches the side was retired, and the Wild Musketeers prepared to bat.

First up was the third baseman. Although he usually went down swinging at anything, his odd, choppy swipe quite a sight to behold, in a miraculous moment his reactions and his arthritis worked together and locked him up long enough to watch four pitches go by for a base on balls. Obviously, Reggie's arm was getting tired. Who wouldn't understand, though—Reggie was seventy-six if he was a day. The Pirates' catcher called to his bench for someone to take the drink bottle out to the mound so Reggie could wet his whistle. Although the Musketeers' bench jokingly objected on the grounds he wasn't really thirsty but just old and tired, they didn't object diligently enough to disallow the pause, and neither did the umpire. After a few swigs, play resumed.

Next, the right fielder for the Musketeers limped toward the batter's box, having strained her back bending over to pick a dandelion during warm-up in the second inning. "Just do what you can," Shelby kindly said to her as the pained woman grunted when she bent over to pick up the bat.

"To heck with what you *can!*" Jessie said. "Get in there and do what you HAVE to! There's plenty of aspirin at the drugstore for later." Sheila grinned a kind of hopeless grin and stepped up to the plate. As luck would have it—at least for the good of the game, although not necessarily for the good of Sheila—she was hit by the first pitch, being too stiff to back out of the box quickly enough. The crowd went wild as she limped to first base, favoring her injured side, even though the ball had actually only clipped her finger.

"Runners at first and second," Reggie hollered from the mound to his players, turning 360 degrees and repeating it three times for those whose hearing and eyesight might be missing this little detail. All that turning and yelling seemed to liven him up a bit, and he struck out the next two batters.

"Two down, two on, tie score," Harold said over the loudspeaker. "It just doesn't get much better than this! Hang on to your hats, everybody. Mugsy Landers is stepping up to bat."

Jessie took her time getting to the plate, playing a bit of a mental game with Reggie. She swung twice to limber, then stepped into the box, then held up her arm to indicate she was backing out again. She bent from the waist to the right and then to the left, slowly stretching. Finally, she stepped into the box for good, only settling into a motionless stance after she'd shuffled the dirt out from under each foot, as though digging herself a stabilizing trench.

"Let 'im have it with both barrels, woman!" Arthur was standing, too nervous to sit. Upon hearing his words, Jessie grinned from ear to ear and spit over her left shoulder, twice. The pitch, which was low and away and exactly where she liked them, had her name written all over it. She swung for all she was worth and nailed it clear over the second basewoman's head.

The runner on second base took off, chugging toward third, but Sheila, who was staring at her finger to see if it was swelling and who now also had a full-fledged back spasm going, could barely get started for second. Jessie was jogging toward her yelling, "MOVE! MOVE!" In the meantime, the ball had finally been retrieved by the Pirates' right fielder, who threw it to the second basewoman, who, being a substitute, wasn't sure what she was supposed to do with it, so she threw it to the first person she looked at, who happened to be the third baseman—whose upcoming cataract surgery hadn't taken place yet, so he didn't see it coming until it rolled through his legs. The base runner coming from second was so winded that even though the third baseman was off the bag to retrieve the rolling ball, he stopped on third to catch his breath.

"RUN!" Musketeers fans screamed. "RUN!" Jessie hollered as she began to move toward second, one linear foot behind the woman whose spasm had just released enough to get off first base. And although he was still so winded he could barely breathe, let alone break into a sprint, finally the winning run left third base and headed toward home plate, plodding along one foot in front of the other.

The Pirates' third baseman had by now picked up the ball and got ready to toss it toward home, where the Pirates' catcher was waiting to tag out the runner. But as fate would have it, the dirt Jessie had kicked up planting her feet before she batted suddenly ignited the catcher's allergies, and a sneezing fit ensued that lasted just long enough for the winning run, huffing and puffing all the way, to cross the plate while the catcher ACHOOed with her eyes closed.

"Now, wasn't THAT worth the drive, Mom?" Josh asked his mother while they were cheering and jumping up and down. But Katie never even heard him. She was too busy watching Arthur throw his arms around Jessie. And then, for the briefest of moments, Arthur kissed his wife—his cantankerous, hardheaded, spittin' and winnin' wife—full on the lips, right in front of everybody. It was yet another first for the books.

21

Dorothy and May Belle sat at May Belle's kitchen table polishing off the last of the ham sandwiches that May Belle had whipped up for them. Earl ate faster than anyone else Dorothy knew (although Arthur ran a close second), and as soon as he had finished and the ladies had begun to settle into lengthy conversation, he'd cleared his plate and glass to the sink, then gone out to the backyard to get their lawnmower and walk it the couple of blocks to Dorothy's. She would hire him as her steady groundskeeper, she had told him. He asked daily, sometimes more than once, if it was time to mow again until he nearly wore May Belle out with the question. Finally Dorothy explained to him that it wouldn't be time to mow again until she told him it was. "Now, honey, listen to me. You shouldn't fret, because I won't forget. Oh, MY! And I'm a poet and don't know it!" She'd broken out in hearty laughter after tickling herself with that one. Earl just studied her, subtle humor nearly always escaping him. Nevertheless, he understood from past experience that Dorothy would keep her word. As soon as he'd finished his sandwich, Dorothy had told him that today was the day, and off he'd gone.

"I'll tell you what I miss the most, May Belle, and you're a dear friend to even ask, considering all I've left behind lately. Why, we might just need another pitcher of iced tea before I even reach the end of my list!"

"Never you worry about running out of iced tea. You know me—I've always got an extra pitcher in the refrigerator. Earl and I go through it like water this time of year." May Belle's house had never been air-conditioned. "What's the point of shooting cold air into a kitchen that's always got the oven running?" she would ask in sincerity. Although there were many who would argue the point, as their area of the country fairly well sweltered with heat and humidity come mid- to late summer, Dorothy wasn't one of them. She just nodded her head in agreement, knowing that in all the livelong days she'd known May Belle, she hadn't been one to be bothered by the heat—not even when everyone else thought they were surely melting. No matter what the thermometer said, May Belle would fire up her oven and bake all day if she got a hankering or someone was in need of refreshments. "The good Lord's given me very few gifts, but baking is one of them. Please let me use it!" she'd say time and again when folks hesitated to ask her to contribute a pie or plate of cookies when she'd barely put her hot pads away from her last bout. "It gives me such joy to measure and stir, test and serve. Such joy!"

Now it was her turn to serve Dorothy another tall glass of iced tea, but not before wrestling with one of her stubborn metal ice cube trays, then using her old claw-tonged server to plop a half-dozen cubes into Dorothy's glass. As for May Belle, she liked her "iced" tea room temperature.

"Here's what I miss, friend. I miss the feel of the earth under my feet, May Belle. And even when I was in my bedroom on the second floor of the farm, I knew my house was resting on its richness. I miss the stars that don't show up in town around the streetlights. I miss the smell of hay and the view from my favorite spot and the rustle of pigeons when the big door is opened. I miss the creaking sound of my stairs when I walked up to my office, and the rattle of gravel on The Tank's undercarriage as I headed for home. I miss watching Sheba's tongue flapping in the breeze in my rearview mirror. I miss *driving*. The independence of going where and when I want. As *fast* as I want."

The women sat staring at each other, then May Belle nodded her head up and down in acknowledgment of Dorothy's statement.

"Yes, Dorothy, I imagine you do. Although I never did find it necessary to drive, I always knew *you* liked driving, whether you had anyplace to go or not. You liked driving just to be driving, about the same way I like watching teaspoons full of cookie dough spread on the cookie sheet in the oven. Or the smell of peach juice on my fingers when I quarter them for a pie. Or the steam rising up out of a pan of homemade chicken and noodles when I lift the lid."

Dorothy stared hard at her friend and tears welled in her eyes. "You know one of the things I've always liked best about *you*, May Belle?"

"What's that, dear?"

"Your way with words."

"Oh, Dorothy," May Belle said, covering her mouth with her hand. "What on earth do you mean? Why, I can't even as much as spell."

"I mean the way you so quickly bring all the bigness of life into the smallest details. The way your words have always been a balm to my soul. Your words, your friendship . . ." A tear trickled out of Dorothy's right eye and rolled down her cheek.

"My double fudge brownies?" May Belle asked, lightening the moment.

"And them, too. The fact of the matter is, I like you. I imagine it's been way too long since I told you that I just plain old like *you*. I simply cannot imagine my life without the good company and friendship of you and Earl." Dorothy reached across the table and picked up May Belle's plump hand and drew it to her own cheek. "Thank you, May Belle, for putting up with me. I know sometimes I'm a pistol, but never once have you given me cause to worry I might lose our friendship, even when I've behaved badly."

"Dorothy Wetstra! When have you behaved badly?" May Belle rubbed her index finger against Dorothy's wrinkled cheek to wipe a tear away while Dorothy continued to hold her hand to her face. "Okay, sometimes you may have borderline been a bit frisky, but . . ." May Belle snickered, as did Dorothy.

"I mean it, May Belle. Your loyalty and honesty have helped sustain me during some of my hardest times. If it hadn't been for you, I don't know what I'd have done when I lost Henry and Caroline Ann. What I'd have done when Vinnie moved away. What I'd have done when I've had all those leftovers without you to come for smorgasbord night." Again they chuckled, falling into the familiar pattern of their friendship that mixed meaning with levity.

May Belle sighed when Dorothy set her hand back on the table, allowing her to now swipe at her own nose, prompted into running by her own tears. "Well, since we're having true confessions here, I guess it's my turn now." May Belle placed her hands on top of Dorothy's, which now rested on the table, fingers folded together. "You, Dorothy Jean Wetstra, have blessed me in uncountable ways. I reckon my life would have been downright boring without your lively presence in it. Earl and I have about the truest friend one could have. Thank you from *both* of us, our *Dearest* Dorothy, for not only shuttling us from here to there ever since Homer died, but for always being so happy to see both of us. You know, although everyone in Partonville accepts Earl, not everybody treats him the same. Oh, it's not that they're not good to him, but you, Dorothy, have always treated him like an equal."

"And why *wouldn't* I?" she asked, incredulous.

"Some just have a harder time than others."

The distant sound of a lawnmower started up in the background. "Well, I guess my faithful groundskeeper is fast at work!"

"That's what I'm talking about, Dorothy. Earl isn't just mowing your lawn—you've honored him with a title." May Belle choked out the last word, then tears began to just pour out of her eyes. "My Earl, a groundskeeper!"

By the time the two women stopped blubbering, each had blown her nose no less than twice. "Aren't we a sight?" Dorothy asked as they looked into each other's reddened eyes.

"Let's get to something happier," May Belle said. "Let's talk about what you *don't* miss so far, even though you've only been here a few days now."

"Let's see. I don't miss fretting about how inconvenient it's been for so many people to have to come out to the farm to handle all I've grown too old to handle. I don't miss worrying what's going to happen to the farm when I die. I don't for a moment miss that! I tell you, it gives me more peace than you can imagine just knowing my affairs are in order." May Belle shook her head up and down, and a far-away look flashed across her face. Dorothy knew May Belle worried what would become of Earl when she passed. There'd never been a scrap of extra money, and she had no idea how Earl would ever survive another's supervision or even *if* anyone would take him, other than the county home.

"But let's move on to what I've *gained*," Dorothy said. "I've gained the security of neighbors close by, especially you and Earl. I've gained a ham sandwich just for walking two blocks. I've gained a fire engine red ceiling and the perkiest kitchen I've ever seen! And May Belle, for the first time in my life I've gained the chance to decorate a place myself. I'm beginning to think that red ceiling is only the beginning!"

"You mentioned that before, Dorothy. And here I thought you were kidding about wanting that red ceiling! I have to say, it kind of makes me feel like I'm walking into a cottage. I liked it much better than I thought I would when I heard you talking about it. Have you got any other plans?"

"I think I'm gonna take me a walk to Swappin' Sam's."

Swappin' Sam's was on the outskirts of town and was a combination salvage and antiques place that overall appeared more like a junkyard. Sam had officially received more than his share of complaints over the years about the condition of his establishment. Nevertheless, if you couldn't find it anyplace else, whatever *it* was, odds were—even if you might have been one to complain about his place—you'd find yourself there one day. If you had enough time and patience, you could likely find your *it* at Sam's, and most who'd lived in the area for more than a decade had, at least once if not more often.

Occasionally when Dorothy'd been out bombing around in The Tank, she would drop in just for the conversation. Sam Vitner had more stories than anyone else she'd ever heard, and he just loved telling them. "Sam, you missed your calling. You should have gone on the circuit and made your living as a storyteller," Dorothy had told him one fine, crisp afternoon last fall.

"Dorothy, why do you reckon people buy this old stuff? Because it's that special? Nope. They buy it because I tell them the stories. The story sells the product. Story sells anything, in fact."

And by golly, he was right. The last time she'd been there, she'd seen some dandy, intricately carved dining room table legs, and Sam had told her their story. They'd been the legs on the dining room table that used to sit in the governor's mansion in Louisiana—before the fire, so he explained. With great animation, Sam acted out how one Christmas season the maid had left a hand-dipped beeswax candle burning in the center of that shiny table. She had surrounded it with pinecones and bits of fresh holly, fragrant cloves and dried acorns. Wouldn't you know there was a meteor shower that very evening and everyone convened to the backyard to watch, forgetting about the candle. The next thing they knew, the table was on fire, and by the time they put it out, the only things left were the legs. "As the story goes," Sam said, "'You don't have a leg left to stand on' is certainly a saying that doesn't ring true this evening, now does it?' the governor joked as they stood gathered around remnants of smoke, staring at the legs that were still standing because of their stabilizing cross members." What governor, what year and how Sam had come by the legs were facts that were suspiciously never offered. But the story . . . ahhh, the story . . . Dorothy hadn't forgotten, so, of course, neither had she forgotten the legs.

"I'm gonna go pick me up some old dining room table legs, if he's still got them," Dorothy said to May Belle. "And who knows what else I might find."

"Table legs? What on earth for?"

"I was standing in the doorway to the guest room last night just staring, trying to picture what kind of bed I might like to buy. You know I'm putting Caroline Ann's bed in the auction, right?"

"No!"

"Yes, I am, May Belle. I realized it's time a new little head had the chance to sleep tight in that beautiful old set. I tell you, it just made me feel good to speculate what the next little girl might look like."

"So what's that got to do with table legs?" May Belle asked.

"So I was standing there in the doorway staring, and suddenly, plain as day, I recalled the day Sam Vitner told me about those table legs and *voilà*! I just imagined what a great headboard and footboard they might make! And what a story I'd have to tell about them," which of course she then went on to repeat to May Belle.

"You say you're going to use those table legs for a guest bed?"

"Yes, ma'am. If you turned those upside down . . . think about it. They'd look just like posters on a four-poster bed!"

May Belle glazed over and stared into a hole in space somewhere above her kitchen sink. For the longest time, she just stared. Then she smiled and slapped her knee. "By golly! You're *right*! How on earth did you come to that on your own?" May Belle asked without waiting for an answer.

"But Dorothy, you can't be walking down the hard road out to the edge of town. It must be two miles from here. And you certainly can't be dragging table legs back home with you!"

"You're right. I'll just call Arthur. He's always asking me if there isn't something he can do for me anyway. I'll tell him to bring his truck. Who knows what else I might find. I want to talk to him about something anyway."

"Oh?"

"The Tank."

"What about The Tank?"

"I'm talking about her smashing last ride."

"Dorothy! You're not still thinking about that demolition derby?"

"I am."

"I thought you'd gotten that notion out of your head."

"What made you think that?"

"You haven't mentioned it for a good long while."

"I've been waiting for Arthur to examine her and tell me if he thinks she can make it through the startup. That's all I'd need to make me happy is to see her go down running in a good battle, giving it all she's got, even if she's the first one out."

"Dorothy! Please tell me you're not thinking of driving!"

"I'm telling nothing more. And don't you ask me either, you hear?"

For all the decades May Belle had been Dorothy's friend, she knew that when Dorothy wagged her finger with that tone of finality in her voice, one thing was for sure: *that* was *that*.

22

When Josh and Katie arrived in Partonville on Thursday evening, they headed directly to Dorothy's new home for an up-close-and-personal look-see, as Dorothy referred to it. From all Jessica had told Katie on the phone, and from all Dorothy had shared with Josh in their daily e-mails, Dorothy was making the transition with flying and fire engine red colors. "You just won't believe how swell things are shaping up, Joshmeister!" Dorothy had typed in a flurry, sitting in her yet-drab-but-new combination computer and guest room. No doubt about it, Katie and Josh were eager to see that kitchen ceiling. It had, however, come as quite the stunning surprise to her sons and grandsons when they'd arrived, since Dorothy hadn't even mentioned it to them—figuring Jacob would lecture her, which is exactly what he did. Truth be known, Katie was as excited to see Jessica and *her* artistic handiwork Dorothy'd bragged about as she was to see Dorothy *or* the ceiling.

Katie began marveling at the transition the moment she pulled up in front of the little house. She sat in her Lexus just staring for a moment before she even turned off the engine, thinking back to the day she had first arrived in Partonville, soon after Aunt Tess's death. She recalled with emotion how stunned she'd been at its horrid, run-down and overgrown condition. But now . . . between all the yard sprucing and the new mailbox and front porch decorations, it was hard to believe this was the same dwelling. The entire place seemed to radiate the happy and refreshing presence of new beginnings.

Once inside the door, after Dorothy's generous hugs and chatting a moment about their Chicago brownstone closing and pack-up, Katie acknowledged Dorothy's family seated around the room. As much as Katie was not looking forward to being around Jacob again, she had made up her mind that she was going to be tolerant. There was just no sense in fueling an obvious, spontaneous and mutual animosity, not when everyone involved was, deep in his or her heart, really concerned for the well-being of the same woman. After giving the room a quick scan, she thankfully spotted everyone but him.

Drawing her attention back to the room itself, Katie continued to be in awe of the transformation. What she had first beheld as the piled-high chaos of Aunt Tess's mounds of possessions, and then, after the massive cleanup and dispersal, had left behind as a clean albeit lonesome space, was now shaping up into a modest but cheery home. Aunt Tess's old floor lamp with the fringed purple shade was the perfect accent to Dorothy's couch. The massive mahogany desk that had been Dorothy's father's—the one she wasn't sure she could even fit in the tiny house—stood proud and strong against the back wall as though it were overseeing the room. A man's pocket watch encased in a glass dome was displayed on the end table, and the pervading and steady ticking of Dorothy's old regulator clock on the wall reminded Katie of a beating heart.

Katie had neither noticed the clock nor its prominent sound in Dorothy's old place—now *her* place, she had to keep reminding herself. After Katie inquired about it, Dorothy replied, "I assure you it was there in our living room since nearly the beginning of time itself." They agreed that it must be the acoustics of the smaller space that brought its heartbeat to life, as though the house itself were alive.

They rounded the corner into the kitchen, Dorothy first, then Josh, followed by Katie. Bradley, Steven and Vinnie jumped out of their seats to follow them, just to witness their response to the red ceiling. Katie didn't even notice Jacob sitting at the table, so uplifted was her head. For a moment, everyone was stone still.

"This ROCKS!" Josh shouted, startling them. "Dorothy, this absolutely ROCKS! What do you say, Mom? Doesn't this ROCK?"

Everyone looked to Katie, who was now running her finger along Jessica's beautiful floral-and-ribbon design. She looked again at the ceiling, then back to the trim. "Joshua, much to my own surprise, I quite agree!"

"You're just being polite," a doomful male voice she recognized as Jacob's said. For the first time, she made eye contact with him. Forcing herself to paste a broad smile on her face, she responded, "No, sir. I mean that with all that's in me. And you can believe this, too: I don't say *anything* just to be polite."

For the rest of the evening's visit, Katie and Jacob kept their distance, positioning themselves across the room and speaking civilly to each other. The boys spent a considerable amount of time together in front of Dorothy's computer, playing some of her games. When Josh and Katie left around 8:30 P.M., sighing that it was going to be a big day tomorrow since it was Josh's first day of school, Dorothy and her grandsons walked them to the car. Vincent's boys exchanged quips with Josh about how happy they were that *their* school didn't start until *after* the holiday.

"We'll probably see you around the Lamp Post," Steven said to Josh.

"Aren't you staying here with your grandmother?" Katie asked.

"I guess you didn't notice, huh?" Bradley asked, but he didn't wait for an answer. "Grandma doesn't have any bed in there yet. Besides, for all of us to be at the farm for the sale by 7:00 A.M. Saturday would mean there'd be five of us trying to use the bathroom before we're barely awake. Dad said it would just be easier to stay at the motel. Uncle Jacob's gonna stay here and sleep on the couch, though."

Katie sighed with relief. Somehow, Uncle Jacob didn't need to be encroaching on *her* relaxing hideaway. No, 7:00 A.M. on Saturday would be plenty early to have to be in *his* company again.

At nine o'clock Friday evening, the volunteer phone tree had spread the word: all workers were to arrive at the auction site no later than six the following morning. Dorothy called Jessica, who passed it along to all her pertinent motel guests. Even though it would mean a tremendous amount of last-minute work, they'd decided, since it was promising to be a clear day after all, that it would be best to separate the Social Concerns Committee's Fall Rummage Sale from Dorothy's auction as best as possible. Containing the sale to the upper barn and the auction to the yard, house and lower barn would do that nicely.

There was already a line of buyers forming at the end of the driveway at 5:45 A.M. Signs had been posted the night before saying that until nine o'clock sharp nobody but workers was allowed beyond that point. A couple of Scouts were ordered to post themselves at the mouth of the long lane by five o'clock just to make sure folks followed the rules and weren't trying to sneak in ahead of schedule. They had been duly warned about antiques dealers who would ask for special permission to view the goods early, and they had been given strict orders to say no. Sure enough, the antiques dealers *were* the first to arrive and the first to ask, but the Scouts stood their ground in spite of the dirty looks.

Wilbur from Your Store had arrived—hauling his homemade trailer containing the steamer table and serving tables, folding chairs and all the food—at 6:00 A.M., the time Swifty and everyone on the committee had promised to be there. Wilbur figured the working troops would be hankering for coffee and doughnuts, and he was right.

Shelby's golden hair was tucked up under her Wild Musketeers baseball cap, which rested backwards on her head. She wore baggy coverall shorts over a pale blue tank top, and Josh thought it was the most beautiful outfit on the most beautiful girl he'd ever seen. It was all he could do to watch his step as the two of them carefully carried a heavy coffee table for the auction out of the upper barn, down the hill and into the yard while they chatted about yesterday's "bogus day of boring teacher introductions." Shelby commended Josh on having found his way around the school so quickly, and he thanked her again for being so helpful. He beamed brighter than a halogen headlight. He could almost hear Alex saying, "Geesh! Turn on your low beams, please. You're blinding me!"

Although it was already seventy degrees, humid and heading for the upper eighties, there was neither a cloud in the sky nor one in the weather forecast. The clear day seemed nothing short of an answer to prayer since all week the weather channel had kept predicting thunderstorms for their area this Saturday. But at the last minute—and as though blown by the very breath of God—the storm had suddenly veered to the south.

Dorothy was glad her sons, grandsons, Josh and Earl were around to supply younger muscle power. Her sons drove the tractor to maneuver the trailer loads from here to there. They kept looking at one another, saying, "Didn't we just move all this stuff a few weeks ago so we wouldn't have to move it today?" Then they would all shake their heads in exaggerated disgust, continuing to move things from here to there yet once again.

Everyone knew it would take them every bit of their three hours to set up and get things in order, especially with all the last-minute moving for the auction. One by one they looked at their wristwatches, fretting how surely it couldn't be seven-thirty already; then suddenly, it was eight-forty-five.

"NOW HEAR THIS!" Gladys shouted into the microphone from atop the trailer turned auctioneer stand.

"You gotta turn it on, Gladys!" Swifty hollered from the refreshment area, where he was already downing his third cup of Wilbur's powerful, eye-opening coffee and polishing off a home-made cinnamon roll May Belle sneaked him for free from the bake sale table. Gladys's raised voice was so loud that Swifty could hear her without the microphone.

"And WHERE, exactly, do I do THAT?" she screamed back, causing folks standing at the foot of the platform to duck and cover their ears.

"On the BOTTOM of the microphone!"

Gladys fumbled with it, finally finding the little black switch at the base of the cordless instrument. She began whapping it with her knuckle to see if she heard the thumping over the loudspeakers, which she did.

"NOW HEAR THIS!" she yelped into the mike.

"YOU DON'T NEED TO HOLLER INTO THE MI-CROPHONE!" Swifty screeched back at her the moment her voice boomed so loudly it made his expensive speakers rattle.

"Now hear THIS!" Gladys said again, this time leveling her voice a bit.

"FOR GOL-DERN SAKES, WOMAN!" Arthur yelped from inside the barn. "I IMAGINE THEY CAN PLUMB HEAR YA IN ALASKA! TURN YOUR VOICE DOWN, WOMAN!"

"Arthur Landers," Gladys said quietly into the live mike, "I *need* to be heard. What I have to say is important."

"That woman thinks *everything* she says is important," Arthur complained to Nellie Ruth as the two of them were making sure the cash box was in order and their checkout volunteers were in place.

"Now, Arthur," said Nellie Ruth, "it isn't easy being Gladys."

Arthur's mouth flew open and he looked up to respond.

Then it soaked in what she'd said, and he noticed that Nellie Ruth was grinning from ear to ear and winking at him. "I guess yer done right 'bout *that*, now, ain't ya?"

"If I could have everyone quiet down for a moment. *Please*." Gladys paused until the din waned. "The Scouts, *if* we can count on them to *not* steer vehicles into mowing us down rather than heading them toward the designated parking areas"—and she paused just long enough here to raise both eyebrows at her brother, who stood staring at her from alongside the top portion of the driveway next to the giant arrow that pointed toward the field—"will be opening the gates in exactly . . ."—she raised her wrist, then tapped on her watch face—"eight minutes and thirty seconds. That means in exactly eight minutes and thirty seconds, folks will begin storming the barn and the yard and the house, asking a million questions like"—she paused and drew a breath—"what's for sale and what's auction and where do they pay and where do they get numbers for the auction and can they write checks and how late can they pick up items and are there any guarantees or is everything sold 'as is' and can they use the toilet in the house rather than having to use the portable outhouses and . . ."—she stopped to draw a big breath, which most were beginning to wonder about—"and how late are we open and . . . and I just hope we have all the answers. And if you don't, here are a few of the most important ones.

"ONE! NO, they cannot use the toilet in the house, which is why there is a large piece of duct tape across the closed bathroom door saying DO NOT ENTER. No septic tank on earth could handle today's kind of load." Several in the crowd laughed out loud. Gladys ignored them.

"TWO! We are closing the rummage sale promptly,

PROMPTLY, at 5:00 P.M. All small items, that is, items that are smaller than a chair, must be taken today. TODAY!" The microphone squealed, causing her to once again back down her escalating voice. "All large items left behind can be picked up tomorrow between noon and 6:00 P.M. Any items *not* picked up by then will be considered donated, and we will do with them as we see fit. No exceptions.

"THREE. Net proceeds from sale items, as in those that are marked and sold for a *price* rather than purchased in the auction—and ALL *those items* are located in the *upstairs only* of the barn—will go toward this year's charitable causes, and if you can't remember what they are, read the posters in the barn. All items in the auction are Dorothy's, and proceeds will go to her, although she has stated that she will be donating a thus far undisclosed percentage to Social Concerns." Gladys noticed a couple of people tossing her a dirty look, and for the briefest of moments, she wished she hadn't phrased that exactly the way it came out. But after all, if somebody was going to make a donation, it seemed to her that they should commit a percentage *before* they knew how much they were going to make!

"FOUR. Numbers for the auction can be obtained from Swifty's wife, Loretta, whom I'm sure you all know, who is set up at that table"—she pointed with the microphone toward the house—"just over there." She realized she'd kept talking with the microphone away from her mouth, so she drew it back to her lips and repeated, "just over there. Raise your hand, Loretta," which Loretta obediently did.

"FOUR."

"You already said four," Jessie said as she passed by in front of Gladys.

Frustrated and thrown off her concentration, Gladys was forced to look at her index card again. "Please, folks, no more interruptions! We're running out of time! And listen up because this is important: FIVE. Everything is sold AS IS, *no* exceptions. None. Whether it looks like it's broken or not, broken is not our responsibility. Is everyone clear on that?" Heads nodded around the yard as Gladys refused to move forward until after her slow, 360-degree turn on the platform seeking acknowledgment. She looked down at her card again and continued.

"SIX. Yes, Swifty *and* the Social Concerns Committee will take checks but NO credit cards. Checks for sale items should be made out to United Methodist Church, and auction checks should be made out to Sell It Like It Is. Loretta has all the directions folks will need for auction information. If there are any other questions about that, refer them to her. Also, I'm sure Swifty will make any announcements he needs to before he begins, right, Swifty?" Swifty had by now walked up to her side, having been sent by Dorothy. "Use the hook if you have to, Swifty," Dorothy'd implored him. "That woman will talk until dark if we don't stop her!"

Swifty reached for the microphone, but Gladys kept a tight grip with her right hand, clasping her left hand over the top of it when he moved toward her. "The auction will begin promptly at 1:00 P.M. and not a moment sooner," Gladys said. "It will end when items are gone. And you know Swifty! He'll move things right along, ready or not."

Swifty leaned into the microphone curled in both Gladys's hands and said, "Thank you very much, Gladys. Folks, let's all give Gladys a *big* round of applause for doing such a great job of heading up the sale this year." In her moment of receptive glory, Gladys accidentally loosened her grip on the microphone, and the next thing she knew, it was gone from her hands.

Swifty looked at his watch, then looked toward the driveway, then put the microphone to his lips. "HERE THEY COME! Good luck, folks. May Social Concerns *and* Dorothy . . . may ALL of us have a safe, fun and profitable day."

Although Katie had neither volunteered for nor been appointed to any specific task, she spent the entire first two hours of the sale running herself nearly ragged, scurrying from here to there as cars swarmed her property and people invaded the land. She was astonished at how proprietary she felt, considering she hadn't even moved in yet. She also became aware that a portion of her anxieties was for Dorothy. She didn't want Dorothy to have to witness any destruction or incident on this day, which must make her move now seem very final. It was obvious from their brief meeting in Dorothy's new home last night that she was beginning to settle in, but Katie noticed a pining look in her eyes once in a while when they talked about the auction.

The moment she'd arrived at the farm this morning, Katie also noticed that Jacob Wetstra looked amazingly fit— long, well-defined calves, tight abdomen, substantial biceps—in his cutoffs and tightly fitting white cotton T-shirt. Try as she might not to stare, she'd caught herself doing so on more than one occasion.

23

⚜ ⚜ ⚜

Maggie Malone stood in the lengthy checkout line, two brightly colored throw pillows tucked under her left arm and another under her right. She wore a lemon yellow sleeveless shirtwaist dress with a wide lime green belt and yellow sling-back slippers. Her banana boat earrings danced above her shoulders as she wrangled around, trying to keep the pillows from escaping her grasp. Arthur jabbed Nellie Ruth and said, "Look what's a-comin' down the pike. Me oh my, if it don't look like one of them big tropical birds!"

"Do you think you could move it along here, fellow?" A well-to-do young stranger held his wallet in one hand and carried a heavy basket of items in the other. "The auction's going to be starting in twenty minutes, and I'd like to get these things to my car first—which is parked about a *mile* away!"

Arthur, who didn't take kindly to anyone's lip, started to stand up, but Nellie Ruth grabbed his arm and quietly yet emphatically reminded him he was representing the Social Concerns Committee and that he'd better behave. "We're sorry, sir," she said to the rude gentleman. "Here, I'm all ready for you." Arthur eyeballed the guy a good one, then gave a loud humph, one grand enough to rival even Gladys's best.

By 2:15 P.M. the entire lawn surrounding the auction items was filled with people. Swifty had lived up to his reputation, moving things right along as they worked their way toward the furniture remaining in the house, which would come last. But even though he'd been at it for more than an hour, more remained than did not. As he'd explained to Dorothy when she signed the contract—though she was already quite familiar with auction procedures—if you auction off the best stuff first, nobody sticks around until the end. "You gotta keep them waiting. And furniture is always a hot item."

Arthur, now off checkout duty and assigned by Gladys to "whatever you see needs to be done," sidled up behind the crowd, casting his eyes around for Dorothy. He'd walked the entire barn, upstairs and down; the house, upstairs and down; the whole yard, scanning this way and that, looking for her. May Belle hadn't seen her since she'd stopped by the bake sale at noon for a double fudge brownie. Her sons, who continued to haul items out of the lower barn and hand them up to Swifty, hadn't seen her. He'd checked with everybody he could think of, and *nobody* knew her whereabouts. The last time anyone remembered seeing her was right after the auction had begun. A prickly feeling began to run up his spine. It wasn't like her to disappear.

"Oh, LORD," Dorothy wailed. "Hear my prayer." She had retreated behind the barn, away from the crowds. At first she thought the sounds of people bidding on pieces of her past wouldn't bother her. After all, she herself had decided to do without whatever items she'd put up on the block.

First up had been a box of miscellaneous linens, most of which she hadn't used for decades. Nothing. She felt nothing. Next came a selection of bowls nested one in the other. The only time she dragged many of *them* out was for the annual Christmas party, and she would no longer be the hostess. When the bidding began, a slight pang of sorrow raced through her heart.

But then Swifty held up an apron. He'd stuck his hand down into a box of aprons—which would go, in its entirety, to the highest bidder—and grabbed hold of the first thing his fingers touched. Dorothy remembered that when she was packing kitchen items in the pantry, she'd simply selected her favorite apron—the only one she ever wore anymore—out of the folded stack and then just grabbed the rest of the stack off the pantry shelf and stuffed it into a box without a bit more thought. She was shocked to notice what Swifty now held in his hands. This particular worn and faded blue apron with ruffles around the neck and at the lower hem had belonged to her mother. The hem was coming out here and there, and one of the ties around the back was nearly ripped off.

Dorothy went deaf to the sounds of bidders, lost in her recollections of her mother wearing that apron while she was standing in front of her washer, patiently feeding clothes through the wringer with what she used to call her dipping stick; wearing that apron while rolling pie dough; wearing that apron while serving country fried chicken to her family, whom she so happily and selflessly cared for. The sound of her mother's humming began to play in her head, and a giant knot began to form in Dorothy's throat that she could not for the life of her swallow.

BANG! "SOLD to bidder number eighty-five for four

dollars!" The words pierced her awareness. "Four dollars for all those memories," she whispered under her breath. It was then she started striding toward the back of the barn, toward the field, the earth . . . air! When she arrived, she leaned back against the old wooden barn slats, staring toward the tree line down near the creek at the horizon. Feeling weak in the knees, she allowed her body to slide down the sturdy building until she sat. It was there she still remained, unable even to pray—until this very moment.

"Lord, as sure as I know you exist, I know I'm doing the right thing. But I am overwhelmed with how it feels like my very blood sprouts up through this land and pumps through my veins. At eighty-seven years of age, I'm suddenly racked with loss and missing my mother, my father, my sweet Caroline Ann. I am wracked with memories that are racing inside me, vying for attention, fearing they won't come my way again once I say my final good-byes to the only home I've known for my entire life." Dorothy began to cry uncontrollably, covering her eyes with her hands.

"I know," she said through sobs, "that it is time. I *know* I am relieved to have my things in order. Good Jesus, I so appreciate the way You answered my prayers as I cried out for help in my decision. So why, *why* is this so hard?"

Just then, a ray of sun worked its way past the edge of the barn and warmed her face. It was as though God had reached down and touched her with the warm palm of His hand. "'Not by might, nor by power, but by My Spirit,' says the Lord of hosts." The words in Zechariah were suddenly in her mouth. "Yes, by Your Spirit, not my pitiful pity party," she said, chuckling through her tears.

Then she thought about Noah and the ark. On more than one occasion, she'd stopped at one particular passage while reading Genesis. "So they went into the ark to Noah, by twos of all flesh in which was the breath of life. And those that entered, male and female of all flesh, entered as God had commanded him; and the Lord closed it behind him." *And the Lord closed it behind him.* The words danced in her head, reminding her that she had sought God's help; he had provided an answer; she had followed his directive. Just like Noah, she was building her own ark on Vine Street.

"And the Lord closed it behind him," she said aloud, repeating it three times, her voice getting stronger each time. The next thing she knew, she was weeping tears of gratefulness for memories that could never be stolen and for having given her trust to the One who deserved it, knowing full well that the Lord Himself would close the door to her wounds. Her body went limp as the sun lavishly splayed its warmth over her entire being.

It was 2:40 P.M. By now, Arthur had alerted Josh, Katie, Jacob and three church members that Dorothy seemed to be missing, and a search party was discreetly activated. "We'll meet right here in ten minutes," Arthur said, pointing to the very spot near the silo on which he was standing. He'd designated a direction for each of them. Before they dispersed, Katie and Jacob—at the very same time and with the exact same cadence—said, "Don't worry. I'm sure she's fine," even though they were trying to calm themselves more than anyone else. After the awkward, wide-eyed double take, off they went.

It was Josh who jogged straight toward the back of the barn, intending to run down to the creek near Willy, Woodsy and Willoway, Dorothy's favorite three trees she'd named decades ago. He figured if Dorothy went anywhere, that's where it would be. Before he had walked five paces past the barn, he saw her out of the corner of his eye.

"DOROTHY!" he shouted as he raced to her side. Josh hadn't even noticed Sheba, and she startled him when she awakened and jumped over Dorothy's lap to come running in his direction. Dorothy's outstretched legs before her on the ground, her upper body limp against the barn, her head tilted slightly to the side and her mouth agape presented a startling image. "DOROTHY!" Fearing the worst, he felt his heart pounding even harder than it had when he'd heard she was missing. He squatted down in front of her just as her eyes began to flutter open. "*Dorothy!* Are you okay? What are you doing down here on the ground? Do you need a nitroglycerin tablet? Have you taken one? Do you have them with you?" The nonstop questions flew past his lips as he fretted before her, whiter than a sheet.

"Joshmeister," she said in a weak voice. Being neither fully alert nor completely awake, she wondered why he was making such a fuss. When she finally registered his questions about nitroglycerin, then took stock of where she was and how she must look, she understood. "I'm fine, Josh," she said, her voice gaining strength as she pulled her knees up a bit and lifted her head from resting against the barn. "I must have dozed off."

"What are you *doing* back here? It's too hot back here, Dorothy. Let's get you to the shade. There's a whole pack of people looking for you."

"What on earth for?"

"Arthur gathered us up. He was worried, Dorothy. Nobody had seen you for so long . . . *Can* you stand up, do you think? Here, take my hand and I'll help you, but *don't get up too fast*! Or maybe you should just stay here and I'll go get somebody to help . . ."

"Don't be silly, Josh," she said, her voice sounding stronger with each word. Dorothy reached out and took his extended hand, then slowly he helped her to her feet. She brushed off the back of her pants and steadied her equilibrium. "Alrighty, then. Outta my way! It's time to get back to business!" Slowly her unsure legs steadied themselves, and she and Josh headed toward the silo. By the time they appeared at the meeting spot, the rest of the party had already reconvened, shrugging their shoulders and looking more concerned than before.

"Mom!" Jacob said breathlessly as he rushed toward her, then threw his arms around her so powerfully that he had to steady both of them. "Are you all right? *Where* have you *been*? I was worried sick!"

"Why, Jacob, calm down. I'm just fine, dear, as you can see for yourself." Dorothy proceeded to shuffle her feet as if she was tap dancing. "See?"

"Okay, Mom. That's quite enough dancing for one day," he said, holding tightly to her elbow.

"Lordy BE, Dorothy!" Arthur said. "I never would have thought for a hog's hoot ya'd still have *that* in ya!" Although he joked around, his face revealed his concern.

"Arthur, I've got lots in me you couldn't even imagine. But right now I'm taking it all to the auction, right after I get me a hot dog smothered in ketchup and drowning in pickle relish. I've had a nice refreshing chat with the Lord and a catnap to boot, so I reckon I'm good to go, as the kids say today, for at least another couple hours." Before any of the rest of them had a chance to say another word, she'd left them in her dust—albeit a slow-shuffling dust. But as she walked away, she wondered what in the world *had* happened to her. By the time she reached the hot dog stand, she'd dismissed the concern, deciding that she had, indeed, simply dozed off. After all, she hadn't been sleeping as well as usual in her new home, and that would surely explain it.

Katie stood frozen, staring at Jacob, still surprised at his outward emotional response upon learning that his mother was okay. From what she had seen previously, he barely cared about her. But now . . . now she'd seen something more.

Swifty was working his way through the last platform of items before moving toward the house. Most of the serious buying crowd had already headed indoors to stake their positions around the furniture objects of their desire. Arthur had pressed his way through the crowd still remaining outdoors to stand beside Dorothy, just feeling a little more at ease at her side since her disappearing act.

"I'll tell you," she said, "there's no better place to study human nature than at an auction."

"By golly, I know what ya mean. For some folks, auctions is nothin' more than a big gamblin' game. Why, I just heard a woman say, 'I WON!'" Arthur laughed a cynical laugh. "They ain't won nothin'. They done bought it, and probably paid more fer it than they shoulda anyways!" But indeed, one's desire for an object, coupled with the long wait until they finally got to it—peppered by a quickened spirit of competition—often caused people to run smack up against their better judgment. And since their internal triggers—not to mention their conscience—sometimes had only a split second to decide whether to go a notch higher than they'd promised before the gavel came down or to find themselves aced out by the last person with the guts to raise their bidding number that one more time *was* a fine and sometimes hair-raising line. Then, of course, if they *did* go that extra notch and cause the last of their opposition to drop out, they *did* feel as if they'd won.

"You goin' in the house, Dorothy?" Arthur asked.

"No, I don't believe I will. Too crowded in there. Besides, I think I'd just be stirring up a heap of emotions, watching people scalp the place clean. No sir, I believe I'll just stand here until Swifty goes through that last little bunch of whatever he's standing in front of, then I'll head back to the rummage sale before it closes and see if there's anything I can do to help. First, though, I'm gonna stop back by the bake table and pick up a bag of snickerdoodles, if May Belle's got any left."

"I reckon I'll see ya later, then," Arthur said as he started to walk away.

"Arthur! Wait! So? Can she make it? And you *know* who I'm talking about."

Arthur removed his engineer's cap, twirled it around in his hands, swiped at his mouth with the back of his hand holding the hat, then replaced the cap on his head. "Honest truth?"

"Honest truth."

"We'd have to tow her to the fairgrounds fer sure. No sir. No sir-ee-Betsy, she couldn't make it to the fairgrounds on 'er own, even if she wanted to—which I'm sure she does. *Then*, if we're lucky and if she's in a good mood—and I say *if*, as in IF—I'd say we'd have us one good chance at gettin' her to crank over, but just one, 'cuz when she dies after that, she's probably a goner. A cracked engine block can only take so much afore she plumb seizes up tighter than a lug nut around a boiled egg." Dorothy was leaned in close to Arthur, hanging on his words as though *her* life depended upon them. Her mind tried to form a picture of a lug nut around a boiled egg. She wisely decided to dismiss that fruitless endeavor and simply keep listening.

"Lots of big ifs here Dorothy. 'Cuz if she *would* keep her jets a-firin', well, it would only be a short matter of time afore, like I said, she'd die, just like a chicken who ran into a bear trap. That would be the end." Now, *that* Dorothy unfortunately could picture.

"But she'd go down fighting, right, Arthur? She wouldn't go out with a whimper or a final image of a garbage truck in her headlights, right?"

"I reckon so, Dorothy. But them was a lot of ifs, woman."

"Sign us up, Arthur! Find out how you go about it, and sign us up!"

"Dorothy, you're not thinkin' of drivin', are ya?"

"That's for me to know and you to find out, Arthur."

"Well, I can promise ya *one* thing for sure, it ain't gonna be ME!"

"Folks, right here is the last item up for bid before we head into the house," Swifty said. "It would seem I've saved the most, um, *unusual* for the last." Laughter rippled throughout the crowd, and Dorothy turned her head to see what was so funny. Gosh darn if it wasn't the bedpan stuffed with plastic poinsettias! She'd forgotten all about it. It had surely gotten tucked into the wrong pile, since it was supposed to be in the rummage sale. But it was a mistake too late to rectify, since Swifty was already set in motion.

"Who'll give me a five-dollar bill, five dollars, five, five, who'll give me five?" Swifty's cadence always reminded Dorothy of the kids who used to sit on the baseball benches and holler, "Hey, batterbatterbatter, SWING, batterbatterbatter . . ." He held the bedpan high over his head and flat across the bottom to keep the dirty plastic flowers from falling out. "Come on, folks, it's an object of art you're lookin' at here. A Christmas wonder. Who'll give me five, five, a five-dollar bill?"

"How about you start with a quarter?" a voice from the back yelled.

"How about I start with a dollar. One-dollar bill, one dollar, one dollar, one, one, one-dollar bill. Who'll bid just one lousy dollar?" Silence.

"How about you start with a quarter?" the voice from the back yelled again.

"Who'll give me half, half a dollar, half a dollar bill. Who'll give me a half?" Silence.

"I'll give you a quarter," the voice said. Swifty saw an arm rise in the air, holding a bidder's card with number 124 on it.

"One quarter, I've got one quarter. Who'll give me a half? Quarter give me half, half a dollar bill!"

Dorothy saw Swifty reach for the gavel he kept tucked in the back of his belt. "Arthur! Do you have a number?" Dorothy hadn't bothered to register for a number since everything in the auction was hers to begin with, or so she thought.

"Yup. Why?"

"QUICK, ARTHUR. RAISE YOUR NUMBER!"

Arthur reached into his coverall pocket, pulled out his number, lifted it in the air and yelled "HERE!" so Swifty didn't miss that there was another in the hunt.

"I've got a half, half a dollar, who'll give me one dollar bill? Half give me a dollar!"

"HERE!" came the voice from the back.

"I've got a dollar, who'll give me two, one dollar looking for two!"

Dorothy poked Arthur in the ribs. "RAISE YOUR NUMBER, ARTHUR!" Dutifully, Arthur pierced the air with his card.

"Two dollars I've got two, two, two, who'll give me three?"

"HERE!" While Swifty noted the stranger's bid, Arthur asked Dorothy, "What in the jumpin' jupiters are ya gonna do with that thing, woman?"

"Hush up and just hold your arm in the air, Arthur. And don't put it down 'til I tell you to!" Arthur did as he was told. Swifty acknowledged Arthur's three-dollar bid and asked for four.

"YUP!" said the voice from the back.

"Four, who'll give me five? Do I have five dollars?" Arthur supported his raised right arm with his left, acting like the bidder's card weighed a ton. "FIVE, now I've got FIVE DOLLARS!" Swifty said, pausing a moment in his own astonishment. A mumble rippled through the crowd. "Who'll give me a TEN-dollar bill? Five I've got five, who'll give me ten?"

"What happened to SIX?" asked the bidder in the back.

"Just trying to speed things along so I can get a potty break in before we move inside," Swifty said. Everybody laughed, since it was a potty he held in his hand.

"Well, I'll give you SIX!" said the sarcastic voice.

"Dorothy, why don't ya just let that piece of junk go? What's gotten into ya, woman?" Arthur stared at her long and hard, wondering if she hadn't lost her mind back there behind the barn.

"Arthur Landers! Do *not* lower your hand! Don't even LOOK like you're wavering! Can you see who in the world that is bidding against us?" Dorothy craned her neck, but from her perspective, the face of the bidder that belonged to the arm could not be seen, and she didn't recognize the voice. Arthur kept his hand held high as he turned to see if he could get a gander at who was bidding against them while Swifty acknowledged their seven-dollar bid. At that moment the crowd jostled just enough that Arthur could see it was the stranger who'd given him some lip.

"HERE!" the stranger yelled when Swifty asked for eight. Although he'd previously determined he wouldn't pay more than six dollars tops for this gag gift for a golfing buddy who'd recently suffered a bladder infection, when he saw he was bidding against the testy, burly man who'd nearly refused to wait on him earlier in the day, his nostrils flared, and he set his good sense aside. The two men glared at each other for a brief moment until the crowd closed their view again. Never mind the gag; now it was a matter of wills.

"I'LL GIVE YA TWENTY DOLLARS!" Arthur yelped, trying to stare a hole through the crowd in the stranger's direction.

"*Arthur!* What in the world are you *doing*?" Although Dorothy wanted the bedpan and flowers, she surely hadn't thought about having to pay twenty dollars for them.

"There's only one thing I know fur sure right now, Dorothy, and that's that *that* fella ain't a-gonna git that ugly bedpan!" Although Dorothy had no idea as to the why of Arthur's sudden determination, she was glad of one thing, that Arthur was on *her* side. And on her side he was, clear to the finish when the bedpan and poinsettias went to bidder number four, which was Arthur's number. Yes, the bedpan was all hers, but not before she had to pay thirty-five dollars to get it!

"WE WON!" she yelped to Arthur when the gavel finally came down.

"Yup, we won, Dorothy! We beat that sissy pants good, by golly." He reached into his pocket and pulled out a crisp twenty-dollar bill and handed it to her. "I reckon fer what we paid for that dented piece of garbage and some plastic flowers, we oughta have joint custody, don't ya think?"

Dorothy stuck out her hand to shake, and Arthur accepted. "Deal!" she said. And they both laughed for a solid thirty seconds.

24

❦ ❦ ❦

It was the end of a second day of exhausting but fruitful work, during which time the cleanup committee—who'd arrived immediately after church—waited for final pickups, often having to help people load. All the auction items had been cleared away, except for a couple of miscellaneous boxes of stuff from which owners had obviously retrieved their choice item, having been forced to bid on a box-lot of goods. As if arriving direct from heaven, Dorothy's mother's old apron had been stuffed into one of them. She reclaimed it with utter joy, deciding she would display it on a wall in her new home. All looked forward to the next day's holiday when they could catch their breath.

Dorothy told the committee just to go ahead and toss the rest of the odds and ends of leftover auction items in with the leftover rummage sale boxes of stuff. They needed to get rid of them somehow, and Dorothy had already rejected them once. Then everything that had been boxed was donated to Now and Again Resale, whose owners happily came and loaded every last scrap into their old horse trailer. The committee then tidied up the grounds, depositing debris in the Dumpster.

Sometime just before the last pickup truck roared its way down the Crooked Creek lane, Caroline Ann's bedroom set strapped in the back—while its dimple-cheeked, curly-haired, blonde new owner giggled in the front seat next to her daddy—the Wetstras made the decision to have one final bonfire together at day's end. Dorothy suggested they invite Katie and Josh and make it an Official Good-bye/Hello to Crooked Creek Farm Event. Everyone agreed. But this evening they would settle for nothing less than a creekside gathering rather than their usual fire pit up near the barn. Dorothy's men had dutifully loaded everything needed on the trailer behind the tractor, even though they groaned about once again getting stuck in the loading/unloading cycle.

Katie had purchased the tractor-trailer duo fair and square at the auction. Although she wasn't sure exactly why, she knew it needed to stay. The old John Deere's official first duty under its new ownership had been to tow them all— lock, stock, firewood and benches—through the wild grasses and flowering weeds down to the feet of Willy, Woodsy and Willoway.

The sound of crickets, rustling water and quiet conversation permeated the warm Sunday evening air. Nostrils were treated to dew-laden, earthy aromas intermingled with the fragrance of smoke from the bonfire. Some of the stars actually winked, appearing like blue and reddish jewels luring the eye to behold them, and from near the horizon a full moon watched over it all. Katie and Josh, Dorothy and her sons and grandsons all sat around the fire, realizing that sooner or later they'd have to get up and say their official hellos and good-byes to the now empty estate—empty, that is, aside from the Dumpster.

The group spent the fireside evening talking about recollections from Dorothy's youth, as well as from those of her sons and grandsons. Josh gave them a replay of his first crawdad hunt with Dorothy, and they all laughed about

Josh and Alex's adventure when they wore their T-shirts tied around their heads.

"As long as you didn't get wet, everything was okay, right?" Vinnie teased. "Right. I mean, come on! Who among us hasn't gotten wet in Crooked Creek?"

Flatly and with perfect enough timing to make his point, Josh answered the redundant question. "My mom."

"What?" Steven asked incredulously. "Your mom hasn't gone crawdad hunting?"

"Nope."

"Too bad it's too dark to find the little buggers now," Vinnie said.

"But it's never too late to get wet!" A hint of a threat rose in Jacob's voice. "I'm game if everyone else is. And he—or she—who *isn't* game is a chicken liver." Although Katie couldn't see his eyes through the reflection of the fire in his glasses, she had a feeling he was talking directly to her.

"Jacob Henry," Dorothy said. "I do believe you're trying to cause trouble. We don't even have any towels down here with us, let alone up at the house now."

"Chicken Liver," he said to his mom while he looked right at her. "Chicken Liver," he said to Katie, turning his head in her direction. With that, all three boys began unlacing their shoes, as did Vinnie, then Jacob. Although Jacob had just intended to taunt Katie a bit, it seemed the rest of the clan was taking action. In a flash, Dorothy bent down to untie her pink laces.

"You can't be *serious!*" Katie said. "You're all liable to trip and slip in the dark and injure yourselves. Think about your mother here," she implored.

"Whose mother are you talking about?" Josh asked. "Theirs or mine?"

"She who doesn't *volunteer* to get wet gets wet anyway!" Vinnie said.

"Now, boys!" Dorothy reprimanded, as if they were all five years old. But they were already cautiously heading toward the creek, the full moon lighting their paths just enough to keep them from stumbling over branches.

"Come on, Mom. I'll guide the way." Jacob, who had now peeled off his shoes and socks and rolled up his pant legs like the others, came over and took his mother's hand, helping her up from the chair. Dorothy glanced over at Katie, who was still sitting on the bench, her spanking new white cross-trainers tightly laced. "Come on, dearie. I think it would be best for you if you join us voluntarily, lest this group of wild and woolies takes you hostage."

"Really, Dorothy," she said stuffily. "This just isn't my thing." Katie trusted that her firm statement would be respected.

"Wet feet don't have to be your *thing*," Jacob said sarcastically. "They just need to be your wet feet."

By now, the boys and Vinnie were kicking water at one another and whooping and hollering, their voices echoing in the darkness. Jacob was guiding Dorothy one step at a time as he backed his way into the creek, holding one of her hands in each of his. Her eyesight surely wasn't what it used to be, especially in low light. "Whoo-*ee*, that's chilly water," she said when her feet squished into the familiar and comforting muck. "But it wouldn't be so refreshing if it wasn't!"

Katie, sitting all alone, stared into the fire, the sounds of laughter encircling her. For a moment she began actually to pout, feeling abandoned by juvenile behavior. But at the exact same moment it struck her that she had *chosen* to stay behind—an insight that would never have occurred to her

several months ago—a chorus of relentless "Chicken Liver!
Chicken Liver! Chicken Liver!" came her way from the
creek.

Off went the shoes. Off went the designer socks. Off to
the water she bravely strode, ouch-ing her delicately pedi-
cured feet across the rocks and into the waters of Crooked
Creek. Before they finally doused the fire, packed up and
piled back onto the trailer, every one of them was sopping
wet. Katie couldn't remember when she had ever laughed
harder.

"Let's begin upstairs in my office," Dorothy said to the
damp and motley-looking crew, "and work our way
through, just like we did when we sorted through things."
Dorothy led the way up the stairs, once having to stop and
rest. As they stood on the stairway, Vinnie said, "Mom,
maybe we should have skipped the bonfire and splash
party. I imagine you were worn out enough already."

"Don't be silly, Vinnie. Why, you can't begin to imagine
how that restored my very soul. I wouldn't trade that new
memory for anything, not even for all the crawdads in the
creek."

Room by room, they entered and, as instructed by
Dorothy, formed a broken circle around the periphery.
With ceremony, Dorothy stepped into the middle of the
empty room, her voice sounding a bit hollow with nothing
to absorb the sound, and announced, "Office, I am saying
good-bye. Thank you. You have served me well." Then she
motioned Katie and Josh to step forward into the circle
with her. "Office, this is Katie and her son, Josh. They're
your new tenants. Thank you for all the memories you are

already beginning to impart to them." Although Katie at first felt awkward and silly, not to mention the fact that she looked disastrous, by the time they were done with the first two rooms she had forgotten about her vanities. An acute awareness of a deeper meaning now grew in the pit of her stomach. Occasionally Dorothy would thank a room for a specific memory, especially in her bedroom, the room in which she had been conceived and born. Everyone choked back a tear before they left there.

When they got to the last room, the kitchen, Dorothy had them form a tight enough circle to hold hands. It was time for a prayer of thanks. In the middle of the empty kitchen in the empty farmhouse, she began:

"Lord, giver of life, of all that is seen and unseen, I am overwhelmed with gratefulness for the folks gathered here with me in this circle. *Thank you* for sparing me trying to say my good-byes by myself when I first moved out awhile back, for surely I would have broken under the weight.

"But now, now with the people I love gathered around me, and the promise of new life and stories standing right here beside me"—she squeezed Katie's hand when she spoke—"I don't feel so much like I'm leaving something as I am just moving along and turning things over to the next loving hands." She paused for five seconds, contemplating. "I imagine that's what heading for heaven will be like. A feeling of just moving along to the next better place, making room for those who will come to this earth even long after I'm gone.

"Thank you, God, for seeing us through so many trials. For feeding us off the land. For loving us, even when we didn't love You with our whole hearts. Thank you for a sturdy homestead and the hands that built it.

"Thank you for the uncountable memories I take with me and the joy that fills my heart when I sift through them. Thank you, God. Thank you. And that's it for now. Amen." Her voice had stayed strong and steady throughout.

By the time they let go of hands, Katie's nose was running like a faucet as tears streamed down her cheeks. When Jacob noticed her trying to wipe her entire face with her damp shirtsleeve, he reached into his back pocket and handed her his monogrammed cotton hanky.

Before Dorothy got into Jacob's car, she told everyone she needed to have a quiet moment by herself in the barn. "Please, dear, open the big door a crack so I can squeeze through. I'll only be a minute." Jacob held her elbow in his hand as they ascended the hill, past the silo, into the barn. He rolled back the door for her, then stood watch outside while his mother said her personal good-byes to the barn.

Katie started up her Lexus, desiring to leave to give Dorothy space for her final farewells. When she turned the wheel, the Lexus's headlights flashed directly on Jacob, revealing the fact he was wiping tears from his cheeks. Quickly she cut the engine, feeling as though she'd broken into the hidden heart of a man.

Inside Dorothy stood silent, not even praying. She concentrated, willing her senses to absorb as much of the surroundings as she could. Oh, it wasn't that she wouldn't be back to visit. But it would never feel quite the same again, of that she was sure. For decades and decades, this place had been nothing short of God's holy ground, where Dorothy could drink of her maker's magnificent creation and melt into being nothing more or less than *her* complete self. "Just as I am, Lord. You've *always* accepted me just as I am."

Suddenly, the words she'd heard God whisper to her just a few short months ago when she stood nearly in the same spot as she did right now came to her again. *Remember well all you see, for these splendid images will sustain you in the days to come.* She closed her eyes and meditated upon the words. Favored verses from the first chapter in Second Peter rose within her. *". . . I shall always be ready to remind you of these things, even though you already know them, and have been established in the truth which is present with you. . . ." "His calling and choosing you . . ."*

"John fourteen, twenty-six. Lord, I thank you for my Sunday school teacher who helped me memorize *that* one." She spoke the verses aloud. *"But the Helper, the Holy Spirit, whom the Father will send in My name, He will teach you all things and bring to your remembrance all that I said to you."*

"THANK YOU, sweet Jesus, for reminding me I don't even have to worry about remembering, other than to remember You were, are and will always be with me, no matter where I stand." Dorothy Jean Wetstra then blew a kiss to the heavens. With the eyes of her heart, she fully understood the power of living in the moment. Her merry heart then delivered a huge smile to her face, and in that instant, Dorothy knew that no matter where she roamed, her very own smile would proclaim her memories—the very spirit—of Crooked Creek Farm.

25

Josh was happily off to his third week at Hethrow High and his first week getting on the bus at the end of the lane at Crooked Creek, the place he and his mom had now moved into. Katie'd had her concerns for his transition alleviated early on when he returned to the Lamp Post day after day rattling on a mile a minute about how Shelby had spent every free moment in the halls introducing him to this one and that, and how she seemed to know just about *everybody*. He engaged in nonstop, upbeat chatter for a solid twenty minutes nearly every day.

Tucked in with all the good news, however, Katie thought she discerned a bit of a jealous note in his voice when he talked about all the guys Shelby'd introduced him to. But it was clear Josh himself was encouraged by all the new acquaintances, some of whom even stopped by the Lamp Post and invited him to join them in after-school French fries at Harry's. "And Mom, the *best* part is that the majority of them are just regular guys, not a bunch of geeky, boring college preppies!"

Now that Katie and Josh had moved into the farm, Katie sought out every opportunity she could to spend time with Jessica. She missed their nearness from all those stays at the motel. It turned out that since the Lamp Post had had such steady bookings for the last few months, thanks to the city slickers, a little extra money was in the till—at least for the moment—for Jessica to hire a cleaning lady for the rooms one day a week, and today was the day.

Jessica sat cuddled in a corner of Katie's posh, mud-colored, kid-leather couch, legs drawn up under her. Katie marveled at how young Jessica sometimes appeared, especially with her sassy new hairdo, which Katie *still* couldn't believe Maggie Malone had given her. Sarah Sue slept in the new portable crib Katie'd purchased for her, saying she'd never before had a chance to give Sarah Sue a gift. Katie also selfishly knew the lightweight contraption would enable Jessica to stay out at the farm for longer periods without having to worry that Sarah Sue was going to roll off the couch, even though she wasn't even scooting yet, or catch a draft from lying on the floor.

Jessica got up off the couch and started surveying the living room, walking from here to there and holding her fingers up, looking through the box she made with them. Katie had simply been unable to arrange her furniture so that it felt right. She was shocked at how out of place her African décor looked in the old farmhouse, deciding she must have had her head in the clouds to have ever imagined it would work. But even though Jessica's eyebrows had shot up in the air the first time she saw the room, she finally convinced Katie that with a little ingenuity, she was sure they could tie everything together and make it just beautiful. Shortly after Jessica had arrived today, she called the visit *Let's Imagine.* "No ideas will be off limits. No colors ruled out. We'll just brainstorm."

"I'm not good at brainstorming," Katie replied. "I'm good at high stakes and deal closing."

"Don't be silly. Everyone can brainstorm. It just takes a

little practice." Jessica walked backward into the entryway to the living room and cast her eyes about. Suddenly, a look of excitement leaped across her face. "What if we could find an area rug that had all the right colors and we moved the furniture off the walls a bit, drawing everything into kind of a conversation pit? I saw something like that in a *House Beautiful* at the checkout line at Your Store."

"Oh, I don't think we could ever . . ."

"NO, *no*, no! The first rule of brainstorming is that you don't ever say, 'I don't think that will work' or that 'we could never.' All ideas are bounced around. Hear me out, now." Jessica had come alive with her idea. Katie marveled at her uncontained enthusiasm. "It just struck me that African décor and homey farm colors are very similar in tones," she said almost breathlessly. "Earthy. I think the right rug . . . one that had a little red in it . . . YES! That's IT! A rug with a little red, and then a few red accents here and there . . ."

"Jessica, I think you've been brainwashed by Dorothy's kitchen."

"No, I'm sure I'm right. Stare hard, Katie, and try to imagine." Jessica crossed the room and scooted the side chairs away from the wall. "Grab the other end of the couch. You'll see what I'm talking about." Together they grunted, pushed and arranged the furniture into Jessica's vision. Then in a flurry of activity Jessica began rearranging end tables and accent pieces, moving them from here to there, once again rearranging the side chairs, standing back and squinting, then moving things just a tad more.

"THERE! THERE IT IS, Katie! If you had the right rug and some throw pillows that picked up the reds and browns, it would be PERFECT! The next time I'm at Now and Again, I'm going to check their fabric roll ends." Katie stood staring at Jessica, thinking about how much her couch and chairs, artifacts and collector's items, had cost her. To even imagine the finishing touches would come from a resale shop was nearly beyond her comprehension.

"I know!" Jessica exclaimed. "Where are the baskets I made for you?"

"In my bedroom."

"Run, get me one!" Although Katie loved the baskets Jessica had made for her motel room, then insisted she take for a house-warming gift, Katie was sure of one thing, and that's that they certainly wouldn't go with her living room. "Go on now, go get me one!" Jessica all but demanded. "I can see what you're thinking already, and that is against the rules of brainstorming." It was beginning to get scary how transparent Katie had become in the company of her new best friend.

When Katie returned, Jessica began tugging at the fabric of the basket until she'd removed it. She all but ran to one of the side chairs and laid the wadded fabric down on the floor, setting the legs of the chair on the edge of it, smoothing the wrinkled, foot-square bulk of it toward the center of the room. "SEE! Oh, Katie, these colors would be PERFECT in a rug! *Squint*, Katie. Look at it through squinted eyes and you'll be able to drown out the pattern and just see the colors."

Katie tried Jessica's squinting method and sure enough, after a few seconds, she caught Jessica's vision. "You, Jessica Joy, are a marvel! How on earth do you do that?"

"Gift. It's a gift."

"Are you sure you've never been to design school? Maybe in your previous life?" The two of them chuckled, and Jessica assured Katie she'd barely made it through high school. "Well, you have it, lady," Katie assured her. "You absolutely have it. I was going to have my Chicago decorator head down here for a weekend, but I'd much rather pay you."

"Oh, Katie! Don't talk crazy like that." Jessica's face turned bright red. "I don't know what I was thinking, acting like I'd know more than a decorator." Jessica appeared to be shrinking in stature as she spoke. "*Please*, have her come. I'm embarrassed I've been acting like I know what I'm doing when you have a personal decorator you've already worked with. Really, Katie, please forgive my country ignorance." Jessica started to remove the fabric from under the legs of the chair, her face still crimson and her eyes tearing up with humiliation.

"If you remove that, I'll . . . I'll . . . well, I'll never brainstorm with you again. Honestly, Jessica. I wouldn't compliment you if I didn't mean it. You have more natural talent in one bolt of enthusiasm than I have in my entire being. *Trust* me on this—I don't say things like that unless I mean them. I'd much rather work with you anyway. You're . . . FUN!" A few seconds of silence lingered in the air. "And the truth is"—Katie sighed a huge sigh—"my decorator's really a snob." Katie stared hard at Jessica, who had reseated herself on the couch, shoulders still slumped and hands folded in her lap. An odd look crossed Katie's face, then she spoke very quietly. "In fact, it's time I faced facts. I'm a snob, too."

"Katie! What are you talking about?"

"I mean, since way before my aunt died, I had an attitude about Pardon Me Ville, and it wasn't pretty. I think I've judged just about everybody in this town." Katie stared at her interlocked fingers.

"Don't be silly, Katie!"

"Hear me out, now, before I shrink back from the *truth*." She lifted her eyes and looked straight into Jessica's. "I have always, way before my mom died, been embarrassed to think my roots were in a place like Partonville. I bet I broke my mom's heart on more than one occasion, making snide comments about it. . . . My heart *aches* to think how I must have wounded her. And now that I *know* . . . How does one ever make up for such unkind behavior and judgments?"

"Oh, Katie." Jessica rose and took a few steps toward her friend. "We all get some thick ideas in our heads. But now that you've been here, you can see how the place kind of grows on you. Be kind to yourself, Katie. I'm sure your mom understood. There've been times *I've* even wished I'd moved away, lived in a place with more excitement, more opportunities. But then I think about my husband and Sarah Sue, our friends, our church . . . and now you . . ."

Before they knew it, the two women were standing in the middle of the living room hugging. The Good-bye/Hello evening that had taken place less than two weeks ago suddenly popped into Katie's mind. Dorothy had thanked this very room for the memories it would impart to her. Surely this would be one that would last forever, for it was the night Katie Mabel Carol Durbin admitted she'd been a snob and Jessica Joy became someone's personal interior decorator.

Earl stood on a chair, carefully maneuvering into position to make sure he put the thumbtack exactly where Dorothy was pointing. He gently stretched the faded blue fabric toward himself until Dorothy said, "STOP! Right there,

Earl, honey." He didn't want to harm the deteriorating fabric, and twice she had to coax him into believing that it was okay to stick the pin clear through until it stuck to the wall just like the others. "Now be careful getting down off that chair, Earl," she warned.

When he was back down on the floor, Dorothy and May Belle backed to the opposite side of the room to admire their cleverness. "Oh, Dorothy, it's just perfect in here," May Belle said. "*I* remember your mom in that apron, too. The minute I saw it, you didn't even have to tell me where it came from. But then to think what all you went through that day at the auction over it! It's just a miracle, I tell you." Earl stared at the apron up on the wall above the computer, trying to see whatever it was that made them so happy.

"If you think *this* is good, now I'll *really* show you two something," Dorothy said. "Follow me." She headed for the spare bedroom, waiting until May Belle and Earl were in position before she turned on the light. "*Voilà!*"

"For goodness sakes, Dorothy," May Belle said, staring at the beautiful four-poster bed. "Don't tell me those are *table* legs!"

"I'm here to *tell* you they are," Dorothy said. "Arthur picked them up for me, and then Edward Showalter made the simple frame and attached it all together. I'll tell you, I'm beginning to wonder if there's anything that man can't do! The mattress was just delivered yesterday. Then it occurred to me my old dining room tablecloth would make the prettiest bedspread. . . . Can you hardly believe it? I'm so excited about the way the whole thing looks that I could just bust wide open!"

"It's beautiful, Dorothy. You'd just never guess those were table legs."

"Where's the table, Dearest Dorothy?" Earl asked. "I don't see a table."

"Oh, I don't see a table either, Earl. Let's go look in the bathroom and see if we can't find something more fun in there." Dorothy flipped off the light and motioned for them to follow her. "Just get a gander at *that,* Earl!" Even though the walls were white, it was the brilliant accent colors that caught the eye. The wooden trim to the vanity mirror had been painted cobalt blue, and a one-inch border of sunshine yellow zinged mid-wall high around the middle of the room. The towel bar was blue to match the mirror trim, and a basketball-sized sun was painted up in the corner over the tub.

May Belle's mouth flew open, and she looked at Dorothy. Before she could speak, Dorothy said, "Edward Showalter, paint and three hours. That was that. In one day that man can accomplish more than you can shake a stick at." It did not pass by May Belle that the last time Dorothy said the name Edward Showalter, she did so with a girlish lilt to her voice.

Even in the midst of all the decorating, Joshua Matthew Kinney had managed to get his driver's license. He'd logged plenty of hours since he received his permit before they left Chicago, and he had logged many more during two weeks' worth of back-and-forths to Hethrow High before they officially got moved into the farm. Katie finally ran out of excuses to keep him from getting his license, other than "I just can't be old enough to have a son who drives." After he proved himself numerous times driving around Hethrow during thus far fruitless scouting trips for rugs and window treatments, and managed to demonstrate his behind-the-wheel prowess on the gravel roads as well, she finally conceded he was ready.

The day he got his license, after much nagging, Katie broke down and let him take the Lexus for his first solo trip. Although he wanted to go pick up Shelby and take her for a ride, Katie vetoed the idea, saying he needed to concentrate on his first expedition alone, and she was afraid he just wouldn't be able to do that around Shelby. She did, however, let him talk her into going to Dorothy's to take her and Sheba for a ride. When he pulled up in front of Dorothy's house, they were waiting on the front porch.

After Dorothy got all seat-belted in and Sheba finally perched herself on the backseat, head hanging out the window, Dorothy said, "Show me your stuff, kid. You can't go too fast for me!"

"You trying to get us grounded, Dorothy?" Josh said with a laugh.

"Okay, don't floor it. But let's at least go fast enough for me to feel that breeze blowing through my pink scalp, okay? And what do you say we take a spin by Shelby's and at least just toot the horn and wave."

She received not a word of argument.

26

✥ ✥ ✥

"Ladies and gentlemen, boys and girls, welcome to the last event of the season!" The announcer's voice boomed out of the loudspeakers, causing Earl to cover his ears. He and May Belle had ridden with Ben and Maggie to the fairgrounds, where they hooked up with all their kids, grandkids and great-grandkids, who'd been saving seats for them by laying blankets along the bleachers. Lester, Harold, Nellie Ruth, Gladys, Pastor Carol, Pastor's two kids and Jessie sat in the row behind them. Harold's wife hadn't come because she didn't like automobile racing, and try as he might, he could not convince her that demolition derby was not racing but "a test of metal against metal, strength against will and guts against brains. A fight to the death," he'd said. "Oh, Harold, you're so cute when you're dramatic. But I'm still not going."

Another row up, Cora Davis sat next to Jessica and Paul Joy, who had, for the first time, left their baby with a sitter, not wanting to expose her little ears to the loud roar of engines. Pastor's wife had volunteered to baby-sit, and Paul convinced Jessica it was time the two of them had a night out alone. Sarah Sue had gotten plenty used to a fill-in bottle by now, and Pastor's wife, who'd even come to their home, could certainly be trusted. Jessica looked at her watch every three minutes and fretted a bit, but once the announcer began his warm-up, she decided to grab hold of her husband's hand and for one night just try to remember she was a *woman* as well as a mom.

Lawyer Rick Lawson, his secretary and nearly thirty other Partonville folks were seated around everyone else, forming a mighty rooting section for their hometown's favorite. Once Harold's little tidbit appeared in the *Partonville Press* announcing "The Tank's Last Hurrah," nobody wanted to miss it, especially since the driver was listed as Mystery Person. Some were there rooting to pay their last respects to The Tank while others came to cheer because The Tank would never again terrorize their streets.

Since the county fairground stadium was quite large, the Partonvillers were outnumbered by fans from other areas. It was clear from the program listing statistics that most other cars and/or drivers had been racing at the monthly meets throughout the summer. Lester leaned over to Harold and said, "I've always heard that the old station wagons have the best chance since the vehicles do most of their smashing with their rear ends to protect their engines."

"That is correct, Lester. But you are forgetting one thing: The Tank's not called The Tank for nothing! No sir. Those 1976 Lincoln Continentals, back *and* front, were made like brick barges. If they hadn't been, Dorothy would have surely done her in by now!" Everyone sitting around who'd heard the exchange quite agreed.

Arthur was down in the pit area. He'd had to come early to have The Tank checked in an hour before the derby began. "Well, old gal," he said when he hooked her up to the tow bar at his place, "enjoy this ride headin' in the right direction, because fer your last ride—and I do mean yer *last*—you'll likely be a-goin' in reverse. I reckon you can do that 'bout as well as everything else you've done in your life-time. Just give 'em yer best stuff, honey," he'd said.

The pit area, visible to the crowds, was just off to the right of the derby arena. Every once in a while the Par-tonvillers would see Arthur raise the hood and tinker around, then he would close the hood and everyone could tell his jaw was still working as he talked her through what-ever was to come. What everyone was *really* looking for, however, was not Arthur but the driver—who still had not been identified, not even on the evening's one-sheet racing form. Although the *entry* was credited to Dorothy Jean Wet-stra of Pardonville (a typo that did not escape Harold Crabb), the *driver* was listed as TBA, to be announced.

The next time the voice boomed over the loudspeakers, the announcement was made that there was to be a manda-tory drivers' meeting behind the judge's stand, which was across from the bleachers and roped off and invisible to the public. Any driver not in attendance, they were told, would be disqualified since rules were rules, and they didn't want anyone to be endangered. Although the Partonville cheer-ing gallery craned their necks to see if anyone they recog-nized—and hopefully it wasn't *Dorothy*—headed toward the designated meeting area, they didn't see a person they knew aside from Arthur, who'd just taken to whapping the front fender with a sledgehammer, making sure no metal was left within rubbing distance of the tires from her garbage truck escapade. Right after the announcement, he tossed the hammer down in disgust and disappeared behind the judge's stand, causing Jessie's heart to skip a bit. "SURELY he's NOT!" she said to the universe.

"Well, where's *Dorothy*? And for that matter, where's her

city slicker friends?" Gladys wanted to know. "It could be any one of them, maybe even that young fellow I saw parading around the square in that fancy Lexus."

"I'm sure he's too young to drive in a demolition derby," Maggie said.

"No, Maggie, you are incorrect. It says right here in the program"—and Gladys jutted her program right up into Maggie's face—"that you only need to be sixteen years old and have a parent's consent. Although I must say that I find it *highly* unlikely they'd stoop to something like *this*, considering all their uppity airs." Gladys turned up her nose as she cast her eyes around from the crowd to the muddy mess of a derby arena. In fact, she kind of wondered what she, a mayor, was doing at such a questionable event herself.

"For goodness sakes, Gladys! Don't even *think* about DOROTHY being a driver!" Nellie Ruth admonished. "I'm sitting here praying as hard as I can that it's not her. And if you all have an ounce of sense in your heads, you'll do the same."

"I'm going to say a quick prayer myself for who*ever* it is," Pastor said, "because it seems pretty sure they'll be a rookie." Pastor scanned some of the fans from surrounding towns, many suddenly appearing oddly bloodthirsty and burly beyond belief. He decided he needed to stop watching so much professional wrestling on TV.

The derby arena was a rectangular shape about one hundred by two hundred feet. It was surrounded by telephone poles lying end to end, staked into the ground and shored up by dirt. The poles served as a boundary, but they were also an impediment drivers liked to use to try to ram other cars over—at least one tire's worth—thereby hanging them up and causing them to be out of the race. As soon as a car could not move for more than sixty seconds—whether it was hung up, overheated or smashed into stillness—they were black-flagged by one of the officials, and that was that. Also, if you were running but didn't intentionally hit another car still in the derby for sixty seconds, you were also out, for acting like a chicken.

The only other thing that could disqualify a driver was to ram a driver's-side door deliberately, which was an obvious safety violation. You'd get a warning the first time it happened, but the second time, you were not only disqualified but also booed, since most fans didn't take kindly to meanies.

In order to prepare The Tank to abide by the rules and regulations, Arthur had had to remove all the glass from the windows aside from the windshield, which was optional. If you took the windshield out, your helmet had to have a full-face shield. If you left the windshield in, you wore a regular helmet without a face shield. But if the windshield came out during the race, you were also black-flagged. Since the dirt ring was turned into a mud bath before the races began, keeping speeds from getting too out of hand—not to mention the fact that fans just *love* mud—a windshield served its purpose but posed its own risk. Arthur figured The Tank was goin' down one way or the other, so he decided to risk keeping the glass to protect the driver from the blinding mud. When they said all other glass had to be removed, however, that's what they meant; he even had to hammer out the taillights, headlights, reflectors and outside mirrors, during which time he apologized to The Tank on more than one occasion.

The driver's-side door had to be bolted or welded shut, and Arthur went with the bolting since he had all the tools for that. The Tank's radiator needed to be drained and re-filled with clear water: no antifreeze or additives allowed. The gas tank had to be inside the car in the rear seating compartment and secured with a protective fire wall. It also couldn't hold more than five gallons of gasoline. He had to drive to Hethrow to get a marine-type tank, which was most recommended. After he talked around to every "gear head" he knew, they all agreed it was worth the price, which wasn't that much to begin with. Besides, he figured he owed it to The Tank to get her a farewell gift anyway.

One of the most consuming of requirements, however, was the necessity for two eight-inch holes in the hood, one on each side of the carburetor. Fire was always a threat, which explained the gas tank situation, and extinguishers needed to be able to get right in.

The final "gussy up," as Arthur called it, was to paint both her front doors with the large black numbers of Dorothy's choice. She'd opted for 23, since that was the day her Caroline Ann had gone to heaven. "Wear them numbers proud," he said when he finished painting, even though he'd used an old can of spray paint he'd found in the shed and the paint had run in several spots.

All drivers had to wear an approved seat belt, no ifs, ands or buts about it, and an approved helmet, which Arthur had borrowed from Melvin Jack, Edward Showalter's friend who owned a Harley. Cars had yardsticks taped up the frame of the driver's window, and when they were out, they had to break the stick off. This way cars still in the derby were signified by their sticks, and cars that were out were out of bounds as targets.

Between programs, printed rules and announcements, all the important stuff was finally covered. The water truck was giving the ring one last dose of spray. No doubt about it, the ring was now one solid mud bath, since a summer storm had come through the day before. It had been quite entertaining to watch the truck slipping and sliding a bit itself. So entertaining, in fact, that by the time it pulled out of the ring and the announcer's voice came over the loudspeaker asking everyone if they were ready to rumble, the Partonville gang was stunned and aggravated at itself for watching a dumb water tank truck rather than striving to sight *who* had gotten behind the wheel of The Tank!

There were to be eleven cars in The Tank's heat, which was the first of three qualifying heats for the night. The final three cars in each heat to remain moving would advance to the championship round later in the evening. One by one the cars revved up and made their way from the pits to the ring entrance. When it was The Tank's turn to fall in line, the driver was still trying to crank her over. Arthur motioned for the next car to go around them, then the next. He popped the hood, yelped around the side of the car, instructing the driver to do something—although no one could hear over the roar of the engines and the crowd—and then he tinkered a moment.

"It looks like number twenty-three, a *real* oldie, is having some trouble, folks." Just then, a big backfire racked the night air and The Tank rumbled to life. "Wait . . . there she goes!" If the announcer hadn't said so, Partonvillers would have known anyway by the grin on Arthur's face. As The Tank made her way past Arthur toward the ring, he lifted a thumbs up to the driver and patted The Tank's rear end as she went by.

"Lord, hear our prayer!" Nellie Ruth said as she bowed her head yet again, her heart nearly beating out of her chest. "HAS ANYONE SEEN DOROTHY?" she screamed, trying to be heard over all the noise. Eyes searched this way and that, but all those who had been missing before were still nowhere to be seen.

The Tank pulled up in the last space inside the ring, nose to the poles. Five cars were on one side and six on The Tank's side, rear ends toward the center of the ring. The announcer beckoned the crowd to help in the countdown. "TEN! NINE! EIGHT! SEVEN! SIX! FIVE! FOUR! THREE! TWO! ONE!" Down came the green flags in the flagmen's hands, and into reverse they all went. The Tank's nose was the last away from the poles, but it was clear she was floored from the sounds of her engine.

The Tank's first hit was sloppy, since she'd not been directly lined up with anyone to her rear and she'd backed up at an angle. Nevertheless, it was a hit. The right rear of The Tank crashed into the right backseat door of the Ford that had just been smashed into by station wagon number 00. When 00 had made contact with the Ford, a huge group of fans cheered, yelling a long "OOOOOOOOOO" sound and holding up their thumbs and forefingers in circles, thumb knuckles joined together creating *00*s.

The Tank moved forward away from the pileup, but before she'd gotten back into reverse and readied to pick up speed, 00 had cut his wheel and rammed into the front passenger-side door. Again, the 00 fans went crazy. Partonvillers actually moaned out loud, as though they'd personally felt the impact.

"Who*ever* is driving better get with it!" Gladys barked.

Rather than pull forward to realign this time, The Tank just kept going backward as fast as she could go, striking full bore into the front end of a Chevy whose engine was already smoking. Suddenly the Partonvillers were on their feet cheering. But before they knew it, 00 had blasted into The Tank's front end, sandwiching her between the Chevy and his own backside.

"Number twenty-three just took a good whack!" the announcer yelled. "Looks like zero zero has decided who his competition is! You certainly can't blame him for going after a car made like *that!*"

The Tank just sat there after 00 pulled away. Action was going on all around her, and three of the cars were already out of the race, including the one that came into the ring looking more like an accordion than a competitor. BLAMMO! The Tank took another shot, right into the rear door behind the driver. BLAMMO again! This time a blast to the passenger rear hit so hard that between the two hits The Tank's backside swayed from the impacts as if it were doing the hula.

"Leave it to those brothers to tag-team," the announcer said. "Just like last month!"

"Lord have mercy," Nellie Ruth prayed over and over.

"The Tank's gotta be getting close to the sixty-second mark!" Harold hollered.

"Come on, honey. MOVE!" Arthur yelled from the pits. As though she responded to his command, The Tank bucked forward and the Partonvillers rose out of their seats, cheering at the top of their lungs. Immediately, The Tank was thrown into reverse and whizzed through the sloshy mud, making a 180-degree loop around the outside of the ring, just missing opportunity after opportunity but picking up speed all the while, her engine beginning to smoke. By this time four more cars were out, and it looked like The Tank was threading a needle through what was quickly becoming a graveyard of gnarled metal.

The impact was tremendous, the sound of crushing metal piercing the damp night air like a sonic boom. The Tank, 00 and his brother came together in a major collision, 00 careening right into the driver's-side door of The Tank, caving in the door. A warning flag was pointed at 00; the crowd was now on its feet.

"OH, NO!" Jessica screamed. No matter *who* was behind the wheel, it couldn't have felt good. But if it was *Dorothy* . . . Jessie was holding her breath. She'd known Dorothy long enough to understand she was fearless. It would be just like her to try and . . .

"Only four cars left, folks!" The Chevy had hurled himself up on the poles, missing his target and accidentally catapulting his own left rear wheel over the hump. "Number twenty-three just took a HUGE shot! What a battle!"

Smoke and steam were now billowing out of The Tank's engine, all but encasing her in a cloud. "Keep moving! Keep moving!" Arthur implored The Tank *and* the driver. But eke backward about five inches was about all she could seem to do. The sad fact was, if The Tank couldn't pick up speed, her long front end was surely nothing more than a sitting duck for the brothers, who were positioning themselves, one to each side, for the kill. It had looked sure to them that if they knocked out The Tank and left the sputtering Mercury alone, they'd get rid of their strongest adversary and advance to the finals, taking a weak link with them.

But suddenly, everyone but them realized the Mercury had died and couldn't get restarted, leaving The Tank one of the final three to advance. Partonville fans were going crazy!

Then The Tank backfired, and a lick of flame shot out of one of the holes in the hood. "FIRE!" the crowd called, as they always did—even though the firefighters standing nearby with the extinguishers certainly couldn't hear them over the roar. But the firefighters had seen the flame themselves. Immediately, the flagmen, one to each side of the ring, began waving their flags in the air: the checkered one to show the heat was over and the red one to signal all drivers to stop immediately. Just before ramrodding The Tank, the brothers slid through the mud to a halt. The Tank received several blasts from the extinguishers, and in a moment she was no longer on fire.

The Partonvillers were now stone silent, holding their breath. After a few seconds, the cloud around The Tank settled and an arm reached out the window, breaking the yardstick in half, the driver obviously unaware that the race was over and that The Tank had advanced to the finals. In utter relief, the Partonvillers, who were still on their feet, began to hoot and holler and cheer themselves silly!

The sad fact of the matter was that The Tank could not advance; she was done in. The Tank was out of the derby. But the clear fact was that she had not been defeated; she had gone down a winner. Standing brave and alone in the middle of the ring, in a *Whoosh!* of sound, flames and courage, she had taken *herself* out, and no one would ever convince Arthur otherwise.

Now all Partonvillers needed to know was who was going to emerge from The Tank. They all stood, watching the lengthy process as the tow trucks hauled the mounds of wreckage out, one at a time. Finally, The Tank was the last auto to be deposited in the pits, the driver still behind the wheel.

After a few breath-holding moments, the driver's left arm slowly reached out the window and hooked itself over the roof. Arthur held up his hand, signaling the driver to stay put. Suddenly Josh was at Arthur's side. The two men had to pull the driver out of The Tank through the twisted window—the same way the driver had gone in—since the driver's door had been bolted closed and was now completely concave. Little by little, the limp form, still wearing a helmet, was extracted from the vehicle. Too woozy, fatigued and in shock to stand, the figure sat on the ground.

Just then, Dorothy appeared, having been escorted over from where she'd watched the race from inside the judge's stand, two of her long-time-past flute students insisting she shouldn't be climbing around up in the bleachers, from what they'd heard. It was then, after they were all assembled, that Katie Mabel Carol Durbin, a city slicker now *definitely* worth her salt—and who had, with this act (at least in her opinion), officially paid penance for any traces of being a snob—removed her helmet and shook her head.

"*Great* drivin' there, woman!" Arthur said to Katie in earnest as he stroked The Tank's roof. "Yeah, Mom!" Josh added. "Alex will *never* believe *this* one!"

"There was nothing to it!" Katie said. "I just closed my

eyes and figured every hit I took knocked a bit more country girl into me. That, and I kept the pedal to the floor the whole while."

"Well now, Katie," Dorothy said, "welcome to my world. I guess you've finally figured out the best way to go through *life*! Look out *now*, everybody! A brand new Outtamyway is taking to the streets of Pardon Me Ville!"

A Note from the Author

I am happy to have this chance to share, since I, too, am always curious about authors. Here's what I've learned from this side of the pen: Writers are no more fascinating than any reader I've ever met. The only difference is, writers never seem to run out of words!

I didn't begin writing until I was in my forties (talk about a backlog of words), and I haven't stopped since. Our two sons are grown and gone; my husband, George, faithfully cheers me on, and leaves me alone when necessary. I once left him a note on the kitchen table that said, "I'm not here, not even when you see me." Yes, he's used to me by now.

I love what I do, which is to write (and speak) about life. One thing that never changes is the power of story. I believe God speaks to us through stories—ours, others', fiction; good, bad, dubious—and that each moment of each day delivers the potential for us to listen, learn and grow through them. As with my fictional characters, in real life we don't always get it right, but God is always there to shine a light on a better path while loving us all the while.

'Tis that sovereign presence and graciousness of God, Dear Readers, that keeps me writing.

—Charlene Ann Baumbich
www.welcometopartonville.com